About the Author

Hayley Louise Macfarlane has spent most of her adult life pretending she wants to be a scientist, whilst secretly hoping that she could go back to her creative roots and become a writer/artist/sensationally popular singer. Since two of the three of those options seemed far more viable, she went with them.

Hayley sincerely hopes that you enjoy her first foray into writing and that her scientific background hasn't gone entirely to waste in the making of this book.

For my granny, who would have been proud; and to my family (by birth or by choice) who are everything.

To Ana,

Hayley Macfarlane

CARELESS ASSASSIN

I hope you
enjoy the madness,

H.L. Macfarlane

AUSTIN MACAULEY PUBLISHERS™

LONDON • CAMBRIDGE • NEW YORK • SHARJAH

A CIP catalogue record for this title is available from the British Library.

ISBN 9781786128430 (Paperback)
ISBN 9781786128447 (Hardback)
ISBN 9781786128454 (E-Book)

www.austinmacauley.com

First Published (2016)
Austin Macauley Publishers Ltd.
25 Canada Square
Canary Wharf
London
E14 5LQ

Acknowledgements

I never really knew how authors went about writing an acknowledgements section. I mean, surely there are so many people that they want to give thanks to that putting those people into some kind of order is damn near impossible? So here's my best shot at 'putting those people into some kind of order'.

To my family – I love you all, and you all know that, so I won't go through all of you one by one (though I'd like to!). To my mother for once telling me that I had an inflated sense of my own self-importance whilst also being supportive of everything I do…thank you for keeping my feet (somewhat) on the ground. I learned how to be an independent, functioning adult because of you which is no minor feat. To my father who essentially let me do whatever I wanted – thank you for being the counter-balance to mum! You didn't really know I was writing a book but when you found out you weren't surprised at all; honestly, I could tell you I had been chosen by NASA to fly off into space and you wouldn't blink an eye, because you would never have doubted for a second that I could do it.

To my siblings – of whom there are many! To my "grown up" sisters, I'm sure you'll see aspects of all of you in the female characters in Careless Assassin, and that's not coincidence. Exploring the sister bond is something which is very much prevalent in this novel, and I literally could not have been able to write about that without any of you. You have taught me when to let it go that you've stolen my clothes and when to go absolutely mental that you just won't leave my flat (looking at you, Rach). You have taught me about wanderlust without me ever having travelled all that much and that, sometimes, the only thing left to do is to get drunk. To my younger siblings, you have taught me that the only thing you need to get over a massive age gap is a common interest – be it Pokémon, Lego, manga, rabbits or classic PlayStation games. You have taught me how to be a mother (whether I wanted to learn or not!) and with it how to have endless patience and find joy in seemingly the most insignificant things.

At this point I'd like to acknowledge that I couldn't have written Careless Assassin without the stellar science education I received at Dunoon Grammar School and, of course, at my home away from home – The University of Glasgow. I don't know if I'd love genetics quite so much if not for Glasgow Uni!

My acknowledgements section wouldn't be complete without giving a massive thank you to the Cecilian Society, without whom I may well have broken down halfway through my PhD and never gotten back up again. You are the massive, absurd, insanely talented and incredibly incestuous (don't ask) family that I chose for myself, and you have made my past few years in Glasgow a joy, even when we were re-enacting the sinking of the Titanic. You are my oldest established comfort and joy, the hero I was holding out for to make me feel alive (this is probably the worst musical pun sentence I have written to date). You are all the strangest, the bitchiest and the most amazing people I have ever met.

To my friends, I am fortunate enough to have so many good ones that I couldn't possibly make it through you all without writing another novel about it! But in particular, I'd like to thank Gillian and Hannah, for baking and drinking and always being there for a gossip or a cry; Amelia, for all of the inappropriate drinking sessions, dress borrowing and complaining about lab life; Hazel, for being absolutely mental and being the enabler of every stupid plan I have; Lisa, who will never forget my worthless pride; the anime night crew, for doing exactly what is said on the tin and a whole lot more…and Kirsty. Kirsty, my hetero life partner, without whom this book would likely never have been written. You shot dubious alcoholic substances that I throw at you even if you hate them because you love me, and what is friendship if not that? You are always there for me and I love you, love you, love you.

To Jake – and the bunnies. You are my home. I don't need to tell you how much I love you all. I can't wait until we have our castle with a menagerie of pets (sorry Jake, they're simply not negotiable).

Finally, to Austin Macauley for giving me the opportunity to publish my book, and to my readers. I have readers?! This is an absurd, wonderful concept. I hope you enjoyed Careless Assassin, and are willing to stick around to read the rest of the story as this failed scientist writes it.

CHAPTER 1
Don't Go Knockin' on My Door

Ichi

Ichi split people into two groups: those who had something interesting to say before they died...and those who didn't. When Ichi was sent to assassinate Claire Danvers he was assuming she would be the latter.

It was an ordinary enough job on the surface. Two famous scientists had run off with all of their secret (Ichi read this as morally grey) research that his boss had funded privately. In revenge, his boss wanted one of their daughters killed and, if they failed to return the research, he would have their other daughter killed too. Unfortunately for Claire, her sister was on holiday and Claire was looking after their parents' house whilst they were busy being runaways. Life really was unfair for some.

Vic was driving. That was Ichi's only inconvenience, really. Vic was good with knives and killer with a wide array of guns, but he was too emotional for Ichi's liking. Why their boss put Vic on a job to slaughter an innocent girl rather than someone who had directly wronged him, Ichi had no clue. He could see the other man flex and un-flex his leather-gloved hands on the steering wheel, a vein pulsing in his temple – Ichi could practically feel Vic preparing a pre-kill rant. *Oh, fantastic,* he thought derisively.

"Seriously, Ichi, I really don't like this," Vic complained. "We don't even know what the research *is* and we're killing off their daughter for it? I don't like it."

Ichi sighed. "It's clearly worth killing for; leave it at that. She's just another girl," he replied. Vic threw him a look which Ichi dutifully returned. Ichi didn't care anyway. A kill was a kill, a job was a job and money was money. Vic really was too soft.

"You're a heartless bastard, Ich!" the other man said. "Just because you act like a psychopath on the job doesn't mean none of this affects you. I know you have feelings…deep down." Vic paused, considering Ichi for a moment before laughing. "Okay, very, very deep down, but they're there somewhere, I'm sure!"

Ichi chuckled. Vic was a fool. In all honesty, he just couldn't understand why Vic was an assassin in the first place. He was distracted from his thoughts when the car made a left onto a long driveway. It opened out onto a gravelled courtyard to the back of a very large, whitewashed, Victorian-era house, complete with ornate bay windows framed by black windowsills. Vic slowed to a halt before they hit the gravel, stopping by the only other car present, which had to be Claire's. An ornamental copse grew close to what looked to be the kitchen windows.

Vic let out a low whistle. "Okay, bigger than I was expecting. I'll go round front and scope out the ground floor. You can put your hereditary ninja skills to good use –" Ichi glared at him, "– and use those trees to get through the open window above the kitchen." Ichi nodded in assent. "What's the chance that that's her bedroom?" Vic wondered, eyes on the window. Ichi could hear music playing through it, though it was so generically pop that he had no idea who the artist was supposed to be.

"Pretty damn high, I'd say," he replied mindlessly to the other man, head already absorbed in the job. Ichi gave the copse a calculating look. One of the gnarled-looking trees grew so close to the wall of the house itself that climbing it would allow him to literally step through the open window frame. *This is going to be so simple that I'm almost disappointed,* Ichi thought.

Then he heard a click behind him and scowled; Vic was loading his pistol. "Seriously? You're going for a gun on this one?" Vic shrugged his shoulders in response. Ichi rolled his eyes.

"Hey, I don't take any joy in killing an innocent girl – I'm gonna make this as painless as possible for her!" Vic retorted, affronted.

Ichi felt his scowl deepen. "It's such a crude weapon though," he said. "You really take no pride in your knife skills, do you?" Vic gave him a measured look which Ichi didn't understand.

"Okay, I was wrong, you have no feelings. Let's just get this over with," he sighed. Ichi glanced at him before stalking over to the copse like a cat.

"Gladly," he replied softly, before making an almost silent ascent up the gnarled tree.

When he reached the window, Ichi could see that it really was Claire's bedroom inside; a pair of pyjamas, a laptop and a Kindle had been thrown haphazardly onto the unmade bed. He could hear the sound of running water coming from an adjoining door. A bathroom. Claire Danvers would walk out of that bathroom soon, completely unaware of her impending doom. She wouldn't even see Ichi coming.

This was going to be so easy.

Claire

Claire was excited. Very excited. She had been on a self-inflicted 'single year' whilst she finished her undergraduate degree so that she had no distractions. But now, having graduated with a first class degree with honours in genetics, she was free to do as she pleased. *Genetics, to match my prodigal parents,* she thought. *Who are gone.* Claire berated herself; she had forbidden all thought of her parents for now. Because tonight she was finally going on a date with the man she had been watching wistfully from afar for months. He was a geography PhD student in the final year of his doctorate who spent increasing amounts of time poring over his thesis in the library, which suited the library's almost permanent tenant Claire just fine. His name was John. John! It was so delightfully ordinary that Claire couldn't help but love it.

Claire's last boyfriend had self-styled himself as 'Zeke the hipster', who seemed to have strained with every fibre of his being to be as unusual as the name he had given himself. All it did was make him a dick. Claire had put up with him for six months (five months too many) before getting out of the incredibly one-sided relationship. John's only very vague nod to anything out of the ordinary was that he kept his blonde hair a little longer than Claire would have expected given his personality, but with his sharp jawline and steely blue eyes it only served to accentuate how God damn beautiful he was. She liked to watch him rake his fingers through his shoulder length hair as he mulled over his thesis, whilst simultaneously tapping out the beat of the song he was listening to on his tightly-jeaned legs. She badly wanted to be the one to run her fingers through his hair and relieve him of those jeans in the process…Claire stopped her thought process abruptly as she realised that she was letting her imagination run away with her. *Okay, maybe 'wistfully' isn't how I've been looking at him*, she mused. *Perhaps* lustfully *is more accurate.*

Claire knew she was getting ready far too early but the pre-date butterflies wouldn't let her sit still. So there she was, having showered, shaved and applied her make up in the bathroom, trying to decide whether she should get dressed or dry her hair first. So mundane a choice to make. *How glorious!* she thought happily.

Even acknowledging how great making a boring decision was forced Claire's mind back onto the ever-pressing, decidedly non-mundane issue of her runaway parents once again. It was taking its toll on Claire, who was expected to have all of the answers to why they disappeared, but of course had none. And that *stung*. How many weekends had she spent working with her parents? How many summers? She had thought they were close. Olivia was the party animal, the one who couldn't care less about science, the one who had responded to her parents' disappearance with an impromptu trip to Ibiza. And yet she had received no warning or reason for their swift and silent departure. Maybe Olivia's take on the situation was better than Claire's – pretend nothing has happened and run away to some place warm. Lots of music. Lots of alcohol. Lots of boys. Suddenly Claire was very envious of her younger sister.

"Snap out of it, Claire!" she berated her reflection. She would deal with her runaway family in her own way; by getting on with her life. She wandered through to her bedroom to get dressed, having decided to let her long, dark brown hair air dry. She had been sleeping in her sister's room because it was cooler to sleep in at night and got the morning sun, but both bedrooms connected to the bathroom Jack-and-Jill style for convenience (and so their parents didn't have to hear them thumping up and down the corridor to the bathroom in the morning when they were teenagers). She would have gotten dressed in Olivia's room too, if it weren't for the fact that Claire's own room benefitted from floor-length mirrors, which was exactly what she required to ensure she looked perfect for her date.

Suddenly Claire missed her own flat in the city, where most of her clothes were. She studied the dress she had brought with her – dove grey with an embellished strappy bodice, a keyhole back and a flouncy lilac skirt that fell to just above her knees. Claire hoped it was just the right amount of classy and sexy for a first date. She had chosen a dark grey, satin-feeling underwear set to match the dress – she wanted so much to go strapless so that the delicately beaded dress straps could be shown off without thicker bra ones ruining the look, but to Claire's chagrin, her chest was too large to wear any kind of strapless underwear. The only way around the matter was to wear a basque or corset but she couldn't wear one of them with a half-backless dress. *Oh the dilemma!* Claire thought happily. Something that used to genuinely infuriate her felt pleasantly banal now.

Having dressed, Claire fastidiously inspected herself in the mirror. She had gone for smoky purple eyeshadow and cat-eye black liner to frame her eyes, with a touch of silver just inside her lash line. It brought out the almost-violet tones in her dark blue eyes and complimented her dress, which cinched in flatteringly around Claire's admittedly already slender waist. Her dark brown hair hung half dry, slightly wavy; she was considering putting it up in a French twist. Claire was weighing up the pros and cons of finish the look with fragile silver sandals or heels when she heard the door to the bathroom from her sister's bedroom open.

She froze. Nobody had come up the stairs (they were creaky; Claire would have heard something) and no one but her family knew of the old, rickety staircase hidden behind the newer hallway panelling, a relic of the house's décor prior to her mother's avid remodelling of the place. *It can't be Olivia,* Claire reasoned. She had only spoken to Olivia on the phone an hour ago, and her sister had gleefully told Claire that she was two thirds of the way through her fifth mojito. *She's probably on her seventh now. So who else could it be?* Claire's parents were long gone, leaving Claire with no other conclusion to reach than the fact that the person currently in her bathroom was an intruder.

It took Claire only a second to rush out of her bedroom door into the hallway, just as the intruder entered her room. She saw a flash of silver as she bolted down the hall, feeling the wooden panelling of the wall for the secret stairwell until she heard a click. *Got it,* she thought as she slid the panelling open. Not pausing to glance behind her, Claire slammed the panelling shut behind her and bolted down the stairs, three at a time. *Just get outside, get in your car and GO*, she repeated to herself. Claire silently thanked God that she had left the keys in her car, a bad habit her parents had often admonished her for before they disappeared. But as she exited the stairwell and ran across the downstairs hallway, she noticed another intruder standing by the front door, looking straight at her, pistol aimed at her head. Claire panicked; how could she outrun a bullet? She heard the gun go off and threw herself to the ground. Outright terror left her clutching to the floor for dear life.

"I got her, Ich!" she heard the second intruder say. *He couldn't possibly...?* Claire thought. But he had! *He thinks he hit me!* Claire had to bite back a sigh of immeasurable relief.

"Yeah, I'll bring the car around," she heard the man say. *He must be talking to the other intruder through a radio,* Claire's terrified mind concluded. When she heard footsteps on gravel growing fainter, Claire knew it was probably her only chance to escape with her life. She ran down the hallway towards the downstairs bathroom, which contained a window that a seventeen-year-old Claire had often used to sneak out late at night. Not even acknowledging how strange it was that she had never heard the first intruder run down the stairs or exit the house, Claire unlatched the window with adrenaline-unsteady hands and vaulted herself out of the bathroom and onto the courtyard outside, ripping the skirt of her dress in the process. Claire flat-out sprinted past the trees in the courtyard toward the driveway, blood roaring loudly in her ears, when she realised a second too late that the intruders' car was blocking access to her own.

"Checkmate," Claire heard a man say, as she felt a hand grab her hair and press a knife to her throat.

Ichi

Ichi could feel the pulse in Claire's neck throbbing against his knife. Erratic, fitful. He could barely contain himself, he was so excited. His own pulse was racing; he could practically feel his pupils dilating. What a thrill it was, to have another life in his own hands for him to extinguish! Ichi could feel little beads of Claire's blood on his hand as he pressed the knife a little harder against her neck. She was his. But she so nearly hadn't been.

"Vic, you fucking idiot! This is the most alive dead girl I've ever seen!" he allowed himself to growl through gritted teeth, not trusting himself to look at the man in question lest he slit his throat open too. Vic had the sense to look ashamed as he muttered something that included the phrases "low lighting" and "she fell". But even Vic's idiocy couldn't destroy Ichi's high. No longer did he feel like simply slitting Claire Danvers' throat, killing her in seconds. He was going to enjoy this. He turned Claire around roughly by the shoulders and flung her to the ground – Ichi wanted to see the look on her face as she realised she was going to die.

And what a face it was! Claire's dark blue eyes were wide as a deer's caught in headlights, tears welling up between her lashes and threatening to ruin her make up. Her skin was deathly pale, her hair plastered to the sides of her face. The beads of blood around her neck looked like a macabre necklace, slowly running down to ruin her delicate collarbone. Ichi shivered just thinking about that blood soaking into her little dress as the life drained from her eyes. And then –

"Please – no – d-don't do this!" Claire begged, words barely coherent beneath her panicked, laboured breathing. Despite how exhilarated this young woman was making Ichi feel, she still fell under the category of 'nothing interesting to say'. Ichi almost sighed.

"I'm sorry, princess, but orders are orders," he barely heard Vic say. Ichi sincerely wished that Vic wasn't there to ruin his beautiful kill.

"N-no, you don't understand. I'm not – I don't want to die! I'm not ready to die!" Claire pleaded. She was shaking with fear, eyes roaming wildly between Ichi and Vic. *Don't look at him, look at me, only me,* Ichi thought. He crouched down in front of her, the better to look at her petrified face. He ran the edge of his knife slowly up the centre of Claire's body to her neck. Claire let out an audible gasp, her chest heaving as she struggled to stay conscious. The terror she was clearly feeling was almost palpable; to Ichi, in this moment, Claire Danvers was the single most magnificent being he had ever seen.

But then something changed, as if a gear clicked into place inside Claire's head. She looked straight at Ichi as she said, calmly and clearly, "I'm the only one who can give Michael what he wants." Ichi froze, stunned. He could feel Vic staring at Claire, just as dumbfounded as he was. He took a breath.

"What exactly did you say?" Ichi asked, very slowly.

"Michael doesn't know it yet but I'm the only one who can give him the data," Claire replied with cool indifference. Vic was staring at Ichi now, aghast. Ichi's high crumpled. Why did this damnable girl have to go and say something interesting *now?*

"Ichi, we're going to have to bring her in – Michael will literally kill us if we don't," Vic said, stating the obvious. Ichi never took his eyes off of Claire.

"How do you know Michael's name?" he asked her, completely on edge.

Suddenly, Claire seemed to revert back to her previous, terrified state. "I-I don't know. I just don't know! Please, I don't want to die! I need to speak to Michael!" she babbled hysterically. Ichi groaned. His kill was ruined; completely destroyed. How he would love nothing more than to slit Claire's beautiful throat and watch her bleed to death.

Instead, he grabbed Vic's gun and violently pistol-whipped her across the back of her head.

CHAPTER 2
Dance with the Devil

Claire

She woke up tied to a chair, head throbbing and lights dancing behind her eyes. Disoriented and confused, Claire's eyes roamed wildly from side to side as she tried to get her bearings and attempt to recognise something or someone. Unfortunately, that someone was the man named Ichi, who was leaning against a wall to Claire's right. Claire had to suppress a sudden overwhelming desire to throw up.

"Deep breaths, princess," she heard a man say behind her. His voice was soothing, his advice practical. Claire closed her eyes, despite her brain yelling at her to never lose sight of the man who wanted her dead, and began to take slow, deep breaths. She counted to ten. When the pain in her head had marginally subsided, Claire opened her eyes again. The man with the soothing voice was now kneeling in front of her, a slight frown of concern creasing his brow. Claire realised that he was the other man sent to kill her – the one called Vic. And by all accounts, Claire should have been terrified of him as well, but she found that it was impossible. Even more unlikely was that he was actually putting Claire at ease. He smiled at her.

"That's better, princess, that's better." He paused. "Sorry about knocking you out earlier, it's not how I would have done it –" Ichi glared at him, his expression all venom and malice, "– and sorry about the duct tape now," he continued. Vic's pale blue eyes never left Claire's. He paused for a second before continuing, during which time Claire concentrated on the too-fast beating of her own heart. "What you said before, Claire," Vic finally said, "Do you know what you meant by it? About how only you can give Michael the data?"

"That's enough, Vic, I'll take it from here," interjected another male voice from behind Vic; Claire hadn't even realised anybody else was there. Vic stood up and stepped away from Claire.

"Are you sure?" he asked. The man was sitting behind a mahogany desk. He laced his fingers together before responding.

"Quite." Vic took his cue to leave. He gave Claire a pat on the shoulder and a reassuring half-smile before exiting through what Claire could only assume to be a door behind her. She heard it gently close. "You too, Ichi," said the man behind the desk, but Ichi looked like he desperately wanted to protest. "Not now, not now, Ichi!" the man added on before Ichi could vocalise said protests. "I'll talk to you later. This is private." Ichi glared at the man but eventually turned to leave, giving Claire a hungry, lingering glance before swiftly departing from the room.

"What nerve, that one, glaring at me like that," the man smiled. Claire could do nothing but stare back at him. The room wasn't well lit, save for a lamp on the man's desk which gave off a warm, amber glow that left deep shadows in the corners of the room. He was thin, his dark blonde hair swept back expertly from his face, and he was dressed smartly in a sharp grey suit that matched his equally sharp jawline and his eyes. Though whether his eyes were indeed grey or not, Claire couldn't actually tell in the low light. She figured that he must be around his mid-thirties, and that if he stood up he would be tall. It all left Claire feeling entirely inadequate in her ruined dress, bloodied neck and no doubt running mascara.

But as she thought this, the man chuckled and removed his suit jacket and loosened his tie. "I suppose there's no need to be so formal for a meeting such as this," he murmured. He looked at her critically. "Do you know who I am, Miss Danvers?" Claire swallowed, not trusting her voice.

"No, but I can make a pretty good guess," she replied. He smiled again, waiting for her to elaborate. Claire swallowed once more. "You're Michael."

"Very good, very good. And now here's another question – why did I send Vic and our dear friend Ichi to have you killed?" Claire flinched at the question, at the way Michael so casually brought up the subject of her own assassination. She decided to throw caution to the wind and spoke honestly.

"That one's easy. You have something to do with my parents' research. I don't really know what. But you want it, and they've run away. You're trying to force their hand; kill their first child as a warning and kill the second if they fail to comply with your demands," she said. Claire had no idea how she could possibly have worked this out, yet she had nonetheless.

Michael grinned at her. "Oh I like you, you're sharp –"

"But it won't work," she interrupted. Michael matched her stare.

"And that is why you are here," he said, in a soft, slow murmur. His gaze sharpened. "Now, you are going to tell me precisely why you are convinced of your absolute importance in obtaining this research for me…or I will send our dear Ichi back in and let him do as he pleases until you are begging for him to end your life."

Ichi

Ichi was lingering outside Michael's office, mutinous that he had been sent out like a petulant schoolboy.

"I wouldn't try to listen in if I were you. You know Michael would admonish you for that, big time," scolded a familiar female voice off to his right. It was Alexis, Michael's body guard/personal assistant, Ichi wasn't sure which.

"I'm not listening in; I'm waiting for Michael to tell me I can kill her," Ichi replied, restless.

Alexis gave him a look. "As heartless as ever, I see. Has it crossed your mind that he might spare her?"

"Once. I ignored it." Alexis laughed softly at that.

"I wouldn't be surprised if Michael spares her just to spite you," she said.

Ichi shook his head. "As tempted as Michael would be to do just that, it's not in his best interests. And we both know –"

21

"That Michael only does what's in his best interests," Alexis finished for him. She regarded him curiously for a second. "Anyway, when this Claire girl invariably proves how important she is and Michael spares her life, you know where I'll be if you feel like releasing that murderous frustration of yours in a more…healthy manner. It wouldn't be the first time!" she grinned at him. He glared at her.

"Just shut up and let me wait in peace, Alexis," he glowered. Alexis seemed oblivious to the venom in his voice.

"Aye aye, Captain," she joked, and resumed standing in silence.

Claire

Claire had to weigh her words carefully. *Say the wrong thing and…*she didn't want to imagine what would happen. But how could Claire explain her situation when she herself didn't entirely understand it?

"Clock's ticking, Miss Danvers," Michael commented casually, keeping his steady, impassive gaze on Claire. Claire shook her head to clear her thoughts. She didn't want to die. She didn't want Olivia to die if she failed and her parents never showed up. They had abandoned her to save her own life, so save it she would. Claire took a deep breath.

"My parents don't have access to their research unless I'm around – I'm the only one who knows the password to access the files," Claire began.

"So give me your password," Michael replied simply.

"I can't."

"And why is that?"

"Because I don't remember it."

Michael frowned. "Being contrary will not aid your situation, Miss Danvers," he said.

Claire shook her head again. "I'm not being contrary, I'm being truthful. My parents, they – they did something to me."

A spark of interest lit up Michael's previously blank eyes. "They experimented on you?" he asked.

It was Claire's turn to frown. "I'm not sure exactly…possibly," Claire admitted. "I don't even know why I know about this *now* – I didn't this morning. But my point is that I *do* remember them doing something to me after the password was created and now it's buried deep in my subconscious. I think my parents have – I don't really know the best word for it – a buzzword of kinds that allows me to remember what it is…this sounds insane." Claire looked at the floor, but brought her head back up abruptly when she heard Michael chuckle.

He raised an eyebrow at her. "Quite the contrary; it sounds precisely like something your parents would do." Claire let the meaning of that sentence sink in. *Michael knows my parents well, then?* she thought. Claire didn't know why she felt like that piece of information was important, but she knew it nonetheless. Michael continued: "I don't suppose you are well versed in their research yourself?"

Claire thought about that for a moment. "Well, that's what's strange for me. I *did* know all about their research – I helped them out with some of it after all – but now I can't recall any of it! I don't even know when I forgot about it!" Claire shook her head for the third time in frustration at the realisation of how far this memory loss had gone without her ever realising it.

Michael gave Claire a sympathetic smile that didn't quite reach his eyes. "It appears you may be the biggest victim of us all, Miss Danvers, so I propose a deal." He paused and regarded her closely. "I will find your parents, and when I do you will have them activate your buzzword and then you will give me all of their research. In return I will give both you and your sister Olivia your lives to do with as you please. Until then, you must stay on my complex here where I can have you watched. Do you agree to my terms?" He left his chair and crouched in front of Claire's to cut away the duct tape that bound her wrists together as he spoke. Claire kept her eyes on his. Some part of her brain confirmed that Michael's eyes were indeed grey, and very, very cold.

I don't want to die.

She took a deep breath. Exhaled. "Yes," she said. Michael grinned and held out his hand, amusement finally breaking his calm expression. Claire didn't hesitate as she took it.

"Then welcome to my base of assassins."

Ichi

Ichi straightened up as he heard the door behind him open; it was time. He felt his heartrate accelerate at the very thought of getting his hands on the girl finally leaving Michael's office. "Ah, Ichi, no surprises that you're still here," Michael commented as he entered the hallway. He glanced at Alexis before looking at Ichi. "Kindly escort Miss Danvers up to suite 1202 please. Alexis, could you see to it that she gets some more…suitable clothes?" Alexis nodded in assent and swiftly left, leaving Ichi to stand there, dumbfounded. Michael frowned at him. "*Now*, Ichi," he warned, leaving no room for argument. He pressed a key into Ichi's hand. Ichi ignored the warning and protested anyway.

"But you can't be serious? And 1202 is –"

"The room next to yours. Yes, I am aware of the layout of my own complex, Ichi. Now *go*." Michael grinned, taking immense pleasure in the swath of emotions that were no doubt plastered across Ichi's face. Ichi hesitated for a moment before storming down the corridor towards the elevator. "You'd be best to follow him, Miss Danvers," he heard Michael comment to the girl – the girl who should be dead or dying even as Ichi watched the elevator number decrease from floor to floor until it reached the basement.

He could tell that the last thing she wanted was to be stuck in an elevator with him, but she obliged Michael's orders anyway and followed him into it as the doors crept open. Ichi considered killing her during the ascent, despite his orders. However, he knew that that would be his life too, and Ichi somewhat valued his own life. But there was something else he could do, something else he knew Michael would turn a blind eye to.

Ichi was broken out of his tumultuous reverie by the noise of the elevator reaching the twelfth floor. Without looking at the girl, he walked calmly towards door 1202, unlocked it and waited for her to reach the door. Then he flung her unceremoniously into the glorified prison, locking the door behind her.

He stalked down the corridor to his own rooms, a maniacal grin slowly spreading across his face as he mulled over all of the ways in which he could break Claire Danvers.

CHAPTER 3
Stolen

Claire

Claire lay on top of the covers of her new bed for hours, curled up motionless with her knees up to her chest. *This isn't happening, this hasn't happened, none of this is real,* she found herself desperately repeating. She clenched her eyes shut; begging for the world to return to the way it was before her parents disappeared.

Claire's brain was going over and over her meeting with Michael – how had she known half of the things she had said to him when she had forgotten so much about everything else? How was it only now that Claire *knew* that she was missing large portions of the past three years of her life? How had she forgotten it in the first place? How was she supposed to make sense of anything when Claire didn't even know which things she had forgotten and which things she genuinely had never come across before? Claire's brain felt like a horrible, foreign object in her head.

She stared blankly at the wall in front of her and tried to clear her thoughts of everything, but it was useless and Claire knew it. Resigned to a sleepless night, Claire decided that she was as well exploring the prison that she was contained in. Naturally, she wandered over to the door first on the off chance it was somehow unlocked but, of course, it wasn't. Claire sighed and scanned her surroundings. The room had no windows, but it did have warm ceiling lights that lowered in their brightness at some point when Claire was lying on the bed. A quick flick of the switch by the door turned them off and then back on again at full power. In front of her was a couch with a glass coffee table presiding over a dark brown rug in the centre of the room; the bed, a wardrobe and a chest of drawers lay adjacent to this living space behind a Japanese screen door. She noted that there was also a small kitchen area situated in an alcove to her right. Claire had noted earlier that there was a shower room off of the 'bedroom'. In reality, suite 1202 was altogether bigger, nicer and more expensively furnished than Claire's one-bedroom flat way back in her old life.

She headed back to lie on the bed, sighing, when she heard the door click. Claire stiffened, but then she heard a knock on the door and a female voice gently say: "Claire? I'm Alexis, I have some clothes for you. Can I come in?" Claire gulped. Her throat was so dry; it took several attempts for her to reply with an 'okay'.

The woman called Alexis let herself in, a small bundle of clothing in her arms. Claire allowed herself to look Alexis up and down. She was slender and tall, with dark brown, shoulder length hair and dark eyes to match. Claire concluded that she was beautiful. *Why does any of that even matter?* Claire thought morosely. *She's probably a trained killer.* It took her a moment to realise that Alexis was also looking *her* up and down, as if she were sizing Claire up. Alexis frowned.

"…what?" Claire asked somewhat nervously.

"Never mind," was all Alexis responded with. It was Claire's turn to frown. *I suppose I'm going to find every facial expression of every single person living here to be suspicious, all things considered,* she mused. Claire glanced at Alexis before delicately perching on the edge of the couch in the living space of her prison. Alexis followed her and sat on the table, facing Claire. For a long moment neither of them said a thing. Eventually, Alexis' stare began to make Claire feel incredibly uncomfortable and she looked away. Alexis laughed.

"What do you want?!" Claire shot at her. Alexis grasped Claire's hands before she had an opportunity to pull them away.

"I'm just making sure you're okay," Alexis replied, keeping her voice soft. She smiled slightly. "I was expecting you to be curled up in the shower, crying your eyes out, to be honest. I must say I'm impressed; you're holding yourself together much better than anyone could expect." Claire supposed that the other woman meant it as a compliment.

"It appears I'll have a lot of time for crying over the next few days; why get it all out of my system in one night?" Claire replied dryly, before frowning. "It *is* night time, isn't it? That's why the lights dulled a few hours ago, right?"

27

"Well observed!" Alexis said. "It's pretty late, or pretty early depending on how you look at it. Which means that you need to be getting some sleep! Vic wanted to come and check up on you but I told him he could wait until tomorrow. Really, even I was leaving it a bit late to give you those clothes. I figured you would need a few hours by yourself to recover from the shock of everything though. It appears I wasn't wrong." Alexis gave Claire another once-over before saying: "Though by the looks of things, a shower and about two days' worth of sleep would be far more helpful than a few hours curled up in a ball, wondering why any of this happened, you know." Claire winced; she knew it was true.

Alexis stood up and placed the clothing she had brought with her on top of the table. "I'll be heading over to your flat tomorrow to get some of your *own* clothes but, until then, these will have to do. They should fit you okay…maybe just a little tight in the chest." She grinned at Claire, whose face had flushed with embarrassment at the comment. Alexis smiled sadly at that, and it made Claire feel odd. "A bit of colour in your face makes you look much more alive, Claire," the other woman said, "And keep that in mind – you *are* alive. You saved your own life, by the sounds of things. Not everyone has the mentality to go through what you did today and survive. So don't think of yourself as a dead girl walking. Just stick to your deal with Michael and I can assure you, you'll walk away from this like nothing ever happened. You just need to hang on until then..." Alexis turned and headed towards the door. Just before she left, she glanced back at Claire.

"…despite your next door neighbour."

And then she was gone, leaving Claire with a bundle of clothes and a mountain of thoughts to mull over. She knew she should do exactly as Alexis suggested and have a shower and then attempt to get some sleep, but Claire found that she didn't even have the energy to walk to the bathroom. Instead, she collapsed onto her side, lying on the couch, goose bumps prickling every inch of her bare skin at the very thought of her new 'next door neighbour'.

Ichi

Ichi had been pacing his own room for several hours. His entire being was on edge, completely wired; he *had* to see Claire again, to witness her terrified expression as he looked into her eyes with the intent of a predatory cat. And that's exactly what he would be – a cat, who played with its prey until they decided to kill it. Or, in Ichi's case, when he got the 'okay' from Michael to kill her.

The very notion that he had to follow somebody else's orders irked him. However, Michael's employment was Ichi's only means of being paid an inordinate amount of money for doing what he loved best. Not to mention that Michael provided the highest level of protection for his 'agents' against most global governments, allowing Ichi to continue with his work just about anywhere, without having to worry about his next hiding place.

Michael had also insisted on Ichi learning how to work undercover for extended periods of time, but he had little interest in such charades. *Leave the suspect vetting and information gathering to Vic and Alexis,* he had said. Michael had made him undertake the training nonetheless.

He was snapped out of his reverie by the sound of Claire's door being knocked upon, followed by the soft murmur of Alexis' voice. Ichi flicked his head around to check the time on his clock – it was just after two in the morning. He wondered why Alexis had waited nearly five hours to bring up some clothes for Michael's new prisoner; it was probably something idiotic to do with giving her some time to cry. *But she's a dead girl,* Ichi thought. *Why give her new clothes or 'alone time' or any other luxury? It's so pointless.* And besides, Ichi didn't much like the idea of anybody else talking to his prey. Claire was *his*.

Only a few minutes later, he heard Alexis leave Claire's room and lock the door behind her. Ichi glanced at the key Michael had given him to let Claire into her room in the first place. A grin spread across his face. *It's almost as if he* wants *me to do something to her,* he thought, verging on gleeful. He wondered how the oxymoron that was Vic, the moral assassin, would react to the thoughts currently circulating Ichi's head. He didn't care.

Ichi's pacing became faster, more erratic. He forced himself to wait another half an hour before he finally grabbed the key to room 1202 and vacated his own room to stalk over to Claire's prison.

She was so lost in her own head, curled up like an infant on the couch that Claire didn't even seem to notice Ichi waltz in until he was almost upon her. It was in that moment, when Claire properly saw him, that she sat up stock straight and her eyes widened in fear. Ichi took slow, deliberate steps towards her, letting the half-light in the room work deep shadows across his face, obscuring his features. Paired with his tall frame, black clothes and the knife on his hip, Ichi knew he was painting an intimidating picture. He allowed Claire to stand up from her couch and back away from him. She stumbled in her retreat, near knocking down the screen door that blocked the bed off from the living space. Ichi almost laughed.

The girl who had saved her own life was gone.

Suddenly, Ichi lunged at Claire and pinned her to the bed, both of her wrists in one of his hands. He grabbed at the torn hem of her bloodied dress and ripped it further. Claire's eyes were roving wildly from side to side, looking for a futile way to escape. Ichi allowed himself a dark chuckle.

"What, no clever words to get you out of this? I'm almost disappointed," he growled into the nape of her neck, feeling her pulse beat frantically against his eyelashes. He ran the tip of his tongue over the thin trail of blood that his knife had left on Claire's neck where he had cut her earlier. He could feel his hand roaming up her thigh, her waist and then over her chest, but he was barely conscious of the action. He couldn't take his eyes off of Claire's, forcing her to, finally, look at him. He could feel her entire body shaking under his; it was exhilarating. He ran his free hand through her hair, yanking it back to expose more of her neck.

"What do you want from me?" she half whispered, half sobbed. Ichi levelled his face with hers until their noses were almost touching.

"Everything," he replied. Claire's eyes went even wider than they had been before, fresh tears running down the sides of her face into her hair. He wiped them away with a finger, ever so gently, before murmuring into her ear, "And once I've taken everything, I'll kill you."

Claire

Claire had been sitting in the bottom of her new shower cubicle for half an hour, back pressed against the glass to allow the steaming water to run down her front. She knew no amount of soap and water could wipe away what Ichi had done, yet it was the only thing she could do. The sound of the water also helped to drown out her sobbing, and she'd be damned if she was going to allow that *monster* to hear her cry. Even the thought of him ran an icy shiver down Claire's spine, despite the scalding water.

Ichi had left her crying, shivering and helpless on the bed, a positively triumphant expression on his face. Claire had been so terrified of him that she had been unable to move even in the hour after he had left. It had taken every inch of willpower that Claire had in her to eventually drag herself to the shower.

I wish I were dead, she thought. *I wish Vic had shot me and taken away the victory from that son of a bitch.* But even as she said it, Claire could feel the vague beginnings of anger piercing her bleakness, and if she could be angry…then maybe she could hope to override her fear with it. *I can't let Ichi see me this vulnerable ever again. If I do that then I've lost.*

Claire forced herself to her feet, washed her hair, her face and her neck and then turned the shower off. She towelled herself dry, threw on a t-shirt and a pair of shorts that Alexis had brought up to her and grabbed the duvet from the bed. Claire couldn't face sleeping on something that Ichi had touched her on; she'd sleep on the couch tonight. Then Claire poured herself a glass of water and drank it in one go before setting up on the couch. She sighed.

For what felt like the millionth time today, Claire felt completely and utterly lost. *How could it have been only a few hours ago that I was getting ready for a date? An ordinary date?* She couldn't even recall what John had looked like now. But Claire knew she couldn't think of any of that right now, not if she was going to survive here. So she shook the thoughts from her head, closed her eyes and resolved to get some sleep.

Ichi

Ichi left Claire's room on a massive adrenaline high, his heart thumping faster and faster until he could hear the blood rushing inside his ears. He couldn't believe that intimidating Claire Danvers had elicited in him the same reaction that killing another human being incited. Except this was better; Claire was still alive, which meant Ichi could terrify her again and again and again, until eventually he would top it all by draining the light from her eyes permanently.

Ichi mentally noted that he would need to rig Claire's room up to spy on her – in order to continue his torment, he would need to learn everything he could about her routine, from the moment she woke up in the morning to the moment she fell asleep at night, for all of the days that she was left alive for him to break. He knew that meant laying low for a few days but he also knew that every moment that he had to leave Claire alone would be worth it.

He was going to make killing Claire Danvers the most beautiful moment of his life.

He felt inclined to find Alexis, to channel some of his marvellous high into fucking her senseless, but all he could see in his mind was how it felt to have every inch of Claire react to him, how every little hair on her body stood on end as he touched her and how, near the end, she couldn't take her eyes off of his. No. He couldn't ruin any of that on Alexis.

So Ichi jumped in the shower and tended to his own needs, all the while thinking about how it would feel to rip Claire's clothes off and take everything away from her, just as he had promised.

CHAPTER 4
Roll to Me

Claire

Claire was dreaming. Even in her unconscious state she knew that she must be dreaming, because it was about what she should have done as soon as her parents disappeared. In her dream, Claire had emptied her savings account and was gallivanting across the globe with Olivia, relaxing on beaches with cocktails and riding donkeys up mountains. All of the things that she had wanted to see in the world she was finally seeing, and they were all incredible. Olivia prevented Claire from getting too serious, Claire prevented Olivia from making too many stupid mistakes and they prevented each other from thinking about their parents too much. It was as close to bliss as Claire could imagine.

So when she started to hear knocking, way back in reality, Claire's subconscious furiously clung onto her dream; her escape. "Claire?" she vaguely heard in the back of her mind. "It's Vic. I'm going to let myself in – I have breakfast and *you* have to eat, like it or not." Claire could feel her dream rapidly run away from her, the sound of Vic's voice dragging her back to reality.

"I'm not here," she complained, as if she were talking with Olivia and not a man who had nearly killed her. *Ah. Damn.* The very thought jolted her to complete and utter alertness, and Claire opened her eyes. Due to the lack of windows in her prison, it was hard to tell the time, but the ceiling lights that had glowed a warm, orange colour the previous night were now bright and dazzling. She peered up at the towering figure that was Vic; he was holding a tray of food in his hands and was gazing back at her with a smile on his face.

"I *knew* you'd be sarcastic, I just knew it. Keep your wit sharp and you'll fit right in, princess," Vic commented. Claire sat up on the couch; it hadn't made for a particularly comfortable sleep.

"One wonders why any sane person would want to *fit right in* in a place like this," she replied.

Vic laughed. "Looks like apparently all you need to get over a traumatic experience is a few hours of sleep," he commented, then his face grew serious. "Can I sit down, Claire?"

Claire gave him a look. "I don't exactly have a choice, do I? I'm a prisoner here," she sighed. *I shouldn't have the mental capacity for sarcasm and rhetorical questions right now,* Claire found herself thinking. She wondered how talking to Vic already felt so much like a normal conversation that she would have had any day in her old life, despite the subject matter. Vic held his serious gaze steady.

"Claire, you may be here against your own volition, but trust me when I say this: I will *never* do anything that you don't want me to do. I hope you'll give me the opportunity to prove that to you." Claire looked at the floor.

"You tried to kill me…I'm pretty sure I didn't want that," she murmured. She glanced back up at Vic – the expression on his face would have broken Claire's heart if it wasn't currently made of steel. She waved a hand at the couch. "If you have something to say in your defence, no doubt I'd *love* to hear it," she said, in a manner that reminded her so much of the way her mother used to scold a young Claire and Olivia when they had done something wrong. Claire flinched internally at her continued, entirely situationally inappropriate use of sarcasm. *The subject of my own death isn't casual…I'm not Michael,* she thought.

Vic hesitated for a second, placed the tray of food he had brought with him on the coffee table and then sat down on the other side of the couch, leaving as much space as was physically possible between them. He took a deep breath in. "Claire, what I'm about to tell you…is something I shouldn't tell you. There's a certain someone who couldn't handle having this piece of information, so you *have* to keep it to yourself. Can you do that?"

Claire looked at him quizzically. "Someone who couldn't *handle* knowing? You don't mean –"

"Yes, that's exactly who I mean. Our friendly neighbourhood psychopath, Ichi," Vic answered, so casually. Too casually. Even Claire, who knew Vic for all of five minutes, could tell that he was trying to turn the idea of Ichi into something that Claire could laugh at, like a pantomime villain, rather than someone to genuinely be fearful of. She could tell that even Vic knew that it probably wouldn't work.

"You don't have to lighten the mood before saying something serious, Vic, just tell me," Claire said.

Vic kept his pale blue eyes on Claire's dark blue ones as he said, "I wasn't sent to kill you." Claire looked back at him, nonplussed. How was she supposed to respond to that? Just as she was about to reply, Vic continued: "Well, I *was*, as a team with Ichi, but my orders from Michael were not to kill you. I was to create a situation in which it *looked* like we had killed you –"

"But what's the point in that? Ahh…" Claire interrupted, though she reached the correct answer even as she did so.

"To upset your parents, as you've just worked out, yes," Vic said. "Obviously, considering your current position, you can work out that we – "

"But wouldn't kidnapping me upset them in a similar manner? Wouldn't they be more willing to give Michael the information he needs if –"

"Claire, if you keep interrupting me like a five-year-old child then I'll never get to the point," Vic laughed. He ran his fingers through his blonde hair. Claire allowed herself a sheepish smile.

"Sorry," she chimed. "I guess I'm just being swept up in the story of my own almost-demise. It's quite fascinating, if I pretend it's not about me." She looked up at Vic through her eyelashes. He looked so forlorn; Claire couldn't help feeling bad about her comment. *But why should I feel bad about it? So he didn't try to kill me, personally. He was only sent to kidnap me. So much better.*

"So my point," Vic continued, "is that, right now, your parents will be getting the news, wherever they are, that Michael has killed their daughter.

If they have any hearts at all then the news will shatter them. They'll become easy to emotionally manipulate. They may even make mistakes in covering up their tracks as they try to protect your sister Olivia. So when Michael, finally, lets out the information that you are, in fact, alive and well and entirely in his captivity, they'll be so deliriously happy that you're not dead that they'll do anything Michael needs to get you back to safety. Especially since they'll know how awful it feels to have lost you already. There's no way they'll want to feel like that again." Claire looked at him, a frown on her face.

"You don't buy it?" she asked. Vic looked surprised.

"Very perceptive, princess. No, I don't. What kind of parent leaves their child in such a dangerous situation in the first place? If they had these bleeding hearts that Michael is so depending on then they'd never have left you. They –" Vic stopped talking, looking surprised again. He glanced down; Claire had placed her hand on his arm as if on reflex, trying to soothe him. *And why the hell did I do that?* Claire asked herself. *He's angry on my behalf, which is sweet. But he and Ichi are still the reason I'm in this situation that he apparently doesn't want me to be in in the first place. Speaking of which...*

"So why can Ichi not *handle* the truth then?" Claire asked aloud, averting her eyes from Vic as she awkwardly withdrew her hand. He continued as if nothing had happened, which Claire was grateful for.

"You're sharp enough to figure out that Ichi's…not quite *right* in the head," he said. Claire's expression darkened at the understatement, a chill running down her spine. Vic looked as if he was regretting this whole train of conversation, so Claire just stared at him pointedly until he carried on. "He doesn't seem to have the capacity to hold back when it comes to any of Michael's jobs for us," Vic carried on reluctantly. "Michael tried to train him in undercover ops, but Ichi didn't have the patience to learn. Don't get me wrong, he's an excellent assassin –" he looked at the very alive Claire "– ninety-nine percent of the time, but I think it bothers him if he can't get the job done quickly. And that's exactly why Michael likes him – he's efficient and quick and never careless." That confused Claire.

"So why send him on a job that he was required to fail on? Why not just send you to do it?" she asked.

Vic shook his head. "Who knows what Michael wants? I'm around eighty percent sure that he did it simply to terrify *you* into submission. I hardly seem to elicit the same reaction from you, do I?" he said, stating the obvious. Claire decided to throw caution to the wind and speak her thoughts.

"But why is that?" she asked. "You fired a bullet at my head, kidnapped me, are part of an organisation clearly up to something terrible *and you kill people for a living*. If anything, I should be more terrified of you, who acts so like a normal person, than Ichi, who's obviously...something else." Vic laughed at her. "What?!" Claire bit out, indignant.

"Well, I wouldn't be a very good undercover agent if I acted like *him*, would I?" he explained. "And let's set one thing straight; I very rarely kill. That's not to say I'm not good at it, because I am –" Claire raised an eyebrow at the bizarre boast "– but I don't like it. I much prefer getting a job done through cosying up to important people and convincing them to give me all of the information I need...or I can steal it, either/or, really," he chuckled. He looked at Claire. "So, no, I'm not a psychopath, but the paycheque for working for Michael is a whole lot better than working for some government somewhere. Much more freedom too."

Claire considered all that Vic had said. "How do I know that this whole open and friendly act isn't exactly that – an act?"

"You don't! But you're a smart girl, Claire; I'm sure you can figure out what's genuine and what's not, given time." He smiled at her. Claire leaned back against the sofa. *This guy should* not *be putting me at ease,* she thought. *So why is he?* Something else that Vic had just said came to her mind then, and Claire felt her face grow paler as she thought on it. She glanced nervously at the door out onto the corridor. Vic's eyes followed her gaze.

"What is it, Claire?" he asked, concerned. Claire dragged her eyes away from the door to stare at the food Vic had brought with him; she found that she had no appetite.

"It's nothing, not really. It's just...do you really believe that Michael set Ichi up so that he would terrify me all of the time? So I'd stay...obedient?" she asked in a small voice. Vic's face grew stormy.

37

"That little fucker…has he done something to you *already?!*" Vic exclaimed. "What the hell, I was joking about the psycho stuff; I thought that was just how he acted on the job! Jesus, Claire, I don't want you up here on your own. I'll get you moved, I'll guard your bloody door if he's –"

"No, Vic, stop, it's nothing…really. I was just worried about it," she reassured him. *Why am I lying to him?* Claire wondered, but she stuck to her guns anyway. "The whole of yesterday freaked me out, you must understand that. I'm *still* freaked out, all things considered. But Ichi hasn't done anything to me, apart from fail to kill me," she added on with a sarcastic smile. Vic didn't look convinced.

"You'll tell me if anything happens, okay? I know you're a big girl, you can take care of yourself, but he's a trained killer and you're not in the safest of situations as it is…just being honest, Claire," he remarked, in answer to the look she gave him. "But I'll tell you this: I don't want you dead. I didn't want you dead when I didn't know you and I especially don't want you dead now that I do."

"You don't know me at all, Vic," she pointed out. Vic pretended to be horrified.

"Well you certainly know how to put a dagger through a man's heart, figuratively speaking. As it happens, I actually have." Claire winced at the thought. Vic rolled his eyes and snickered in response to her expression.

Laughter comes so easily to this man.

"Well okay, Claire, you say I don't know you. I would very much like to remedy that." He held out his hand. Claire looked at it, confused. Vic laughed again.

"Don't tell me you've forgotten how to shake a person's hand?" he grinned. Claire couldn't help but smile back. She held out her hand, which Vic grasped in his much larger one. His grip was firm but gentle.

"I'm Claire Elizabeth Danvers, newly graduated geneticist, at your service," she announced.

"Vic Winters, trained assassin and undercover agent," he replied. Claire raised an eyebrow quizzically.

"That *cannot* be your real name," she retorted. Vic chuckled; it was a low, throaty sound that reminded Claire of the way her father used to laugh, in a time in her past when she was happy.

"I guess that's for you to find out, princess," he challenged. He stood up from the couch and gestured towards the untouched tray of food on the coffee table. "Now, for the love of God eat something, or I'll be forced to feed you. And you won't like that…probably." He grinned. "I'll be back up with more around lunch time anyway, so there's no escaping food if you were planning on starving yourself out of here." He headed towards the door.

"Vic," Claire heard herself say. He turned his head around to face her, an eyebrow raised in question.

"I'm not a princess," she said simply. He smiled at her, the forlorn look he had been wearing on his face earlier creeping back up into his eyes.

"That depends on where you're standing, Claire." And then he was gone, leaving Claire, once again, alone.

Ichi

Resisting the urge to 'visit' Claire had been much harder that Ichi had anticipated it would be. He had thought that his willpower was able to withstand far longer than four days without satisfying his urge to torment the girl…he was wrong. Ichi felt his blood start to pump faster through his veins simply by looking at the door to suite 1202, and he could feel his feet walk him right up to it before his brain yelled at him to stop. *If I bother her too frequently then she'll come to expect it, and that might…ruin the fun,* Ichi had to remind himself. Constantly. Oh, how he had wanted to creep into her room in the small hours of the morning for the past four days, to bring to life all of the horrible things that he was fantasising about that were keeping him awake. But he had to learn Claire's routine first, and he couldn't do that whilst she was locked up in her room. *Well, not until I've rigged it with cameras,* he thought, though that also required Claire vacating her room for at least ten minutes.

Ichi knew it wouldn't be long now before Michael decided that Claire could have more freedom in the complex; Alexis had commented that she had recovered from her ordeal as well as anyone could expect to recover, and that was two days ago when she had brought round a collection of Claire's clothes and other belongings from her flat and her parents' house. Ichi had considered visiting Claire's flat too, to learn more about her, but Michael had firmly denied his request and warned him against finding out where the flat was on his own. Ichi valued his life too much to risk directly disobeying one of Michael's orders, so he begrudgingly gave up on the idea.

He had considered questioning Vic about Claire – he had spent a large portion of each of the past four days with the girl, holed up in her prison together. Ichi had nudged his anger at that to the back of his brain. However, he hadn't spoken to Vic since the day Claire was brought in; he was still furious that Vic had missed the shot that should have killed this girl who was plaguing Ichi's every waking moment. *If she were already dead, I could go on satisfying my urge to kill by assassinating other people. Now that'll never be enough.* It was a catch twenty-two, and Ichi knew it, for if Claire were already dead, Ichi would have been pissed that he wasn't the one to kill her and he would never have known how much of a thrill it was to torment her.

He blasted the conflicting thoughts from his head with a cold shower. Ichi decided his best course of action would be to go about his normal routine; that way, when Claire was finally let out of her rooms, she would constantly be looking over her shoulder for him and he would simply be ignoring her…which would put her on edge even more. It was perfect! Ichi couldn't wait to see that terrified look on Claire's face again.

Resolved to exercise out all of his pent-up energy at the gym, Ichi dressed in a black t-shirt and grey jogging pants before heading out of his room.

Just as Vic was leaving Claire's.

Oh, for fuck's sake, Ichi cursed internally. He planned to simply walk past Vic and ignore him, but Vic seemed to have decided that now was the moment to break their four-day silence.

"You did something to her the first night she was here," Vic said accusingly.

Ichi kept his composure and answered, his voice cool: "And did she tell you this directly?"

Vic frowned at him. "No, she didn't need to –"

"Then I didn't do anything," Ichi interrupted. He allowed himself a glance at Claire's door; Vic caught on to it immediately.

"You want to know how she's coping," he said.

"No I don't," Ichi lied smoothly. Vic pondered that for a moment and then seemed to remember who exactly he was talking to.

"You want to know if she's thinking about you," he stated. *Bang. Hit the nail on the head.* Ichi didn't respond. "You're a dick, Ich," Vic muttered. Ichi started to walk away from him.

"Tell me something I wasn't supposed to know already," he responded. Then, out of the corner of his eye, he saw Vic flinch at his retort. Ichi narrowed his eyes. "What was that?" he asked, suspicious. It looked like Vic was internally cursing himself at his reaction.

"Michael might let your actions fly because you're so good at your job, but that doesn't mean that *I'll* let you get away with doing whatever you want. So don't you dare lay a hand on her, Ichi, or you might find it missing when you wake up the next day," Vic threatened. Ichi couldn't tell if he was deflecting or not; maybe Vic's flinch was genuinely directed at Ichi's demeanour and didn't mean anything else. Ichi didn't care enough to work it out. He continued to walk down the corridor.

"I'll keep that in mind, Vic," he answered sarcastically, choosing to take the stairs over the elevator, for want of silence.

Looks like I'll have to factor in avoiding a guard dog into my plans, Ichi mused, as he jogged effortlessly down twelve flights of stairs in order to take out his frustration in the gym.

CHAPTER 5
A New Life

Claire

Claire was beginning to suffer from extreme cabin fever. For four days, she had been confined to her room and it was more than beginning to wear thin. During that time, Vic had visited her three times a day to bring her food and make sure she was eating, as well as providing her with much-needed human company. Vic tended to spend as long with her as possible, for which Claire was grateful; what else did she have to do, after all? Alexis had dropped by two days prior – with her came several of Claire's belongings as well as what felt like half of her wardrobe from her flat. Alexis had had the good sense to bring Claire her laptop, Mp3 player and Kindle for which Claire had thanked her profusely. Of course, there was no way in hell that Michael was allowing her anywhere near an internet connection, so Claire had to placate her boredom with any music or films that she already had on her hard drive (which Claire assumed had been scoured by Michael before being given to her). Claire was glad that she had thousands of books on her Kindle, which her father had given her the previous Christmas for fear that her flat would be overrun with physical books.

But it didn't matter what Claire tried to do to distract herself; her thoughts were always drawn back to the far more interesting (and terrifying) situation that she herself was in. Why hadn't she had any more 'visits' from Ichi? Claire had been certain that he was going to continually plague her whilst she was locked in a room that she couldn't escape from…but he hadn't. Claire was, of course, relieved about this, but it was beginning to make her incredibly paranoid. When was he going to show up? What was he going to say? What was he going to do? What could *she* do about it? All those thoughts and more raced through Claire's head on an endless loop, tormenting every moment that she was awake, and often when she was asleep too.

Claire feared to fall asleep nowadays; not least because of who currently presided next door. Her fitful sleep was littered with horrible nightmares no matter how many times she woke up and fell asleep again. Only they weren't nightmares; it was merely Claire's brain replaying what had happened to her in real life over and over again. *How are you supposed to chase the nightmares away when they actually happened?* Claire found herself constantly wondering. The whole experience left her both drained and restless; she couldn't help but believe that all she needed was an actual, real life distraction to help her sleep and feel less on edge.

Claire hoped to God that that distraction wouldn't come in the form of Ichi.

Claire still didn't know why she had lied to Vic four days prior about Ichi terrifying her. He had offered to protect her several times since then, not buying her lie one bit. But how would that look to Ichi, getting someone else to act as her bodyguard? It would only make her look weaker. Claire knew that the only hope she had of coping with Ichi whilst she was here was to act as though he didn't bother her, and she couldn't do that by having Vic baby her all the time. Still…Claire felt a hell of a lot better when he was around, and that wasn't just to do with his tall, lean stature and tightly muscled arms. She had only been able to fall asleep for the past three days because he had been there, a fact that Claire was ashamed of. She still wasn't sure why she trusted and even liked Vic when it so easily could all be an act. But what choice did Claire have? She had no one else. Claire had half hoped that Alexis would show up again, just to keep her company, but the other woman hadn't. Alexis had acted strangely when she had given Claire her belongings, as if she was expecting Claire to know something that she simply didn't. *But that might be because that's how I feel about everything right now,* she thought, sadly.

Claire jumped in surprise as she heard a knock on her door, but relaxed again as soon as she heard Vic's voice announce that he was coming in.

"I'm pretty sure it's not lunch time yet, Vic," Claire said when he entered through the door. Though she had no access to a clock (her laptop was currently set to an entirely different date and time, which she suspected was Michael's doing), she had grown accustomed to Vic's thrice daily visits and based the time of day on when he showed up. So by her estimate, it couldn't possibly be later than noon, and that was stretching it.

"Maybe I just couldn't wait to see you again. Five hours is such a long time to go without gazing upon your face," he replied melodramatically. Claire rolled her eyes. *Why is he so interested in me? Right from the beginning, he's made that obvious,* Claire thought, not for the first time. *It really could all be an act...but then again...* Vic had told her himself that he was sure she could figure out what was real and what was not with him. But how was she supposed to do that when she had no basis for comparison? Claire pushed the thought out of her head.

Vic was grinning at her, his perfect white teeth gleaming in the light of the living room. "...what?" Claire asked, nervously.

Vic's smile grew even wider. "I have some good news," he began. Claire cocked her head to one side expectantly.

"Which is...?" she prompted. Vic rushed over and spun her around in a circle. Claire was surprised, but laughed nonetheless.

"Now you're just being a tease," she remarked. Vic gave her a look, the one he had started giving her whenever she said something that could resemble flirting...which had been becoming more and more of a frequent occasion, considering Claire had nobody else to talk to. And Vic was very attractive. Claire had a feeling he knew it, with his easy smiles and the way he swept his blonde hair back from his eyes so that she could see his face properly when they were speaking.

"Michael has hereby decided that you have earned your roaming rights of the complex...well, except for the lab, for obvious reasons," he said, finally. Claire simply looked at him; she didn't know what to say. The very thing she had been hoping would happen only five minutes ago was now true...but what was she actually supposed to *do?* She vocalised those thoughts to Vic. He responded by ruffling her hair. "Don't worry; he's got plenty for you to do," Vic said, "As it turns out, this place is in dire need of a repaint...apparently. Personally, I don't really see why the white walls need to be painted white again. But those are his orders. I'm sure it'll make for *fascinating* work." Claire blew stray strands of hair out of her eyes as she considered Vic's words. He watched her do so as if it was the most interesting thing in the world to him. Claire couldn't help but look away, face reddening.

"No, it's exactly what I need, Vic. Some honest to goodness hands-on labour will do nicely, thanks. Only…" she paused.

"What?" Vic asked. Claire frowned.

"I don't suppose you have any headphones? Alexis never brought mine over and I imagine I'm going to need some musical company if I'm going to be conversing with a wall all day," she said. Vic laughed at her.

"I'm sure we can wrangle a pair from somewhere, princess," he replied, before walking back over to the door. He glanced over his shoulder when he realised that Claire wasn't following. He looked at her pointedly.

"Oh, I get to leave *now?*" she asked, surprised.

"Well, I imagine you'll want to know where everything is first to satisfy your curiosity," he said, smiling. Claire nodded in agreement and made for the door. But as she was about to leave, Vic stuck his hand out, blocking the doorway. Claire looked up at him, confused.

"What is it?" she said. Vic ran his eyes up and down Claire's body, making her blush again.

"Are you seriously going to leave your room wearing *those*?" he inquired. Claire looked down at herself; she was wearing a white strappy camisole top and some very short turquoise shorts (room 1202 was very warm). She considered Vic's question for a moment, before shaking her head.

"Fuck it, I'm already a prisoner here; I'm not going to start dressing like I'm going to my own funeral every bloody day," she replied, trying to sound nonchalant whilst inwardly thinking she was making a huge mistake. *I need to be brave; I can't let* him *affect me. If I do I've lost,* Claire repeated, like a mantra she was clinging on to for her sanity.

Vic let out a low whistle. "Language, princess," he laughed. "Not that I'm complaining about the clothes, personally…" Claire whacked him on the arm.

"Keep your eyes to yourself, Mr Winters," she scolded.

"Ha! Not when you're dressed like that, Miss Danvers," he chimed back, running his hand through his hair as he did so.

That was how Ichi came across them in the corridor, laughing and flirting with each other, as if Claire wasn't a prisoner and Vic wasn't one of her captors. For one horrible, drawn out second, all Claire could do was stare at him, the laughter dying on her lips. He was staring right back, eyebrows lost in the dark hair that fell over his forehead, they were raised so high. And then –

"Vic," Ichi murmured, as he turned his back on them and lurked towards his own room.

"Easy, Claire, easy," Vic said softly. Claire realised she was gripping Vic's arm far too tightly, her nails digging into his skin. She took a deep breath and let go.

"Sorry…I just wasn't expecting that," she replied truthfully.

Vic sighed. "Claire, you're going to have to get used to him being here. But I've said it a hundred times before – I'll never let him do anything to you. If you feel unsafe, just say the word and I won't leave your side, I promise." His tone was serious, all of the previous frivolity long gone. Claire forced herself to smile up at him.

"No, I'm fine, really. It's just that I haven't seen him since, you know, he tried to kill me." *And then he snuck into my room, pinned me to the bed and told me he was going to take everything from me before killing me,* she added on silently. She suppressed a shiver. *I need to get better at hiding my reactions to things, for my own sake.*

They waited on the elevator in silence, both of them too wrapped up in their own thoughts to speak. Claire knew she had to change the subject to something more banal. "So…why so many floors to this place?" she asked tentatively. Vic shrugged.

"Most of it is just apartments for anyone staying here. There are two suites per floor from the second to the twelfth floor. Currently only six are occupied – most of Michael's…agents…are out doing somewhat permanent undercover work or come back between jobs so infrequently that their rooms may as well be vacant," he answered, stepping into the lift as he did so. "The ground and first floors are taken up by a rec hall to stop us being bored to death and for those of us too lazy to make our own food, and yes, we have a permanent chef here," he said in response to Claire's 'I'm about to interrupt and ask a question' face. "There's also a shooting range, the gym and a swimming pool, and numerous…classrooms, for want of a better word." Claire looked confused.

"Classrooms?"

"Rooms where we can research in peace and quiet and debrief others on assignments. Some of them are physical practice rooms for specific weapons, though. As you can imagine, they're used quite a bit."

"What about below ground? That's where Michael's office is, right?" Claire asked. The elevator screen showed her that they had just passed the fifth floor.

"Well remembered, princess," he replied. "The basement floor is all for Michael, and the sub-basement floor is the lab and…other rooms. Both floors are off-limits, obviously." Vic glanced at Claire out of the corner of his eye. Claire didn't bother asking what 'other rooms' meant; she imagined they weren't used for anything that she particularly wanted to know about if she was going to get any sleep that night.

"So which rooms am I painting then?" she asked instead.

"All of the classrooms, basically. The gym is mirrored and the rec hall is way too high for you to be able to paint all of it, so they're both out. But trust me…there are plenty of classrooms. It should keep you busy for a few weeks, at least! If you want any help, please don't ask me," he chuckled. "Though I'll happily come along and watch you whilst doing absolutely nothing myself." Claire raised an eyebrow at his comment, smirking slightly.

"Can I use the gym? Can I get food ordered in that I can cook up in my room myself? Do you think Alexis can get me a swim suit so I can use the pool? Is there a window *anywhere* in this building?" Claire had many more questions than that, but Vic held up a hand to stop the torrent before it could continue.

"One thing at a time!" he exclaimed, laughing at her excitement. "Yes, you can use the gym. No, you can't cook in your room because Michael's cut the wires and the gas to your kitchen so you don't deliberately set something on fire…haven't you noticed?" Claire shook her head, surprised that she hadn't actually tested anything in the kitchen whilst she had been confined to her room. *Michael really has thought of everything, hasn't he?* Claire mused. Vic continued: "Yes, I'm sure Alexis can get you a swim suit; hell, *I'll* get you one if I get to pick it," he joked. Claire didn't even bother admonishing him for it. "And if there's a window anywhere, I haven't found it yet. Though I should point out that I get to go outside of my own free will." Vic grinned like an idiot at the look Claire gave him for his blatant disregard of her captivity.

"Speaking of Alexis, which floor does she stay on?" Claire asked suddenly.

"She's on the fourth floor, suite 401." Vic looked at Claire as if he was expecting her to ask something else, but when she didn't, he sighed. "Right, here we are; first floor. After you, princess." He gestured towards the slowly opening elevator doors. Claire cautiously stepped out onto the corridor floor.

There were several doors on her left, all numbered. On her right there were far fewer of them, but there were double doors that led to what Claire could only assume was the rec hall. *I'm not even sure what a rec hall for assassins should look like,* she thought. Her confusion was met with an answer after Vic led her through the double doors; it was a conglomerate of various facilities for the people living in the complex. There was a giant kitchen in one corner with a mix of long and circular tables situated in front of it. It reminded Claire of high school, except the smells coming from the kitchen were far more enticing than those from her teenage memories. Against the other wall were pool tables, arcade games, a basketball hoop…*this feels like it's come straight out of an American teen summer camp film,* she mused. She looked up at Vic.

"What, not what you were expecting?" he joked. Claire rolled her eyes.

"It feels very nineties teen summer camp," she replied, voicing her thoughts. Vic chuckled. He turned Claire around, to look at the side of the rec hall that they had just come through; Claire had completely ignored it by only looking forwards.

"Is that a *bar?"* she exclaimed, rushing over to examine the various optics hanging on the wall. There was a collection of glasses on the shiny surface beneath them, a fridge full of wine and a tiny freezer with an ice bucket lying on top of it. On an adjacent floating island table there were a couple of sinks and a draft soft drinks machine.

"Grown up enough for you?" Vic inquired, eyebrow raised.

"I guess it's too early in the day for a drink…" Claire muttered, eyeing up the rum. Vic grasped on to her shoulders and wheeled her around.

"Booze isn't the answer, Claire," he said, and marched her over to examine the kitchen.

"That depends on what the question is," she replied sarcastically, knowing full well what he was referring to. *It's not for him or anyone else to decide how I cope with my situation. But I'll hardly be keeping my wits about me if I just get drunk,* she thought dolefully. As she approached the kitchen, Vic gestured to a man who Claire could only assume was the chef he had mentioned earlier. The man couldn't have been much taller than her, with broad shoulders and dark, curly, slightly receding hair. His face was plain, the corners of his eyes slightly crow-footed. Claire thought that he might have been around the same age as her parents.

"Roger, this is Claire, our new…resident," Vic said. Roger smirked at the comment, eying Claire up critically. Claire looked away; she didn't like how all of these people felt it was acceptable to so blatantly size her up. Roger laughed, the crow's feet by his eyes creasing up as he did so.

"You're going to have to get used to the guys here looking at you, Little Miss Captive. Have you seen yourself in a mirror?" he remarked. Vic ruffled her hair.

"Told you that you should've changed," he said. Claire chose to ignore it, swatting his hand away. *I am not some weak-willed, little girl dependent on everyone else,* she thought, irritated.

"Yes, I'm Claire Danvers, currently being held against my will," she said to Roger, holding her hand out as she spoke. "I hope your cooking's good because apparently I'm not allowed near fire for fear of burning the place down in protest." Roger took her hand and shook it, laughing.

"Oh, I *do* like her, Vic. And I'm betting the other guys will too. You better be keeping an eye on her!"

"Both of them," he replied, smiling. Claire frowned.

"I can fob off unwelcome attention just fine all by myself, thank you very much," she muttered, sounding entirely like a five-year-old girl being scolded by her father. Roger looked at her sympathetically.

"Unfortunately, some of them just won't take *no* for an answer," he said with a sigh, and Claire's mind went straight to Ichi. She repressed a shiver at the thought. Then she felt Vic's fingers brush against her own, as if he was going to take her hand but then thought better of it.

"I need to show her around the rest of the place, Roger. See you in a couple hours! What's for lunch?" he asked. Roger seemed to think about it for a moment.

"Probably pie; there's leftover chicken from last night." He smiled at Claire. "Give me a list of things you like to eat and I'll make them for you. Doesn't matter what it is. You should at least be able to *eat* what you want here." Claire decided in that moment that she liked Roger; his act of kindness was likely to be one of few she experienced here.

"Thank you," she replied, as Vic took her out of the rec hall and down the stairs to the gym. They walked in silence for a few moments, until Vic eventually broke it.

"He's a good guy, Roger; I'd go so far as to say you can trust him," he said in a low voice. "Though I know that that trust will be hard earned with you in this place." Claire regarded Vic; his expression was odd.

"So you're saying I shouldn't trust *you*?" she asked, confused. Only four days ago Vic had been commenting on how he had hoped to earn it. Vic smiled at her, but it didn't meet his eyes.

"Just don't trust everything I say," he replied. *Oh great,* now *he decides to be enigmatic.* Vic sighed when Claire did nothing but stare at him in response to his answer. "Don't think about it too much," he added on. "Well, at least, not now. Ah, here's the gym." Claire knew that Vic was happy for the change in subject, so she chose not to press the matter of his confusing statement further. *Well, for now, anyway,* she thought.

The doors to the gym were made of glass – Claire could see right through to the equipment. Alexis was on a treadmill, along with two men and a woman that Claire, understandably, did not recognise. "Isn't that, like, half the people living here right now?" Claire asked.

Vic chuckled. "Most of us basically live down here. What use is an out-of-shape assassin?"

"I'm sorry if spending all of your time with me has interrupted your gym routine," Claire replied dryly. She didn't mean it at all. Vic merely looked at her.

"Interrupting them in the gym to introduce yourself would not be the best way to go about things, so I won't bother taking you in," he said. Claire managed to catch Alexis' eye through the glass door, however, but the other woman averted her gaze almost immediately. *I wonder why she's acting so oddly,* Claire thought. Then Claire realised that the other gym occupants had noticed her through the glass and were regarding her curiously. She didn't know what to do, so she looked away. "And that's our cue to leave. You can deal with prying eyes later, princess," Vic said, as he gently pushed her further down the ground floor corridor. "The swimming pool is accessed through the gym. There aren't any changing rooms so you just have to change clothes in your room. For my sanity though, please don't go flouncing about in a bikini outside of the pool." He grinned at her mock insulted face.

"Give me some credit…a bikini isn't practical swimming gear for me at all. So it'll be a swim suit I'm *flouncing* about in," she joked. Claire glanced at a door to her left.

"What's in there?" she asked. Vic went over to open the door and gestured her in. It led into a narrow room, the upper half of one of its walls covered in windows that overlooked a large gym hall with mirrored walls. There was another door to Claire's left that clearly led into the hall itself.

"This hall is for self-defence and hand-to-hand combat practices that need a larger space than the classrooms," Vic explained. "We're standing in the viewing gallery just now. It serves us well to watch each other practice sometimes." Then they exited the gallery back out onto the hallway and Vic showed her into the next room. The objects inside made it look just like a classroom straight out of Claire's high school: white board, over-head projector, desks and chairs. The four walls of the room were unadorned and plain – Claire felt boredom creep over her already. Vic laughed at the resigned look on her face.

"I told you your work would be fascinating. White paint on white walls…riveting stuff," he said.

"How many of these rooms are there?"

Vic's eyes looked up at the ceiling as he mentally counted. "Five down here, thirteen upstairs. The ones above are smaller though, if that's any consolation," he joked.

Claire sighed. "Well, I may as well start now and work up an appetite for Roger's pie," she said. "Where are all of the painting supplies?" Vic took her out into the hallway and pointed to a door at the end of the corridor.

"Everything you need will be in there. If you need anything else, just go and ask Roger. He's in charge of all of the general food and supply orders for this place." Claire looked down at her clothes, considering what she was wearing.

"Can I go upstairs and change into something I don't mind ruining? I'm rather fond of these shorts," she said. Vic rolled his eyes at her.

"You're not going to be stuck in a room all day and forced to paint, Claire; it's just work to keep you busy. Feel free to go back up to your room or to the rec hall or gym whenever you want." He glanced at her clothes. "And I agree; I don't want you ruining your shorts either," he added on, winking at her. *Winking*. It struck Claire that Vic was just about the only person she had ever met who could get away with it without looking like a fool.

She wandered back into the classroom they had just vacated and stared at the blank walls within. "Vic," she said.

He turned to look at her. "Yes?"

"Please find me those head phones…fast," she requested, in a tone far more serious than her words required. Vic laughed. "As you wish," was all he said, before making to head down the corridor. But then he turned around again, clearly having thought of something else he needed to say. "Claire, please be careful around here," he said, genuine concern in his pale blue eyes. Claire responded to his words with a faint smile.

"Don't worry, Vic, I haven't forgotten where I am, despite your efforts to take that off my mind." Vic seemed to take comfort in that. He regarded Claire for a second, looking as if he might say something else, before actually walking down the corridor to leave this time. It took Claire a couple of seconds to realise that she had another question only made obvious by Vic's absence, and rushed out of the classroom after him to ask it. "Vic!"

she half yelled down the corridor. He turned around, surprised. "Where's *your* room?"

Vic's face lit up. "I thought you'd never ask," he grinned. "I'm up on the fifth floor in 502. Dinner at my place tonight?" Claire could tell that he was chancing his luck. She decided she could throw him a bone...this time.

"It's a date," she replied, giving Vic a half smile before returning down the corridor.

CHAPTER 6
Toxic

Ichi

Ichi hated it. Ever since Claire had been given roaming access of the complex, everyone was talking about her. Not that he talked to any of the others often, but they were loud and brash and he couldn't help overhearing everything they said about her: why she was here; what she could possibly have done to have ended up here; how well she was coping. Ichi didn't want them to be talking about her – he wanted Claire's attention to be on him and him alone. He wanted her to be terrified of what he'd do next. And yet…

And yet Claire seemed fine. Better than fine, if Ichi was being honest with himself. Since Michael had decided that she could repaint all of the classrooms, Claire spent most of her time covered in white paint, running in and out of the storeroom, singing along to the music coming through her headphones. But when she wasn't painting, Claire was exercising in the gym or swimming in the pool and talking with everyone else in the rec hall. It seemed as if she attempted to spend as little time as possible in her own room, preferring to eat with the others or, more often, with Vic in his room. Ichi told himself that this was because her kitchen was non-functional, but he knew that that wasn't just the case.

Ichi hadn't wasted a minute after Claire was allowed to leave her room. Directly after he had run into her and Vic in the corridor two weeks prior, he had gotten all of his equipment together to rig up Claire's room so that he could watch her. He frowned at the memory of them together that day. It irked Ichi immensely – the way Claire had been holding onto Vic's arm and laughing whilst he did that idiotic sweep of his hair thing that he reflexively did when he saw something he liked. Ichi wondered when he suddenly became so interested in what all of Vic's hand gestures meant; did he always know what they had meant but simply hadn't cared before? Ichi didn't spare it another thought. Claire had been dressed in those ridiculously short blue shorts that day that showed off her long, pale legs. He imagined that if she was allowed outside underneath the summer sun, they would tan. But the very appearance of her looking happy and unafraid and *alive* had shocked him so much that Ichi had been unable to move for a moment. Claire's clothes, or lack thereof, had hardly helped. It was all he could do to stalk away from the two of them, only mildly satisfied with the way Claire's eyes had widened and her grip on Vic's arm had tightened at the sight of him. Ichi had thought that her reaction meant that she was still terrified of him.

Clearly he was wrong.

Since that day, Claire seemed completely unperturbed by his presence. He was dutifully ignoring her too, hoping that she would become paranoid and on edge as he had wanted. In reality, that wasn't the way Claire Danvers was acting at all, causing Ichi to become increasingly frustrated. Because she didn't spend much time in her room, he hadn't managed to glean very much information about who Claire was when she was by herself. Ichi would sit on his bed at night, watching the various hidden camera feeds he had rigged up in her room (cursing the fact that he didn't have any waterproof cameras set up by her shower…he would rectify that soon), waiting for her to do or say something that he could use against her. But Claire didn't cry, she didn't speak out loud and she didn't try to break anything in despair. All she did was listen to a ridiculously eclectic range of music, from Irish folk to Japanese rock (Ichi found this incredibly amusing), whilst reading various books on her Kindle. *And that's all essentially boring, pointless information,* Ichi thought, irritated. The only thing Ichi had learned of note was that Claire wasn't sleeping. And when she did, she didn't sleep well. He drew some kind of satisfaction from the fact that she couldn't control her terror when she was unconscious. Ichi had hoped against hope that Claire would cry out in her sleep, to give him some indication of what she was dreaming about, but she never did. Claire would merely toss and turn and thrash about on her couch, finally waking up when she fell to the floor. Ichi wondered why Claire didn't sleep on the bed; he liked to assume it was because of what he had done to her upon her arrival to the complex. That was the information that Ichi clung on to; it suggested that how Claire was acting on the outside was exactly that – an act.

55

Besides watching her through cameras, Ichi also spied on Claire in person when she was around the complex. He noted that she was always out of her room by half past seven in the morning to go to the gym or the swimming pool – she alternated them, presumably so she didn't get bored, although for the last three days she had chosen only to swim. After this, Claire would come back to her room to have a shower and change into 'painting clothes'. These usually consisted of an oversized t-shirt and denim shorts, which always resulted in her showing off her damnably great legs whilst concealing her chest. It only took a couple of days of ogling from the other male assassins for her to wear the t-shirt; before that, it had been little strappy tops that he could tell Vic couldn't tear his eyes away from, as gentlemanly as he attempted to be. Then Claire would have breakfast in the rec hall with Vic and the others who were here, but never Alexis. Alexis seemed to be avoiding her; Ichi could see that Claire was confused by this and was trying to work out why she was doing so. *Maybe she's simply uninterested,* Ichi mused, although considering how everyone else seemed to be obsessed with the new 'resident' in Michael's complex he couldn't help but wonder whether there really was something more to Alexis ignoring Claire.

After she had eaten, Claire would paint. And paint. And paint. She often didn't stop until Vic found which classroom she was working in to remind her that she had skipped lunch entirely. She'd then overcompensate by eating too much at dinner and would subsequently be groggy and tired for the next few hours. Claire disappeared during those few hours onto the stairwell; where exactly Ichi wasn't sure, not without giving away the fact that he was following her. There were a few more obvious places she could be, Ichi knew – there was an alcove of sorts underneath the stairs on the fourth floor where cleaning supplies used to be stored, and another one on the tenth floor. But the stairwell was very quiet from the fifth floor upwards, so Ichi supposed that Claire could be holed up literally anywhere on the upper floors. Ichi considered the idea that she had managed to break into another suite, but a cursory search around the other rooms (which involved breaking into them himself) confirmed that she hadn't. It also caused Michael to call Ichi into his office to warn him not to do it again. *So I can't break into anybody else's room but Claire's? And I can get away with installing cameras in her rooms?* Ichi was confused about what Michael considered to be 'acceptable' behaviour or not. But when he voiced this opinion, Michael merely smiled at him and told him that that wasn't for Ichi to know.

Claire would return to painting at about nine in the evening until nearly midnight before she would, finally, retire up to her room. Once there, she would shower again in order to remove the paint from all over her person before reading and listening to music until the small hours of the morning. By Ichi's count, Claire rarely slept more than four hours in any one night. *That'll catch up to her eventually,* he thought. *And when she's exhausted beyond belief, that's when I'll strike,* he decided. Even the idea of cornering Claire again caused Ichi's pulse to accelerate in his throat and his pupils to expand and contract in quick succession.

There was one major problem: Vic. Always Vic. The damn man seemed to shadow Claire as much as he dared to, considering how she had asked him not to. Ichi wondered why she had said as much. They seemed to get on incredibly well and Claire even seemed to, infuriatingly, react positively to Vic's flirtations and, more rarely, return them. Ichi couldn't stand it; Vic was successfully monopolising her, making it near impossible for Ichi to do the same...but with rather different intentions. He knew that Vic's presence, as well as Ichi not knowing where Claire's stairwell hiding place was without making it obvious that he was tailing her, resulted in him having very few windows of opportunity in which to accost Claire on her own. Ichi didn't want the next time he did so to be in her room again – that's what Claire would expect the most after all – which meant that Ichi would have to go after her when she was painting, at a time when Vic was sure not to show up unannounced and in a room that was far enough away from the rec hall or the gym for anyone to hear her. And, annoyingly, only around half of the classrooms had locks on them. *So, not difficult to set up at all*, Ichi thought wryly. However, once he did get a situation like that set up, it would be plain sailing. Claire listened to music and sang along to it (rather well, Ichi noted) whilst she painted – she would never hear him creeping up on her. Not a single room in the entire complex had a window, and so long as he cornered her in a classroom he could lock, Claire would have no escape from him.

So all Ichi had to do was wait; wait for what felt like a million different parameters to line up in an ideal situation for what he wanted to do. Although the 'what' wasn't a set thing yet. It suddenly occurred to Ichi that that was the only thing he hadn't planned. He had imagined so many different situations in which he did various things to Claire, from the more obvious physical torments to the less obvious, deeply psychological ones. He just needed to work out what he would get most pleasure out of inflicting upon her, and what things would affect her most. Which was no easy thing, considering Claire simply gave nothing away about what she was thinking or feeling.

He was lost in such thoughts when he found himself falling into step a few feet behind the two other men who were currently residing in the complex, Ryan and Imran. He knew Ryan only in the context of him being exactly the kind of person Ichi hated. He was egotistical, misogynistic, boastful and loud. Apparently, that made him absolutely perfect for corporate undercover work. He wished Ryan was back on a job. Imran, he knew less about and didn't care to find out more.

Ichi kept his footsteps quiet; he couldn't be bothered with them realising he was there. "I joined her in the pool this morning, Imran," he heard Ryan say. "My *God* she's got a body to die for! Gotta hand it to Vic, he picked the right girl to fall for. If I wasn't scared of what he'd do to me, I'd try and screw her myself. Still tempted to…she's technically fair game, right?" *Jesus Christ, he's such a sleaze*, Ichi thought, irritated by the other man's very existence upon the earth.

"Hold up, she might be dead in a week or two, you never know. What would be the point in going after her?" Imran countered. *You bet she'll be dead in a week or two,* Ichi agreed.

"Are you kidding? That's exactly why I'd go for her!" Ryan exclaimed, as if it was the most obvious thing in the world to understand. "There wouldn't be any emotional attachments…I bet she's begging for it in case it's the last time she ever gets to bang a guy." Ryan laughed, and Ichi inhaled through his nose so loudly in anger that the two men in front of him turned around. Ryan threw him a lazy smile. "You know, Ichi, skulking isn't nice when you're not on a job. You have a problem with the new girl? I heard you failed to kill her, big time," he mocked.

Nostrils flaring, anger rising in his throat, Ichi's hand instinctively went for a knife at his hip that simply wasn't there. Ryan noticed the movement instantly. He held his hands up in protest. "Alright, alright!" Ryan said, "Someone's super touchy about that. But hey, you should be glad. She's way too hot to kill off without fooling around with for a bit." *You have no idea how spot on you are, you prick,* Ichi fumed. He chose to ignore the comments and walked straight past the pair of them.

"Aw look, Imran, he's ignoring us! Did I hit a soft spot, Ich?" Ryan called out after him. "Are you jealous 'cause Vic got in there first? You could always go for Claire after he's done with her, though I don't know if she'd be in any fit state after him. Vic's *massive.*"

"Height doesn't always correspond to length, Ryan," Imran pointed out, laughing.

"I bet in Vic's case it does. Lucky son of a bitch seems to have everything going for him these days," Ryan replied, his voice trailing away as Ichi walked further and further away from them, jumping in the elevator up to his room. He was infuriated; they had been sullying Claire's image before anything had even happened to her. *Ichi* would be the one to sully her, not anybody else. He felt fairly certain that Claire would never 'go for' a man like Ryan – she came across as far too mature to waste her time on someone so...so...*sexist.* It angered him to no end that Ryan had been talking about her like she was an object to be passed around all of the men in the complex. Claire was human, so beautifully, wondrously human, whose grasp of every emotion from scared to outright petrified was so nuanced that Ichi experienced many new shades of terrified on her face the day Claire thought that she was going to die. *No object can be so magnificent,* he thought longingly, his left hand twitching at the thought of curling his fingers through her hair or around her throat. It occurred to Ichi that he wasn't sure which, and that confused him somewhat.

But Ryan and Imran's snide comments about Vic kept niggling Ichi in the back of his brain. He couldn't possibly have slept with Claire already. *It would be obvious if he had...right?* Ichi wondered. *Vic would throw it in my face.* Ichi realised only then that Vic most definitely wouldn't do that. *He'd keep it to himself. He'd keep all of her to himself.* Ichi would never know. And now Ichi was wondering if that was what Claire was sneaking off to do every evening. It was entirely possible that she was holed up in Vic's room for those few, unchartered hours every evening, letting the other man's hands roam all over her skin. *Or they could be doing it when she has dinner at his place,* Ichi's brain helpfully chimed in.

Ichi held his head between his hands. *Stop thinking about it, stop it.* His mind was going into overdrive, thinking about every situation in which Vic could be screwing Claire and ruining her for him faster than he could chase the thoughts away. Ichi started to grow dizzy; he could see dark spots clouding his sight, and could feel his heart beating erratically.

Get a fucking hold of yourself, he admonished. When the elevator reached the twelfth floor, it was all Ichi could do to drag himself along the corridor and past Claire's door without thrashing it down.

He turned his shower on and blasted himself with icy cold water, not bothering to undress first. "I need to go after her soon…for my own sanity," Ichi muttered aloud, feeling his heartbeat gradually slow down as the torrent of water washed away his unexplainable rage.

CHAPTER 7
A Thousand Miles

Claire

Although painting all of the classrooms in Michael's complex was indeed boring, Claire had found it incredibly therapeutic. During the three weeks since she had been given the tedious work, Claire felt as if she had finally been able to take stock of her situation. Yes, there had been what had seemed at the time a very real attempt on her life, but she was still alive. Yes, she was now a prisoner to a man with a dubious-at-best interest in her parents' research, but so long as her parents remained off the grid, Claire's life was safe. And if they returned…Claire would be responsible for betraying them in order to, once again, save her own life and keep her sister Olivia free from harm.

Claire knew that it was only a matter of time before Michael found her parents. Yet until he did, Claire was in limbo; she couldn't really do anything to improve her chances of survival. That fact had freaked her out at first – Claire had never been in a position before where she had had no influence over what happened to her. At school and university, she had only herself to blame for not studying hard enough if she got a bad grade (which hadn't been often due to her being incredibly competitive). In her social life, it was entirely up to Claire who she talked to and therefore who she liked and spent time with. And with boys…well, Claire had definitely never allowed herself to be treated like a doormat for any of them. Except for Zeke, Claire's one allowance for making a bad decision.

Claire sighed. All of those previous decisions seemed so trivial now. But thinking over and over again about how if she had only done *this* or *that* she might have prevented her current situation only made Claire feel worse. So with every brush stroke of white paint on white walls, Claire resolved to just let it all go and focus on what she *could* do. She could get

61

physically fitter to make herself less vulnerable, so she started getting up and hitting the gym or the pool early in the morning. Claire hated the early morning exercise at first, but now she found herself enjoying the feeling of burning muscles, accelerated breathing and quickening heartrate, and the increase in stamina that came with all of that. She had thanked Alexis profusely when she provided Claire with a swim suit, but Alexis had merely nodded and went on with her day. *What could I possibly have done to piss her off since the first night here when she was so nice to me?* Claire had wondered, not for the first time.

The situation with Alexis was eerily paralleled with Claire's situation with Ichi. He had also been ignoring Claire since that first, terrifying night. The only difference was that he had explicitly told Claire that he was going to take 'everything' from her, whereas Alexis had made no such promises that she would have continued contact with Claire, menacing or otherwise. She shivered at the memory of Ichi whispering into her ear, as she always did when she thought for too long about it. But with the memory came a growing sense of confusion and foreboding. How could Ichi take everything from her if he made no contact whatsoever with her? Claire couldn't help but think he was planning something terrible. Yet on the other hand…Ichi seemed completely disinterested and detached, not only from her but also from everybody else. Vic had told her that that was simply how Ichi was. *Maybe he was just pissed off that he couldn't kill me, so he thought he'd mess with my mind a bit but then realised it wasn't worth it.* Claire had thought this on numerous occasions when she passed Ichi on the twelfth floor corridor, but she wasn't convinced. There was something about him that Claire had felt all too clearly when he was about to kill her, and later, when he accosted her in her bedroom. She didn't exactly know what that *something* was, but it was intense and dark and intimidating and beyond her comprehension. He had looked at her as if nothing else existed but her life. And he wanted to extinguish it.

Stop it, Claire, stop it! she admonished. The thought of Ichi and what he may or may not be planning had been swallowing up Claire's every waking moment since her first night here, preventing her from thinking about much else. But she had so many other things to think about, and so Claire constantly forced herself to ponder only those issues that did not pertain to Ichi as she painted classroom after classroom white, white and white.

She hadn't only been painting and exercising over the past three weeks. Claire spent any time that she was in her own room reading science fiction and fantasy novels whilst listening to a plethora of music from different genres. She was leaning towards classical and folk music right now, to go along with her current rather zen mood, though for her first week or so in the complex she had listened to nothing but Japanese hard rock and metal. Once she discovered that listening to such music only caused her to obsess over what Ichi was getting up to, however, Claire promptly stopped listening to both genres. She also had a lot of showers. Technically they were necessary after the gym and at the end of the day, to get rid of all of the white paint on her skin, but Claire knew she was doing it because the rush of the water helped to drown out all of the unwanted, unwelcome thoughts that plagued her mind.

Claire didn't sleep much. She had resigned herself to this fact for a couple of weeks now; she couldn't in good conscience expect Vic to wait for her to fall asleep every night, to soothe her nightmares away with a gentle stroke of her hair. Especially when she didn't fall asleep until about four in the morning. So Claire worked with what little, fragmented sleep she could get, although she knew that it would come back to haunt her sooner or later. Claire expected sooner. Even now, she could feel her eyelids drooping ever so slightly as she painted the final classroom that required her attention. Claire wondered if she would ever sleep well again.

Claire had tried to exhaust herself as much as possible every day, in the hope that it would cause her to fall into a deep, dreamless sleep, but it never happened. After her morning workout and shower, she'd devote most of the day to painting, only stopping when Vic told her she needed to eat, usually around dinner time. For the first week or so Claire only ate with him, up in his room, but lately she had taken to eating with both Vic and the other people currently residing in the complex. Ryan was American and a typical chauvinistic womaniser; he had recently begun joining her in the pool or gym in the morning. She could practically feel his eyes roving up and down her figure whenever she looked away, but he was funny and easy to talk to once she decided to ignore his obvious misogynistic tendencies. Imran, she couldn't quite place; he was quieter and more reserved than Ryan but the two seemed to get along rather well. Claire hadn't had enough direct conversation with him to decide if she liked him or not yet. The only other female in the complex aside from Alexis was so obviously attracted to Vic that Claire found it painful to watch her talk to him sometimes. Marie was as plain as Alexis was beautiful – she was small of stature with light brown hair and brown eyes, a spray of freckles littered across her nose and cheeks. Claire could only gather that her unassuming, forgettable appearance was what made her so great at undercover work, though Claire couldn't help but feel like a bitch even thinking such things. Maybe she was simply looking for reasons why Vic wouldn't be interested in her. Other than Ryan being obviously American, Claire couldn't place anybody's accents to a particular place, not even Vic's.

Vic. Vic was one of the things that Claire allowed herself to think about in order to push other, far more unpleasant thoughts from her mind. Claire could feel the tension growing between the two of them; how every light touch of the arm or laugh or smile was beginning to mean something else. She wished it didn't, all things considered. But Vic was a gentleman – he made no indication that he wanted to act upon his frequent, easy going verbal flirtations and seemed content with the way their relationship currently played out. For that Claire was grateful. *I imagine that initiating a romantic or physical relationship with one of the assassins sent to kill and/or kidnap me would not make my current situation any less problematic,* she had to keep reminding herself, whenever Vic gave her one of those looks that meant he was thinking about precisely that.

Despite Vic's attempts to keep her company as often as possible, he never interfered with Claire's need to be by herself for those few hours between dinner and the last lot of painting she embarked on before retiring to her room. Claire had found an alcove of sorts under the fourth floor stairwell, discovered after she went wandering up there with plans to knock on Alexis' door, before she decided against it. The alcove wasn't visible when ascending the stairs – Claire only noticed it and how deep it was because she had been investigating every visible inch of the complex that she could get away with investigating. Claire liked to hide right at the end of it in the shadows, thinking about her parents and her sister and her own situation for hours on end. Sometimes she would even find herself falling asleep, if only for about five minutes at a time, especially if she had eaten too much at dinner to compensate not having eaten anything for lunch. The stairwell was barely used in the first instance; the only person who seemed to prefer the stairs to the elevator was Ichi, and that was only occasionally. He had climbed the stairs once whilst she had been hiding in the alcove; Claire had made herself as small and as quiet as she possibly could and, thankfully, Ichi had walked on by.

64

Claire paused from her painting to survey the classroom she was in. She had pushed the desks and chairs against the far wall – she had painted that earlier in the day. By her estimate, it must have been around half past nine in the evening. Or, at least, it was the imaginary half past nine that her circadian clock had made up for her, considering she didn't know what the actual time was. Claire had asked Vic once why she couldn't just know what time of the day it was – he had only replied that that was what Michael wanted, a sad smile on his lips.

Claire had been wearing an old, worn-out t-shirt and shorts for the bulk of her painting job. However, since today was likely the last day of her job as forced resident decorator, Claire had decided to mark the occasion by wearing an airy cotton sundress, which was as white as the walls she was painting. *It's hardly like I can make use of it in the sun,* she had reasoned after the first few drops of paint had seeped into the fabric.

There were more than just a few drops staining the dress now, though they weren't exactly visible considering the colour of the dress. She didn't care about the paint splatter over her arms and legs and no doubt her hair – she could just wash them out in the shower once she was done. Which was perhaps in an hour's time by Claire's reckoning, her head cocked slightly to the left as she considered the wall she had left to paint. She sighed at the fact that she had no idea what she was supposed to do after she had repainted that wall. *Staring at it won't magically make the answer appear,* Claire thought scornfully, so she picked up her roller and began working on what was left to do.

"Olivia would be bored to tears if she had to do this," Claire found herself chuckling out loud, which was followed promptly by a twinge of pain in her chest. She had never missed her sister as much as she did now, now that she was a world away from her. Olivia and Claire had always been close, despite the differences in their personalities, taste in boys or taste in clothes. *This is her dress though,* Claire thought wryly. It was just about the only piece of clothing Olivia owned that looked better on Claire than it did on her. The tie up halter neck of the dress pushed Claire's chest in and up almost as much as a corset would, giving her a cleavage that she knew Olivia had always been envious of. She hadn't even realised it was in her flat and not at Olivia's…clearly Claire owed her sister an apology for when she insisted, months ago, that she absolutely didn't have it. If she ever saw her again.

65

As Claire methodically ran the paint roller up and down the wall in front of her, she wondered whether Michael really would stick to his word. Alexis had promised her that he would; but how much stock could Claire put in Alexis' promises? She didn't know the woman, and she certainly wasn't giving Claire an opportunity to rectify that. She didn't want to think about what would happen if Michael broke his word, so Claire clung to the hope that he wouldn't. She thought about whether her parents were okay, wherever they were, and for one horrible moment Claire wished that they weren't. *If I'm suffering then why shouldn't they?* she thought bitterly. But Claire felt bad as soon as she had thought it; if she had no memory of what happened, how could she possibly know the circumstances under which her parents disappeared? They could have had a reason for doing so that Claire would have supported. *But it's their fault I don't remember anything...isn't it?* She was so confused.

Claire shook her head, trying to get rid of the thoughts that always ended up giving her a migraine if she tried to make sense of them. She picked up her Mp3 player from where she had left it by the paint pots before dinner. After browsing through her music collection for far too long, Claire decided to put on The Killers, with the hope that the anthemic feel of their first album would lift her spirits up as she sang along.

Thirty minutes later, that decision proved to be the correct one. Claire belted out every last lyric to every song as it played, not caring if anybody could hear her. It was only in rare moments like this that Claire could almost forget where she was, and why. When there was no paint left in the pot she was using, Claire wandered over to the stacked desks where she had left an extra pot of paint. She fiddled with the lid, struggling to get it open without the use of a knife to pry it off.

As the last refrain of All These Things That I've Done faded away, Claire thought that she heard the door open from behind her. She smiled to herself, assuming it was Vic coming to check up on her again.

"Vic, I'm fine, I'm practically finished this," she began, turning around as she spoke. "Just give me twenty min –"

The end of the sentence caught in her throat as she realised it was Ichi.

CHAPTER 8
Roxanne

Ichi

Claire heard him enter the classroom earlier than Ichi had expected; he could only assume that he had made his entrance just as whatever Claire was listening to had finished. She spun around, thinking that his interruption had been Vic, a smile upon her face. That smile promptly disappeared when she saw Ichi.

Ichi made no move towards Claire, instead choosing to stand his ground several feet away from her, regarding her carefully. Claire didn't say anything; she stayed rooted to the spot as she watched Ichi in return, her eyes wide with alarm. Finally, Ichi walked very slowly towards her, and Claire seemed to break out of her reverie, her eyes roving from side to side as she tried to identify an escape. He looked her up and down almost lazily as he walked; her hands were clutching at an unopened paint pot, her ears still covered by headphones that were beginning to blare out another song. And her dress…her dress was simply begging to be ripped apart, all virginal white and revealing at the same time.

Ichi came to a halt when he was about five feet from Claire. She stopped looking around, choosing to put down the paint pot in order to remove her headphones. *Well that was stupid,* Ichi thought. Her hair was in disarray, covered in paint and coming undone from the ponytail she had put it in.

"You don't have anywhere to go," he said softly, verging on menacing. His hands were in the pockets of his jeans, making his stance so casual that an onlooker would have assumed he was merely asking Claire how she was. Claire said nothing. Ichi grinned. "What, no conversation for me?" he asked, mock upset in his voice. He took another step towards her. "You seem to have plenty for everyone else. Especially Vic. Tell me; how long did it take you to overlook that he tried to kill you? You seem to have

67

conveniently forgotten that in your hurry to *whore yourself out to him*." Ichi made no attempt to dull the scathing tone to his voice. Claire gulped, her face pale, yet still she said nothing.

Ichi frowned. He hadn't anticipated that the damn girl would stay silent. *Just watch, Claire, I'll make you scream,* he thought excitedly. Ichi took another few steps forward; he was only inches away from her. This time, Claire took a step backwards…and promptly hit the tables that were stacked behind her. She spared herself a glance over her shoulder and Ichi saw, just for a second, her face crumple at the fact that she really did have nowhere to go. Ichi smiled.

"I told you there wasn't an escape." He crossed his arms over his black t-shirt, looking at her through the numerous strands of hair that had fallen over his eyes as he walked. Claire glanced at the door. "You're currently a prisoner in a base of assassins with a ticking time bomb over your head. Everybody knows you'll be dead soon. Nobody is going to rush to your defence right now, not even Vic." He could see Claire's eyes widen even more, fighting back the urge to say something. *Jackpot.* "You think he cares about you?" Ichi continued. "You're wrong! All he wants to do is screw you. Hell, he probably already has. That's all any of the guys here want to do to you. And the girls…well, Alexis is hardly going to show up and help someone she's trying so hard to ignore." Claire flinched. "And Marie is probably so jealous that Vic's fucking you and not her that she'd gladly kill you off herself." Claire looked at the floor, biting her lip. But still, she said nothing.

Ichi, infuriated, closed the gap between them, slamming his hands down on either side of Claire onto the table behind her, pinning her in place. He looked down at her until she finally brought her face up to look back at him. Claire almost looked defiant. Almost. Ichi rested his forehead against hers.

"Is this what Vic does before he bangs you?" he murmured. "Does he look you in the eye and tell you how beautiful you are; how everything will be okay if you just keep your head down and stick by him?" Ichi didn't even know where half of the stuff he was saying was coming from, but he couldn't stop a word of it. He brought his left hand up to drag the band out that kept Claire's ponytail in, his fingers running through her hair once it had come completely undone. "Does he stroke your hair and whisper into your ear not to be afraid of him? Of this place? Of me?" Ichi could feel his right hand crawl up Claire's thigh, bringing her dress up to her waist as he did so. His other hand had left her hair to work on the knot that tied her dress up at her neck. He heard Claire gasp audibly, could feel her tremble ever so slightly like she had done on the first night that she had been brought to the complex. Claire's eyes were bright and gleaming, the dark blue of her irises almost purple in the low light of the classroom. She tried to turn her head from Ichi's and failed, the hand on her neck keeping her in place.

"Go ahead – cry. I can see you want to. It's all you *can* do, after all," Ichi mocked. The knot keeping Claire's dress up was proving too tight for him to untie one-handed; Ichi brought his face down to the nape of her neck to use his teeth instead. To his immense satisfaction, he felt Claire shudder as he did so. His other hand was drawing slow, smooth circles against Claire's hip, his fingers itching to grab at her underwear and rip it off. But Ichi was in no rush, and he had waited for so long for this moment.

He had just about teased out the knot at her neck when Claire lunged to her right to try and grab the paint pot she had so stupidly put down earlier. Ichi stopped what he was doing to fling the pot away with a lazy sweep of his hand, the lid falling off as it came crashing to the floor, spilling its contents everywhere. He wrestled Claire to the ground, her head smacking off of the tables behind her as he did so. She let out a gasp of pain, her eyes watering. Ichi smirked at her.

"I'd like to say that that was a nice try, but you and I both know that it wasn't. You can do *a lot* better than that," he murmured into her ear. Then Ichi finished undoing the knot that kept the top of Claire's dress up, pulling the material down as he sat up to admire her. Claire's face was flushed with humiliation; he could tell that she was fighting the urge to stop herself from covering her chest with her arms. Ichi could feel his dark jeans growing ever more uncomfortably tight, his body reacting to the sight of Claire in her forced state of undress. He grinned maliciously at her as he began to undo his belt. Claire's face grew pale again.

"Go on, say something. Tell me you don't want this. Tell me you want me to stop, so that it's even better for me when I don't," he half-laughed. Ichi lowered himself down until his forehead was resting on Claire's again. She kept her eyes looking down. Ichi frowned. "Look at me, Claire. *Look at me*," he growled softly. *Only look at me.* He used a hand to force her to look up. Claire's eyes were blazing with so many emotions that Ichi scarcely thought that he could name half of them. But he could see the fear, and that's what mattered most.

"You're mine, and you know that. Not Ryan's or Imran's or God damn fucking Vic's. You're not even yours anymore. Until the moment you take your very last breath, all of you belongs to me. And I keep my promises; I mean to take all of you. Starting now." And with that, he tore away at her underwear and pulled down his jeans, his eyes never leaving Claire's.

"I –" she began, but whatever thought Claire had decided to vocalise was lost as Ichi forced his mouth and his body onto hers.

Claire

*Don't cry, don't speak, don't close your eyes. Don't cry, don't speak...*Claire's mind was empty of all else but those words as Ichi continued to exert his authority over her. She had gasped in shock when he had entered her, had winced at the pain, but she was determined to keep everything else from showing on her face. It was all she could do.

I wish I were dead, Claire thought, not for the first time.

Ichi

Claire's body was magnificent. Ichi wished that he had had the sense to pull her entire dress off before he had started so he could truly appreciate all of her. Claire's skin was incredibly smooth, and blazing hot wherever Ichi touched her. Her whole body was reacting involuntarily to him, her spine arching her front into him as he grinded into her. Ichi could tell that Claire hated it, the way her body wasn't listening to her head. Ichi *loved* it. It simply proved even more than Claire was his and no-one else's. He ran his left hand through her hair, holding her head in place as he bit into her neck and shoulders again and again and again. He felt up every inch of her, lingering on her glorious breasts which were so many times better than Alexis'…he pushed the thought of Alexis out of his head. She didn't matter.

Ichi brought his body back up so that he could look down on Claire as he straddled her, his fingers gripping onto her waist as he felt his hips bucking faster and faster. But Claire, to Ichi's dismay, was keeping her expression as stony and neutral as possible, the too-bright shine of her eyes being the only thing that gave away even a hint of what she was thinking and feeling on the inside. Ichi frowned. Claire wasn't going to ruin this for him; she didn't have the right to. He brought his face down to force another bruising kiss on her mouth which he knew she wouldn't reciprocate. He bit into her upper lip until it bled, tasting metal and salt on his tongue. Nothing. He pounded into her, harder than before. Still nothing. Pain and force were doing nothing to change Claire's expression.

Ichi was struggling to come up with some other thing he could do to get her to react, but he couldn't think over the feeling of his own pleasure. And then that very feeling answered his question, and he grinned into the side of Claire's neck as he brought his left hand down between her thighs.

Claire

No, stop it; don't do this, Claire thought despairingly as she felt Ichi's fingers start to work down between her thighs. She could handle the pain as he bit her; she could handle the force of Ichi screwing her senseless, but in no way could she handle him actually making her feel *good. And God is he good,* Claire found herself thinking involuntarily, and she felt ashamed. She could feel her legs begin to shake under his as all of the nerve endings down there sent waves of pleasure up to her brain, could feel her fingers twitch, instinctively wanting something to grab a hold of that was more substantial than air. *Stop it, stop it, STOP IT.* Claire bit back a moan as her body struggled to cope with the feeling of Ichi both inside her and on the surface of her. *This isn't fair, I don't want this,* Claire wailed. She hated her body for giving up on her brain.

Claire forced her eyes up to look at Ichi, hoping that looking at his damnable face would bring her body back in check. Instead it did the opposite; Ichi was looking at her with such an intent ferocity that, for just a second, Claire forgot the exact circumstances that she was in and felt the pleasure coursing through her nerves all the stronger for it. She felt her hands shakily grabbing up for this man whom she both hated and feared, desperate for something to cling onto lest she be drowned in this feeling that *he* was causing. Claire was horrified when she realised what she was doing and tried to draw her hands back, but it was too late; Ichi, wide-eyed with surprise for a moment, regained his composure for long enough to press his body even closer to hers, preventing her from doing so.

Stop it stop it stop it stop it, Claire thought, as her head got ever dizzier and the protests of her brain were rapidly drowned out by Ichi's assault on her body.

Ichi

Pressed together this closely, Ichi could feel Claire's accelerated heartbeat against his chest, pounding faster and faster even as his own heart did the same. It was exhilarating. He loved the feeling of Claire squirming beneath him, her body eagerly reacting to the feelings pulsing through her nerves to her brain. And her hands…Ichi couldn't believe that Claire had reached out for him, desperate for something to cling to. He knew it was involuntary and had prevented her from drawing her arms back, so now he could feel her hands shaking mere inches from his shoulder blades, unwilling to grab on to him. He wanted so badly to feel her fingernails dig into his skin; Ichi wished he had taken his t-shirt off.

Too late now, he thought as he bit into Claire's earlobe, nuzzling into her neck to smell the scent of paint and shampoo in her hair. He knew he couldn't last much longer but he was determined to finish Claire off first, making it all the more humiliating for her. So he grabbed Claire's hip and pushed her pelvis up, changing the angle of her body to his and making every feeling that much more intense.

Ichi was deeply satisfied when he felt Claire's fingers grip into the back of his t-shirt, her legs shaking beyond control. Her mouth was open, like she was about to beg him to stop, but when he looked at her again Claire clenched her teeth together and buried her head against his chest so that he couldn't see her face as he caused her to climax. *The bitch*, Ichi fumed to himself, so he grabbed Claire's hair and pulled her head back so she could see his face as *he* finished, seconds later.

It was the most amazing feeling; fucking Alexis just couldn't compare. But Claire's face still gave nothing away, not even at the moment Ichi exploded into her and collapsed on top of her body, putting all of his weight on her.

Ichi lay there for a long time, letting his heart rate slowly fall back down to normal. He could feel Claire's doing the same, yet her face stayed alert...and empty. He bit into her neck again, her ear; he brought his face level with hers until his lips were millimetres from brushing hers. This time, Claire matched his stare without being prompted. He didn't know what to make of her expression; it simply gave nothing away. She looked as if she might cry but Ichi knew, instinctively, that she wouldn't. Claire's face was still flushed from what had happened – Ichi supposed that his was too, from the heat he could feel in his cheeks.

Then they lay there even longer still, simply looking at each other. Ichi had decided that he wouldn't leave until she said *something*. Eventually, just as he was concluding that she was going to stay silent until the very end, Claire spoke.

"Are you done?" she asked him, her eyes blank, her voice devoid of all emotion. Ichi could have slapped her; he nearly did. Instead he kissed her, hard, let her go and hoisted his jeans back up. As he reached the door he looked back at Claire, lying on the floor in a splatter of white paint, her neck and shoulder already beginning to bruise from where he had bitten her.

"I'll be back, don't forget it," he promised, so softly. He didn't specify *when* he'd be back. *Let her have something to worry about when I'm not there,* he thought, as he unlocked the door and left, riding the biggest adrenaline high of his life.

Claire

I wish I were dead, Claire thought again, as she cried silently to herself long after Ichi had gone, clutching the top of her dress to her chest with shaking hands.

CHAPTER 9
Mr Brightside

Vic

He found Claire after midnight, having knocked on the door of her room to no answer. Vic knew Claire didn't sleep until well after three in the morning and so he figured that she must still have been painting if she wasn't answering her door. Which was odd, because she had told him she'd be done nearer eleven that evening.

When Vic found her, dishevelled and bruised, half undressed with paint literally *everywhere*, he knew immediately what had happened. He nearly turned away from Claire, the blood boiling in his veins so badly that he wanted to find the bastard who had done this to her and bash his skull in right that very second. Vic was stopped dead in his tracks by the quiet, tremulous sound of Claire's voice.

"Vic," was all she said, the word nearly lost in a sob as she tried to sit up and failed, fainting immediately where she lay on the floor. Vic felt his breath catch in his throat as he rushed to kneel down beside her; Claire's neck and right shoulder were littered with teeth marks, the skin around them blossoming into dark purple bruises even as he watched. Her face was flushed, like she had the beginning of a fever, but the rest of Claire's skin was icy cold and so pale that it was difficult to see all of the paint that had dried into it. Vic gingerly tied her dress back up at her neck, trying his hardest to avoid both the bruises and her exposed breasts as he did so.

Vic scooped Claire up into his arms as if she weighed nothing at all and took her straight to the elevator and up to his room. Once he got there, he laid Claire gently on his bed, covering her with a blanket whilst he headed to the bathroom. He prayed a silent thank you to Michael for giving him one of the only rooms with an actual bath as he ran one for Claire. When he returned to his bedroom, Vic saw that Claire had regained consciousness and was looking up at the ceiling, wide eyed and terrified. He ran over and held her hand, smoothing her tangled hair back as he did so.

"It's okay now, princess, it's okay," he soothed, as Claire's breathing grew rapid and shallow. She turned her head to look at Vic, but she didn't quite seem to see him. Vic felt a frown crease his brow. "Claire, I've run you a bath, do you think you can handle it? Or do you just want to lie down? I can leave you alone if you want me –" he felt Claire grip his hand hard, her nails digging into his skin.

"No, don't go, please don't go," Claire begged, her voice hoarse. She coughed several times, so Vic jumped up and ran to his kitchen and poured her a glass of water. Claire finished it in seconds, the glass trembling in her hands as she forced it down. Then she looked at Vic again, and seemed to actually see him this time. "Thank you," she said. "I can handle a bath. I don't think I've ever wanted one more than I do now." Vic smiled at her and pointed towards his bathroom with a thumb.

"Bath's right through there. I've put fresh towels in for you too. Take all the time you need," he said. Claire, somehow, managed to return his smile as she made herself sit up and swing her legs over the side of the bed. The motion seemed to make her dizzy; she held a hand up to her forehead as she swayed a little. Vic reached out to touch her shoulder to steady her, but Claire flinched away from his hand, her eyes widening in fear as she did so. Vic couldn't keep the shock from his face at the unexpected reaction. Claire's eyes widened further as she realised what she had done. *Ah, damn, I'm a terrible person,* Vic cursed inwardly.

"Vic, I'm sorry, I'm sorry, I –" she began, but Vic held up his hand to stop her.

"Don't think for a second that you have *anything* to apologise for. I'm in the wrong; *I'm* sorry. Now get yourself in the bath while it's still hot," he said, keeping his voice as gentle as possible. Claire looked as if she might say something before she slowly forced herself up from the bed and walked over to the bathroom. Before she closed the door, Vic made a spur of the moment decision.

"Claire, I'm just going down to Roger's kitchen to grab some food for you whilst you're in there. I'll run up and get you some clothes from your room too if you, you know, don't mind staying here tonight instead," he said, his voice almost trailing off at the end of his sentence as he realised how inappropriate it was of him to assume that she *would* stay with him. But Claire's face seemed to relax at his words, and a genuine smile played across her face.

"Thank you," was all she said before closing the bathroom door, leaving Vic to his errand run. *And first on the list is to crush Ichi's skull with my hands,* he fumed as he waited on the elevator. But as the doors slowly opened to let him in, he saw that Alexis was waiting inside.

"Ah, I was just coming to get you," she said as he walked in and stood beside her. "Michael wants to see you." Alexis regarded him curiously. "Why are you covered in paint? Did you and Claire have too much fun in the classrooms?" she joked. Vic punched the side of the elevator; a knee-jerk reaction that he immediately regretted. Alexis looked at him, shocked. "Okay, okay, not in the mood for jokes tonight. God, you're no fun if you act just like Ichi."

"Don't compare me to that fucking bastard!" Vic raged at Alexis' face. "How can you stand to be anywhere close to that son of a bitch? Do you know what he's gone and fucking done, Alexis? *Do you?*"

Alexis' face darkened. "He didn't…" she began, but let the very notion of defending Ichi trail away to nothingness. "Is she okay, Vic? Tell me she's okay," she said, her face all genuine concern.

Vic glared at her. "What do you even care? You don't seem to give a shit about her. And no, she's not bloody okay. How in seven hells could she be?" Vic replied. Alexis slapped him. Vic looked back at her, shell-shocked.

"You are not in a position to dictate my feelings on anything, Vic. Now get a fucking hold of yourself. You're not going to be any use to Claire if you're like this." The elevator screen showed that they had reached the basement floor. "Now go and see Michael, cool your head down, and when you get back to Claire be the shining white knight she needs you to be. And go get her Mp3 player; it's full of Irish lullabies that'll calm her right down," Alexis demanded as they walked out of the elevator and down the corridor. Vic looked at her – she had the strangest expression on her face.

"How do you –"

"I'm not ignoring her as much as you think," Alexis interrupted. "And I'm far more observant than any of you give me credit for. Why do you think *I'm* Michael's right hand man? Just trust me on this."

Vic shook his head. "I don't understand your angle on this at all, Alexis," Vic admitted.

Alexis smiled. "Then I'm doing my job right," she replied, before knocking on Michael's door when they reached it. "Vic's here," she announced, raising her voice slightly to be heard through the door.

"Let him in," Vic heard Michael reply. He gave Alexis another glance before leaving her to enter the room. Michael was sitting behind his mahogany desk as usual, his expression haggard and harassed.

"What is it?" Vic asked immediately, his foul mood cutting through all sense of courtesy. Michael raised an eyebrow at him.

"Given the nature of what just happened to our guest, I'll forgive your bluntness on this occasion, Mr Winters."

"How do you know what happened already?" Vic asked, but then he remembered that Michael had cameras all over the complex, so he moved on to the far more pressing issues that he wanted to address. "You *knew* something like this would happen," he said, knowing it to be true. "I was right from the beginning – you *wanted* Ichi to terrify Claire! She would have done what you had asked without setting your psychopath on her!" Vic knew he was stepping over the line with his accusations; he didn't care.

Michael's gaze sharpened. "That's enough," he replied, in a cold, steely voice. "It is not for you to decide how I run things around here. I could not for certain know that Miss Danvers wouldn't get curious and start looking into things that didn't concern her. Keeping her both busy with menial work *and* scared to go looking around elsewhere for fear of running into Ichi was the best way to keep her in check. As it happens, it worked splendidly."

Vic looked at him, aghast. "How could you let him do that to her?" he asked, disgusted.

Michael sighed. "Ah, Vic, that's why you were there too. Why would I keep my best undercover agent out of duty for a month? Your job was to ensure that nothing as…drastic…as what happened tonight occurred. You failed," he admonished.

"I could hardly stay by her side every moment of every day! She didn't let me!" he protested, although as he said it Vic realised that it was a terrible excuse.

Michael frowned. "And you think that should have stopped you from doing so? Vic, no more arguing, it's not productive," Michael said in response to Vic's imminent interruption. "As much as you seem to think so, I do *not* find Ichi's behaviour tonight acceptable. I'm sending him out to do some work for me for a while. I want you to go up and tell him to come and see me." It was Vic's turn to frown. "Why me? You know I'm going to pummel his brains out," Vic replied honestly.

Michael smiled.

"Exactly. By all means, let your anger out; just make sure he's capable of heading out to work tomorrow. Try not to damage his pretty face too much – it'll be his redeeming feature on this job," he said, so casually. Vic nodded before turning to leave, but as he reached the door Michael spoke again, his voice soft as he said: "Vic, this should be obvious, but don't tell anyone about what happened tonight. I'm sure Miss Danvers would rather this was kept quiet."

"How could you possibly know what she would want?" Vic replied, daring to be bold one final time.

"Have you ever met a twenty-two-year-old woman who wanted everyone around her to know that something like this happened?"

Vic sighed, knowing that Michael was right. "I'll send the son of a bitch your way once I'm done," he said before leaving Michael's office for the elevator, but Vic stopped off in the rec hall to grab some supplies first and forced himself to enter the classroom he had found Claire in to grab her Mp3 player. Vic felt his skin crawl just looking at the white paint still spattered across the floor, so he turned his back on it and swiftly left the room. After that, he made his way up to the twelfth floor to pick up some of Claire's clothes and left the small assortment of items he had collected in a pile by the elevator.

Then he walked over to Ichi's room and smashed the door open.

Ichi was lounging on his couch, engrossed in something on his laptop. He stood up suddenly as Vic stormed into his room, eyebrows raised in surprise. He didn't have enough time to react as Vic reached him and bodily flung him against a wall. Vic didn't give him a second to retaliate as he pressed his arm up against Ichi's neck, cutting off his airway.

"*What the fuck is wrong with you?*" Vic hissed into his face. Ichi seemed to regain his composure then, despite his failing air supply.

"Do you want a list? I'm sure it's rather long," Ichi replied sarcastically, voice hoarse from lack of oxygen. Vic dropped his arm to punch Ichi in the gut, over and over again, the ferocity with which he did so bending Ichi over double. Vic had to force himself to stop before he rendered him unconscious. When he was done, Ichi coughed a few times and took a shallow, ragged breath; a thin trail of blood ran down his chin from the corner of his mouth. He glared at Vic as he stood back up and wiped the blood away with the back of his hand.

"What was I supposed to have done to merit this?" Ichi asked, feigning ignorance. He swept his hair back from his face, acting as if Vic hadn't practically torn a hole through his stomach. Vic couldn't quite believe that, even in a situation like this, Ichi would pretend to be innocent of all charges.

"You know exactly what you've done, you fucker! God, I knew you were pissed you failed to kill her, but how did you ever think it was acceptable to exact your revenge like this? *Or at all?!* Claire's done nothing to you!"

Ichi grinned. "That's what you think," he replied, his response infuriatingly vague.

"You're lying. She hasn't gone near you," Vic said, furious that Ichi was baiting him like this.

"It's amazing what someone's body will do even when their head is screaming at them not to do it," Ichi continued, looking half crazed as he continued to taunt Vic. Suddenly, he squared up to the taller man, and spoke in a soft, low voice. "But you won't hear about what happened from me. And you won't hear it from her, either. What's between me and Claire is between me and Claire. I dare you to ask her to see if she'll say anything to the contrary." Ichi smirked, an air of superiority about him that Vic hated with a passion.

"Besides," Ichi said as he made to turn away from Vic. "You're just pissed because you didn't get to screw her first." He was spun back around by Vic grabbing his t-shirt in order to punch him in the face, causing his nose to bleed profusely.

"Michael wants to see you, you fucker," Vic said, before turning around and leaving Ichi's room. *I'll apologise to Michael later for hitting his face…eventually,* Vic thought to himself, knowing full well that he wouldn't. When he got back to his own front door, Vic stood outside it for several minutes, forcing himself to calm down. *Alexis was right; I'll be no use to Claire if I'm angry. I need to grow up…how I feel about what happened is irrelevant right now.* And so Vic exhaled slowly and opened his door, only to find Claire curled up on his couch in one of his t-shirts. She looked up at him, a sad smile on her face. Vic had to use an inordinate amount of mental power to stop his face from growing red at the sight of Claire in his clothes, on his couch. *Get a grip – this isn't the time for those kinds of thoughts!* he admonished.

"I'm sorry, you took so long so I ended up raiding your drawers," she said quietly. Vic smiled back at her apologetically.

"Michael wanted to see me; I didn't think I'd be gone so long." He held out the clothes he had brought down from Claire's room. "Here. I didn't really know what to bring so I just grabbed the first things I saw." Claire gingerly took the clothes from him, wincing, presumably from the pain in her right shoulder, as she moved her arm. Vic desperately wanted to touch her again, to make sure she was okay, but he didn't want to elicit the same reaction he had gotten earlier. He moved over to his kitchen.

"Do you want some toast and hot chocolate? You must be starving," he asked. Claire's eyes lit up like a child's would at the mention of hot chocolate.

"Yes please…oh…no toast. I don't have much of an appetite, sorry," she mumbled, looking at the floor.

Vic sighed. "Claire, you have *nothing* to apologise for, so don't." He continued to make up her drink in silence, sitting down at the other end of his couch once he had given it to her. Claire had put on some shorts whilst his back was turned but she hadn't removed his t-shirt. Vic internally decided that it was now and forever hers.

Claire held the steaming mug between her hands, seeming to revel in its warmth. She gave Vic a sideways glance. "You haven't sat that far away from me since the day I got here," she commented. She was trying too hard to make casual conversation; Vic knew it. When Claire had finished her drink, she put the mug down onto the table in front of them and was quiet for a moment. "Thank you, Vic," she mumbled quietly, after a while.

"You know I'm not doing any of this for your gratitude, princess," he replied sadly. He stood up, stretching his arms as he did so. "Okay, you're taking my bed tonight. God only knows you need some sleep. I'll take the couch, so up you get," he said, trying to sound more cheerful. Claire seemed to falter for a second. "There's no use protesting, Miss Danvers. Now off to bed!" Vic scorned. Claire smiled at him before walking slowly over to his bed; she regarded it carefully before curling up under the duvet. Vic followed her to sit on the end of the bed.

"Please try to get some sleep, Claire," he said seriously. Claire looked up at him through her eyelashes.

"Yes, sir," she said, trying to sound upbeat and failing. Vic stared at her for a moment, wishing he could ask her more about what had happened to her but knowing that it was a terrible idea. Then he wandered back over to his living space, pulling the screen door that was identical to the one in Claire's room shut behind him. He flicked the lights off.

"Good night, princess," he called over to her as he settled on the couch.

"Night, Vic," came a small voice in return.

*

He was awoken by the sound of crying sometime later, and for a moment Vic was confused about what was going on. *Claire*, he remembered, and he knocked his screen door over in his haste to reach her in his bed. He fumbled with the light switch on the bedside lamp. Claire was white as a sheet, her eyes wide and unfocussed and full of tears. The duvet lay at the end of the bed, having presumably been kicked off by Claire. Vic sat beside her, daring to hold her hand.

"Claire, Claire, it's okay! It's me, it's Vic, I'm right here," he soothed. Claire turned her head to look at him.

"Don't leave me," she sobbed, the tears welling up in her eyes until they broke and ran down her face. Vic lay down on the bed beside her and hugged her gently.

"You know I won't," he replied, stroking her hair. They stayed like that for a while until Claire's sobbing had subsided somewhat. "…do you want to talk about it?" he ventured hesitantly. Claire looked up at him through strands of still-damp hair, her blue eyes too bright and red around the edges.

"Never," was all she said, before turning her gaze downwards again. Vic brought the duvet back up to cover Claire; he lay on top of it.

"Then I'll never bring it up again," Vic promised softly. *Looks like Michael was right,* Vic acknowledged begrudgingly. Then he thought about someone else whose idea might be right, so he left his bed abruptly, much to Claire's surprise.

"What are you –" she began, but Vic was back with her Mp3 player and a pair of speakers before she could finish the question.

"I hear you like lullabies," he said, flicking through her music as he talked until he found what looked like a promising album. Vic plugged the player into his speakers and set the volume on low. Claire allowed a genuine smile to play across her face.

"How did you know?" she asked. Vic smiled in return.

"A little bird told me. Maybe one day I'll know why they know too." Claire's fingers brushed against his hand ever-so-lightly before looking up at him.

"Could you…could you hold me again, please? Just for a while," she asked, her eyes shining with the tears she was trying to hold back. Vic lay down again and pulled the duvet over himself this time.

"Any time, princess," he replied, hugging her tenderly against his chest. "Any time."

CHAPTER 10
Keep Holding On

Claire

Claire slept for two days. She hadn't thought it was possible for her body to sleep for so long, even taking into account the drugs that Vic ended up having to give her when she was still awake at God knows what time in the early hours of the morning after she was attacked. She had clearly needed the rest, both physically and mentally. But after having just woken up, instead of feeling rested, Claire's muscles felt stiff from disuse, her neck and right shoulder stung and the inside of her mouth was parched. Claire had to blink several times to restore focus to her vision, before attempting to sit up and look around, her sleep-slow brain reminding her that she was in Vic's bed in an assassin complex in the middle of who-knows-where and not in her own bed, back in her own flat in her own city.

Vic had rushed over to her, telling her to take things easy. He had poured her a glass of water which she had swiftly drank, so he poured her another. Claire drank that one far more slowly, whilst Vic filled her in on what had happened since she fell asleep. He had hardly left her side or slept himself, by the looks of the dark shadows under his eyes. Now she was lying in a bath Vic had insisted she take, letting her head sink below the water's surface as she tried to process everything.

Ichi had been sent away to work undercover for a while, Vic had told her. And he wasn't expected back for several months. *Maybe I'll be gone by then, safe with my sister somewhere warm and obscure,* Claire thought, revelling in the idea of Ichi returning to her not being around for him to torment anymore. She resurfaced when she ran out of air, sighing. Claire forced herself to sit up and inspect her right shoulder. It was heavily bruised; she imagined her neck was too. *How the hell am I covering this up?* She shivered despite the hot, soapy water that enveloped her. *I'll just have to work it out,* Claire thought, *though at least* he *won't be around to see the damage he caused.* She could feel her heart rate accelerate in fear at the memory of Ichi biting into her skin, refusing to let her escape. *So stop thinking about it,* Claire told herself, knowing that she was doomed to replay it over and over in her head until her brain was done with it. Claire looked down into the water at her own body. She hated it; hated herself – how could her own body have reacted to Ichi in the way that it had when her head was screaming at it not to? She felt ashamed.

"This isn't my fault," Claire reminded herself, in a small, fragile voice. She hugged her knees to her chest for a moment, suddenly freezing, so she turned the hot tap back on and dunked herself under the water again, to try and suppress the shiver that ran down her spine at a very obvious and undeniable realisation. *I need to see a doctor.* Claire should have demanded to see a doctor the evening Ichi had attacked her, but she had hardly been in any fit state to do so. *How do I even get to see a doctor here?* Claire wondered. She assumed she'd have to see Michael, which was not a meeting she cherished happening. *I just have to suck it up and tell him I need to see a doctor as soon as possible.* Claire looked down at her stomach and felt her eyes sting with the beginnings of tears.

"I can't…I just can't," she stammered, not even willing to vocalise her thoughts for fear of making them true. Back in her old life, Claire had been so careful about everything. She was always on the contraceptive pill; she took it every morning when she woke up, like clockwork. She never missed a day. She'd insisted that any boyfriends she had go for a check up to make sure they wouldn't give her any STIs before having unprotected sex with them. And she got checked herself every six months, just to be sure. Olivia had called her paranoid. Claire had called her reckless. *I'm sure she wouldn't be mocking my old habits if she knew what had just happened to me,* Claire thought, upset and worried. She wished she had thought to ask Alexis to pick up her supply of the pill when she had gone to Claire's flat. *How was I supposed to know I'd need it* here?

Claire sighed. Lying in the bath for hours wouldn't solve anything; she had to keep busy if she was going to push the memory of what Ichi had done to her to one side, but she had no more painting left to do. Vic had told her that Roger had cleaned up the mess that was left in the classroom that Vic had found her in, no questions asked. Claire consciously decided to thank Roger for doing so. *I never want to go near that damn room ever again.* But if she couldn't paint, what could she do to keep busy? Claire mulled over the question as she dragged herself out of the bath, towelling herself dry and pulling on the one pair of jeans she owned and her favourite oversized blue jumper. She cleared the steam from the mirror above Vic's sink to inspect her neck. No amount of make up was going to cover the purple-blue mess that was her skin. *I'll just have to wear a scarf until it clears up, like a fourteen-year-old trying to hide a love bite.* She grimaced at the thought. But her only scarf was up in her room, and Claire didn't want to go back up there, even though she knew she had to. *What kind of message am I giving off if I cower away in Vic's room?* Claire reasoned. *And Ichi's not even here right now.* She looked at her face in the mirror. Her skin was pale, despite just having left a scalding hot bath, her eyes furtive. She slapped both of her cheeks gently, frowning.

"Claire Danvers, for your own sake, you will get over this. No man has dictated your thoughts and feelings before, and this one won't either," she said to her reflection in a serious voice. It was time to get whatever life it was that she had here back in order. *And with any luck, I'll be long gone before* he *returns.*

When Claire exited the bathroom, Vic jumped up from his couch. He looked as if he had been sleeping. "How do you feel?" he asked her, anxious. Claire gave him a smile.

"Much better, thanks. You were right about the bath; it really did clear my head," she replied.

"Do you want something to eat? You haven't eaten anything in days, literally. You must be starving. I'll go and –"

"No, Vic, it's okay," Claire interrupted. "I'll go down and get something from Roger myself. I need to thank him anyway." Vic looked like he might have protested, so Claire pressed on with everything she needed to say. "Vic, can…can you arrange a meeting for me with Michael today? The sooner the better."

Vic raised an eyebrow. "Am I allowed to ask what for?" he inquired. Claire shook her head slowly.

"I'd rather you didn't, all things considered. You'll probably figure it out anyway," she said, sadly. Claire kept her eyes on the floor, not wanting to look Vic in the face for fear of what might be there once he realised why

Claire needed to see Michael. She saw Vic shuffle his feet; Claire figured that he was probably trying to think of something to say to break the uncomfortable silence.

"I brought you down some more clothes," he finally said. Claire glanced up at him through her eyelashes.

"Thank you, but...I need to get back up to my room. I shouldn't stay in yours for any longer," she replied, quietly.

"Claire, you can stay here as long as you need to! Don't force yourself to –"

"Vic," Claire interrupted again. She gave him a level stare, keeping her face as composed as possible. Vic returned the stare, clearly resisting the urge to speak. "You have done so much for me already. I'm not forcing myself by going back up there; I'm just getting on with things. I can't stay holed up in here forever...however appealing that idea is," she added on with a smile, for Vic's benefit. "Besides," Claire continued, trying to sound nonchalant, "Ichi isn't even here right now, and for all we know I'll be long gone by the time he gets back. So there's no danger in me returning to my room, is there?" Claire's words seemed to darken Vic's eyes; there was no warmth to his expression anymore.

"The last time you told me he hadn't done anything to you, you were lying," he said. It wasn't a question. Claire shifted on the spot and struggled not to look away.

"If you knew I was lying, why didn't you force me to tell the truth?" she asked. Vic sighed, running a hand over his face.

"Forcing you to do anything would make me no better than that son-of-a-bitch," he half-growled. Claire flinched at the anger in his voice. For once, Vic didn't make any apologies for startling her. "My point is, Claire, how am I supposed to protect you if you won't let me? If you just pretend that everything's okay? You say I've done so much for you already, but I haven't. Let me do more. *Please*," he begged. Claire's face softened – all of the anger had dissipated from Vic's face as quickly as it had arisen. Now he just looked vulnerable. Claire couldn't help but feel a twinge of guilt, knowing that she was the one who caused him to look like that. She walked over to him and placed a hand on his arm. He looked down at it, surprised. *This feels like my first morning here all over again,* Claire thought, wryly.

"I'm sorry," she said to him. Vic opened his mouth to protest her words, but Claire put a finger to his lips to quieten him. His eyes widened with even more surprise at the gesture. "I know you're going to say I have nothing to be sorry for. But I do. I'm sorry I've ignored your feelings. I know I'm important to you for some reason that I don't quite understand, and that you want to protect me because of it. And I know that I haven't let you do so regardless of that." Claire fidgeted with the damp ends of her hair, turning her gaze away from Vic. "It's just…I like being independent and in control of my own life. But I haven't been in control of my own life for months now, thanks to my parents and Michael and the fact that I don't remember a *damn thing.*" She felt her grip tighten on Vic's arm; he put a hand over hers and squeezed it gently. Claire looked up at him, knowing that her eyes were full of tears that she mustn't let fall. Vic was looking at her like she was the most precious thing in the world.

"I need some control back," she said, quietly. "I can't let what *he* wants to do dictate what I can or cannot do here. But he's stronger than me. Hell, I'm pretty sure he's a damn bit smarter than me too. So I need to work out how to deal with him, *without* relying on someone else. Otherwise he'll just wait until that one moment when I'm by myself to do something again. Do you understand, Vic?"

Vic made himself smile. "One hundred percent, princess." *He looks so sad. Not like Vic at all.* "So, Michael. You need to see him. I'm on it," he said, forcing himself to sound happy. Claire reached up on her tip toes and just barely managed to reach his cheek to kiss it.

"Thank you. You know I mean that," she said, resting her head against his chest for a moment. Then she moved away from him and walked towards the door. "If I'm not in my room I'll be speaking to Roger, okay?" Claire smiled at Vic. His hand was touching his cheek where she had kissed it, his face ever-so-slightly red.

"Roger that," Vic replied, letting out a chuckle. *That's better,* Claire thought. *Always laugh for me.* Then she left Vic's room and headed up in the elevator to her own.

Claire didn't linger long, staying within the confines of her room only long enough to locate her scarf. It was made of lots of wispy material, all dark blue and violet swirls. Claire liked to wear it in spring and autumn, when the weather was too warm for a woollen scarf but too cool to go without one. *It must be nearly autumn now,* Claire mused. She wrapped it around her neck, inspecting herself in the mirror to make sure it covered all of the bruised skin before promptly leaving her room to head down to the rec hall.

She found Roger washing dishes. It occurred to Claire that even her made-up notion of what time it was was all messed up now from having slept for two days, so she ventured for an answer to that question. "Hey Roger, what's for lunch?" she asked, trying to sound casual. Roger turned at the sound of her voice and smiled, washing his hands of soap suds and drying them off before walking to meet Claire by the entrance to his kitchen.

"So you're awake then, Miss Danvers. And it's nearly dinner time." He grinned at her. "You didn't think you'd get an exact time out of me that easily, surely?"

Claire laughed. "It was worth a try…so what's for dinner?"

Roger calmed his grin down to a soft smile. "Anything you want, dear." Claire looked away, averting her eyes to look at the floor. *No. You're not doing this anymore. You're going to stand your ground and take care of yourself.* She brought her gaze back up.

"Pizza. And carbs. Lots of carbs please. And ice cream. And about two litres of orange juice," was her answer.

It was Roger's turn to laugh. "I think I can wrangle that. Just give me a couple hours to make up some dough. And if you're going to drink that much orange juice, I'm going to have to start ordering in a lot more," he replied.

"Then order more. Put it in the fridge in the bar. It's not like I get to use it for booze, anyway. Vic would preach at me for hours if I did," she muttered. Claire allowed herself a moment to be more serious. "Thank you for cleaning that room up, Roger."

Roger's smile faded. "Don't worry about it; it's my job to keep this place in check, after all." He had a slight frown on his face. "I did warn you though, Miss Danvers. Some people don't take 'no' for an answer. You were naïve to think that you alone could take care of yourself here." Claire flinched at his words. *When he speaks like that, he almost sounds like Michael,* she thought.

Roger's face relaxed when he saw how uncomfortable he had made her. "Oh, don't mind me, I'm just a grouchy middle-aged man. But so long as you don't understand your own limits, I'll continue to be that grouchy man. Let Vic help you or you might not be so lucky next time," he admonished.

"I don't feel like I was so lucky," Claire mumbled, before matching Roger's stare again. "I know I need to take better care of myself. I'm working it out. Thanks for your concern, Roger," she said, before turning to leave the rec hall.

"I'll get Vic to tell you when your carbs, carbs and more carbs are ready," he called from the kitchen.

Claire turned her head to smile at him. "Roger that," she replied, taking Vic's previous parting words as her own.

"That got old thirty years ago, Miss Danvers!" she heard him reproach as she exited out into the corridor. As she was waiting on the elevator, Claire vaguely heard footsteps through the door by the elevator that led onto the stairs. *Don't let it be any of the others,* she thought desperately. *Let it be Vic.* To her immense relief it was indeed Vic, and he ushered her over to the stairwell when he saw her.

"Good timing, princess. Michael can see you now, if you want," he said, smiling. He didn't seem as upset now, though Claire wondered whether he was simply hiding it better. He still looked exhausted.

"Thanks Vic. Yes, I'll see him now. Care to lead the way?" she asked, gesturing down the stairs.

"It'll be my pleasure," he said, smiling at her fondly.

"Please go and sleep after this Vic," she commented as they walked down the stairs to the basement. Vic looked at her out of the corner of his eye.

"I'm the one looking after you, remember? Not the other way around. I'm heading to the gym after this, otherwise I'll feel guilty when I steal half of whatever it is Roger's cooking for you later," he joked. Claire rolled her eyes. Vic sighed. "I promise I'll go to bed like a good boy after dinner. Ah, here we are," he said, when they reached the door to Michael's office. He knocked gently upon it.

"Send her in," came Michael's voice from the other side of the door.

Vic regarded Claire for a second. "You sure you don't want me in there with you?" he asked, worried.

"Definitely not," Claire replied immediately. *It'll be just about as awful and awkward as I can take without you there, never mind if you heard everything I had to say.* She gave Vic a quick smile to hide her thoughts before entering Michael's office, closing the door shut behind her.

His office was exactly as Claire had remembered it, empty but for the dark mahogany desk at the far end of the room, warm orange light emitting from the lamp that sat on top of that same desk. There was a computer monitor sitting on the right hand side of the desk, though if it was a new addition or had been there before Claire could not be certain. Michael was sitting behind the desk, fingers laced together over a closed folder of paper. He looked tired, his sandy coloured hair pointing in all directions, as if he had run his fingers through it continuously all day. Claire figured he probably had been. She glanced at the chair that sat in front of Michael's desk and wondered whether she should sit down.

"No need to take a seat, Miss Danvers, I have a notion as to why you're here," he remarked, cutting through Claire's thought process. She looked at him.

"And that notion would be?" she replied, knowing as she said it that it probably sounded childishly confrontational. Michael smiled at her; it didn't reach his eyes.

"I imagine, being the careful person that you are, that you want to see a doctor," he said.

Claire frowned at him. "How would you know that I'm a careful person?" she asked. Michael's smile grew a little wider, and this time it seemed to meet his eyes, just a little.

"Because you take after your mother more than you'll ever know," he said softly, getting up from his chair as he spoke. "I'm sure there will be time for reminiscing and exchanging stories of your parents another day, however," he added on, when it became apparent that Claire was going to press him for more information. "But for now, if you'll kindly follow me to the laboratory, let's have you talk to a doctor."

As Claire followed Michael out of his office and down another flight of stairs, she thought about how her meeting with him had gone a lot smoother than expected. She couldn't even call it a meeting, really, since he seemed to have anticipated exactly what she had needed. Claire wondered whether Michael knew her mother from outside of funding her research, since to her it certainly sounded as if he did.

She was broken out of her reverie as they reached a large glass door, which Michael opened by typing in a long code into a keypad. "Ladies first," Michael said, gesturing through the open door. Cautiously, Claire stepped into the lab and couldn't help but gasp. It looked identical to her parents' own research lab, right down to the pipette tips on the work benches.

"Look familiar?" she heard Michael comment behind her. She could hear the smirk in his voice. Claire didn't bother to ask him to explain why this lab looked the way it did; she would only be disappointed when Michael invariably didn't answer her question.

"I'm only in here for one reason," Claire replied, as much as a reminder to herself as it was a response to Michael. She heard him laugh behind her – it was mirthless, sardonic and cruel and it cut right through her. Claire turned to face him.

"Yes, you are indeed only in *here* for one reason, and that reason is your parents," he said. Claire felt her mood darken. Subconsciously she reached for her scarf, to pull it more tightly around herself. Michael noticed the movement immediately. "And whatever it is that Ichi did, you know that you only have your parents to blame for it. Don't forget that, Miss Danvers, when you lie awake every night cursing the day that he ever came into your life." Michael kept his tone casual, much like the way he had spoken to Claire about her own death on the day that she had arrived at the complex. Claire could feel her eyes beginning to sting, so she looked away from Michael's hard stare.

"Just let me see a doctor…please," she added on, knowing that courtesy was a better bet than disobedience in this situation.

Michael gave her one of his empty smiles. "As you wish. She's through here," he said, and Claire followed him through to an office exactly where her dad's had been in her parents' lab. Michael didn't bother knocking on the closed door; he simply let himself in. A woman who looked to be about the same age as Michael was sitting on top of an exact replica of her father's desk, fishing through some documents, presumably looking for something. When she heard Michael enter, she looked up and smiled.

"So this is your house guest," she said, giving Claire a quick once-over. She stood up. "Right, off with you, Michael. I'll see to her myself, thank you." Claire was shocked at how quickly and colloquially this woman spoke to Michael. He merely laughed – a genuine one this time or, at least, as close to genuine as Claire ever imagined he got.

"Just make sure you walk her back up to ground level for me when you're done," he said. Then he turned and left, leaving Claire with a stranger in a place that was so familiar and yet so alien at the same time.

"Well, don't just stand there, have a seat," the woman commanded. Claire promptly sat down.

"I –" she began, but the woman cut through her.

"I know what you need. The morning after pill is far less effective if you take it two days after the morning…or evening after, as the case may be. You're a smart girl, you understand this, of course."

Claire nodded. "Can you –"

"Yes, I can put you on contraception," the woman interrupted again, "– I don't imagine you want anything to happen again, but it's best to take action against every possibility. I'll put you on the implant so you don't have to remember taking any pills but I'll need a day to get one for you. Can you come back tomorrow evening to see me?" Claire nodded, nonplussed at the speed at which the woman in front of her spoke. "If you come back to see me in six weeks or so I'll test you for all of the usual suspects that you're no doubt worried about. Though I should point out that all of the…residents, shall we say?" She looked up at the ceiling for a moment, considering her word choice before looking back at Claire. "Yes, all of the residents here were checked out when they began their employment with Michael. They all sign contracts to ensure that they will not partake in any unnecessary activities that could endanger their health. Michael likes his employees fit and functional, after all…regardless of what it is he needs them to do." The woman looked at Claire thoughtfully. "My point is that you don't really have to worry on that front."

"But –"

"Yes, I know," the woman said, interrupting Claire for the third time. "I'll have you take a pregnancy test too. And if worst comes to worst…well, we can cross that bridge when we come to it." She motioned Claire over. "Take off that scarf," she ordered, and Claire complied. She fastidiously inspected her neck, clucking her tongue as she did so. "Were you hurt anywhere else?" the woman asked. Claire slowly nodded her head.

"On my shoulder too but…but that's it," Claire mumbled. The woman spared her a sympathetic look.

"That's all that's on the surface, you mean. But I'm no psychiatrist; I won't be any help with anything else. Wait here a minute," she commented, before leaving Claire in the exact replica of her father's office with only her thoughts for company. *Where are you, dad? Mum? I need you both.* She closed her eyes, forcing the imminent tears back.

"I will not cry," Claire said aloud.

"What was that?" the woman asked as she re-entered her office. Her office, not Claire's father's, Claire had to remind herself.

Claire looked away from her. "Nothing, I was just talking to myself," she replied.

"Well, whatever gets you through this, I suppose. Here," she said, handing Claire a white paper bag. "The morning after pill. And witch hazel, for the bruising. Just apply it topically and they'll heal up in no time." Claire murmured her thanks. The doctor glanced at her watch; Claire had to resist the urge to try and look at it to see what the real time was. "I better take you back upstairs. I don't have much time to waste." She gestured for Claire to leave her office and then the lab, locking the glass door with what looked like the same code Michael had used to open it in the first place. Claire subconsciously counted sixteen characters to the code. *Why even try to work it out?* Claire thought, feeling rather nihilistic. *What's the point?* She glanced back through the glass. She couldn't help the twinge of longing she felt in her heart for this place that looked so like home to her. The woman ushered her up the stairs to the ground floor.

"I'll call for you tomorrow, then," she said, before making to turn around.

"Wait!" Claire called. The woman looked at her pointedly. "Do you have a name?" she asked. The woman kept her face blank.

"Just 'doctor' is fine," she replied.

"Okay, well…thank you, doctor," Claire said. The doctor nodded curtly before descending back down the stairs. *That was the most bizarre doctor's appointment I've ever had,* Claire thought.

Back up in her room, Claire poured herself a glass of water and promptly swallowed the morning after pill. She went over to the mirror above her sink and absent-mindedly brushed her now dry hair before deciding to put it up in a ponytail. Claire looked critically at her reflection – she had lost some weight since arriving at the complex a month ago; it made her look gaunt and sleep-deprived, despite the two days' worth of sleep she had just had. It made her look physically weak. *But that's because I* am, Claire thought.

And then she made a split-second decision and bolted for the elevator, back down to the ground floor. Claire walked quickly towards the gym, her ponytail swishing left and right behind her with every step. She marched into the gym, straight past Ryan and Imran and Marie and even Alexis, towards the weights. He had his back turned, working a knot out of his shoulder.

"Vic!" Claire called out.

Vic turned around, surprised. "What is it, Claire?" he asked. She looked at him, a determined expression on her face.

"You say you want to do more for me," she began, "You say you want to protect me. So teach me how to fight. Teach me how to defend myself." Vic grinned; a wide, genuine smile that gave him the most beautiful face Claire had ever seen. That grin turned mischievous as he unexpectedly grabbed Claire and flipped her onto the floor, catching her just before she hit it.

"I thought you'd never ask, princess," he chuckled, mussing her hair up as he helped her back to her feet.

CHAPTER 11
In Sleep

Ichi

Well he didn't put up much of a fight, Ichi thought, wiping the blood from his forehead before it could get into his eyes. It wasn't his; it belonged to the now-dead man that lay at his feet. There wasn't much left of the corpse's face to distinguish that he was the boss of the cocktail bar in London that Ichi had been forced to work in for the past two months. Before, he had been a fat man, with a bland face and a genial smile that hid the fact that he was keeping money off-books so that his patron, Michael, didn't get a cut of it. Ichi had slashed that smile right off of his face. And most of the rest of it, too.

Ichi's heart was racing from the thrill of methodically slicing into a person so that they were alive right up until the end, when he finally slit their throat with his knife. But as his heart rate slowed back down to normal, Ichi frowned. He had wasted more than eight weeks of his life for this kill. Sixty-one bloody days, acting as an empty-headed cocktail waiter, allowing giggling, idiotic girls to flirt with him over the bar top and pawing off the continued, sometimes aggressive advances of the owner's son. That made his frown deepen; Ichi didn't think he would ever forgive Michael for that one. But he had had to stay in character until he could prove beyond a reasonable doubt that the bar owner was indeed sluicing money from the top to pocket for himself, no matter how uncomfortable the situation was. *Then make him pay,* Michael had said. *Make sure the son knows not to repeat the father's mistakes.* The man's son had been in on the whole scam from the beginning; Ichi had suspected that it was his idea in the first place. Ichi had asked Michael if he could kill him too, not least because of the way he had prowled around the bar when Ichi was working, looking him up and down like he was getting ready to jump on him the second Ichi was alone…the irony wasn't lost on Ichi. But Michael had refused – who would

96

continue to run the bar if Ichi killed its inheritor? That Ichi hadn't understood; why couldn't some other fool just run the place instead for Michael? But orders were orders, and Ichi couldn't be bothered with the repercussions of breaking them.

Ichi leaned over the dead man's body, wiping the blood from his blade on the two inches of the man's shirt that had somehow survived the blood spatter. He heard a door slam shut from behind him. *How odd,* Ichi thought. *We're not due to open for the evening for another hour.*

"This time, Ryou, I'm not taking 'no' for an answer —" Ichi heard the man's son begin to say from behind him. He turned his head to glare at him. The other man grew pale once his brain had processed what had happened in front of him, his right hand clutching at the bar for support. "R-Ryou?" he stammered. Ichi stood up and walked over to him slowly; the man backed away. Ichi grabbed his shirt and punched him in the face. He fell to the floor, his face terrified.

"Michael says congratulations on your new promotion and he looks forward to working with you," Ichi said menacingly. The man's face got even paler, somehow.

"You-you work for *him,* Ryou?" the man whispered. Ichi looked down at him, disgusted.

"That's not my name. And if you even think of continuing your little embezzlement scheme or whatever it was, just think of what I've done to your father and I'm sure that'll stop you," Ichi replied, scathingly. Then he left him there, shell-shocked on the floor. Ichi grabbed his leather jacket from the bar top before he walked out and got into his car. He drove calmly back to the flat he had been living in for the past two months. He didn't have much there that he cared about, but he needed a shower before he left for Michael's complex. When he got back, he called the man himself to inform him that the job was done.

"Will the son comply?" Michael asked.

Ichi chuckled. "Have I ever disappointed you before?" he replied. It was Michael's turn to laugh.

"You're in a good mood, Ichi. Maybe I should put you out on undercover work more often." Ichi cringed at the idea.

"Do you know how many people I could have 'taken care of' for you in the space of sixty-one days?" he said. He heard Michael laugh again. Ichi shrugged out of his jacket and threw it on the floor of his sparsely furnished flat, heading towards the bathroom to turn on the shower.

"So you *were* counting the days. How very like you, Ichi. And here I thought I was doing you a favour, getting you out of the complex for a while," Michael chided. Ichi glared at his phone.

"I can take care of myself," he replied, annoyed.

"Ah, how apt. That's exactly what she said." Ichi gaped at his phone, too shocked to respond. "Report in with me when you return," Michael added on, before hanging up. Ichi continued to stare at his phone for a minute or two, cursing Michael for baiting him like that before he threw it on top of his jacket, took off the rest of his clothes and jumped into the shower. The water pressure was awful; Ichi couldn't wait until he returned to the complex and had one that actually made him feel *clean.* He rested his head against the tiles, watching the blood that covered his arms and face slowly wash away down the drain.

Having an objective and an inevitable kill once he completed that objective had helped Ichi immensely in keeping his mind off of Claire Danvers. Initially, when Michael had sent him away, he had been furious. *How dare he pull me away when I had her right where I wanted her?* Ichi had thought on numerous occasions. For the first week or two of his undercover job, all he thought about was Claire. The way her whole body had responded to him; the feeling of her skin growing hot under his fingertips; the way she had grabbed on to him in the end, desperate for something to cling to, to keep from losing herself. Ichi felt himself growing hard at the very thought of it, even now, two months later. But there was an overarching feeling of dissatisfaction that had crept over the memory, sullying it. Claire had barely said a thing. She had hardly put up a fight. And, most infuriatingly, she had kept so many of her reactions to herself. Ichi had wanted to hear Claire cry and beg for him to stop. He had wanted her to be furious and terrified at the same time. He had wanted her to scream for him to get off of her when he had finished. Claire had done none of those things.

Well, now I'm coming back. We'll see if she can 'take care of herself' like Michael said, Ichi thought, excited at the prospect of tormenting her again. Ichi cleaned his skin and hair as best as he could in the terrible shower, dried himself off and put on a fresh pair of dark jeans and a white t-shirt. He burned the clothes he had worn earlier, save for his leather jacket, and smashed the phone he had used as 'Ryou' to pieces. Then he grabbed the jacket and a small bag full of his own belongings before he left the abysmal flat for the final time.

He had to destroy the car he had been using too once he, finally, reached his pick-up point for returning to the complex. Ichi waited by its smoking remains in the middle of nowhere, some distance outside of London for just over fifteen minutes before a car showed up, a hand gesturing him in through its open front window. The driver said nothing to him as he drove Ichi to a large expanse of flat ground, where a helicopter was waiting. Ichi grimaced.

"Helicopter *again?* I swear Michael does this to me only because I hate them," Ichi muttered aloud. Still, he got on the helicopter nonetheless, watching the car that took him there getting smaller and smaller as he rose higher into the air. He braced himself for a boring, several hour-long journey that was likely to be more than a little turbulent, if the stormy nature of the night sky was anything to go by. So Ichi closed his eyes and thought of how Claire would react when she saw he had returned, several months earlier than Michael had originally anticipated. He opened his eyes again and slid his glance down to the bag at his feet, feeling a grin slowly spread across his face. Ichi's coverage of Claire's room was soon to become much more expansive than it currently was. He had missed those camera feeds immensely whilst he had been away, but a personal laptop was definitely not something Ichi was willing to bring with him on a job, just in case anybody got a hold of it. Ichi felt his hand twitch with the desire to click open those camera feeds. *Not long now,* he thought. *And they're about to get much, much better.*

He allowed his mind to wander aimlessly as he closed his eyes again. Killing that idiotic man earlier had certainly abated Ichi's desire to murder anyone who crossed his path, but the feeling had not altogether vanished. Ichi wondered why he even felt like that. He wasn't a fool; he knew it wasn't normal, not in the slightest. He didn't care. Ichi satisfied himself with the knowledge that he was a hell of a lot smarter than most people. He could speak several languages; was adept in the fields of maths, physics and chemistry; he was exceptional with various weapons and hand to hand combat. He could run for miles and never tire. He thought of something else that he could do for a long time without tiring and smirked for nobody to see. In almost all respects, Ichi was a superior human being. Was it a consequence of that that he wanted to kill anybody who wasn't? Ichi didn't believe that. His desire to run a knife through a person's heart did not take into account how clever or stupid they were, or how beautiful or ugly. He simply needed to *kill*.

Or fuck, he added on as an afterthought, for that was the only other thing that dulled his desire to extinguish a life. He thought of Alexis and considered finding her when he got back, but he shook the notion out of his head. He didn't want to waste any of his dangerous feelings on her. When he got back, all he wanted to do was focus his efforts on *Claire*.

A few hours later, he felt the helicopter land on top of the complex. Ichi figured that he must have fallen asleep by some miracle; he didn't remember much of the journey. He nodded his thanks to the pilot, grabbed his bag and headed through the only door on the roof that headed to the elevator and the stairs. Ichi considered using the stairs, but the urgency with which he desired a proper shower forced his hand, so he took the elevator down to Michael's office.

He didn't bother knocking; he rarely did. "You know that that's bad manners, Ichi," Michael said, not looking up from the laptop he was working on. Ichi sat down.

"I'm too good at my job for you to bother with my bad manners," Ichi replied. Michael looked up and smiled.

"As arrogant as usual. I trust the journey back went smoothly?" he asked, returning to his laptop.

Ichi grimaced. "You know I hate helicopters. But I slept through most of it, somehow." Michael didn't say anything for a while. Eventually, he closed the lid of his laptop and returned his gaze back to Ichi.

"You have to reign it in with regards to Miss Danvers, Ichi."

Ichi frowned. "Why should I? I'm not trying to kill her, am I? You only specified that you needed her alive." Michael gave him a hard stare; it made Ichi feel uncomfortable.

"Stop looking for loopholes," Michael reprimanded coolly. "I never said to stop keeping her in check, only to be…less extreme. That young woman is important to more than just your ego, Ichi."

Ichi closed his eyes for a moment, bringing his fingers up to rub his temple in irritation. "Is that all?" he forced himself to ask instead of protest.

Michael smiled. "I'm sure that that's plenty for you to deal with. You've certainly given Miss Danvers a lot to cope with whilst you have been absent," he added on as an afterthought. Ichi glanced at Michael before looking at the floor.

"Like what?" he asked, trying to sound like he didn't desperately want to know how he had affected Claire. Michael laced his fingers together.

"Let's just say it involved several trips to our resident doctor. She's a careful young woman, after all," Michael commented, as if he were discussing the weather. It took Ichi only a second to catch on to his meaning.

He stood up. "Why would she think I'd given her anything?! Who does she think I am, some whore who sleeps around?" he exclaimed, outraged. Michael continued to stare at him, a neutral expression on his face.

"I think she was more concerned about getting pregnant, Ichi," he said, quietly. Ichi gaped at him, speechless. He didn't even have a counter-argument. Michael's point was fair, and Ichi had not once in the past two months considered the possibility.

Ichi looked at his feet. "…is she?" he dared to ask.

"You know better than to ask for confidential information. If you want an answer, ask her yourself." Ichi cringed at the thought of having to ask Claire about it. Michael didn't let up his stare an inch. "Considering how uncomfortable this knowledge has made you, surely you must see why I need you to *reign it in*," he added. Ichi looked up at Michael and nodded, slowly.

"Understood," he replied. He glanced at the door. "Can I go?" It was Michael's turn to nod.

But just as Ichi was about to leave, Michael spoke again: "From what I've learned of Miss Danvers in the past three months, you're in for some difficult weeks ahead." *Oh, how cryptic,* Ichi thought.

"And what have you learned?" Ichi asked, knowing that he wouldn't get anything close to a useful answer from him.

Michael grinned. "More than you." Ichi scowled. "Close the door on your way out," he added on, but Ichi had slammed it shut behind him before Michael could finish the sentence. Ichi decided on impulse to grab some food from the rec hall before heading up to his room, knowing that he had nothing in his own kitchen. The entire conversation with Michael had left him angry and confused. *What did he mean when he said I was in for 'some difficult weeks'?* Ichi wondered, irritated. *And how am I supposed to work out if Claire's bloody pregnant or not? I can hardly just walk up and ask her, can I?*

Ichi's head was full of such thoughts as he entered the rec hall and spied Claire herself, sitting on a table, playing with Vic's hair and laughing as if she didn't have a care in the world. Ichi dropped the bag hanging from his shoulder in surprise, the thump it made as it fell to the floor turning both Claire and Vic's heads. He stared at them for a moment, not sure what to do. Then Claire turned her head away and continued her conversation with Vic as if nothing had happened. Ichi picked his bag up off the floor, feeling his fingers clench around its handle before he forced himself to wander over to Roger's kitchen; the resident chef was nowhere to be seen. Ichi went over to the fridge, grabbed a plastic tub of whatever was left from the dinner the man had made and a carton of milk. He swigged from it as he stalked past the pair, glancing at Claire as he did so. She made no move to even acknowledge that he was there. Vic glared at him.

Ichi went straight for a shower when he got up to his room, fighting the urge to punch the tiled wall. It looked like he hadn't affected Claire at all, and Ichi couldn't stand it. *Is this what Michael meant?* Ichi thought, frustrated. *How can he expect me to 'reign it in' if Claire continues to act like I don't exist? When I'm dying to get a reaction out of her?* Ichi rested his head against the tiles, as he had done in that terrible shower in the dingy London flat what felt like a million years ago. *This is going to be a hell of a lot more difficult that even Michael thinks.*

Vic

Vic couldn't quite believe that Ichi had returned months before anyone had expected him to. He begrudgingly acknowledged the fact that Ichi really was great at his job, though he took some grim satisfaction from the fact that Ichi had been chosen for the job because he looked exactly like the type of man that the bar owner's son was attracted to. *I hope that was fun for you, you prick,* Vic thought. Normally, Michael didn't share the details of jobs that he sent other people to work on, but Vic had worked for Michael longer than anybody else. He was always privy to the more *interesting* aspects of everybody's undercover work, even if Vic never knew what exactly they were doing.

He was proud of Claire for having successfully ignored Ichi when the other man had appeared in the rec hall. He couldn't have done it better himself. Or, rather, Vic chose not to, instead opting to glare at Ichi until he left. *After all, it does me no harm to openly hate him.* Vic was even prouder of how Claire was coming along in her training. She took to working with both guns and knives surprisingly quickly, almost always hitting on target with both. Claire put this down to always playing darts with her father; Vic simply put it down to her being a natural with both weapons. He had warned her that throwing knives were no good as an *actual* weapon choice unless you always hit on target, since failing to do so was as good as handing your assailant the knife and telling them to take their best shot. Claire had laughed at that. *Then I'll just have to make sure I never miss,* she had said in reply.

However, Claire was terrible at hand to hand combat and self-defence: not once in the past two months had she managed to overthrow Vic. Claire had complained that it was because Vic was so much taller and stronger than her, so Vic had pointed out that she would hardly be able to *choose* who attacked her in the future, if anybody ever did. *But you're taller than he is,* she had muttered. Vic had smiled sadly at that. He knew Claire still couldn't shake Ichi from her mind, but Vic continued to do his damnedest to make her forget, nonetheless.

He had been worried that Ichi would be so bold as to try and attack Claire as soon as he returned, but Vic's worry had not come to fruition. He had come straight up to Claire's room the following morning, deciding to bring her breakfast directly so that she wouldn't have to risk the rec hall after she had gone to the gym. Claire was fresh out of the shower, dressed in the t-shirt that Vic had given her after Ichi attacked her, and those tiny blue shorts that Vic loved so much. She had smiled broadly at Vic when he came in to her room with a tray full of food, and assured him that nothing had happened since Ichi's return. Vic had mirrored her smile when he realised she was speaking the truth.

Now they were both lounging on her couch, allowing their breakfast to hit their stomachs whilst vaguely listening to the music Claire had playing in the background. She was nestled against his side, sighing contentedly. Vic loved it.

"Vic, how long have you worked for Michael?" Claire asked him suddenly. Vic glanced down at her, surprised. He thought for a moment.

"About…six years, maybe? As soon as I finished university, I suppose," he replied.

Claire's eyes widened. "So that would make you, what, twenty-eight? Or I suppose that would only be the case if you went to a Scottish university, like me. So…twenty-seven?" It suddenly occurred to Vic that he had never told Claire how old he was. He wondered how long she had been thinking about it.

Vic smiled at her. "Twenty-seven, princess. I was seventeen when I started university," he said.

Claire looked at him curiously. "Where did you study then? It must have been in Scotland."

"Edinburgh. Why do you ask?" Claire smiled sheepishly.

"Just curious. I went to Glasgow, like my parents. What was your degree in?"

Vic sighed. "I can't believe you've waited three months to have 'small talk' with me," he joked.

Claire made a face at him. "I just wanted to know," she responded, pretending to be annoyed. Vic ruffled her still-damp hair.

"Geography," he replied, eventually. Claire's almost seemed to flinch for a second, before her eyes lit up with another question.

"So is that where you're from? Edinburgh? You don't sound like you're from there. But then again, I can't work out where *anyone* is from in here," Claire mumbled.

Vic laughed. "I'm definitely not from Edinburgh, Claire. My father was Russian and my mother was English. But I was brought up in France until I was fifteen, then I moved to Cambridge with my mother when my father died. I moved up a year in school because I was ahead of the English curriculum." Vic looked at Claire. "I could be making all of this up, you know," he said, running his hand through his blonde hair. Vic noted that it was getting a little long, even for him. It was past his shoulders now; he toyed with the idea of tying it up.

Claire shook her head at his statement. "No, you're telling the truth for sure." She smiled slyly up at him. "You're not the only one who's worked out when one of us is lying," she added on, laughing to herself.

"Well, since I know when you're lying, tell me honestly; do I cut my hair short or leave it as it is?" Vic asked, inspecting the ends of a few strands of it as he spoke.

Claire looked horrified. "Don't cut your hair; it's gorgeous!" she gasped. Vic was surprised by her reaction.

"I didn't realise you liked it so much," he murmured, almost to himself. Claire's face reddened just a little. She seemed to fish for another question.

"So…six years working for Michael. What about everyone else?" she asked, keeping her gaze down until her cheeks had stopped flushing.

Vic laughed. "I'm not going to jump on you for paying me a compliment, princess," he remarked. "I'm happy just hearing you think I'm attractive." He grinned and promptly ducked as Claire threw the pillow that she slept on at his head.

"No need to be such a dick about it," she said, hugging the pillow after Vic threw it back to her. "So, how long has everyone else worked for Michael, then?" Claire repeated. Vic had to think for a minute.

"Marie joined maybe a year after me. Ryan and Imran a few months later. Ryan spent most of the first couple of years away on a long-term job though, so it doesn't feel like he's been here as long as he has been." Vic paused, considering something. "Alexis joined maybe nine months ago,

Ichi a month or so later." Claire whipped her head around suddenly to look at Vic, her eyes wide.

"Wait, what?" she exclaimed. "I thought that they had both been here much longer than that! I thought they –"

"Yes, they're Michael's favourites," Vic interrupted. "I know, it's strange," he added on in response to Claire's confused face. "I don't know why Alexis became Michael's right hand man, or woman as the case may be. I've never thought to ask. Michael does what he wants, after all. Ichi…well, who knows with him? He's good at his job. Michael used him for just about every short-term job he had that needed done until you showed up. He clearly made an impression on Michael, somehow. Ahh, I don't care," Vic finished. Claire was looking at him strangely.

"What?" he asked, somewhat concerned.

"Give me a second," was all she said, before she rushed away to her bathroom and returned with her hairbrush. "Sit on the floor," she commanded.

"Claire, I'm not your My Little Pony," Vic joked, but he sat down on the floor in front of her couch nonetheless. As she ran the brush through his hair, easing out the tangles that were in it, Vic closed his eyes and let himself relax.

"I'm okay now, you know," he heard Claire say, quietly. "Really, I am. I wasn't before, not by a long shot, but now I am. Thanks for being so patient with me in training." Vic opened his eyes and turned his head up to look at Claire sitting above him.

"That's good to hear," he replied, smiling. "But don't think that saying that will make me go easy on you this afternoon. I'll keep throwing you to the ground until you learn how to use my weight against me." He felt Claire's hands on the side of his head, making him look forwards.

"I can't do your hair if you look up," she said, so seriously that it made Vic chuckle. He could feel her fingers braiding his hair.

"Claire, what are you –" He began turning around, but Claire's laughter drowned out the rest of his words.

"Ah, you really do look like him. You're much too tall though, and your eyes aren't golden," Claire managed to say through fits of giggles.

Vic frowned. "Look like who?" he demanded. Claire waved his question away with a hand.

"It doesn't matter. You obviously don't know who I'm on about, otherwise you'd get the joke," she remarked. "Come on, turn back round, I'll put it in a ponytail instead." Vic rolled his eyes but did as he was told. "There," Claire said when she was done. "Now you won't have to constantly run your fingers through your hair to push it out of the way," she grinned. Vic made a grab at her and missed, Claire jumping up onto the couch as she dodged him.

"Maybe I like running my hand through my hair," Vic commented, pulling the band out of his hair as he spoke, shaking his head to return his hair to its usual, expertly windswept state. Claire made to sit back down again, so Vic took the opportunity to grab at her, pulling her to the floor with him.

"Vic, what the –" Claire began before she started to laugh. She looked up at Vic, smiling. "Your hair is ticklish," she commented, as strands of it just barely swept over her cheeks. Claire's face was flushed; Vic knew his was too. He didn't say anything for a while, not daring to push the moment forward but not wanting it to break either. "Vic," Claire said, eventually. She reached her face up a couple of inches to kiss the end of his nose. "Self-defence lessons aren't until after lunch…it's too early to throw me down." Vic lingered over her for a moment, before grasping her right arm and helping her to her feet.

He grabbed the now-empty tray of food from Claire's coffee table and made for the door. "I'll see you at eleven in the shooting range then," he said, smiling.

"The time I've made up in my head, or the real time? Because you know that I don't know when that is," she said, slight sarcasm colouring the tone of her voice. Vic sighed.

"You've been doing a pretty good job of it so far," he replied, before making his exit. Out in the corridor, waiting on the elevator, Vic could have hit himself. "I shouldn't have done that," he muttered aloud.

"Done what?" came a voice to his left. It was Ichi; Vic hadn't even heard him leave his room. He felt an immediate flash of irritation go through him just by looking at the other man's face.

"That's none of your damn business," he replied scathingly. Ichi looked at him, suspicious, before he chose to take the stairs instead of waiting on the elevator. Vic was glad; he had nearly punched Ichi in the face simply for existing.

He's up to something already, Vic realised. He didn't know what, only that he was. *Then I better make sure Claire is ready to deflect it,* he thought, as he entered the elevator, a frown creasing his brow.

CHAPTER 12
I Can't Read You

Ichi

Ichi was sitting cross-legged on his bed, looking at the new camera he had bought. This one was waterproof, and as high-resolution as they would come. All he needed was an opportunity to slip into Claire's room and set it up somewhere inconspicuous by her shower. Ichi had meant to try his luck to rig it up that afternoon; unfortunately, after staying up for all of the previous night and well into the morning, he finally fell asleep around lunch time and found himself wide awake in the middle of the night. Ichi felt the vein in his temple twitch in irritation at the fact that he'd have to map out Claire's daily routine *again* just so he could set the camera up when she was absent from her room. *Unless...* but no, he couldn't just waltz in regardless of whether Claire was in or not. It was reckless, and certainly not a decision that Michael would be happy about if Ichi acted on impulse whilst he was in Claire's room if she was there. *On the other hand...* Ichi glanced at his laptop screen, and brought up the camera feed of Claire's living space. She was asleep on her couch, still refusing to use the bed; Ichi smirked at that. Ichi looked at his clock – it was after three in the morning. Claire was unlikely to wake up if he slipped into her room *now*. And he would be in and out in five minutes, after all.

Knowing that it was a terrible decision, Ichi grabbed the camera and quietly headed out of his own room anyway, carefully unlocking Claire's door with the key that he still hadn't returned to Michael when he reached it. He closed it silently behind him so that the light from the corridor didn't shine through and wake Claire up, then crept over to her shower room, inwardly thanking Claire for not putting the screen door up to block the way. Ichi worked quickly and efficiently, wiring the camera up in the corner right beside the extractor fan unit and angling it so that its lens was aimed directly into her shower. Once he was done, Ichi inspected his work. The camera was well hidden by the extractor unit; Claire would never know it was there unless she looked for it. Satisfied, Ichi took his leave of the shower room, honestly intending to stalk straight back out of Claire's room entirely. But just as he walked past her couch, Claire rolled onto her side, facing the coffee table. Ichi couldn't help himself; he walked around to sit on the table, staring at this girl who stole all of his thoughts.

She wasn't wearing much, just a thin sleeveless top and shorts, and the blanket she was using was mostly wrapped around her legs. Ichi didn't blame her; her room was far too hot. Ichi wondered why. But all of Claire's exposed skin caused Ichi's brain to think back to the last time he had seen her before he was sent away, and he felt the blood rush down past his navel as a result. *Jesus, I don't think about sex for nearly six weeks and now I can't get it off of my mind,* he cursed.

Some of Claire's long, dark hair had fallen over her shoulder to tumble across her chest in loose waves, so Ichi dared to sweep some of it away to look at the skin on that same shoulder. There was no indication that he had ravaged it two months ago, or on Claire's neck either. Ichi knew that there couldn't have been, not after all of this time, but it irked him nonetheless. Sleeping as she was, all dishevelled and defenceless and God damn sensual as hell, Ichi felt more than ever that he wasn't having any effect on Claire at all.

His eyes roved down to her stomach. It made Ichi feel incredibly uncomfortable thinking about the idea of Claire being pregnant. *And even if she was,* Ichi thought, *surely she would get rid of it? She's not stupid.* His attention was brought back to the present as he heard Claire sharply inhale. He looked back up at her face; she was wide awake. They stared at each other for a long time.

"What do you want?" Claire finally demanded, her voice quiet. Ichi knelt down in front of her, crossing his arms on the couch seat to rest his head on top of them, bringing his eyes level with hers. He mentally inhaled as sharply as Claire had done in real life.

"...are you pregnant?" he asked, keeping his voice as quiet as hers. Claire's eyes widened slightly at his question, but she stayed silent.

Ichi was considering asking her again, more forcefully, when she replied, "No." Ichi let out his breath in a whoosh of air; he couldn't help but be visibly relieved. He ran a hand through his hair, taking it temporarily out of his face. Claire kept her face blank.

"Get out, Ichi," she told him. Ichi didn't move.

"I'll leave when I want to," he countered, daring to be contrary despite Michael's warning. When Claire made to turn around on her couch, Ichi instinctively grabbed at her shoulder, stopping the movement. He pinned her back down onto the couch with the same motion, placing his left hand on her other shoulder. The hair that he had only just swept back now hung mere millimetres from Claire's forehead as he brought his face closer to hers. Claire looked mildly irritated. Ichi frowned, searching her face for any kind of clue about how she was actually feeling.

After a while, Claire spoke. "Are you done?" she asked, echoing the only words she had uttered to him the last time the two of them were alone. Those words went right through Ichi, causing him to blindly react with no regard for Michael's previous warning. He kissed her, gripping Claire's chin with his hand to prevent her from turning away. He bit into her lower lip until she opened her mouth in shock, and stuck his tongue in when she did. But instead of trying to either push him away or simply do nothing as Ichi had expected, Claire kissed him back, ferociously, running a hand through his hair as she did so. Ichi was so shocked that he stopped what he was doing, and that was all Claire needed. She grabbed a handful of his hair and yanked his head back to punch him, full force, in the neck. The assault left Ichi clinging to his throat, breathless and in pain. Claire pushed him off of her and onto the floor. "Get the fuck out of here," she said, her eyes glittering in the darkness of the room.

Ichi rolled over onto his feet, taking a moment to get his breath back. For a few seconds he considered using his full strength and attacking Claire again, but the pain in his neck stopped that idea. He looked at Claire one last time before, finally, stalking out of her room and into the corridor. He heard the door slam behind him.

She punched me. In the fucking neck, Ichi thought, almost in disbelief. He couldn't help but be impressed; it was a clever move. He brought his fingers up to his mouth, still in shock over the fact that Claire had kissed him back. He knew she had done it to distract him which was, again, a very clever thing to do on her part, but it made Ichi feel odd. And angry. Claire had treated him like he was merely a fly buzzing around her head; a nuisance, but not of any importance.

Ichi let himself fall onto his bed when he got back to his room, staring up at the ceiling, thinking of nothing but Claire, and Claire, and Claire.

Claire

Claire sat back down on her couch after Ichi left, her fingers on her lips. She didn't know why she had kissed him back. Claire reassured herself that it was just a self-defence tactic that had worked incredibly well, but some small part of her brain told her that that wasn't all there was to it. She pushed that thought away.

Claire wrapped herself back up in the blanket which Vic had given to her after she told him her room was too warm for the duvet, thinking hard. *Ichi looked so relieved when I told him I wasn't pregnant.* Claire had obviously been relieved when all of her test results had come back negative, leaving her in the clear. But why had Ichi been? Why would he care? He couldn't possibly be thankful on her behalf that she wasn't carrying his child.

"He's probably just glad there's nothing to complicate things for him," Claire muttered. She stared up at the ceiling, knowing that it would be many long hours before she fell asleep, her head full of thoughts she didn't want about the psychopath living next door.

*

Several weeks later, Ichi hadn't so much as looked at Claire since he had let himself into her room. Claire was glad; it helped her keep her head focussed on what was important – training herself to keep him fully at bay the next time he decided to attack her. She was relieved to not run into him as she wandered down to the pool for her morning swim. By some stroke of sheer luck, Claire had managed to avoid seeing Ichi every time she

112

headed to the pool, which was something she was thankful for given that the only towel she had in her possession barely covered her swim suit as she walked through the corridors on her way to swim. She had asked Vic for another, longer one (having long since given up on asking Alexis anything, who continued to dutifully ignore her), but he had teased that a big one wouldn't look as good on her, and that had been the end of that conversation. In the back of her mind, Claire reminded herself that she quite liked the way Vic looked at her as she wandered down the corridor towards the swimming pool with very little on, anyway. The sensible part of her brain ignored that.

When she reached the pool, Claire unwrapped herself from her towel and placed it on the bench that sat by the water's edge. She heard someone wolf whistle behind her. She turned around; it was Ryan, of course.

"Well, if it isn't my favourite swimming buddy," he exclaimed. Claire slid into the water.

"Hello to you too, Ryan," she replied, giving her arms a stretch.

He swam over to her. "How energetic are you feeling this morning then, beautiful?" he crooned in his American accent.

Claire rolled her eyes. "Very. I'm feeling like I could swim for hours," she commented. Ryan positioned himself against the wall of the pool; Claire did the same.

"Why not just start with forty lengths and see where we go from there?" he suggested, a deliberately sleazy grin on his face.

"*We* are not going anywhere," Claire countered, before kicking off from the wall of the pool and starting to swim. She ended up swimming closer to fifty lengths, but Claire lost track of the number after her thirty-fifth. When she was finished, Claire leaned back against the wall of the shallower end of the pool and closed her eyes, breathing heavily.

"You weren't lying when you said you were feeling energetic," she heard Ryan say to her left. "That was your quickest time yet for the number of lengths you did." Claire half-opened her eyes to throw him a sideways glance.

"You were counting them?"

Ryan laughed, sitting up on the edge of the pool beside her as he did so. "I always count them. You did forty-eight today. You were about…4 seconds faster per hundred metres than you were three weeks ago. That's impressive, even taking into account that you weren't that fast to begin with," he replied. Claire allowed herself a small smile. She was pleased with herself; she was much better at swimming than she was running or rowing or cross-training in the gym.

Claire flinched suddenly as she felt Ryan's hands on the back of her head. She made to turn around, but he stopped her. "Calm it, I'm fixing your hair. It's fallen out of your up-do," he said to her, before she could ask.

"You could have just told me it was loose; I'd have fixed it myself," Claire grumbled. She heard Ryan chuckle.

"What, and miss an opportunity to touch you? Never," he said lecherously. He jumped back into the pool before Claire had an opportunity to protest. Ryan stood in the water only a foot or so away from her – it made Claire feel uncomfortable.

"You're not interested in my welfare here, are you?" she asked him. Ryan looked up at the pipes lining the ceiling, high above them.

"Not particularly," he answered honestly.

"You just want to screw me," Claire ventured.

Ryan brought his gaze back to her and grinned. "That I do; I won't apologise for that. Why, was that an offer?" He chuckled, taking a step towards her.

Claire ignored the advance. "But if Michael told you to, you'd kill me in a second." It wasn't a question.

"That's the nature of the job, sweetheart," he replied. "But know I'd be at least a little sad about it." Claire snapped. She raised her hand to slap him, but Ryan caught a hold of her wrist before it got anywhere near his face. "I wouldn't do that if I were you," he said in a low voice, his tone dangerous. "Don't ask me about something if you don't want to hear the answer." Claire's hand twitched; Ryan's grip on her wrist was too strong for her to get out of. Suddenly, he twisted her arm, spinning Claire around and bringing it down painfully behind her back. She breathed in sharply, trying to remember how she was supposed to get out of an arm lock like this from her training with Vic. But her mind had gone blank, all training forgotten. Ryan's other hand was on her shoulder now, his mouth at her ear.

"Don't forget what we are here, what we *all* are, even your dear Vic," he growled into her ear. "He's a trained killer, just like me. He could crush the bones in your wrist with one hand and you wouldn't be able to do a thing about it." Ryan's grip tightened even more on her arm, making his point clear. Claire could feel her heart beating too fast, the fear in her system being converted into adrenaline that she couldn't use.

Just when Claire was beginning to think Ryan was either going to break her arm or make her beg for him to let go, she spied the last person she wanted to see on earth appear out of the corner of her eye. "Don't mind me, I'm just here to use the pool for its actual purpose," Ichi remarked casually. Claire felt the pressure on her wrist vanish as Ryan let her go. She vaulted herself out of the pool and grabbed for her towel, knowing that there was no way to hide from Ichi how vulnerable the situation had made her feel.

"Don't forget what I said, Claire!" she heard Ryan call out to her, almost cheerfully, as she rushed out of the door.

Ichi

He shouldn't have interfered. He should have let whatever was happening between Claire and Ryan happen. But Claire had looked so terrified when Ichi had spied her through the glass panel in the door, and Ichi knew that, with Ryan involved, whatever was going to happen would be nothing good. For Claire, anyway. *She's mine to torment,* Ichi had thought as he opened the door. *That's the only reason why I'm stopping this.*

But Claire spared him only a half-second's glance when he entered the pool room, and didn't look at him at all as she made her escape. *So much for gratitude, you bitch.* Ryan sized Ichi up after she left. "Didn't have you pegged as the knight in shining armour," he commented as he hauled himself out of the pool.

"I'm not," Ichi replied, nonchalant. Ryan laughed.

115

"Go on and believe that, if you want. You're not going to ask what we were doing?" he asked Ichi, trying to bait him.

"Why would I care?" Ichi replied, mentally attempting to stop himself from punching Ryan in the face.

"I think you do," Ryan countered. He picked up his towel from where he had left it on the floor. "I was just reminding her of a few home truths, is all. Hell, she tried to hit me first!" Ryan laughed, incredulous. "As if I'd let her do that. She said all I wanted to do was screw her. Ha! Can you believe that? She actually went out and said it. And here was me thinking she was all proper. Well, if she's thinking about it, maybe I'll give it a try." He looked at Ichi out of the corner of his eye, grinning lazily. "Unless you have any objections?" *He's trying to bait me. Again.* Ichi turned away from him and stepped into the pool to hide the rage that was written all over his face.

"Be my guest," he answered. "I'd watch out for Vic, though." He heard Ryan laugh again.

"He can't be around her every minute of the day. I'll work it out. Bye, Ich," Ryan said, before making his exit. *Don't act like you're so familiar with me, you dick.* The only people who called him Ich were Alexis and Vic, who had started using it to annoy him when Ichi first started working for Michael. Not that Ichi and Vic were on any semblance of good terms right now.

It was only in thinking that that Ichi realised he and Vic *had* been on good terms…right up until Claire's failed assassination. He wondered why he had ever bothered with him in the first place. Or maybe it had just been Vic, pushing friendship on him whether Ichi wished it or not. *Well it doesn't matter now,* he mused as he began to swim. He only hoped that Vic's presence would indeed be enough to keep Ryan away from Claire, but that very hope irked him. *How can I hope for him to do that whilst also wanting him to fuck off so I can do what I like to her?*

Cursing himself, Ichi resolved to swim until all such thoughts had been exercised out of his system. He was behaving himself right now, after all, for Michael's sake. But in reality, Ichi knew that that couldn't go on for much longer. He frowned at the memory of Claire not being able to fend Ryan off. *What is Vic teaching her, if not to defend herself from the likes of him?* Ichi decided it was about time he started observing some of their sessions, to make sure she was being taught properly. The thought caused Ichi to stop swimming, mid-way across the pool.

"Why do I even *care?!*" he shouted in irritation, his voice echoing off of the tall ceiling. Claire learning to defend herself would only make her more difficult to handle, for both Ryan *and* Ichi. *Or it could make things more interesting,* he realised suddenly. He grinned. "Okay then, Claire, let's see what you can do," he uttered, before continuing to swim.

Claire

Claire was sitting in the rec hall, alone. It was well past lunch but she couldn't force herself to move from where she had been seated for nearly three hours, the food in front of her having been left mostly untouched since she sat down. She didn't even have her Kindle or her music or her laptop down with her; the events of the morning were more than enough for Claire to concentrate on. She couldn't believe that she had Ichi to thank for getting her out of the situation with Ryan, accidental or not. Claire believed it to be the latter. She wondered what she would have done if Ryan hadn't been there and Ichi had shown up to find her…alone. It would have been the first instance in which they were alone since he had broken into her room. *Well, having a key hardly counts as breaking in.* Claire was angry at that; why hadn't Michael insisted on Ichi returning it? Maybe Vic had been right all along and Michael really was using Ichi to scare her. Claire supposed that Ichi would literally just break in if he didn't have a key, so it was probably for the best that he had one. Claire's face grew stony as she realised what she was thinking.

"Hell *no* it's not for the best," she said out loud. Living in this place was seriously twisting her idea of what was acceptable behaviour or not, and Claire didn't like that at all. Her mind went back to what Ryan had said to her in the pool, after she had tried to slap him. *Everyone here really would kill me in a second if they were told to…even Vic.* But would he? Claire hoped that he wouldn't. However, if his orders hadn't been to prevent her death four months ago but instead to cause it, what reason would Vic have had to *not* kill her? Thinking about it made Claire's head hurt.

117

Ryan's statement had made something perfectly clear, however: Ichi had been right on target with his words when he had forced himself on her. Claire shivered, trying to ignore the memory as it came sweeping over her regardless. She was beginning to wonder if he was simply right about everything. That notion chilled her more than him attacking her did. But Ichi couldn't have been right about Vic, when he said that all Vic wanted to do was sleep with her. It just wasn't who he was. *He's still a killer, though,* her brain reminded her, unbidden. Whether he hated it or not, the fact that Vic chose to murder people for a living was a cold, hard truth. It made Claire feel weird; if she broke the essential parts down, what truly separated Vic, whom she trusted, from Ichi, whom she absolutely didn't?

Only literally everything else about them, Claire thought with a frown. Vic wasn't a psychopath, for one. Although the more that Claire thought on it, the more she considered the possibility that that wasn't exactly what Ichi actually was. He seemed to make a lot of emotionally spontaneous decisions, such as on the occasions where he had broken into her room, after all. He knew exactly what to say to get a rise out of Claire, like saying that Vic only wanted to sleep with her and mocking her by doing the things he assumed Vic would do to her if that were true. If Claire wasn't so good at hiding her own reactions from him, he'd have broken her already. *How could a psychopath make decisions based on emotions if he doesn't understand them?* But Ichi was clever, so Claire could also argue that he was merely manipulating Claire's weak points rather than making any emotional decisions.

The problem was that, if Ichi wasn't a psychopath…then it meant exactly that – that he wasn't. Which meant Ichi had genuinely emotion-based reasons for every little thing that he had done to Claire so far. *Can a person be so cruel?* Claire was upset at the idea. But why else would Ichi have forced himself on her? Claire could only think of one rational explanation – that Ichi was jealous. And possessive. The possessive part Claire had concluded already, from the numerous times Ichi had reminded her that she was his. But jealous? Claire could feel her face grow red.

"Stop thinking about it; he's just a messed up, dangerous person who's not worth your time," Claire reminded herself.

"Exactly," came a female voice from behind her, so Claire turned her head to see that it was Marie. Claire was surprised; she assumed Marie disliked her. "Who exactly are you referring to though?" Marie added on as she took a seat beside Claire. She had a sketchbook with her.

"Can I have a look at that?" Claire asked her, curious. Marie moved it out of reach.

"Only if you don't deflect my question," she answered. "So who were you talking to yourself about?" Claire looked down at the floor, ashamed.

"Ichi," she mumbled.

Marie laughed. "Ahh, I *thought* so! Imran owes me big time," she cackled happily.

Claire looked back up at her, eyebrow raised in suspicion. "What do you mean?"

Marie put her sketchbook down in front of Claire. "Here, have a look. I'm free to deflect your questions all I want," she said, grinning. Claire sighed, turning her attention to Marie's book. She gasped when she opened it, turning the pages over slowly as she took in drawing after glorious drawing of people, animals, flowers…

"You're so talented, Marie," she said, in awe of her skill. Marie didn't bother to feign bashfulness at the comment.

"You work in the field that I do, you find yourself something that can take your mind off of it completely in your down time." She smiled at Claire. "For me, that's drawing. People, mostly. I find them far more interesting to draw than to listen to, generally." Claire snickered at the comment.

"I get why you would feel that way," she replied. "Is that – is that *Edward Elric?!*" Claire asked excitedly as she turned the page to a gorgeously drawn image of one of her favourite fictional people. Marie's eyes widened in interest.

"So you're an anime fan too? Huh."

Claire narrowed her eyes at her. "What does that mean?"

Marie smiled. "You just don't look the type, is all. I figured you'd be far too busy with real boy attention to watch Japanese cartoons." Claire laughed.

"If all guys were like Ed, maybe I'd spend more time talking to them. As it happens, they're not."

"Except Vic," Marie pointed out. Claire looked away.

"Well…yes. But he's more than a foot taller and lacks the golden eyes," she joked. Claire looked wistfully at Marie's drawing, sighing again.

"What is it?" the other woman asked.

"I don't have any anime here," Claire answered. "I wish I did…I've gone through every film I have on my laptop."

Marie grinned. "I can help you with that." Claire gaped at her, shocked.

"You would lend me some?!" she replied, not able to cover the surprise in her voice.

"Why, would you expect me not to?" Marie asked, looking a little put out.

Claire ran a hand through her hair, embarrassed. "It's just…well…I thought you didn't like me much. Because of –"

"What? Because of Vic?" Marie interrupted. "Don't make me laugh. Vic wasn't interested in me long before you showed up. I've accepted that for years. I'm content with my golden-eyed anime alternative." She chuckled. "So do you want to borrow Brotherhood or not? Please tell me you think it's better than the first anime series," she said, changing the subject. Claire smiled at her. *I got her all wrong. So did Ichi. Maybe he* isn't *right about everything.* The thought comforted Claire immensely.

"Of course," she agreed. "Thank you, Marie, I really mean it."

Marie smiled, but her eyes were sad and sympathetic. "I really hope you get out of here soon, Claire. You clearly don't deserve to be locked up here."

Claire stared at her curiously. "How would you know –"

"Ahh, you're not the only one who talks to Vic," Marie interrupted, laughing. "He shouldn't tell me what's going on with you, and he doesn't, not really…but I can read him like a book. He wouldn't like you so much if you had done something terrible." Marie's face grew serious. "But despite that, Claire, when you get to leave, forget about all of us. Even Vic. Even Ichi. Just get on with your life."

120

She got up to leave, and was halfway towards the door when Claire replied, "That's the best advice I've heard since I got here, Marie." She paused before adding on quietly, "I only hope I get to take it."

Marie nodded her acknowledgement of Claire's statement. "You're up on the twelfth floor, right? I'll come by later with Brotherhood. Don't watch it in two days, like I did!" She grinned, laughing as she took her leave. *That's what I did too,* Claire thought with a smile. Claire realised in that moment that she genuinely liked Marie.

But they're all killers, Claire thought, and the air around her seemed to grow several degrees colder. Claire didn't understand how she could so easily laugh and talk and flirt and even *like* these people. It disturbed her. *It can't disturb you whilst you're here, idiot,* Claire scolded herself, getting up to throw her mostly uneaten lunch in the bin.

"You can just forget about them when you're gone, like Marie said," Claire mumbled aloud as she washed her plate in the sink. She stared out at the rec hall, seeing nothing. "That's never going to happen," she whispered, but whether she was referring to forgetting Ichi or Vic or getting out of the complex in the first place, even Claire didn't know.

CHAPTER 13
Undisclosed Desires

Ichi

After a full month of observing Vic and Claire's training sessions, Ichi concluded that he hated them. The pair of them were so *close*, both physically and emotionally. Especially physically. Claire spent half of her afternoon every day being arm locked and grabbed around the waist and flung to the floor, over and over again, until she could successfully save herself from the situation. She didn't look like she wanted saved from where Ichi stood, watching. Or maybe Claire was just really bad at self-defence; Ichi liked to think that Claire was not so air-headed that she would be performing badly in her training simply so that she could end up lying underneath Vic after he threw her to the floor for the hundredth time. But the more Ichi watched them, the more he wasn't so sure. The only thing he took out of Claire's afternoon lessons that consoled him was that she was clearly not sleeping with Vic…yet. There was too much tension between the two of them, and a lot of that was coming from Vic. *He wouldn't be so on edge if he was already screwing her,* Ichi found himself thinking almost every single day.

Claire's morning training sessions were easier to watch, mainly because learning how to handle a gun and knives didn't involve as much physical contact between teacher and pupil. And Claire was good with both weapons – ridiculously so, considering how long she had been learning. Ichi couldn't help but be impressed. And pissed off. Claire was learning how to use *his* weapon of choice, but not from him. Which meant she'd never be a match for him. Vic was excellent with knives, yes, but Ichi was in a whole different league when it came to using them. *Why would I even want her to be that good with them? It's not like she'll ever have an opportunity to even try to use a knife against me.* The thought excited him, somehow, though Ichi didn't understand why.

Claire didn't even seem phased that Ichi had been watching most of her training sessions for the past four weeks, which infuriated him. But Ichi wasn't the only one who watched; Ryan and Imran and occasionally Marie came along to observe, from behind the safety of the bulletproof glass that separated the viewer's gallery from the shooting and target range and the large practice hall. It annoyed Ichi that other people came to watch, but it was a habit of everyone here that they came to see just how good any new recruits of Michael's were. They had watched both him and Alexis train for several weeks after they had joined, Ichi had to remind himself. But Claire wasn't a new recruit; she was likely going to be dead in a few months at most. *So why bother watching her train?* Ichi never voiced any of his questions – the other assassins were likely to simply ask him the same questions straight back in response, and Ichi had no answer for them that made any sense.

Vic tended to look at Ichi with open hatred whenever he came along to watch, but Ichi pretended that he didn't notice. He was fed up of Vic acting like he would love nothing better than to put a bullet through his head; it was making Ichi's life at the complex uncomfortable. It wasn't like he had ever been particularly sociable with any of the other residents, but Vic's open animosity towards Ichi left him unable to sit down in the rec hall whenever Vic was in there, either on his own or with Claire. *He should just hurry up and get over it; he has no business being angry at me anyway. It's got nothing to do with him.*

Ichi knew he was correct on that front – Vic hadn't tried to beat Ichi to a pulp when he had returned from his undercover work, which meant Claire had *definitely* not told Vic about what exactly Ichi had done to her, four months ago, nor about the night that Ichi had crept into her room just after he had returned from his undercover work and kissed her. It reminded him of the fact that Claire had also never told Vic about how he had accosted her on the very first night that she had been brought to Michael's complex, either. Ichi felt some twisted sense of victory for that; if Claire was keeping all of these encounters to herself, then that meant she didn't want anybody to know about what Ichi got up to with her when nobody was around. Ichi could monopolise on that…if he could only work out how. He was surprised that he had managed to keep himself from cornering Claire in her secret hiding place under the fourth floor stairs after he worked out that that was precisely where she ran off to in the evenings a couple of weeks ago. Ichi supposed he was just keeping by Michael's orders to 'reign it in' until he identified where exactly the line was that he wasn't allowed to cross, but Ichi felt like there was more to his reluctance to attack Claire on the stairwell than just that. He didn't dwell on the thought; it pissed him off that he couldn't bring himself to corner her there.

Ichi shook his head to bring himself back to the present. He was watching another Claire-and-Vic self-defence lesson, even though he hated them. He had been channelling that hatred into all of the one-off jobs Michael had given him lately; not a week had gone by that Ichi hadn't killed off at least one person for him in the past month. It helped Ichi to keep a handle on his desire to accost Claire in her room every single night. He forced himself to be content with his live camera feeds to her room, which were made both much easier and much, much more difficult to watch now that he had a camera over Claire's shower. He pushed the attractive thought away to concentrate on what was happening in front of him.

Vic had grabbed Claire around her waist, pinning her arms to her sides so that she couldn't use them to fight back. Claire attempted to grind her heel into Vic's foot, but he twisted her leg around his and flipped her onto the ground. Though Ichi couldn't hear what either of them were saying, he could see Claire's expression and she was very clearly annoyed. Ichi couldn't help but smirk at that. *I guess even* she *is getting fed up with these sessions,* Ichi thought with a sense of satisfaction. He vaguely heard the door behind him open, followed by the sound of Ryan and Imran talking to each other as they stood off to Ichi's left to watch what was going on. Ichi's brow furrowed slightly in irritation, then his eyes widened in surprise as he felt a hand touch his right shoulder. He turned his head and saw Alexis, who was smiling.

"Didn't hear me come in, did you?" Alexis laughed. "You're off your game, Ich."

Ichi returned his focus to Claire. "I don't need to be 'on my game' here," he muttered in reply. Alexis laughed again, then hailed Marie over when the other woman appeared through the door. *Great, now everyone's here,* Ichi thought, exasperated. It hadn't escaped Vic and Claire's notice – Claire was grinning and waving at Marie from her position on the floor before Vic hauled her up. Marie waved back, a small smile on her face. Ichi was confused. *When did they get so close?* He was surprised when Alexis voiced that exact thought.

"Common interests," was Marie's reply, a sly smile playing across her lips as she glanced over at Vic, who was tackling Claire to the ground once more. She burst out laughing at the shocked expression on Ichi's face that he couldn't quite conceal fast enough.

"Aw, Ichi, your face is priceless. I'm not even going to bother correcting what you're thinking in your head. Have fun with that chip on your shoulder," she joked. Ichi frowned; he didn't know what to say in return. The woman turned to Alexis, not waiting for a response from Ichi. "Michael wants to see us, Alexis. He needs us both for some job…it might take a couple of weeks, he said."

Alexis nodded. "I'll be with him in a minute – you go on ahead, Marie," she replied. Marie gave Claire another wave through the viewing glass, waited for it to be returned and then turned around and left. Ichi was glaring at Vic, the way Vic often glared at him. He didn't know enough about Marie to know what any of her 'common interests' with Claire could be out with that damn man. For the first time since he started working for Michael, Ichi regretted not getting to know his boss' other employees better. He felt his fingers subconsciously grip the ledge underneath the glass a little too tightly.

"Ichi? Hello, Ichi?" he heard Alexis say. Ryan and Imran were looking at him too, amused expressions on their faces.

"What?!" Ichi snapped at all of them. Ryan chuckled before saying something to the other man that Ichi couldn't hear, before returning their attention back to Claire and Vic. Alexis put her hand on Ichi's cheek, forcing his eyes away from the glass. Ichi swept her hand away, but kept his gaze on Alexis, as she wanted. "What?" he asked again, quieter this time.

Alexis frowned at him. "It's not like you to be this pissed off when you're offing a person or two every week," she commented, so casually.

"What of it?" Ichi fired back, not caring much for an answer. He ran his left hand through his hair to clear it from his eyes. Alexis watched the motion, the sides of her mouth upturned slightly.

"You know where I am if you need an extra vent for all of that anger. It's been too long." She grinned for a second, and then frowned at him. Ichi saw that she was worried about him; he didn't care. "It's not healthy,"

Alexis continued, "You know it's not. When was the last time you slept properly? You look like you haven't slept more than four hours a night since you got back from that undercover job."

"Maybe that's because I haven't," Ichi answered, not bothering to lie.

Alexis' frown deepened. "Why aren't you sleeping?" she asked. *Because I'm watching that damn woman on camera not get any sleep either,* Ichi answered silently, glancing at Claire.

"It's none of your business, Alexis," he responded, which was the truth.

Alexis gave him a searching look, then sighed. "Fine. Be that way. We'll see how well you cope without another outlet when I get back. See you in two weeks, Ich," she said, leaving before Ichi could respond. Ichi saw Ryan and Imran gaping at him.

"Seriously, do you not have anything better to do than to stare at me?" Ichi asked, annoyed.

Ryan shook his head. "I don't get it, man. How can you turn Alexis down? She's smokin' hot!" he lamented.

"Didn't have you pegged as a one-woman kind of guy, Ichi," Imran exclaimed, sparing Claire an obvious glance as he said so.

Ichi's eyes widened slightly at Imran's words before turning away. "Maybe I just don't think with my dick," he replied, imagining what it would feel like to break both of their necks in the next ten seconds.

Ryan laughed. "Looks like Alexis was right. You need to get laid, man. Big time. You're no fun to anyone all pissed off and moody as hell," he said.

Ichi turned back to face the two of them, rolling his eyes as he did so. "I thought that that's what I was like all of the time?" he replied sarcastically.

"Only about seventy percent of the time," Imran countered. He watched as Vic helped Claire up to her feet once more. "But you've been a brooding little shit ever since you and Vic brought Claire in."

Ryan guffawed with laughter. "Didn't know you had it in you to be so blunt, Imran. His point stands though, Ich." They all watched as Claire seemed to argue with Vic about something. Ryan threw a sidelong glance

126

in Ichi's direction. "What is it about her that you're so effing obsessed with, man? Yeah she's hot, but so is Alexis. And Alexis is basically handing herself over to you on a plate!" He raised an eyebrow at Ichi. "Or is that what it is? Alexis isn't a challenge? Ah, so you *are* a player, after all!" Ryan grinned from ear to ear, pleased that he had found a comrade.

Imran shook his head. "Nah, no way is Ichi a player. He isn't the type who can be bothered with all that crap just to get a girl. They're probably all throwing themselves at him anyway, like Alexis, the lucky son of a bitch." Ichi looked from one man to the other – they were leaving no room for him to defend himself.

"I don't get why girls go for that dark, moody thing either way, anyway. He's –"

"Will you both stop analysing me as if I'm not here?" Ichi interrupted, He didn't even have the energy to be angry at them anymore; their casual onslaught had simply made him tired.

Imran grinned. "Not until we at least get your sense of humour back, Ichi. Nobody wants to even be in the same room as you right now because you just seem to get pissed off at every little jest someone makes," he said.

"And you won't even go near us if Claire's around," Ryan added on. "Get a grip, man; this isn't high school. Just screw her or I swear I will, just to piss you off. So screw her or get over it."

"What if I have, and I haven't?" Ichi muttered, more to himself than in answer.

Ryan frowned at him. "If we were supposed to be able to hear that, neither of us did."

"But whatever, Ichi," Imran said, "It's up to you if don't want to talk to anyone whilst you're here. Must get pretty boring though."

Suddenly, Claire came bowling out of the glass door that led into the viewing gallery, Vic not far behind. "I'll try it again tomorrow, Vic. I just need to let off some steam," she called over her shoulder, not looking at anyone as she disappeared through the door that Marie and Alexis had exited through earlier.

Ryan put out an arm to stop Vic from following her. "Whatever it is you did, you're gonna make it worse if you go after her," he said in response to Vic's outraged expression.

Vic sighed. "She's just pissed because she can't beat me," he said, running a hand over his face. He glanced at Ichi, his eyes narrowing. "Why are you even here, Ichi? I don't get your angle. You're not intimidating Claire at all," he remarked sharply.

Ichi glowered at him, about to counter, but Ryan interrupted. "Are you really just going to start a fight with him because he watches you two practice together, something we *all* do, Vic?" he asked. "Let it go, man." Imran nodded in agreement, but Vic continued to glare at Ichi nonetheless.

Imran frowned at both of them. "Okay, I'm fed up of all this," he said. He looked at Vic. "Whatever it is that Ichi's done to so royally piss you off, just remember what you both do for a living and consider whether what he's done is worse than what he *could* do." He turned to Ichi. "Ichi, stop being such a moody prick."

Ryan laughed. "You're on point today, Imran. I say we should get our old blackjack game up and running once the girls get back from their job. If anything it'll force you guys to speak to each other," he said. Ichi looked at the three men, feeling exhaustion wash over him just by listening to them all talk about such insignificant things.

"Fine, whatever. You know I'll win anyway. I'm off to grab some food," Vic said, before taking his leave of the viewing gallery. Ryan and Imran both turned to face Ichi.

"Can't say no now, Ich," Ryan said. Ichi brought his hand up to his temple, as if rubbing at it with his fingertips would somehow make him more alert.

"Then I won't say no," was all he said, before leaving the two of them to head back up to his room. He took the elevator, feeling too tired to walk up twelve flights of stairs. *I can't believe having a conversation for longer than ten minutes has left me this fucking exhausted,* he thought. Ichi knew that he had to stop watching the camera feeds from Claire's room until the small hours of the morning, for his own health, but he wasn't so sure that he could resist the urge to wait until Claire had fallen asleep before he did so himself. It was like a ritual to Ichi now; something he *had* to do. *It would*

be so much easier if she would just fall asleep before four in the morning,
like a normal person.

Ichi ran a hand through his hair as he stepped out into the twelfth floor corridor, and was surprised to see Claire standing in front of the wall opposite her room, a look of concentration on her face. Ichi felt his resolve to head straight to bed crumble. "What are you doing?" he couldn't help but ask. Claire glanced over at him, pushing loose strands of hair out of her blue eyes as she did so, but she didn't say anything. Ichi crossed his arms over his chest. "I seriously won't leave until you give me an answer," he said, astute.

Claire looked as if she might simply ignore him again, until Ichi took a step towards her. "Why would anybody build a twelve-storey-high building with no windows?" she mused, keeping her eyes on the wall. The question surprised Ichi, but then he realised that, for somebody who hadn't been outside in five months, wanting to look out of a window was probably a recurrent desire. He strode over to the wall, standing a few feet away from Claire.

"You're looking at the wrong panel. If you look here –" he pointed to the thin join line between the two panels in front of him, waiting to see if Claire would come over and see. Eventually she did, keeping as much distance between herself and Ichi as possible. "– then you'll notice that there's a very slight colour difference between the two, see?" Ichi left her there to wander further over to his left. "It's the same over here." Claire looked at him, an eyebrow raised, waiting for him to elaborate. Ichi walked back over to where she stood. "There are windows behind the lighter panels," he explained. Claire's eyes widened slightly in understanding. "Michael had them put in a little while after the building was constructed. What's the point in having just anybody being able to look in, after all?" He looked at Claire, who was still looking at the wall, wary about what happened next. It was the most normal interaction Ichi had ever had with her, and far more civil an interaction than he had ever planned to have. *I'm too tired to actually do anything, that's all,* he thought.

"Huh," he heard Claire say.

Ichi frowned. "What's that supposed to mean?" he asked, irked at her barely-a-word response to his explanation.

Claire didn't look at him; she was completely spaced out. "I wonder why Vic never told me," she replied, quietly. She put her hands up on the wall, as if she was hoping that doing so would somehow make the window behind it appear. Ichi leaned against the wall beside her. *I'm so tired.*

"Maybe he doesn't want you to get any ideas about how to break out of here," he half-joked. "That's how I'd do it. Not on the twelfth floor though." But Claire didn't seem to be listening; her eyes were slightly unfocussed. Ichi frowned, annoyed. He couldn't believe that Claire was ignoring him having a normal conversation with her. He was about to force her to turn around and face him when she spoke.

"You miss your freedom almost as much as I do," Claire said, voice low. "You just don't know it yet. It was like that before…" Claire seemed to sway on the spot a little, before Ichi had the sense to catch her as she fell. He brought her down to kneel on the floor, holding onto her arms to keep her up.

"What are you talking about, Claire? When was the last time you ate? Or slept?" Ichi knew the answer to the latter question, but he couldn't let Claire know that he did. Claire's eyes seemed to refocus, and her gaze sharpened as she realised that she was being held upright by Ichi.

"What are you doing?" she asked immediately, her voice suspicious. Ichi frowned at her.

"You were all spaced out by the wall and spouting a load of stuff about me and freedom," he replied, honestly. He told himself that he was too tired to lie. Claire tried to move away from Ichi's grip, but he tightened it to stop her.

"Let me go, Ichi," she said.

"Not until you tell me what you meant," he exclaimed, curious to know the answer. Claire looked at him, genuine upset and confusion flashing in her eyes for just a second before she masked it completely.

"I don't even know what I said," she replied. "I was clearly half-asleep; I've been training all day. But you knew that already, since you seem to have nothing better to do than to watch me every day." Her voice was scathing by the end of the sentence. *And now we're back to normal Claire,* Ichi thought, resigned. He stood up, sighing; he was probably never going to understand what Claire had said. Ichi leant his hand against the wall and put most of his weight on it, keeping his gaze on the floor. He was too tired for a confrontation. Claire stood up, slowly, looking at him with an odd expression on her face. Ichi glanced at her through his hair.

"What?" he asked. *That's my response to a lot of people, lately.*

"What's wrong with you today?" she ventured. Ichi stood up a little straighter and took a half-step forward, brushing against Claire's arm as he did so. He leant his head against the wall, eyes closed. His fingers lingered on her wrist; he could feel the blood pulsing through it, slightly faster than normal. Claire didn't move.

"Everything's wrong with me all of the time. But you knew that already," Ichi replied quietly, mirroring Claire's words from a minute ago. Claire made to move away from him, but Ichi grabbed her wrist to keep her in place.

"Ichi, what the –" Claire began, but Ichi interrupted her.

"Don't move for a minute. Just a minute," he said, not bothering to open his eyes. He held on to Claire's wrist, listening to her pulse, pretending in his exhausted state that it had quickened because of an emotion other than anger or fear. Then Ichi let her go and wandered over to his room, closing the door behind him and falling straight onto his bed, fast asleep almost as soon as his head hit the pillow.

Claire

Claire had never been so glad that Ichi had had his eyes closed for most of their conversation in the hallway. *What would he have thought of me blushing at him acting like that?! I'm a fool,* Claire admonished. But she had not expected Ichi to ever act the way he had, and she had no idea why he was behaving like that in the first place. Right up until ten minutes ago, the two of them had been ignoring each other as usual. Even though Ichi had taken to watching most of her training sessions, he continued to say nothing to her. It unnerved Claire; she had no clue what he was thinking or what he was up to. All she could do was dutifully ignore him in return.

131

So what was all that about? It freaked Claire out that she couldn't remember the first half of their conversation…unless Ichi had simply been lying about her having said anything out of the ordinary. Claire remembered reluctantly asking Ichi about the lack of windows because he wouldn't go away, and him explaining about the different panels, and then her mind was blank until Claire found herself sitting on the floor. *How does a person simply forget five minutes of their life that just happened?* Claire couldn't help but let out a bark of sarcastic laughter at the thought; she had somehow managed to forget most of the past three to four years of her life, and she was freaking out over five minutes. But even that didn't worry Claire nearly so much as the way Ichi had been acting. What had she said to him that he had demanded she explain? And why had he been so *civil* in the first place? If it wasn't for the fact that it had happened with Ichi, the conversation had been almost pleasant. Almost normal. *Well, if I ignore that we were discussing the head of a group of assassins hiding the windows in his massive, twelve-storey building,* Claire thought, bemused.

Claire brought the wrist that Ichi had held on to up to her face. Had he felt her pulse quicken and worked out what it meant? But he had been so tired; that much was clear. Claire wondered, not for the first time, why Ichi hadn't been sleeping lately. She tried to imagine what a person like Ichi would do in the middle of the night, when everyone else was unconscious, and subsequently stopped the thought before it went too far. *You're not sleeping either, idiot.* But Claire had an excuse, surely. She had so many things to dwell upon, worry about and overthink to death. What could Ichi possibly have to think about that was on par with what was going on in her life?

He might be thinking about you. Claire forced the thought away, far to the back of her mind where the notion that Ichi was jealous of Vic's relationship with her was hidden. She didn't want to think about it; couldn't *afford* to think about it. But despite all of that, Claire could feel her heart accelerate ever-so-slightly at the thought of how gentle Ichi had been in the corridor and how worried he had looked when she had regained consciousness on the floor. *He looked like he was close to passing out himself. He should worry about his own health, not mine. If he even does, which would make no sense whatsoever.* Claire slapped her forehead with her hand, a little harder than she meant to.

"Snap out of it, you stupid girl," she muttered aloud, wincing. Claire decided to attempt to get a couple of hours of sleep before dinner, then find Vic and apologise for her sudden and snappy departure from training. He was only pushing her limits so that she could defend herself, after all. *Against the guy that my subconscious can't stop thinking about. My brain is messed up.* Sighing, Claire entered her room and crawled onto the couch, curling up into a ball and wishing for what felt like the millionth time that her life could go back to the way it had been before her parents disappeared.

*

Three weeks later, Alexis and Marie still hadn't returned. Claire had been sad that she didn't get to bid Marie good bye before she left, and to tell her that she was dutifully watching the anime the other woman had given her as slowly as possible. Claire missed the female company, especially considering that she was surrounded by hot-blooded males. She was still a little wary of Ryan after he had forcefully made his point about the profession of the people surrounding her, so Claire had been avoiding the swimming pool for a few weeks. She had chanced a few midnight trips to the pool, but the lights were kept off at that time of night and Claire felt that there were simply too many opportunities for Ichi to catch her unawares whilst she was in there. Imran had also been working on a job for the past week or so, but Claire had overheard Ryan telling Vic that he would be returning in a few days. Claire hoped Marie wouldn't be gone for much longer than that. She had given up on Alexis being any company entirely.

Vic's training was getting more and more ruthless, pushing Claire's level of physical fitness to extremes. But Claire loved it; she found that her mind went clear of all thoughts but the task at hand when she trained. Vic's mind was another matter, however. She could practically see him struggling not to kiss her every time he flung her to the ground or disarmed her or even simply when he wished her good night. *But I can't go there,* one part of her brain said to her. *So stop leading him on,* said another, and though Claire knew that she wasn't leading him on *exactly*, she certainly wasn't telling Vic to stop showering her with all of his attention either. Claire was so comfortable with him, and Vic seemed to understand immediately if she needed to talk about something or not. He helped Claire forget where she

133

was. He felt *familiar,* even though he was as foreign a concept to Claire's old life as a concept could possibly be.

Claire sighed. The only problem with Vic was that, when she wasn't with him, she was almost always thinking about someone else who she really shouldn't be thinking about. *I'm in a place like this and my mind is filled up with thoughts of boys. Olivia would be proud, I guess.* Claire felt her heart twinge in pain at the mere idea of her sister. And that was the crux of the matter for Claire – any thought that wasn't about the goings-on of the complex *hurt.* Claire found herself with a growing frequency avoiding such thoughts, instead allowing herself to think ever more on matters pertaining to Vic and Ichi.

Claire was going for her first morning swim in a long time, hoping to push away her near-permanent tiredness with forty lengths in the pool. Claire was surprised when she got to the gym and saw that nobody was exercising, then remembered that half of the complex's permanent residents were away on jobs. *Please don't let Ryan be in the pool...I can't be bothered with him today,* she silently wished. So when Claire entered the pool room and saw that he wasn't there, she breathed a sigh of relief, which promptly caught in her throat as she realised that somebody much worse was there.

Ichi was in the water, leaning his head on his arms by the raised edge of the pool; he apparently didn't hear Claire enter through the door. *Strange,* she thought, but on closer inspection Claire saw that Ichi had his eyes closed, and his breathing was soft and slow. *Is he sleeping?!* Claire thought, incredulous. She walked over and risked kneeling in front of him, gingerly waving a hand in front of his face to see if he'd react. He didn't. Claire rocked back and forth on the balls of her feet. *What do I do now? Do I wake him?*

"Who falls asleep in a place like this?" she mumbled, taking Ichi's current lapse in consciousness as an opportunity to look at his face properly. Claire found that it was a hell of a lot easier to look at Ichi when he wasn't looking at *her,* with those intense eyes of his that demanded her attention even when she desperately didn't want to give it to him. He appeared so much younger and carefree when he was asleep, all traces of the semi-permanent scowl he wore on his face long gone. Strands of Ichi's dark hair were plastered to his forehead, dripping water into his equally dark eyelashes. *He's as visually different from Vic as you could get,* Claire mused. Claire shuffled over to her right to look at Ichi from another angle. She realised that the entirety of his lean frame that was normally covered by clothes, save for his arms, was littered with tiny, thin scars that Claire could just barely see. *What the hell happened to him?* Claire wondered. After a moment or two, she sat back in front of Ichi and found herself admiring how the lights high above the two of them reflected in his wet hair and accentuated his cheekbones. Then Claire quickly looked at the floor as she realised what she was doing, her face reddening in shame. *Why am I checking him out? He's a terrible person.* She glanced back over at Ichi's sleeping face, stretching her right hand out until her fingers were millimetres from his forehead.

"If I pushed you in right now, you'd drown, you son of a bitch," Claire said out loud, her mood infinitely darker than it had been only moments before. *It wouldn't get me out of this place, but it would make living here a hell of a lot easier.* But after a few seconds, Claire shook the horrible thought out of her head. *I'm not the killer here; it's not in me to do something like that...is it?* Claire knew that her continued captivity in Michael's complex had changed her, but surely not *that* much. *I hope to God not that much.* The thought worried Claire immensely, so she stood up and shook her head again to force it away. She took one more look at Ichi's peaceful face, knowing that it was the first and likely last time that she would ever witness it, then walked over to the other side of the pool and dove in, making as much noise as possible.

She didn't spare another glance in Ichi's direction until he was long gone.

CHAPTER 14
Whatya Want from Me

Claire

Claire was sitting in the far corner of the rec hall, huddled over her Kindle and a bowl of tomato soup from Roger. Imran and Ryan were playing a game of pool on the opposite side of the room from her, discussing the job Imran had just returned from. They had asked Claire if she wanted to join in but she had declined – she wasn't feeling particularly sociable and had only ventured down to the rec hall because she was hungry.

Claire couldn't find Vic anywhere, which was strange; he hadn't mentioned that he was going off to work. Claire considered the fact that, in reality, Vic hadn't worked a single job since she had been brought to Michael's complex. She wondered why. *Stop thinking about everyone else,* Claire admonished. *Just concentrate on your book and ignore the world today.* Claire heard someone enter the rec hall but she resisted the urge to look up, knowing who it probably was. *Concentrate on your book.*

"Hey, Ichi! Come join us for a game – Imran's just about to lose," she heard Ryan call over to the last person on the planet that Claire wanted to see. She balked at the idea in silence. *But there's no way Ichi will join them, surely?* Claire thought. *He's way too much of a loner.*

"Fine, whatever," she heard Ichi reply. Claire stared blankly at the words on her Kindle. Why Ichi had suddenly decided to be sociable she had no idea, and Claire had no desire to find out why either. But if she left the rec hall now, with her soup barely touched, Claire knew that it would be obvious that she had left because of Ichi. *And you're not giving him the satisfaction of knowing he affects you...you've been managing that so far; why stop now?* Claire struggled not to look up from her book, knowing that she most definitely was not going to be able to concentrate on it now. She resigned herself to pretend to read as she ate her soup and listened in to the conversation the three men were having.

Ryan hadn't lied – Imran *was* about to lose. She heard Imran curse when Ryan potted the eight ball and won the game. "Right, your turn, Ich. Hope you're better than him," Ryan chided, resulting in another curse in his direction from Imran. "I'll let you break."

Claire heard Ichi chuckle. "If you insist," he said, which was followed by a loud, cracking sound as his cue hit the white ball.

Ryan let out a low whistle. "Not bad, man. But you potted a spot and a stripe – which one are you going with?"

"I'll go stripes," she heard Ichi reply. Claire couldn't help but wish she could join in. She loved pool, but the last time she had played had been with her father. Claire thought back fondly on the many hours spent in their local pub together, playing darts and pool and laughing frequently. Claire had treasured those moments; now they just made her upset. She hadn't taken up on a single offer of a game of pool from Vic or any of the other residents because of it, but Claire was beginning to think that there was no point in mulling over things that she could not change. *I'm hardly going to get up and join Ryan and Imran now though,* she thought resignedly. *Not when Ichi's with them.*

Her thoughts were interrupted when she realised that the three men had changed the topic of their conversation. "Don't you get bored only doing one-off jobs for Michael, Ichi?" Ryan asked. "I find it way more satisfying to off someone I've been working on for ages." Claire cringed at his words.

There was a pause as Ichi considered his answer. "A kill is just a kill...I'd rather get more of them in." He paused again, then added on, "I can't be bothered with putting up a front and pretending to be something I'm not for it."

"But you must have loved finishing off that guy for Michael a few months ago. I heard he hit on you...I bet you didn't like that," Ryan snickered. Claire almost looked up at the comment in surprise.

"It was his son," Ichi answered in disgust, potting another ball as he spoke. "He came into the bar early the day I killed his old man. Son of a bitch figured he'd catch me alone and force himself on me...as if." He potted another ball as Ryan and Imran laughed at his tale. Claire couldn't believe what she was hearing.

"I bet he wasn't so keen on the idea after seeing what you had done to his father," Imran said. "Would have loved to see the dad's face when he realised you were going to kill him."

"He didn't have a face, by the end," Ichi murmured, darkly. Claire's head jolted up to stare at them all before she had a chance to control her reaction. *Damn it,* she thought, as Ryan grinned at her.

"Yes, beautiful, we kill people for a living. I'm sure I've mentioned it to you before. If you have an issue with it, I'm afraid you're living in the wrong place," he said, taunting her. Claire was speechless; she didn't know what to do. She glanced at Ichi for half a second, but he was too busy potting yet another ball to look at her.

Imran clucked his tongue. "Play nice, Ryan. You don't need to throw it in her face, you know," he admonished his friend. Ryan walked over to Claire, placing his hands on the table right in front of her. Claire held her gaze steady, knowing that if she looked away then she lost.

"Oh, but I think I do. She forgets it, sometimes, you can tell. It's really in her best interests to remember what we are," Ryan said, making a grab for Claire's wrist that he had twisted so painfully weeks ago in the swimming pool. Claire recoiled, hitting her bowl as she stood up and spilling its contents all over the blue dress she was wearing. She glared at Ryan, face flushed as Ichi finally stopped playing pool to look up at her, one eyebrow raised. *I can't believe this is happening.* Ryan laughed at her, before returning to Imran and Ichi. "Which reminds me," Ryan continued, acting as if he had never bothered Claire in the first place. "The girls are due back tonight; how about that game of blackjack tomorrow evening?"

Imran shook his head. "I can't tomorrow – Michael wants me to fiddle about with some surveillance footage that Vic's picking up for him today," he said. *I suppose that explains where Vic is,* Claire thought numbly as she looked down at the mess that her dress had become.

"The day after, then," Ryan suggested. Imran nodded in agreement. "Ichi?" Ichi was still looking at Claire, waiting to see what she would do. He forced his eyes away from her to face Ryan.

"Yeah, fine, that works for me," he muttered, not paying attention.

Ryan smirked at Claire before he spoke again. "Fantastic. Prepare to drink, guys," he said. He glanced at the pool table. "You've won this one, Ich. I'm not even going to try now."

"I wasn't aware that you were trying in the first place," he countered, his eyes back on Claire again, who still hadn't worked out what to do with her dress.

Imran chuckled. "Good to see the return of Mr Sarcastic," he said. And then: "Okay, I'm off to go and see Michael," before taking his leave once the others had bid him good bye.

Ryan looked at Ichi. "What say you to another game? No distractions this time," he grinned.

Ichi wrenched his gaze away from Claire again. "I don't see why not. I'll just win again, though." The two men turned to face the pool table as Ryan organised the balls. Claire glanced at her upended soup bowl before staring back at the front of her dress again. *That's the third dress that's been ruined by these people,* she cursed angrily, thinking about the lilac one she had been kidnapped in and Olivia's beautiful, white sundress that Claire just couldn't look at any more. She had repaired the lilac dress as best she could, but all Claire could see when she looked at it was her own blood that Ichi had spilled down the bodice, even though it wasn't there anymore.

Claire was furious; why was she continuing to let these *men* dictate what happened to her? She wished she could do something that would shock them all. So as Claire continued to look down at her dress, she considered doing something insane. *It would certainly shock them,* she thought. Before her brain could convince her that it was a terribly stupid idea, Claire pulled her dress up over her head in one quick, fluid motion so as not to get any soup in her hair. She silently thanked her meticulous self for always putting on matching underwear as she caught Ryan's eye. He stopped what he was doing to gape at her as Claire rolled the dress up and threw it in the nearest bin, before returning to the table for her Kindle. She'd have to beg Roger's forgiveness for all of the soup spilled on the table later. Claire wandered over to the pool table, placed her hands on its edge and leaned over it, just like Ryan had done to her only minutes before. She saw Ichi to the right out of her peripheral vision, not even attempting to hide his shock as he stared at her.

139

Ryan smirked at Claire again. "And what's all this for, then?" he asked. "I didn't know being mean turned you on; I would have tried it earlier if I'd known." He made no effort to hide the fact that he was blatantly looking Claire up and down. She heard Ichi cough beside her, clearly trying to cover up something that he was going to say but thought better of. Claire spread her hands out, leaning over the edge of the table a little more towards Ryan. She smiled seductively, bit her lower lip slightly and let her dark, wavy hair tumble over one shoulder.

"I think it's in *your* best interests, Ryan," she began, softly, repeating his words from earlier, "To remember that you want to fuck me senseless, and that you never will." Her smile widened as she saw the man's face darken. As Claire turned around, she noticed Ichi grinning, struggling not to laugh at what she had done. It was such a rare expression on his face that Claire paused for a second, and all she could think of was that it made him undeniably handsome. Ichi caught her stare for a second, raising an eyebrow at her before she sauntered off, elated that she had finally put Ryan in his place.

Well that's the easy one dealt with...now to handle the other two, she thought, her mind wandering to Vic and back to Ichi again, though Claire had no idea how she was supposed to do so.

*

Several hours later, Claire was curled up under the fourth floor stairs, mulling over what had happened in the rec hall. Vic still hadn't returned from whatever he was doing for Michael to distract her. Her mood was considerably worse than it had been after waltzing away from Ryan and Ichi earlier. Once the delight at finally winning against Ryan had faded, Claire realised that her bold move had maybe not been the best one to make after all. What if she had simply made Ryan angry? What if he *actually* went after her now? *I don't need any extra stress right now,* she mused. Claire had to hope that what she had done was sufficiently humiliating enough for Ryan that he wouldn't risk being in the same situation with her again. She hoped Ichi would remind him of it, if Ryan ever tried anything despite that.

Claire felt her face flush. In her anger earlier, she had decided to ignore the fact that flouncing about in her underwear in front of Ichi was most definitely a stupid idea. She had seen the way he looked at her; as if he couldn't believe Claire would even dare to take off her clothes in front of other people. She had also noticed his hand twitch ever so slightly in her direction, as if he was forcing himself not to grab her. But his expression had changed after Claire had put Ryan in his place. He had almost looked as if he *respected* her for what she had done.

"I don't understand him at all," she murmured, closing her eyes. How was Claire supposed to deal with someone she didn't understand? She had thought Ichi's habit of doing something terrible to her, then ignoring her until he had thought of something else to do would make him easier to handle. She was wrong. It had been so long since Ichi had even attempted to harass Claire outside of the one incident where she had collapsed in the twelfth floor corridor, but he hadn't even tried to do anything to her that time. *What's his angle here?* Claire had no idea. If Ichi was simply trying to ensure that all Claire thought about was him then he was damn well succeeding. Claire hated it. She opened her eyes again, looking up at the stairs that climbed above her.

I need to see Vic. She wanted to have an honest conversation with him, to say once and for all that, whilst she was still a prisoner in Michael's complex, she couldn't reciprocate his feelings. And though Claire knew that she *did* reciprocate those feelings to a certain extent, she knew that it was the right thing to do…she just didn't want to do it. Claire wondered if Vic would still be interested in her once she was finally free, if that ever happened. Marie had told Claire to forget about everyone once she got away, but Claire wasn't sure if she was ready to let go of Vic. All she knew for certain was that she needed time on her own, in the world outside of this building she was trapped in, to work out if her feelings were truly genuine or whether they were due to something like Stockholm syndrome. Claire laughed quietly to herself; she knew her feelings for Vic were not because of it, but also knew that that was probably what most sufferers of kidnap thought about their feelings for their captors as well.

When I get out of here, I'm going to find Olivia and do whatever the hell I want for a while. And then, if I feel like it, I'll work out what my feelings for Vic are exactly. Claire sighed. It was all well and good thinking this in her head, but it was another thing entirely to believe it. And Claire didn't, not a single word of it. *Nothing is ever so simple.*

Finally, Claire stretched her legs out and stood up, deciding to take the long walk up the stairs back to her room. She had to be prepared to make Vic understand how she felt and to respect that; Claire only hoped that Vic was mature enough to take it like a man.

Ichi

Ichi was lounging on his couch, watching Claire shower on his laptop. He didn't feel in the least bit guilty about doing so. *She was basically traipsing about naked earlier, anyway.* He couldn't help but smile in satisfaction at the memory. He had to hand it to Claire – she had certainly gone for a very *visual* way of getting her point across. It was all Ichi could do not to run after her and push her against a wall when she left the rec hall, but he didn't want to do something like that in a public place, where other people might get to see Claire in such a state of undress. He felt just a twinge of annoyance that it was because of *Ryan* that Claire had taken her clothes off, regardless of the reason for doing so.

Ichi was seriously considering going over to Claire's room once she finished her shower, just to see what would happen. But even as he thought it, Claire got out of her shower, dried herself off quickly and threw on some clothes. *Well there's always tomorrow, and the next day, and the next,* Ichi reminded himself. He watched Claire jump in surprise at a knock on her door, then rush to open it. It was Vic, of course; Ichi wondered why he would have expected anybody else. But Claire wasn't letting him in, like she usually did. Ichi searched for a pair of headphones and plugged them in to his laptop to listen to Claire and Vic's conversation at a louder volume.

"…just need some time to myself, Vic," he heard Claire say. Ichi could only see Claire's back from where his camera was positioned; he wished he could spy on them in the corridor without being noticed.

"No, Claire, listen, you don't understand," Vic responded.

"I don't understand what, Vic?" she asked. Ichi watched his laptop screen in shock as Vic reached out for Claire and kissed her. Claire held up her hand as if to stop him, but let it fall as she seemed to reciprocate. Ichi felt his mood darken instantly. He saw Vic smile at Claire when he finally pulled away.

"Sorry, princess, I couldn't help myself. You don't understand how much I care about you. I don't want to have to hold back, but I know I need to." Ichi vaguely heard Vic sigh. "I need to go cool my head…but come by my room later, okay? Just give me an opportunity to change your mind," Vic said, a half-smile on his face. Ichi could feel the vein in his temple pulsing in fury; this was *not* happening.

Vic bid Claire good bye. She closed the door behind him and slid down to the floor, leaning against the frame. Her fingers were on her lips, her face bright red. *He can't do that to you. You're not allowed to let him do that,* Ichi raged at his screen. He stood up, pacing his room restlessly whilst he tried to figure out what to do. *She won't go to his room, she won't. She definitely won't.* Ichi grabbed his laptop from the table in front of him, got up and threw himself on his bed, propping the laptop up on his pillow so that he could continue watching Claire. And for an hour or two, she didn't leave. Claire paced around her room, much like Ichi had done, a frown on her face. Eventually, however, she changed her clothes into something less casual than shorts and a t-shirt and spent five minutes in her bathroom fixing her hair and putting on some make up before leaving. Ichi couldn't believe what he was seeing.

You're mine. He can't have you. Ichi hesitated for a second and then ran to his front door, wrenching it open when he reached it. But Claire was already gone; Ichi could hear the elevator heading downwards. He stood there gaping out at the empty corridor for what felt like forever. Eventually, Ichi retreated into his room, turning off the lights so that he could sit in the darkness and let his anger bubble and simmer under the surface until he couldn't stand it any longer.

CHAPTER 15
Little House

Ichi

Not long after Claire left her room, Ichi decided to let out his frustration by practicing with his throwing knives, so he grabbed them from under his bed as well as his leather jacket, slamming the front door behind him as he stormed out. Ichi spent nearly an hour venting his anger out on the human-shaped targets in the practice room, imagining the various ways in which he could kill Claire and how long it would take for her to die with every throw. He didn't care much for making Vic suffer, only to see him gone, so whenever he aimed for a true kill shot he pretended that the target was Vic.

Eventually, merely throwing knives at empty targets failed to dull Ichi's murderous rage. He knew that, in this state of mind, the chances were extremely high that Ichi would do something that Michael wouldn't like when Claire got back up to her room. Ichi discovered that, in this state of mind, he didn't care. He made up his mind to head back up to his own room and wait for Claire to return, though Ichi had no idea how long that would be. *She might not come back tonight at all,* his brain chimed in helpfully. Ichi felt his vision go red and black for a second at the thought as he struggled to keep in control of his desire to storm into Vic's room and kill them both. Ichi forced himself to breathe slowly for a minute or two before picking out his knives from the dented targets, who by this point he had killed several times over.

Ichi took the stairs back up to his room, like he normally did when he needed to calm down. But just as he began to ascend the sixth floor stairs, Ichi heard the sound of a door open behind him and turned to see Claire, of all people, entering the stairwell. She took one look at Ichi's furious expression before bolting down the stairs, but Ichi vaulted over the handrail and threw her against the landing wall between the fourth and fifth floors before she could get any further. He heard Claire's head crack satisfyingly as it hit the wall. As she winced at the pain, eyes clenched shut for a moment, Ichi put his arm up against her neck, cutting off her airway. He could hear Claire gasping for breath, her fingers clawing at Ichi's arm in an attempt to remove it from her throat.

"You're not going to ignore me if I'm doing this, are you?" Ichi said quietly, his tone venomous. Claire tried to push Ichi away and failed, her fingers grabbing at his jacket as her attempts to breathe got shallower and shallower. Ichi removed the pressure from her neck, just a little. Claire drew in a ragged breath, her lungs hungry for the air. She looked up at Ichi, tears welling up in the corner of her eyes, her expression frantic. Ichi glared at her, bringing his face closer to hers before he spoke again. "Do you really think I'd kill you just like that? Do you really think I'd squander your death by *suffocating* you?" he said through gritted teeth. He laughed humourlessly. "Give me some credit. But just because I'm not going to kill you right now doesn't mean I can't make you feel *pain*." Ichi pushed his arm further back into Claire's airway again, causing her eyes to go wide. Her hands were still gripping his jacket, trying to push him away with strength that was quickly failing. "Go on, tell me to stop it," he whispered. Claire looked up at him, eyes bright with both fear and anger.

"No," she replied, using what little air she had left to speak. Ichi dropped his arm from her throat anyway, shocked at her defiance. Claire was bent double, gasping for air; Ichi could see her whole body trembling. When she had regained her breath somewhat, Claire stood back up, glaring at Ichi as she did so. He closed the gap between them again so that his face was millimetres from hers.

"Why would you say that? Why would you not want to even try and stop me doing that?" he demanded, confused.

Claire's gaze didn't waver from his for even a second as she replied, voice breathless from her near-suffocation, "Because you can't kill me yet. You're Michael's pawn and he won't let you. And so long as you aren't allowed to kill me, stunts like this mean *nothing*." The words hit Ichi like a bullet, because he knew that Claire was right. Until he could kill her, Ichi's threats were empty. But knowing that didn't take away his fury, not at all. Ichi felt his hand grab at Claire's hip, bringing them even closer together. She glanced down at the motion for a second, then brought her eyes back up to look at Ichi.

"Whatever it is that you want to say, just fucking say it," Claire almost spat into his face. Ichi looked at her for a few moments in silence, wondering why the girl in front of him seemed to drive him to insanity simply by doing or saying the most inconsequential thing. But what Claire had done tonight was *not* inconsequential.

"Why did you do it?" he asked, his voice soft, completely at odds with his fiery expression. Claire frowned at him.

"Do what?" she countered. Ichi slammed her against the wall again, curling his left hand into her hair to stop her head from being hit too hard – he could feel blood under his hand from where he had smashed it earlier.

"Why did you screw him?!" Ichi half-shouted into Claire's face. "Why wait all this time and then do it? What changed?"

Claire's eyes seemed to darken. "That's none of your business, and you know it," she replied. Ichi almost slapped her.

"It *is* my business, damn it! I told you before, or have you forgotten? *You're mine!* You don't get to do whatever you like –"

"I can do whatever I fucking want, you son of a bitch!" Claire interrupted, furious. "You don't dictate what I get to do or *who* I do for that matter!"

Ichi decided on a whim to change his angle on the argument. "Oh, so you're fine with using your body to keep him close then? Ha! I almost feel bad for him, he has no idea you're just using him to –" Ichi was cut off as Claire slammed her arm against his chest, using the movement to drive him against the wall before she stabbed a knife through the edge of his cheek, lodging it in the wall behind him.

"You do *not* get to say that!" she screamed. Ichi was momentarily speechless; Claire had managed to completely turn the tables on him. Now *he* was the one pinned against the wall. He could feel the blood begin to snake down along his jawline.

"And why not?" he countered, once he got his brain working again.

"Because that's what you want me to be doing. That's what you *expect* me to do!" Claire yelled, her face flushed in anger. "I'm not wrong, am I? You expect me to go crying for help against you, but guess what? I'm not!"

"You're not –"

"*I'm not sleeping with Vic!* Just because that's what you understand doesn't make it true. Because you don't understand a damn thing, Ichi." Claire's gaze was drawn to the blood slowly crawling down Ichi's face. Then she brought her eyes back up to his again, and they were bright and blazing and dangerous. "The next time you try something like this again, the next time you even *think* of judging my behaviour, I swear…I'll drive that knife right through your eye."

And then Claire removed the knife from the wall and turned around in one swift motion, not looking behind her as she departed down the stairs, though Ichi didn't hear her footsteps. He was too shocked by what had happened; his brain simply couldn't process it. *She's not sleeping with Vic. So what happened in his room? She's not sleeping with him…but then how is she coping?* Claire had been completely correct – Ichi didn't understand her at all. Claire had no outlets to vent any of her fears and frustrations whilst she was here (and Ichi assumed she rightly had many). And yet Vic could be an outlet, a very *willing* outlet, and she hadn't taken him up on his offer. *So how is she coping at all? After all the crap I've put her through? Unless…*Ichi was so furious at the notion that he couldn't even finish the thought, because if Claire didn't feel like she needed an outlet to cope with what he had done to her…then he truly hadn't affected her at all. And that meant that Claire wasn't thinking about him, not to the extent that Ichi wanted. It meant she wasn't replaying the time Ichi had forced himself on her over and over again in her head, the way he was doing. It meant he didn't *matter*.

It took Ichi another five minutes to realise that the knife Claire had used against him had been his own, feeling its absence from his hip. *When did she even take it? Why didn't I notice?* It unnerved Ichi to no end. And excited him, which confused him; he didn't understand how he could feel two completely contradictory emotions at the same time. Just as he was deciding to head back up to his room to mull over what had just happened, Ichi saw Alexis walk up the stairs towards him. She raised an eyebrow as she saw the open wound on his face.

"Well, looks like someone has claws," she joked as she reached the landing. She gave him a smile. "Miss me?"

To hell with Claire, Ichi thought, as he grabbed the other woman and pushed her against the wall. "No," he replied roughly, before kissing her.

Alexis let out a low chuckle from underneath his lips. "Such contrary words and actions, Ich. Not that I'm complaining," she added, seeing the scowl that grew on his face as she spoke.

"Do you want to do this or not?" he asked bluntly. Alexis smiled slyly up at him, before kissing him passionately. *I matter to* her, Ichi thought angrily. He vaguely felt Alexis rip his jacket from his arms, throwing it to the floor without once breaking from his lips. Ichi ran both of his hands through her hair, bringing her head back to bite into her neck. Alexis held up a hand to stop him.

"Watch the neck, Ich. It's not very *professional,*" she laughed. She glanced down the stairs. "Neither is doing this here. Come on, my room's closer." Ichi paused for a second, knowing that he was about to do what he swore to himself he wouldn't do anymore.

And who the hell was that promise for? I'll do whatever I damn well please. And so he rushed down the stairs after Alexis to her room, not thinking to pick up his leather jacket from where it lay, abandoned, on the floor.

Claire

Claire had never left the scene; not really. In her haste to get away from Ichi as quickly as possible, Claire had gone downstairs instead of up and realised too late that she didn't know where she was heading. She couldn't face going back up to her room, anyway. And she definitely couldn't face Vic. So Claire had crawled into her spot beneath the fourth floor stairs, hoping that Ichi wouldn't wonder why the sound of her footsteps had disappeared much too early.

And so it was in this way that she heard the entirety of Ichi and Alexis' conversation. *Or whatever it was.* Suddenly, Claire understood a hell of a lot more about their relationship than she wanted to. It even served to help explain a little as to why Alexis ignored her, if she didn't like the attention that Ichi gave Claire. *She can have him! I never wanted his attention, never,* she raged. Claire was too furious with Ichi to consider the possibility that she was jealous.

She winced at the God-awful migraine that was building up behind her eyes. She brought her fingers up to test the growing bump on the back of her head, bringing them back to see blood upon them. *I need to get this seen to.* But it was late; Claire hardly thought that Michael would find it acceptable for her to bother him to see the doctor just for a bump on the head (never mind the fact that she simply didn't want to see Michael in the first place). She would have ordinarily gone to Vic, but...*I can't. Not right now.* When Claire had gone to his room earlier, she had been tempted to throw caution to the wind and sleep with him regardless of her situation. But as the elevator had lowered to the fifth floor, Claire had realised that that was the wrong thing to do, and she really did need to make sure Vic understood exactly what she wanted from him right now, and what she didn't. He had protested at first, but once Claire had told him that she wanted to wait until she was free of everything to pursue whatever it was that she and Vic could become, he had quietened down and conceded defeat. There had been something in his eyes that seemed to let on that there was more that he wanted to say, but was resisting the urge to say it. Vic had kissed Claire for the second time that evening then, gently, and she had reciprocated again.

"You know yourself that it's not fair to expect me to be in any fit state to do this right now, Vic," she had told him, softly but firmly. He had smiled at that; of course he knew. He had simply forgotten it for a moment, he said. Claire had asked Vic what had caused that to happen, but all he did was continue to smile and say that he wished he could tell her. Claire believed him, but had to wonder why he *couldn't* tell her.

Vic had promised her that he wouldn't try anything on with her again – not unless she wanted him to. Claire had thanked Vic for that, and meant it. And then they had talked about menial things for a while, trying to laugh away the lingering awkwardness to no avail until, eventually, Vic had suggested that Claire try and get some sleep earlier than four in the morning and she had left, planning to use the stairs to head down and grab some orange juice from the rec hall before going to bed.

And there Ichi had been, mere feet above her on the stairs, a mutinous expression on his face when he turned to see Claire standing there. She had had no clue about how Ichi could possibly know that something had happened that he could be angry at, yet somehow he knew nonetheless. Claire glanced at the knife in her hands, the blade stained with Ichi's blood.

Screw him, you have to stop thinking about him, idiot. He nearly killed you again, *just because he thought you were sleeping with Vic. Just ignore him...ignore him.* But Claire couldn't; Ichi's reaction to her possibly having slept with Vic was too explosive for her to forget.

And now he's using the same hands that he held on to me with to take Alexis' clothes off. He's a hypocrite. The thought made Claire feel stormy and impulsive, and she got out of her hiding place to rush up the stairs to barrel down Vic's door. But when she reached the landing where Ichi had attacked her and then met Alexis, Claire paused. She looked at the blood on the wall where she had stabbed Ichi in the face.

"I'll just be doing what he wants if I sleep with Vic now," she thought out loud. Then she noticed Ichi's jacket on the floor, lying in a crumpled heap. *Huh. Well they didn't waste any time.* Claire felt a renewed flash of irritation simply by looking at the jacket, yet she found herself picking it up regardless, wrapping the knife she had stolen from Ichi up in it. "Serves him right for leaving it here," she mumbled.

Claire suddenly realised that Roger might be able to help clean her head up for her if he was still in the rec hall. Not thinking about the fact that she should have taken Ichi's knife and jacket back up to her room first, Claire quickly descended the stairs to the first floor, hoping against hope that it wasn't too late for Roger to be in the kitchen.

To Claire's immense relief the resident cook was indeed in the kitchen, cooking something that she couldn't see from where she stood. But as Claire wandered over and Roger looked up and made to wave hello, a sudden wave of dizziness washed over her, and she grabbed for the nearest table to help support her weight.

Roger rushed over, a frown of concern on his face. "Miss Danvers, what happened? Are you al-why is your head covered in blood?!" he asked, shock and concern in his voice. Claire looked up at him and tried to smile.

"I may have had an altercation with someone," Claire replied, trying to sound as if she didn't care and failing miserably. Her head hurt so much. Roger's gaze moved from her head to the jacket she was holding.

"Something tells me you shouldn't have that, or whatever it is you're hiding in it," he said, suspicious.

"Whatever it is I've got hiding in it is what got me out of the situation," Claire said, trying to answer Roger's suspicions without revealing that she now had a knife in her possession. "Could you...could you help me clean up my head, Roger? Please."

Roger's face softened as she winced at the pain in her head. "Of course. Give me a minute and I'll go get my first aid kit," he replied, a small smile on his face. Claire let him clean up the wound on her head in silence when he returned.

Eventually, however, Roger spoke. "Do you want to tell me what happened, Miss Danvers?" he asked as he gently washed away the blood that had found its way onto Claire's face and neck.

"I'd rather not tell anyone, including Michael, if it's all the same to you," she said, her tone astute on the matter.

Roger let out a soft chuckle. "I'd wager he already knows, dear. He has his ways." Roger gave Claire's face a cursory glance before standing up. "There, you're all cleaned up. Your head's stopped bleeding already but you should head up to your room and go to bed as soon as you leave me, okay?" He fumbled in the first aid box for a moment and took out some pills. "Here," he said. "For the pounding headache you are no doubt experiencing. If you keep feeling dizzy or the pain doesn't go away, go see Michael. That's not a request," he added on sharply, when it looked like Claire was going to protest. "Michael needs you both alive *and* in good health, Miss Danvers. Ichi knows that too...though he's clearly ignoring that fact." Claire's eyes widened at his words, before glancing at the jacket in her arms and putting two and two together. "Yes, I'm not stupid," Roger said, smiling. "Now off to bed!"

Claire thanked him before gingerly getting to her feet. When she reached the bar by the door, she grabbed a carton of orange juice before she took her leave. But then she turned back to Roger, suddenly curious as to why he was cooking so late. When she asked him as much, he laughed, eyes creasing up with the sound.

"I'm taking a personal day tomorrow...but I can't be leaving you without any food now, can I?" the older man answered. "You can thank me for all of my good deeds when you get to leave," he answered. "Now *go to bed*." Claire smiled at him, grateful for all of the help he had given her so far, and took the elevator back up to the twelfth floor. When she entered her

151

room, she flung Ichi's jacket to the floor and washed his knife before carefully placed it under her pillow on the couch. Then she flung herself on to the couch as well and closed her eyes, knowing that her brain wasn't going to let her go to sleep for a long, long time.

CHAPTER 16
Misery Business

Ichi

"She's getting pretty damn good with those knives," came a voice far to Ichi's right. He was sitting in the rec hall at the very end of one of the long tables, eating a bowl of cereal. It didn't fit with his dark image at all to the point that it was almost comical, but he was hungry and it was half past eight in the morning – there was hardly much else to eat that was appropriate for the time of day on Roger's rare morning off. And Ichi was feeling far too lazy to cook a fry up in his room.

He identified the speaking voice as Ryan with a quick, almost imperceptible glance in the other man's direction. Ryan was sitting with Marie and Imran at the opposite end of the table that Ichi was sitting at, laughing away as if they hadn't a care in the world.

"Although she still can't work out how to beat Vic in self-defence," Imran pointed out.

"Personally I'd be content with letting him throw me to the ground all day," snickered Marie. "Maybe that's her ploy to get up close and personal with him."

Why must they always discuss that damn girl? Ichi thought, irritated. The previous night's encounter with Claire had left him furious with her, even more so than normal. And sleeping with Alexis hadn't helped calm him down; if anything, it had made things worse. Ichi had also left his leather jacket in the stairwell and it had mysteriously gone missing, which only served to further piss him off.

She hasn't slept with Vic, Ichi found himself thinking again. But why hadn't she? Ichi just didn't understand. *How can she be so close with a man obviously interested in her and not do anything about it? Hell, why isn't*

153

Vic *being more insistent?* Vic wasn't one to ignore his own feelings; he certainly hadn't earlier yesterday evening. Ichi swirled his cereal around in its bowl, trying to ignore the conversation going on to his right but knowing full well that he wanted to hear it.

"Ha! If she's doing that then she's stringing him along for sure. Claire only has eyes for that psycho, but God knows why," Ryan laughed, gesturing at Ichi just as Ichi glanced up to look at him again. *Just ignore him; he wants you to react,* Ichi had to remind himself, stopping himself from replying to the comment just in time.

"I'd noticed that too," Imran agreed. "Hey Ichi, you can't have both Claire *and* Alexis, you prick!"

"That's clearly what they're both after...he's hardly got the sunniest disposition," Ryan joked. Ichi rose from the table suddenly, a slight frown creasing his brow. He wanted to punch them all in the face.

"You're mistaken," he said to them all with a cool, level voice. But Ichi couldn't help but fish out an answer from them as to why they thought Claire was interested in him, so he added on, "She doesn't even acknowledge that I'm here." *Unless I corner her on a staircase and demand her attention, and then she finds a way to make me feel like I matter even less than when she ignored me.*

Marie gaped at him, eyes wide. "Oh, you can't be serious Ichi. You've really fallen for that 'I'm ignoring you' act? God, how old are you, fourteen?" she asked, incredulous.

"She makes eyes at you all the time; I'm totally jealous, man!" Ryan said, his tone suggesting that he was congratulating Ichi on something monumental that he had just achieved. Ichi worked hard to keep the confusion he was feeling from his face.

"He can hardly see her looking at him if she's staring at his back, though," Imran interjected.

"Well, if you have any sense at all you'll go and find her and throw her down on a bed," Ryan said. "We've given you a heads up and everything! If you do nothing, I swear you're not a man." Ichi kept his eyes on the table in front of him. *You know nothing, you idiot. You know nothing at all.* He swept up his half-eaten cereal bowl, dumped it in the kitchen sink and swiftly left the rec hall, to the infuriating sound of the three other assassins laughing at him.

Ichi used the stairs to get up to his room, needing the extra time it would take to walk up all of the stairs to cool his head off. *They're all wrong, they were just baiting me; they had to be. Claire made it clear that I wasn't worth thinking about.* But then why would Ryan have gone on about her looking at him? Ichi hadn't noticed anything of the sort. Claire was always looking at Vic; Ichi felt a familiar twinge of anger cloud his eyes for a moment at the thought. *She needs to be gone. I need to get rid of her, Michael be damned.* But Ichi knew that he couldn't kill her, at least not yet; what would be the point in killing Claire if it also meant his own life? For one irrational moment, Ichi considered the idea that losing his life in order to end hers would actually be worth it. He shook his head to get rid of the thought. *If I do that then she wins. She'll win despite the fact that she's not even playing the game.* Ichi had wanted Claire to be his victim for the entirety of the last few weeks of her life. And yet months later here she was, not a victim at all. And not thinking about him.

But then why would the others have said all of that? Ichi thought furiously, punching the eleventh floor wall in frustration. He winced at the pain in his knuckles, yet it had done nothing to stop his endless train of thought. Ichi's own mind was driving him insane. His thoughts came to a sudden halt, however, as he walked through the stairwell door out onto the twelfth floor…and straight into Claire's path.

Claire had just come out of the elevator, dripping wet and with what Ichi could swear was the shortest towel he had ever seen barely covering her body. Somewhere in the back of his mind, the logical part of Ichi's brain told him that she had clearly just been swimming and so must also have a swim suit on under her towel, but Ichi ignored that. He couldn't help but stare at her and imagine ripping the towel away to reveal all of her. Claire matched his stare with one of cold indifference and stalked straight past him; Ichi stayed rooted to the spot for a moment, wondering how on earth she could still remain that carefree after he had accosted her the night before. His hand crept up to the cut on his face from where she had stabbed him with his own knife.

"I hope you had a good time with Alexis last night. It must be nice to not care about being a hypocrite," Claire suddenly called over her shoulder.

155

Her voice brought Ichi back to reality, and he ran after her and spun her around by the shoulders, forcing her to look at him.

"How the hell do you know that?!" he shouted at her, though Ichi didn't really care how she knew; only that she *did*.

Claire looked at him scathingly. "Because you're careless," she answered, glaring at him. "Next time you want a private conversation, don't do it right above a place you know I go to…and don't pretend like you don't know that that's where I go. Now *leave me alone*." She tried to shrug off Ichi's grip on her shoulders but he continued to hold on, staring at her, trying to figure out why Ryan and the others had been so convinced that she wanted him. Claire's soaking wet hair was starting to come undone from the bun that she had put it in, strands of it falling over her face. And Ichi couldn't help but clear the hair from her eyes, tucking it behind her ear. His left hand froze by the side of her face. *What the fuck did I just do?* he thought, panicking. But as he continued to look at Claire, Ichi could feel her skin warm up under his hand; could see her face flush ever-so-slightly before she flinched away from his touch. Ichi let go of her to lurk off to his room so suddenly that whatever retort Claire was about to throw his way was lost as he slammed the door open and shut behind him. Then he leant against the door frame, sighing. *Why is my heart beating so fast? Why did she react like that?* Ichi wondered whether he had simply imagined Claire's skin heating up underneath his fingertips because of what the others had said.

Ichi rushed to the bathroom, threw his clothes off and jumped in the shower. He could feel his whole body trembling underneath the hot water, the blood rushing from his head and down, down, down to that other organ that seemed to have decided that Alexis wasn't enough. Ichi realised that she'd never been enough. His mind turned straight back to Claire as he began to touch himself. *I want to fuck her*, he thought. *I want to kill her, but I want to fuck her*. But he had already done that, back when Ichi had thought he was capable of taking everything from her, and although the initial high from that had been immeasurable, he had felt entirely dissatisfied afterwards. Claire hadn't visibly reacted to him at all that time, somewhat robbing him of his victory. He didn't want that again. *Then what* do *I want?* Ichi thought angrily, as the same hand that had swept Claire's hair away from her face tugged at himself, faster and faster. He found himself banging his head against the tiles, frustrated and excited and confused.

For the first time since Claire Danvers had sauntered into his life, Ichi forced himself to admit that he didn't know what he was supposed to do.

When he was finished, Ichi slumped down onto the floor of his shower cubicle, allowing the steam to envelop him as he tried desperately to cling on to the only idea that he had wanted right from the very beginning – to kill her.

Claire

You're an idiot, you're a fucking idiot, Claire kept repeating in her head. Her heart was racing after her encounter with Ichi in the corridor. "Why did I have to go and open my mouth?" she groaned, slumping on her couch, not caring if her wet hair, damp towel and swim suit soaked the leather. Claire could feel a migraine coming on, and not from the slowly receding bump on the back of her head from the night before.

If she hadn't said anything then Ichi would never have gone after her, and he would have ignored her as usual. Claire glanced at the door, half expecting Ichi to storm right through it and demand an explanation for her reaction to his fingers brushing against her face.

An involuntary reaction, it was involuntary! It doesn't mean anything, she tried to convince herself. *He might not have even noticed.* Claire couldn't help but roll her eyes at her own desperate attempt at clutching at straws. Of course Ichi had noticed; she could see it in his face. But why had he fixed her hair in the first place? Claire was confused. It was so at odds with almost everything Ichi had said or done so far, especially after their argument last night. *So what's changed?* That's what Claire was dying to know. What could possibly have happened in the past twelve hours for Ichi to have looked at her with such confusion whilst he did something so gentle? For a split second, he hadn't looked intimidating or dark or predatory at all; he had looked positively innocent, all wide eyed and eager for the answer to a question he couldn't quite understand. Claire could feel her face reddening just thinking about it.

Stop it. You're not allowed to think about him like that. Get a grip. But Claire's brain wasn't listening to her. All she could think about was the way

Ichi's dark hair fell into his eyes as he looked at her; how his own face was flushed just from touching her; how he always seemed to find that one inch of Claire's bare skin to hold on to without realising it, even when he was trying to intimidate her.

He wants to kill you, Claire had to remind herself. Yet Ichi hadn't mentioned anything of the sort for a long time; he didn't even give off a dangerous vibe any more, not even when he had attacked her the night before. He simply came across as *desperate* now. *But that's because I made myself get over it, right? I had to in order to survive here.* Claire wasn't sure if that was even true anymore. Or at least, not completely true – Claire couldn't help but admit that Ichi had definitely stopped looking at her as if she should already be dead months ago, and that had made him easier to cope with than any training she had undergone could have.

He scares you. That was definitely still true. Everything he said or did scared her. But now, thinking about it, the aspect that was frightening Claire more and more was her own reaction to his actions. It wasn't so easy to simply ignore Ichi anymore. If anything, Claire knew that the irrational part of her brain was aching to respond to every little thing he did, like she had only just done in the corridor by commenting on his hypocrisy. She wanted him to notice her glancing at him and to call her out on it, but at the same time she was petrified about what would happen if he did. Claire stared up at the ceiling, focussing on nothing.

"He raped you," she said, in a small, small voice. There. That was it. It was the one thing that Claire couldn't forgive, and why should she? Ichi had done it to prove how much control he had over her – to show that she could do nothing against him. And even though Claire had somewhat robbed Ichi of his victory by staying silent through it all, he had still, ultimately, won that round. Claire hated that he had done it. It didn't matter what Ichi's reasons were for doing it, only that he had.

And yet despite it all here Claire was, imagining what it would feel like to rip *his* clothes off and throw him against a wall. She wanted to know what Ichi's hair would feel like if she ran her fingers through it, and how hot his skin would burn against her own.

"I'm single-handedly setting feminism back a hundred years," Claire mumbled sarcastically. She couldn't help her eyes from scanning the floor for Ichi's leather jacket, the one she had stupidly picked up in the stairwell after he had left with Alexis. She stared at it for about five minutes before finally giving in and wandering over to pick it up. Then Claire lay back on her couch again, clutching the jacket to her face. It smelled of him. *My God Ichi smells good*, Claire couldn't help but think. But this was the jacket Alexis had torn from his body in their haste to screw each other. Claire promptly threw it to the ground.

"She can have him," Claire said angrily. Ichi wasn't worth thinking about. She knew it, but…Claire sighed. She was going to have to try much harder than that to get rid of these toxic thoughts. "I'm going to hell," she mumbled, turning onto her side as she realised that not once had she considered how Vic would feel if he ever got to see what was going on inside her head.

Ichi

Ichi couldn't sleep. All day he had kept himself confined to his rooms, not trusting himself to prevent doing something he might later regret if he walked out of his door. But it meant Ichi was restless and desperate for something to do that didn't involve being trapped inside his own head. He glanced over at his laptop.

Watching her will make you feel worse, Ichi thought, but he couldn't help himself. He grabbed the laptop and sat up on his bed, opening up the camera feeds from Claire's room as he did so. And there Claire was on her couch, actually sleeping for once before four in the morning. *I can't believe she still won't use the damn bed,* he mused. Ichi sighed. Watching her sleep was hardly going to make for a decent distraction from his own thoughts. Then Ichi had an idea, and he rewound the camera feed to just after he had met Claire in the corridor.

He watched as Claire entered her room and, instead of heading for a shower as Ichi had expected (which mildly disappointed him), she immediately slumped onto her couch, staring up at nothing, a frown on her face.

"Why did I have to go and open my mouth?" she asked aloud. Claire looked angry at something; though considering the content of their meeting in the corridor, her expression hardly did much to narrow down the possible subjects she was thinking about.

"Give me *something* to work with, damn it," Ichi muttered at the screen. He could feel the heat rising in his face as Claire swung her legs up to rest over the top of the couch, her towel falling around her waist. She dangled her head over the edge of the seat, her wet hair reaching the floor. Gravity was working wonders on Claire's breasts, pushing them up (or down, considering how she was lying) practically to her neck. *I swear she bloody well knows there are cameras in there sometimes,* Ichi thought, trying to stop himself from physically reacting to her provocative pose before it was too late. He couldn't help but wish she had nothing on at all.

He was about to consign himself to another swift jerk off to follow the one he had had earlier when Claire righted her position back to lying horizontally on the couch, a hand over her eyes as she sighed. What are you thinking about? Ichi wondered again, infuriated.

And then Claire spoke. "He raped you." And then there was silence. Claire admitting to what Ichi had done out loud made him feel somewhat uncomfortable, so he pushed the feeling aside and focussed his attention back on Claire. Her expression was tormented and stormy; Ichi imagined that that was exactly how he looked when he thought about Claire. But that couldn't be right - why would Claire be thinking of Ichi the same way he did her? *Her expression's only adding more credence to what those idiots said earlier in the rec hall, along with how she reacted in the corridor,* Ichi mused. But maybe Ichi was just seeing what he wanted to see; after all, how could Claire possibly be thinking about anything other than her hatred for him after literally just saying out loud that he had raped her? And there was that uncomfortable feeling again. Ichi struggled to ignore it.

He watched as Claire brought her hands up in front of her face, looking at her fingers with the most confused look on her face, her teeth subconsciously biting down on her lower lip. Ichi was fascinated by every movement, wondering what it all meant. Claire looked down at the floor, seemingly looking for something that the angle of Ichi's hidden camera couldn't quite pick up. She stared at the unknown object for what seemed like forever before she finally relented and picked it up, flinging herself back onto the couch after she had done so.

Ichi stared at his computer screen, aghast. Was that his *jacket* Claire was clinging to? It would certainly explain how it went missing after Ichi had left it in the stairwell. But why would Claire have taken it? He half-heard her mumble something about setting feminism back a few years as she clutched the jacket to her face. Ichi couldn't take his eyes off of the laptop screen. What did any of this mean?

He watched as Claire suddenly threw his jacket to the floor, glaring at it with as much malice as she had looked at Ichi with the night before. "She can have him," Ichi heard Claire say, before rolling over on her couch, mumbling something that sounded awfully like, "I'm going to hell". And then Claire said and did no more, not for a long time.

Ichi couldn't take it. He grabbed his laptop and flung it to the floor, furious. "What the fuck do you want, Claire?!" he yelled to nobody, not caring if it woke her up next door or not. Ichi made himself close his eyes and calm down, counting to ten as he slowed his breathing right down. He picked his laptop up off of the floor and placed it gently back on to his bedside table. Incredibly, it had suffered no damage from his sudden outburst. He fast-forwarded the camera feeds in Claire's rooms to the current time. Ichi's shouting hadn't stirred her at all.

Tomorrow, I'll have an honest answer from her, he swore. *Tomorrow, I'll make her tell me everything.*

CHAPTER 17
Your Game

Ichi

Ichi was sitting at a circular table in the rec hall with Ryan, Imran, Marie, Alexis…and Vic. He hadn't bothered to find a way to get out of Ryan's stupid blackjack game, and so here he sat, nursing his fifth gin and tonic as Imran shuffled and dealt the cards. It had been a while since Ichi had drank alcohol – he could feel it hitting him far harder than he would like – but he found that it at least helped him to push thoughts of Claire to the back of his mind and enjoy the game.

Ichi had planned to corner her today, but she had somehow managed to keep herself either in public spaces or surrounded by people, so Ichi couldn't get her on her own. And now, when Claire finally *was* alone, Ichi *wasn't*. But he had thought ahead; he had drugged the last, lone carton of orange juice that sat in the bar fridge that Claire was bound to come down and drink, since she went through about a litre of the stuff most days. All Ichi had to do was wait for her to come down and take it. It wasn't much later than eleven, so Ichi figured that there was still a relatively large time frame in which Claire could appear, given her insomniac behaviour. *So I just have to make sure I keep my wits about me all night…though maybe it's a bit late for that already,* he thought, looking at the drink in his hand.

Ah whatever, I'll just roll with it. Knowing that 'rolling with it' was entirely unlike him, Ichi focussed his attention back on the people around him as they began a new round of blackjack. His hand was pretty terrible, containing a six and a two, so he knew somebody else would likely win this time. Ichi and Vic were about tied for number of rounds won, much to Ryan and Alexis' annoyance, who were both incredibly competitive. Alexis was sitting to his right, constantly sending him sultry little glances and smiles as they played. Ichi ignored them all, though that didn't seem to deter her.

Vic was sitting opposite Ichi, and they were both doing a mighty fine job of ignoring each other, too.

"Ichi?" he vaguely heard Imran say.

Ichi looked at him. "What?"

Imran raised an eyebrow. "Do you want a hit? Or are you standing?"

Ichi downed the rest of his drink and pushed his chair away from the table. "Surrender. Terrible hand. I'm getting another drink – anyone want one?" Everybody at the table looked up at him in unison, surprised. "What?" Ichi asked, again.

Alexis laughed. "I guess we're all shocked that you can actually do something nice for another human being," she answered. "And we'll all have mojitos, since you're asking, Mr 'I was working as a waiter in a cocktail bar'." Ichi rolled his eyes at the dig, but waltzed over to the bar to comply nonetheless. He slid over the floating island by the bar to reach the ice machine to an appreciative whistle from Alexis.

"Somebody's in a good mood," he heard Marie say as he began pouring rum into a shaker. "Cocktails *and* lackadaisical behaviour? Well I never, Ichi."

"Shh, don't ruin it by calling him up on it, Marie," Alexis replied, giggling. "I might never see drunk Ichi ever again." Ichi let them make their jokes as he prepared the mint for everyone's cocktails.

Vic won another round whilst Ichi was at the bar, and then Imran. Ichi wandered over to the kitchen and found a tray, using it to serve the mojitos to everyone playing. Then he ran back over to the bar and grabbed a bottle of silver Patron tequila and several shot glasses. Ryan grinned at him as he returned.

"Now *that's* more like it, man. Pass it over, I'll do the honours," the other man said, so Ichi handed him the bottle. Once Ryan had poured the shots and everyone took one, he made a toast, of sorts. "To what should be a regular night for Michael's regulars," he began, looking at everyone in turn. Then he stared at Vic and Ichi in quick succession. "And to burying the unnecessary hatchets. No girl is worth it, not even one as fiery as our dear Miss Danvers!" he laughed, and downed his shot. Vic and Ichi didn't look away from each other as they followed suit. Ryan saw them do so and frowned. "I'm *serious,* just stop it guys, even if only for tonight."

Vic sighed. "Okay, okay, even I can manage just for tonight. No promises for tomorrow though, Ich," he said, glancing at him.

Ichi laughed. "I can agree to that," he replied, and then: "Right, it's my turn to deal," as he picked up the cards and shuffled them.

And so the night continued on in this way for nearly two hours, with everybody getting steadily inebriated as the night wore on. Imran excused himself to his room for nearly fifteen minutes close to one in the morning – to throw up, everyone assumed. Ichi felt very pleasantly buzzed, having successfully managed to balance the time between each of his drinks to prevent him from feeling sick. Everybody had lost track of who had won more rounds of blackjack than anyone else, but nobody really cared.

Marie was busy regaling them with the last mission she had worked on, posing as a high school teacher. She had been investigating another one of the teachers who was the daughter of one of Michael's business partners. "She was swindling money from her old man, big time," she said, "And that was affecting Michael too, of course. Michael had me deal with her in such a way that her father had no clue he was involved." Marie paused, snickering. "She should really be more careful crossing the road when her booze has been drugged."

Vic let out a low whistle. "That's cold-blooded Marie, even for you," he said, cuffing her gently around the head. She shoved his shoulder in return.

"Just because you're still so soft-hearted, Vic. You wouldn't think like that if you offed more than two people a year," she countered. Imran and Ryan both almost spat out the drinks they had just swallowed.

"Are you serious?!" Imran asked, incredulous. "Ichi's killed more people in the past two months than you have in your entire employment!" Ichi and Vic exchanged a glance at the realisation. Vic's face was slightly red, but from the alcohol or Imran's words, Ichi was too drunk to work out.

"Well, we can't all be a psychopath with all of that pent up frustration," Vic replied, then he smirked and glanced at Alexis. "Alexis, you're clearly not doing your job right." Ryan, Marie and Imran guffawed at the comment. Ichi looked away as he realised Alexis was grinning at him, her face far more flushed than Vic's was.

164

"If he wasn't so bloody fixated on other things, it'd make things much easier for me," she mocked, placing her hand on his knee. Ichi shoved it off.

"No sexual harassment at the table, please," he said, keeping his voice jokingly stern.

Alexis pouted at him. "You're no fun anymore, Ich," she complained, taking a swig of her drink.

"Yeah, well, we all know why that is. Same goes for you, Vic," Ryan said, stating the uncomfortably obvious.

Marie clucked her tongue. "Can you just stop blaming Claire for all of the *entirely their fault* flaws that Vic and Ichi have, Ryan?" she exclaimed, giving the man a frown. Ichi caught Vic glancing at him out of the corner of his eye, and he knew they were both thinking the same thing – that Marie was completely correct. Not that Ichi would ever admit to that out loud, of course.

"Why don't we simply not talk about her at all?" Alexis ventured, her expression betraying the annoyance that she was keeping out of her voice.

Ichi chuckled. "You didn't hear me or Vic bring her up, did you?" he countered. "I'm not aware I've *ever* started a conversation about her." There was another collective group of surprised glances in Ichi's direction as they all realised that he was correct. Except for Vic, who was the only one Ichi had ever come close to actually having a proper conversation about Claire with. Ichi had to wonder whether 'being punched repeatedly in the gut' counted as a conversation, however, even if he *had* deserved it. His drunken brain acknowledged that that was indeed the case, though Ichi didn't care enough to dispose of the drugged orange juice that he was waiting for Claire to drink, even though letting her do so was just as despicable as everything else he had done to her so far. *Vic can just punch me again when he finds out,* Ichi thought sarcastically. *Though that's if he ever finds out.*

"Let's just forget all of this," Imran said. "Marie, it's your turn to deal." Marie took the cards and shuffled them, stopping the awkward conversation before it could go any further. But just after she had dealt two cards to everyone (Ichi felt a sense of satisfaction when he saw that he had an ace and a king), everybody turned their heads at the sound of a female voice singing down the corridor towards the rec hall. Then the double doors opened and Claire came in, singing to herself whilst engrossed in her Kindle. She was swinging her hips to the beat of the song that she was listening to, which had some particularly provocative lyrics. And she was wearing *those* shorts – the tiny blue ones that drove Ichi crazy – along with a low cut, sleeveless top that showed off her cleavage, something Claire so rarely did in the complex. Ichi thought his eyes might pop out of his skull at the sight of her. Claire was blissfully unaware that anybody was in the rec hall, probably due to the fact that nobody normally was at one in the morning. The entire table continued to stare at her as she slid over the floating island, much like Ichi had done only a couple of hours earlier, jumping off of it to grab the last carton of orange juice from the bar fridge. *Aaand jackpot,* Ichi thought to himself, feeling his face flush at the thought of an incapacitated Claire in about an hour's time.

"Hello there, beautiful!" he heard Ryan call out loudly in order to get Claire's attention. She turned around in surprise, her cheeks growing redder than any of the faces of the drunk blackjack players. Claire put her Kindle down to remove her headphones, in a motion that mirrored precisely how she had taken them off the night Ichi attacked her in that classroom, all those months ago.

Claire wandered over to the table, a wary smile on her face. Her smile grew more genuine as she saw Marie and Vic grin at her. "Well…you're all drunk," she ventured, stating the obvious.

Imran feigned surprise. "We didn't know; thanks for pointing it out, Claire," he joked, slurring his words slightly. "Want to join us? We just started a round; it's not too late to deal you in." Claire scanned all of their faces, lingering on Ichi's for a second longer than on anybody else, and he returned the stare unflinchingly. Out of the corner of his eye, he saw Alexis bristle at the shared gaze.

"No thanks guys…Ichi has this round anyway," she replied. Ichi raised his eyebrows at her, whilst everybody else looked at him.

"Do you?" Ryan asked, not convinced. He showed them his cards.

"Huh," Vic said, his expression flat.

Imran laughed. "Now you definitely need to join us. Ichi and Vic have been laying us to waste. We could do with someone who can read how good their hands are!" he exclaimed.

166

Claire glanced upwards. "Thanks for the offer, but I have a date with Edward Elric," she grinned.

Marie looked at her, frowning. "I'd have thought Colonel Mustang was more your type by *now,*" she said. Claire looked a little taken aback.

"...can't they both be?" she replied, sounding unsure of herself. *I have no fucking idea what's going on,* Ichi thought.

And with that, Claire bid them all good night. "Okay, what was that about?" Vic asked Marie. She looked at them all, incredulous.

"None of you have ever watched anime? *None* of you?" She stared at Ichi. "I'd have thought you would have..."

Ichi rolled his eyes. "I'm not a racial stereotype, Marie." She had the sense to look slightly ashamed, before a wide smile slowly spread across her face.

"Then I guess I'm the only one who will ever understand the double entendre behind Claire's words," she laughed, a satisfied look on her face. "Vic, it's your turn to deal," she said, putting a stop to any more questions about what Claire could have meant.

An hour later, Ichi feigned sickness to get out of the game. "Well, you lasted longer than Imran," Ryan mused, looking pointedly in the direction of Imran's empty chair. He had left them to pass out in his room nearly twenty minutes' prior.

Vic looked at Ichi suspiciously. Ichi sighed. "I guess it *is* tomorrow now," Ichi said in response to Vic's stare. "Be pissed off at me if you want, Vic. I'm going to go throw up,"

Alexis glanced up at him and smiled drunkenly. "Sure you don't want to stay up and do something else?" she asked.

Ichi shook his head. "I'm not in a state to do anything else, even if I wanted to."

"I swear, Ichi, you've said more to us in one night that you have in the past half a year, do you know that?" Marie commented, then added on jokingly, "It's not entirely unpleasant."

Ichi allowed himself to smile at her. "I'll keep that in mind," he said, before turning on them all to exit the rec hall, his smile widening into a grin.

He could barely contain his excitement as he waited on the elevator to take him up to the twelfth floor. Claire would be well and truly under a drug-induced stupor by now. So when Ichi opened her door, he was surprised to find that she wasn't on her couch, but on hearing water flowing, Ichi wandered over to her bathroom. Claire was in her shower, the air so steamy that Ichi could barely see. On a whim he removed his t-shirt and shoes and opened the cubicle door to join her.

Claire looked at him when he entered the shower, eyes vacant and slightly unfocussed. "What are you doing?" Ichi asked her. He allowed his eyes to rove up and down Claire's completely naked body for the first time in real life and not from a laptop screen.

Claire frowned. "My head feels weird…I'm washing it away," she said, the logic in her response so childish that Ichi chuckled. Claire turned away from him to stand directly under the shower head; clearly she had no intention of leaving the cubicle any time soon. So Ichi pushed her gently against the wall, taking the brunt of the water gushing out of the shower head himself, soaking his hair and jeans in seconds. He turned Claire around to look at him, resting his arms on the tiled wall on either side of her head. Then he just looked at her.

"What?" Claire demanded, defensive, but the drugs had taken any angry edge out of her words.

"Nothing," Ichi replied, his drunken brain too preoccupied with looking at her to respond properly.

"It's never nothing with you," she countered, and her words were completely true.

"I suppose it isn't. I'm trying to figure you out."

"Then I guess we're doing the same thing."

Ichi frowned slightly. "What, figuring yourself out or figuring me out?"

It was Claire's turn to frown. "Both?" she replied. She shook her head. "I don't know, I can't think…"

"But you think about me," Ichi dared to say.

Claire looked up at him, eyes wide. "All the time." Claire's eyes grew wider. "But you-you-you're not supposed to know that," she stammered, words trailing away to nothing as Ichi ran his fingertips down to her waist, revelling in the feeling of her skin. Then Ichi looked down in surprise as Claire started taking off his belt.

"What are you doing?" he asked, aching for her fingers to work faster on the buttons of his jeans.

"You can't wear clothes in the shower," she answered, matter-of-factly.

Ichi closed his eyes for a second. "For your own wellbeing, I can do," he said. Claire brought her hands up to Ichi's stomach, trailing her fingers all the way over his chest to his shoulders.

"But you don't look out for my wellbeing," she countered, hitting the nail on the head once again.

"If you don't stop, I'll touch you back," Ichi said, voice rough and slightly unsteady. He couldn't quite believe that he was actually trying to get Claire to stop.

Claire brought her hands back down to the half-undone buttons of his jeans. "You are already."

Ichi pressed himself up against her, his lips a hair's breadth from hers. "I'll do more than this," he replied in a low voice. He didn't know how much more of this he could take before giving in to the carnal impulse to screw Claire where she stood.

"You're going to anyway," she said simply. Ichi grabbed her and fireman lifted her out of the shower and over to the bed that she never used, dropping her down onto it before climbing on top of her.

"Do you want me to?" Ichi asked quietly, his left hand trailing down Claire's soaking wet skin to her thigh. Claire shivered at his touch, but in an entirely pleasant way.

She looked away from him. "I'm not supposed to," she answered, avoiding the question in classic Claire-fashion despite the drugs. Ichi nudged her head back up with his forehead to make her look at him.

"But you do."

Claire didn't speak for a moment. "...I can't see," she finally said, blinking several times. Ichi sighed, before rolling off of Claire to grab her a towel from the shower room, turning off the shower and retrieving the rest of his clothing in the process. He sat on the bed and passed Claire the towel.

"Here, dry yourself off and put some clothes on," he mumbled, looking away as Claire obliged. When she was dressed, Ichi pulled the duvet over her. "Go to sleep, Claire. Don't even think to try and avoid me tomorrow," he told her.

Claire yawned, turning on to her side. "So demanding…" she mumbled, before falling asleep faster than Ichi had ever seen her fall asleep since arriving at Michael's complex. Ichi rushed out of her room and over to his own, removing his sodden jeans and collapsing onto his bed as soon as he got there.

I only did that because I'm too drunk to actually do anything, he told himself, knowing it was a lie. *I got all of the information I needed, anyway. I'll just get her tomorrow…*Ichi thought, as he felt his eyelids droop, falling asleep almost as quickly as Claire had done.

CHAPTER 18
Blow Me Away

Vic

Vic was sitting in the rec hall, mulling over Claire's rejection of his feelings. Again. The only break he'd had from thinking about it had been the blackjack game with everyone the previous night, and Vic's stomach was paying for that now. He had consumed far too much alcohol, and he instinctively knew that there was no way he'd keep any food down for at least another hour, even though it was already four in the afternoon.

She does like you, she just wants to be free before she gives us a try. That's what Claire had said, and she had meant it. But…Vic glanced over at Ichi, who was mindlessly playing pool by himself for seemingly no apparent reason. He had been at the pool table ever since Vic had come down to the rec hall nearly an hour ago, and Vic knew that he would have looked foolish if he had simply turned and left as soon as he arrived just because Ichi was there. Ryan, Imran and Marie were sitting in the other corner of the rec hall, nursing terrible hangovers and speaking to no-one, so they hadn't bothered to invite either Vic or Ichi over to join them. Vic continued to stare at Ichi. *We got along well enough last night; it was almost back to the way we were before Claire arrived, so why not keep up the truce?* But the thought irked him. Claire *was* here, and it had caused Ichi to do some completely unforgivable things. Vic didn't want to simply brush those things under the rug and forget about them. But then he flinched as he remembered something else Claire had told him when she rejected his feelings.

"…even you're *a killer, Vic, and I shouldn't just overlook that because I like you. You're all killers, and it's screwing up my perception of what makes a person 'good' or not."* Vic hated that Claire had said that, because it was true; he had almost forgotten that being a killer was not something a

normal person would overlook when choosing a prospective partner. Vic ran a hand over his face, sighing, before glancing over at Ichi again. The other man had never been quite right in the head – could Vic really blame him as much as he was for what he had done to Claire? *Yes, because something's bloody going on with them, and I only realised it last night.*

Vic was frustrated with himself; how had he become so ignorant of what was going on? He knew Ichi was obsessed with Claire, and he had thought that she was simply trying hard to get over her fear of him. Now Vic could see the truth – Claire wasn't scared of Ichi so much as fascinated by him. He had seen that for himself with the way she had looked at the damn man during their blackjack game. How else could she have possibly known that Ichi was going to win that round if she wasn't thinking about and analysing every little thing that he did? What confused Vic was how Claire had found the time to observe Ichi's mannerisms in the first place. Clearly she had done an exemplary job at pulling the wool over Vic's eyes to make him believe she didn't feel anything more than hatred for the other man.

There's no way that her warped feelings for him *aren't getting in the way of what the two of us could be if she gave us a chance.* Vic frowned at the thought, digging his fingernails into his arm so hard that he nearly broke the skin. *I'm not allowed to think like that; it's not fair on Claire. She would never have met Ichi if she hadn't been brought here, and she'd never have given him a second glance on the street if she hadn't.* Vic calmed himself down with what Claire had actually explicitly said to him – that she just wanted out of Michael's complex before she thought about what the two of them could be. And she *had* meant it. Vic only hoped that, when Claire was finally free, she would stop thinking about Ichi entirely.

He was broken out of his reverie by the arrival of Claire. To Vic's immense satisfaction, she outright ignored Ichi and wandered over to Vic, sparing Marie a wave and a sympathetic smile on the way. She sat herself down on the table instead of on a chair, swinging her legs to and fro to some non-existent beat. "Hey, Mr Winters, how's the hangover?" she ventured, as if their conversation from two nights ago had never happened. Vic could deal with that…for now, anyway.

He smiled back at her. "Not as bad as it was this morning," he chuckled. Claire looked wistfully at the bar behind her. "What?" Vic asked.

Claire sighed and shook her head. "Wish *I* could be hungover," she mumbled.

"There's nothing stopping that from happening," came a voice from behind them – Ichi. He didn't even look up from the pool table as he spoke. Claire ignored him. Vic was glad that she did. *So long as she continues to act like he doesn't exist,* he thought, *even if she doesn't feel that way, well…that's good enough for me, at least until she's out of here.*

Ichi

Ichi didn't feel hungover at all. If anything, he felt almost elated. He had the upper hand on Claire, now that he knew how she felt. All Ichi needed to do now was to wait until she was back in her room in the evening – the drugs in her system had kept her asleep until well past noon. He had very nearly barged into her room the second she woke up, but Ichi forced himself to give Claire a few hours to herself to ensure that she was completely in control of her wits. After all, his victory would be ruined if she didn't know what she was doing. Ichi wondered how much of the previous night's encounter Claire would remember, if at all.

He was killing time by playing a solo game of pool, though Ichi didn't care much for what he was actually doing. Vic was sitting a few tables away, literally doing nothing; he looked hungover. Ichi knew that the other man kept throwing glances his way, but Ichi couldn't be bothered to demand an explanation for any of them. He had more important things to ponder, such as what the obscure reference was that Claire had made to Marie last night before she left the rec hall. Ichi had promised himself he wouldn't forget it, and yet in his drunken state he had. Ichi was sure it was something to do with him. Or Vic. Either way, he wanted to know. *I'm sure I can find some way to get the answer out of Claire tonight,* he thought, grinning mischievously.

He could hear Vic sighing behind him; clearly the other man had a lot to think about too, though by the sounds of it his thoughts weren't pleasant. *I don't care. Let him make himself unhappy – it's my turn to get what I want around here,* Ichi thought. After all, Claire was thinking about *him,* not Vic. If Ichi's satisfaction was at Vic's expense, then so be it.

Speak of the devil and she shall appear, Ichi joked as he spied Claire enter the rec hall. He made to straighten up from the pool table, to attempt some kind of greeting that he hadn't quite worked out yet, but decided against it when he saw Claire walk right past him and sit by Vic, completely ignoring him. *So that's how she's playing it again, huh?* Ichi reasoned that if Claire remembered nothing of last night then she'd have no cause to treat him any differently that she had before, so he continued playing his game of pool as if nothing had changed between them.

Ichi found himself listening in to the conversation between Vic and Claire. "How's the hangover?" he heard Claire ask. When Ichi heard Claire's response to Vic's answer being that she wished she could be hungover herself, Ichi couldn't help but chime in with his opinion.

"There's nothing stopping that from happening," he remarked, pointedly. Ichi knew Claire wasn't touching alcohol to keep her wits about her at all times, but since he had gotten her far worse than inebriated last night, he could see no reason for why Claire should bother refraining from getting drunk now. *Well, not that Claire knows that, if she doesn't remember anything,* Ichi supposed once again.

Ichi was irked that Claire ignored his comment, but he continued to act as if he didn't care and brought his attention back to the pool table. *After all,* he thought somewhat maliciously, *you won't ignore me tonight.*

Claire

Claire's head was fuzzy. She wasn't sure *why,* just as she wasn't certain why she didn't remember much of the night before. She remembered sitting up in her room and watching anime, mulling over her stupidity at making any comments to the gambling group of assassins who were getting deliriously drunk, and then a whole lot of nothing. *Why did I ever think it was a good idea to show them all that I paid Ichi any attention?* Claire had a sneaking suspicion that he was somehow responsible for her memory loss, much in the same way that she decided he was responsible for anything bad

174

or shady that happened to her in Michael's complex, but she had no proof. Claire was shocked when she woke up in the bed that she hadn't touched since the first night she had been brought to suite 1202, and it only served to lend more fuel to her fiery suspicion that Ichi was somehow behind everything that had happened…whatever that was.

Now Claire was chatting away with Vic in the rec hall, both of them acting as if nothing awkward had been said at all two nights previously. For that Claire was grateful; she had enough to worry about as it was. Ichi was there, too, but Claire was ignoring him, even when he threw in a comment to her and Vic's conversation. Claire was swinging her legs over the edge of the table she was sitting on, unreasonably happy despite her lack of memory of the night before. *Maybe it's because I slept for at least ten hours in an actual bed,* Claire mused. She glanced up at Ichi through her eyelashes; she was sure he was up to something. Then Claire brought her gaze back to Vic – the bright lights from the ceiling were reflected in his pale blue eyes, making them almost translucent. She smiled at him, deciding to do something dangerous just to see what Ichi would do in public.

"Turn around, Vic," she ordered him.

Vic raised an eyebrow at her. "And why would I do that, princess?" he asked, amused. Claire forced herself not to look up at Ichi, knowing that what she was about to do was purely to piss him off.

"I want to play with your hair. You still haven't had it cut since you said it needed done three months ago, so now there's more to play with. Hooray for me!" she replied, a stupid grin on her face. Vic sighed in resignation.

"You know I can't refuse you," he said, turning around in his chair. Claire sat cross-legged on the table, directly behind him, and started teasing her fingers through his blonde hair. *It really is so damn smooth…I'm jealous,* she thought. She ran her fingertips over Vic's hairline in small circles, which made the man close his eyes and sigh contentedly. *I dare you to react, Ichi, I bloody dare you.* "What did I do to deserve a head massage?" Vic joked. Claire brought her head down to look into Vic's eyes, upside-down. When he opened them and saw her there, he laughed in surprise. "What's gotten into you today? You're so…bouncy."

"Maybe it's because I slept so well. Maybe it's because I felt like being super nice. Or maybe I have a secret agenda," Claire replied, hiding the truth behind those last words with sarcasm and a smile.

"You know I could help you sleep even better," Vic suggested, daring to be outrageous. Claire laughed, bringing her head back up to shake her long hair out of her face.

"You know, that sounds more appealing every –" she began, but the sentence was cut short as Claire felt a hand grab at her hair and pull her away from Vic, followed by an arm circling around her waist to drag her off of the table to slam her against the nearest wall. Claire didn't have to look up to know who was responsible. *Let's see what you do now, you son of a bitch,* she thought rebelliously as she recovered from having her head bashed against the wall.

Ichi

Ichi couldn't believe it. Claire had been ignoring him. She *always* ignored him in public. And yet this one time she did something so obviously intended to rile him up, and Ichi had well and truly sprung the trap. Ichi had Claire pinned against the wall, momentarily too stunned to speak. Ichi was furious at her. After everything she had told him last night, there she was again, flirting with Vic for the whole complex to see. And now Ichi had flown into a rage, for the whole complex to see. Everybody's eyes were on the two of them, startled out of their hangovers. Vic's face was mutinous as he slowly got up from his seat. Ichi's eyes never left Claire's, who was returning his stare with a fury all of her own.

"Get off of me," she bit out in a terse whisper. Ichi's grip on her hair and shoulder tightened.

"Why, so you can go back to acting like everything's normal? So you can pretend you actually get to have a say in what happens to you around here?" he fumed, feeling his fingernails dig into her skin. He was satisfied to see Claire wince in response.

"What the hell are you –"

"You just don't get it, do you?" Ichi interrupted. "You never have! I was supposed to kill you that day, to *wipe* your existence from this planet and yet somehow, *somehow* you managed to delay that." Claire was frowning at him, looking as if she was thinking about what to say. Ichi gave her shoulder a rough shake, as if rattling her brain inside her skull would make his point clear to her. "Do you get it yet? Your life is forfeit; your life is *mine!* You can't waltz around this place doing whatever and *whoever* you feel like! The only one who can do anything to you is *me!*" There. He said it. Shouted it really, for everyone to hear. Now they would all know just how unstable Ichi was. He didn't care. His pulse was racing, his heartbeat frantic. Ichi was *alive*. Claire was looking at him with such venom that Ichi himself was envious of the level of hatred that she had managed to inject into her glare. He could feel her pulse racing too, against the hand he had on her shoulder, yet when Claire spoke it was in a cold, quiet voice.

"You think you can dictate what happens to me for the rest of my life? You think you have even an *iota* of control over it? You don't!" Her voice was getting louder, faster, more passionate. "It's me who decides when I get to die and what I get to do! Me! I could end my life right now and you wouldn't be able to do a damn thing about it, and don't think I haven't thought about it. You think you exerted your 'control' over me when you raped me?" Ichi flinched at the statement, the words making him feel just as uncomfortable as they had done when Claire had spoken out loud about it in her room. Claire pushed her hands against Ichi's chest, making him take a step backwards. "Think again, you psychotic son of a bitch!" Claire snarled. "I could have asked Vic to protect me that day, or any day, and he would have done it in a second! At first I thought it was just some twisted arrogance of mine that made me *expect* you to do something like that to me, but I was clearly right on point." Claire looked away from him then, chuckling darkly to herself for a moment before bringing her gaze back up to his, her eyes bright with anger. "And I could have prevented it. All of your torment, I could have avoided it all...but I'm not the kind of person who takes advantage of the feelings of someone else just so that they can protect me against someone like *you!* So do *you* get it, Ichi? I've taken every decision out of your hands by choosing to let it all happen, no matter how broken each of your encounters has made me. But I've been fixing myself, bit by bit, and nothing you can do will affect me now! The last time you had any kind of control over me was the day you were sent to kill me, and you *failed*." She practically spat the last words out.

Ichi said nothing. Couldn't. Claire took advantage of his stunned silence to break away from his grip and bowl past him. Vic made to follow her, but she shook her head gently to tell him not to. When she reached the bar Claire vaulted over the floating island, grabbed a bottle of Havana rum, and stalked away.

No, you're not supposed to say that, Ichi thought numbly. *You're not supposed to think that I don't affect you. I* have *to.* Claire's impassioned speech threw everything she had said in her drugged state the night before to the wind, leaving Ichi frozen in the wake of Claire's revelation that, really, he couldn't do anything to her and never had.

Vic

Vic was left as shocked by Claire's outrage as Ichi was. He had never heard her openly admit to Ichi's rape before but, now that she had, Vic realised that hating Ichi for it was pointless; it would only detract from how unimportant Claire had just made Ichi feel, as if he wasn't worth thinking about. And yet even so, Vic hated him, for as strong as Vic's feelings were for Claire, as much as he wanted to run after her and explicitly tell her how he felt, to throw her on his bed and do unspeakable things to her, Ichi's feelings for her were a hundred times stronger. Ichi, the psychopath. Ichi, who had no feelings. Ichi, who wanted her dead. A man with no understanding of love and therefore didn't know what it was that he was feeling. And all of the jealousy, lust and anger that came with it when it wasn't reciprocated.

Welcome to the club, you bastard.

And so Vic very calmly walked over to Ichi and, for the second time in his life, punched him squarely in the face. He left him there, bleeding from his nose, looking lost, furious and, above all, helpless. Then Vic took a leaf out of Claire's book and grabbed some vodka on his way out.

CHAPTER 19
The Beast and the Harlot

Claire

Claire was celebrating. She had finally won against Ichi. *Finally!* He couldn't possibly have a counter-argument to anything she had told him earlier. And now he knew that it was pointless even trying to do anything to her, because it wouldn't affect her. It had been a dangerous gamble, but it had paid off. And now Claire could concentrate on getting herself out of Michael's complex, rather than worrying about Ichi or Vic. She decided that she would go and see Michael first thing in the morning and dare to demand some information about what was going on. After all, he needed Claire alive and functional, so what could Michael really do to her that hadn't already happened?

"I'm not going to get anywhere in here if I keep meekly obliging everybody's demands and allowing Michael to keep me in the dark," she said aloud, so demanding some answers from Michael was exactly what she would do. *Right after I've finished getting wondrously drunk.* Claire knew fine well that her growing sense of confidence on the matter was a result of both her win against Ichi and the alcohol in her system – she had been drinking her bottle of rum for nearly three hours now, savouring every last drop of it. It had been hard to drink at first; Claire hadn't touched alcohol in so long, and she had certainly never taken to drinking straight rum before. But after the first few swigs had entered her bloodstream, Claire found every fiery mouthful easier and easier to swallow. She had drank about a third of the bottle, not wanting to drink anymore in case she passed out. *I'm such a lightweight now...Olivia wouldn't be impressed,* Claire joked. *I'll just drink more later; it's only dinner time now anyway. The night is young.*

The person Claire had been half a year ago, before she was kidnapped, would have been ashamed at herself had she known she would be getting drunk on her own simply because she had won an argument. "Well, I'm not her anymore," Claire mumbled drunkenly, grabbing a glass from her non-functional kitchen and pouring a shot of rum into it. She held it out in front of her, as if to make a toast. "Here's to the old Claire Danvers, may she never return," she said, making to down the shot before pausing. Claire put her drink down on the coffee table, thinking hard for a moment. Finally, she headed to the bathroom and turned the shower on. "If I'm giving my old self a funeral, I need to look the part," she said as she stepped under the torrent of hot water.

Claire took her time getting ready, attempting to recreate exactly how she had looked on the day of her sham of an assassination. She shaved, vigorously towel-dried her hair (lamenting the fact that she had no coconut shampoo to complete her reversion to her old self) and fastidiously applied her make-up, taking extra care in applying her cat-eye liner, smoky purple eyeshadow and just a hint of silver around her eye. Lashings of mascara completed the look. Satisfied, and somewhat impressed with herself for having applied make up so well when she was drunk, Claire moved over to the wardrobe where her clothes were stored. Her flouncy lilac dress hung innocuously on its hanger, the rip in the fabric barely obvious after Claire had spent time repairing it – an action she had undertaken months before in an attempt to mentally recover from her kidnapping. But when she held her hand out to take it off of the hanger, Claire hesitated. She had taken so long to get ready that some of the alcohol in her system had dissipated, leaving her very slightly more level-headed. *You swore you'd never wear this again,* Claire thought. *You only kept it as a reminder of how everything started.* Then Claire frowned and grabbed the dress anyway before walking over to the small chest of drawers by the bed to find the underwear set she had also worn on the same night. *The dress has no horrifying meaning anymore; it's just a dress.* Claire knew that that wasn't and probably never would be true, but to force herself to get over everything that had happened to her, Claire needed to face these memories that she was so terrified of head-on. And she could start with the damn dress.

Once she was fully clothed, Claire did a little twirl in front of her bathroom mirror. Her hair was drying in waves as it always did when she left it to air-dry. Claire suddenly recalled that she had been considering whether to put it up or leave it down when she had heard Ichi enter her parents' house all those months ago.

"Well, it was down when they found me, so down it shall be," she said to her reflection. She glanced down at her feet. Claire had never had time to put those fragile little silvery sandals on for her date with John before she was kidnapped. *John. Huh.* Claire hadn't thought about John in months, not since her brain had started to black out all memories of what he was like and how he looked. "I wonder how he felt about being stood up," she laughed bitterly. Then Claire resolved to find him once she was free of Michael's complex, to remind herself of who the man had been that she had girlishly fallen for, back when she could still be carefree.

Claire inspected herself once more in the mirror. Her hair was a bit longer, her body was a little thinner, but in almost every respect Claire looked exactly the same as she had done when Vic and Ichi had kidnapped her six months ago. "All I need are some blood and tears," she murmured sarcastically.

Claire wandered back over to the coffee table, to her bottle of rum and half-forgotten shot that she had poured for herself over an hour ago. She picked the glass up, considering its contents, before deciding to make it a double. Claire held the glass out again, as she had done before. "Claire Danvers is dead...long live Claire Danvers," she announced to the air, throwing the rum down her throat as soon as the words had left her lips.

Ichi

Ichi was slumped against the corridor wall on the twelfth floor. He didn't have the energy to move to his room. He was nursing a half-empty bottle of gin, the alcohol barely doing its job at keeping the thoughts Ichi didn't want at bay. He didn't know how to process everything that Claire had said over the past two days. All he knew was that the words she had thrown at him in their argument stung like hell, and left Ichi feeling utterly defeated. *It wasn't supposed to be like this,* he thought wearily. The realisation that Claire would continue to rebuff his advances like they were nothing had drained Ichi's will to do anything entirely. He found that her words from today were completely overwriting the words Ichi had coerced out of her the night before, as if she had never said them.

But she did, he thought feebly. *She said she thought about me all the time, had all but outright confessed to wanting me.* Yet Claire wasn't going to do anything about it, and would likely never believe Ichi if he told her what she had said. If anything, discovering that he had drugged her would just send Claire into a rage far worse than the one she had been in mere hours ago.

"I can't believe I've lost," Ichi murmured, leaning his head against the wall, eyes closed to the world. His nose stung somewhat from the punch Vic had thrown at him, but Ichi considered himself incredibly lucky that the other man had not managed to break it nor bruise any of the skin surrounding it. Ichi sighed and slumped even further down the wall, any will to do something with his evening long forgotten.

That was how Claire found him when she came rushing out of her room. "I wouldn't do whatever it is you're planning to do if I were you," Ichi mumbled, not bothering to open his eyes. He could tell by the sound of Claire's footsteps that she had headed towards *Ichi's* room, not towards the stairs or the elevator.

"Well, you're not me and I can do what I like," Claire responded childishly.

Ichi sighed again. "Breaking into my room for whatever inane purpose your brain has come up with will not lead to the kind of outcome you're hoping for."

Claire scoffed at his answer. "Of course that's what you'd say. I was only planning to snoop around. It's not like you haven't done it to me, I'm sure." Ichi said nothing – he didn't have the energy to argue with her. He simply continued to keep his eyes shut, hoping that eventually Claire would simply leave. He heard her take a step or two towards him.

"You're drunk," Claire said, stating the obvious.

"And so are you," Ichi responded almost immediately, foreseeing Claire's question before she had said it. "You took the rum, Vic took the vodka, so that left me the gin." He held it up to emphasise his point, swirling the contents of the bottle round and round. Then he lowered his arm and sighed once more. "Leave me alone, Claire."

He heard her take another step towards him, resolutely not leaving him alone. "What is up with you? And who are you to tell me to leave *you*

182

alone?! I'll bother you all I like; it's not like you ever listened to me when I told you to stay the hell away from me!" Claire blazed back. Ichi struggled to bite back a retort as he opened his eyes…and was completely taken aback by what Claire was wearing. She looked just as phenomenally beautiful as the day he had been sent to kill her, with her make up all done up to match the delicate little dress she had on and her long, dark hair framing her face in loose waves.

Ichi raised his eyebrows at her in surprise. "Why are you dressed like that?" he couldn't help but ask, and he saw Claire smirk at the question.

"I'm continuing my celebration of your failures," she replied happily.

Ichi frowned, turning his head to look away from her. "I think you've already made it perfectly clear that I failed to kill you. You're alive, after all," he muttered, keeping his voice calm. Claire was beginning to rile him up again, and Ichi was determined not to give her the satisfaction of knowing that she had.

Claire let out a bark of laughter. "Ha! You don't even realise how much of a fool you are," she said, grinning drunkenly from ear to ear. *If she doesn't get to her point soon, I'm going to slap her in the face,* Ichi thought, beyond irritated with her. He kept his gaze on some obscure point on the floor. "You think you're so smart," Claire continued. "But if you were as clever as you think you are, you'd have worked out that Michael was playing you big time." Ichi turned his head back sharply to stare at Claire, all anger momentarily forgotten. "You think he was going to let you kill me? Seriously? You were just a pawn of his that he can control, to scare me into complying with his demands! He set you up and you –" Claire suddenly stopped talking, a hand over her mouth in shock as she looked at Ichi's face and realised what she had just told him.

"What did you just say?" he asked her, his voice low and dark and dangerous, as he slowly stood up from the wall. Claire's face grew paler with every passing second as she backed away from Ichi towards her door.

"I –" she started to say, before abandoning the sentence to turn around and bolt through her doorway. Ichi was on her like a dog, slamming his arm against the doorframe to prevent Claire from being able to close the door, ignoring the pain in his arm in order to slam the door back open and shut behind him.

"Get the fuck back here!" he screamed at her, as Claire ran towards the couch and grabbed something from under her pillow. It was his knife; the one she had stolen right off of him. Claire jumped onto the couch in an attempt to get around Ichi, but he bowled straight into her, grabbing her around both of her arms and locking them in place to prevent her from using his knife against him. Claire tried to kick at him, struggling under his iron grip, but he was too strong for her. Her eyes looked wildly around, trying to work out what to do, before using all of her weight to push both of them over the edge of the couch, toppling it over into the screen door that separated the bed from the living space in the process. Ichi's arms loosened around her in surprise, and Claire used the opportunity to break away from him and run towards the bed. *Idiot,* Ichi thought angrily as he lunged after her, swiping the knife out of Claire's hand and sending it skittering away across the floor. He knocked into her with so much force that he sent the two of them sprawling onto the floor as well, Claire bringing the duvet down with her in her attempt to grab onto the bed to keep herself up. Ichi regained his composure a half-second quicker than Claire, pinning her down to the floor by her shoulders on top of the duvet. Claire's eyes roved from side to side, looking for something to hit him with, and resorted to using her fists instead, banging them again and again against his chest.

"Let me go!" she demanded, her breathing heavy and her face flushed. In typical Claire fashion, she kept her eyes looking at anything but Ichi. *She only looks at me when I force her to or she has a point to prove. Well the one who has a point to prove here is* me, Ichi thought. He was just as breathless as Claire was, and his head was spinning slightly from the alcohol he had consumed.

"Why the hell would I do that, Claire? Now tell me what the fuck you were on about," he replied, a sharp edge to his voice.

Claire continued to stare off into the distance. "No," she stated, daring to be contrary despite the situation she was in. Ichi almost collapsed on top of her in exasperation. He let go of her shoulders to sit up on top of her instead. Claire raised her eyebrows in shock at the motion.

"What's the point in not telling me? No, seriously," he added on, when it looked as if Claire was going to argue with him. "You know I'm not going anywhere until you tell me. And you've clearly messed up by saying what you've already told me." Ichi ran a hand over his face and sighed. "So what's the point in keeping me in the dark? You've obviously gotten the reaction out of me that you wanted – hell, you've clearly gotten the reaction you wanted out of me all bloody day – so just tell me and be done with it." Claire was staring at him now with the most bizarre look on her face; Ichi had no idea what it meant. But as quickly as she had turned her head to look at him, Claire turned away again.

"…I don't know any more than what I told you," she mumbled. "I'm the one who's being kept in the dark, not you." Her voice trailed away to nothing by the end of the statement. Ichi looked down at her, trying to work out if Claire was telling the truth, and he realised that she was. For the first time in months, Claire looked *vulnerable*, her expression a complicated mix of fear and nervousness and frustration – emotions that Ichi had longed to see on her face as a result of him for so long. But she wasn't feeling them because of him; those emotions were reserved for Michael and her parents and the memory loss that Ichi had initially assumed she had been faking, to avoid her imminent death. Ichi realised for the first time that, in the face of everything happening to Claire, his vendetta against her truly was insignificant. There was something much more important happening that Ichi had no clue about, something that Claire evidently didn't know much about either. But Ichi was too drunk to ponder such things at length. He'd think about them later; for now he had to deal with Claire.

Suddenly, Claire tried to wriggle free from underneath him, pulling herself up into as much of a sitting position as she could with Ichi already sitting on top of her, but he grabbed her and pulled her to him, preventing her from leaving. *As if I'm letting you go now.* Claire glared up at him through flyaway strands of hair that had fallen into her eyelashes, face crushed against Ichi's chest.

"You said you'd let me go if I told you what I knew!" Claire bit out angrily. Ichi chuckled at her, pushing the stray strands of hair out of her face as he did so. Claire's eyes followed the motion of his fingers as he touched her face, and her frown disappeared to be replaced with a look of nervous confusion.

"I never said I'd let you go if you told me what you knew…I merely said I wouldn't let you go if you *didn't*," he replied, a smirk on his face. "I'm not about to go making promises I don't intend to keep."

Claire

The dangerous position Claire had so foolishly put herself in had changed. Yes, it was still dangerous, but in an entirely different way. Ichi wasn't trying to attack her and force her to give him answers she couldn't give him anymore. He was…he was…Claire's drunken brain didn't know how to put two and two together to make four. Was he *flirting* with her? *Obviously not in a normal-guy way; in an 'I don't know how to be normal and tell you I like you so I'm just going to stop you from leaving and brush your hair away from your face and smile in that way that you love but won't admit to' kind of way,* her drunken brain thought. Claire shook her head as much as she could against Ichi's chest at the idiotic thoughts her brain was having. *It's the booze, it has to be the booze. He doesn't know how I feel, I made sure he thought completely otherwise…didn't I?* But Ichi seemed to have found some renewed sense of confidence after Claire had knocked it out of him earlier, otherwise he would have left after she had told him what he needed to know. But Ichi also wasn't simply throwing her back onto the floor and having his way with her, like he had done five months ago. She glanced up at him for half a second.

"W-what's your plan here, Ichi?" Claire could have hit herself for stammering. Ichi tugged at her hair slightly, making her look back up at him.

"Am I making you nervous?" he asked, a sly smile on his face. Ichi's hair had fallen into his eyes, making him look young and drunk and mischievous and – *and definitely not thoughts that should be running through my head right now!* Claire scolded herself.

"Only insomuch as you're not acting like yourself," she mumbled into his chest. Ichi knelt up, taking the pressure off of Claire's legs from where he had been sitting on them. He swept all of Claire's hair over one shoulder, brushing his finger against the artery in her neck and down along her collarbone. Claire felt her skin grow hotter than it already was underneath his touch, and was ashamed. Ichi chuckled again. His other arm was wrapped around Claire's waist, keeping her close. Claire could feel her heart beating far too quickly, but if she ignored it she could hear Ichi's beating just as rapidly against her ear. *It's the alcohol.* "Leave me alone,

Ichi," she murmured, knowing that she didn't mean it and hating herself for it.

"We both know that that's not going to happen," he replied softly as he brought his left hand up to run his fingers through Claire's long hair. Ichi's grip loosened on her waist, allowing Claire to pull back slightly. She forced herself to look up at him, scared of what she would see in his face.

"Then this is no different than the last time," she whispered.

Claire watched as Ichi's intent expression crumbled for a second. "Is that really what you think? Do you really think that that's what I want?" he asked her, his face serious as he focussed all of his attention on their conversation. Ichi sat back down on Claire's legs so that his eyes would be level with her own. Claire didn't respond for a moment.

"What about what I want, Ichi?" she asked eventually. Claire saw a flicker of amusement light up Ichi's eyes.

"I know what you want. So do you."

Claire frowned at him. "How could you possibly –"

"You're not the only one obsessed with learning to read somebody else's face," he laughed, though his words were serious.

"I'm not *obsessed* with –"

"Yes you are," Ichi interrupted again. He glanced downwards and grinned. "Look where your hands are." Claire followed his gaze and realised that she had her fingers laced around his belt, under his t-shirt. Horrified, Claire tried to pull away, but Ichi retaliated by gently pushing her back down onto the duvet, bringing his head down to chuckle into her ear.

"I-I'm *drunk*, I just –"

"You just *what*, Claire? I won't know if you don't tell me properly," Ichi interjected, nibbling on the edge of her ear as he did so.

"Then stop interrupting me," she argued. Ichi's right hand was tracing up her thigh, bringing her dress up to her waist, as he had done to her on the day Claire had arrived at the complex and on the day he had forced himself on her. But it felt completely different now. It wasn't an assault or an invasion against her person anymore; he was simply *teasing* her.

187

"I'm only interrupting you when you lie," Ichi murmured, skimming his lips against the skin on her neck without quite touching it; Claire shivered at the sensation. She could feel him, hard, against the fingers she still had pressed against his jeans, and she was aware of her body getting too hot between her thighs.

"How do you know when I'm lying?" Claire managed to ask, her mind struggling to continue with the conversation whilst she was fixated on other, far more physical things. Ichi rested his forehead against her own and looked at Claire as if she was the most desirable woman in the world. She supposed, to Ichi in this moment, she was.

"Does it matter?" he asked, bringing his lips so close to hers that Claire would barely have had to lean forward to kiss them. She closed her eyes for a moment, trying desperately to clear her head. *You shouldn't do this, Claire.*

"No," she replied, finally. Ichi's left hand was still curled in her hair, the fingers of his right following the line of her hip bone, achingly close to the increasingly wetter region between her thighs.

"Then for the love of God, take my fucking jeans off," Ichi begged her, finally kissing her and closing his eyes as Claire reciprocated, fingers tugging at his belt in her desperation to get it off.

Yes, I'm definitely going to hell for this, she thought, as Ichi threw her dress off whilst she ripped at his t-shirt. But for one night, Claire decided that she simply didn't care.

Vic

Vic had drunkenly gone up to Claire's room, thinking that if she was also drunk then maybe she would do something with him that she was too cautious to do when sober. Vic knew it was a despicable thought; he thought it nonetheless. But when he got to Claire's door, he could hear that she wasn't alone. Vic realised what was going on and felt the anger rising in his throat. He swiftly turned away from Claire's door, cursing Ichi, cursing Claire, but most of all cursing himself, for getting to her too late.

CHAPTER 20
An Honest Mistake

Ichi

Ichi woke up in a bed that wasn't his. It took him a few seconds to work out that he was in Claire's room, in Claire's bed...with Claire sleeping right beside him. Considering Ichi still felt somewhat drunk, he concluded that it couldn't quite be morning yet. He slid out from under the covers as quietly as possible to wander over to the sink in the kitchen and pour a glass of water. When he returned to the bed, Claire hadn't moved at all; she was sleeping on her front, her hair in complete disarray. Her expression was peaceful, as if she didn't have a care in the world. She looked *defenceless*.

Nothing could stop me killing her now, Ichi suddenly thought. It would be so easy; his knife even lay forgotten on the floor. But the thought disturbed him. After what had just happened between them Ichi realised that, for the most part, he didn't want to kill Claire at all, even if a small portion of his brain still desired to see her stop breathing permanently. But for what possible reason could Ichi want Claire dead, after having her actually react to him? After realising how glorious it felt to have this girl physically *want* him, and to act upon it? Knowing that Claire lusted after him the same way he did her gave Ichi an entirely different kind of control over the woman sleeping by his side than when he thought Claire had been terrified of him. So why, then, did that small part of his brain still want to kill her? Ichi had no idea. And he had no clue what he was supposed to do once Claire woke up, or what she would do. What were they now?

There was one thing Ichi was deathly certain of: the assassination of the girl happily sleeping beside him was a far more complicated affair than Ichi had been led to believe. Why had Michael and Vic set Ichi up to believe he was supposed to kill Claire in the first place? Why not just make it a cut-and-dry kidnap job? Ichi thought that that would surely terrify Claire's parents more than murdering her, since Michael could do things to their daughter far worse than simply killing her. Ichi didn't understand it at all; maybe it was because he didn't know enough about the situation. He resolved to grill Claire on every detail she could remember to try and piece the puzzle together. It suddenly struck Ichi that he had no idea how far Claire's memory loss went – how could he have been so obsessed with finding out everything about her but failed to gather any information on that? He'd have to fix that now.

Ichi knew that he couldn't walk straight up to Vic or Michael and demand an explanation for why they had double-crossed him. He also knew that he couldn't kill them on the spot for it, even though he badly wanted to. No, Ichi would have to work out what was going on behind the scenes, and he would start by finding out everything Claire knew, significant or otherwise. He glanced over at her, before giving in to the urge to take her in his arms, burying his face in her hair. Claire barely stirred. *She's mine; she always has been. I'm not going to let anyone else do anything to her.*

Ichi woke up again several hours later with a terrible headache. *And there's the hangover I definitely deserve,* he thought. Claire was still sound asleep. Ichi didn't know what he was supposed to do when she woke up, so he swiftly and silently located his clothes which were littered across the floor, got dressed and departed for his own room. He left the knife Claire had stolen from him where it was, though he didn't know why. Once he reached his room, Ichi promptly changed into another t-shirt and jogging pants, deciding to exercise his hangover away. He swallowed some painkillers before he left, hoping that they would help to abate the pain in his head.

The gym was hard-going; Ichi had to get off the treadmill twice to throw up, but he simply filled his stomach back up with water and carried on. It helped to clear his head. He had been running for nearly twenty minutes when Alexis showed up, stretched out her muscles for a couple of minutes before setting up on the treadmill right by Ichi's. They ran in silence for several minutes.

"You look like you've seen better mornings," Alexis finally said, glancing over at Ichi. He ignored her, but she carried on talking anyway. "I heard you had a public altercation with a certain someone yesterday afternoon."

"What of it?" Ichi replied, keeping his eyes focussed on the digital meters of his treadmill. He couldn't be bothered with anything Alexis had to say.

"It's not like you to get so emotional in front of other people, is all," Alexis said, keeping her voice casual but not quite managing to hide the accusatory tone to her voice. "Did something else happen later on?" she ventured. Ichi swung his head around quickly to stare at her, regretting the movement immediately as it sent waves of nausea to his brain. He slowed his treadmill to a stop and got off of it.

"What would make you say that?" he asked, as he took a swig of water to clear his head.

Alexis frowned at him. "You're not nearly as angry as I thought you'd be after what Claire said to you, if I'm to believe Ryan and Imran's account of what happened," she answered. *Damn it, she's sharper than I gave her credit for,* Ichi thought, surprised and annoyed.

"Why does it matter if something else happened, Alexis? It's none of your business," he retorted. And then, after a pause: "It's nobody's business."

Alexis laughed, but it was a hollow sound. "Oh, not my business you say? Okay, I get it. You have fun with that unhealthy relationship of yours," she said, trying to sound nonchalant and failing.

Ichi didn't look at her as he replied, "We never had a relationship, Alexis, so you don't get to judge what I do."

"You think I don't know that, Ichi?" Alexis fired back, her tone bitter. "Just be careful with what you're doing. Claire's not one of us...she doesn't understand how normal it is for us to go to extreme measures to sort out a situation. I somehow doubt, when she gets out of here, that she'll want to be with a guy who kills people for a living,"

Ichi looked at her, one eyebrow raised. "Who said I wanted to be with her?" he asked. He could see that Alexis was struggling not to slap him.

"Are you that much of a fool, Ichi? Ugh, never mind, don't answer that," Alexis muttered. Ichi decided that his work out was not worth dealing with Alexis in her current state of mind, so he left the gym without so much as a glance in her direction.

"I'll just sleep my hangover off like a normal person," he mumbled, then promptly laughed. *Like a normal person? Ha. When have I ever been normal?* When he got back up to his room, he had a shower to further try and clear his head, before collapsing on top of his duvet. He stared at his laptop. "If Claire wants someone normal, then she shouldn't be so damn *abnormal*," he said, quietly. He was tempted to wander back into her room, to see if she was awake or not in person. But Ichi still had no idea what he was supposed to do or say to Claire, and his head hurt terribly, so he abandoned the idea in favour of sleep.

Vic

Vic was hungover. After he had turned away from Claire's door the previous night, he had continued to work his way through the rest of the vodka he had taken from the rec hall, and that had been on top of the hangover he had had from the previous night in the first place. Vic was paying for it with every cell in his body; in fact, he was fairly certain that the only reason he was managing to stay conscious was because he was running on pure anger.

I can't believe Claire slept with Ichi. He didn't want to believe it, not at all. It meant Vic had failed in protecting her from the other man on every level. *Why would you do this, Claire? After everything he's done to you?* Clearly, being held captive by a group of assassins had taken its toll on her decision-making process. And to be fair to her, how could Vic possibly blame Claire? He imagined just about anyone would change after half a year stuck inside the same building with no sunlight or freedom and killers and psychopaths for company. So no, Vic couldn't hate Claire for sleeping with Ichi. He could be *angry* at her though, for delaying her answer to his feelings until she got free, whilst simultaneously running into the arms of a man who had raped and wanted to kill her.

I should have taken the damn rum off her. Vic knew that a sober, level-headed Claire would never have done what she had done, even if she had wanted to. But when Claire got drunk, she acted far more like her younger sister Olivia that she would ever know. Vic paused mid-thought; he forced himself to stop thinking about Claire's family, something he had promised not to mull over for a long time now. And besides, it was Claire's decision whether she got drunk or not. Vic could hardly take away what little free will the girl had left. He felt his anger at her dissipate. *Damn it, my head won't let me be mad at her, and she hasn't even said a word in her defence yet!* But Vic figured that he simply cared for Claire too much to allow what she had done to sully his feelings for her.

"Doesn't mean I want to see her right now though," he grumbled. Vic was lying on his bed with an ice pack covering his eyes, trying to dull the blinding headache that besieged him. He had only stopped throwing up an hour ago, at nearly two in the afternoon. He wondered if Claire was awake and if she was regretting her actions from the night before. He wondered if he should pretend he didn't know what had happened, but his mind flicked to Ichi and he immediately knew that he couldn't. He only hated the other man more for sleeping with Claire. Vic stood up suddenly, swaying on the spot for a moment before he threw on some shoes and headed up the elevator to confront Ichi. *This is a terrible idea,* he thought, but Vic knew that he'd go through with it nonetheless.

When he tried the door handle to Ichi's room, he was surprised to find the door unlocked, so he let himself in. Ichi was collapsed on his bed, seemingly fast asleep, but his head turned at the sound of somebody entering his room. "Oh. It's you. Should've known," Ichi complained, making to roll over and ignore Vic entirely. Vic stopped when he reached Ichi's bed, looming over the man until he finally sat up to acknowledge him.

"Why the hell did you sleep with her?" Vic demanded, cutting straight to the chase. "Why couldn't you leave her alone?"

Ichi frowned at him. "I'm not even going to ask how you know what happened," he said, running his hand through his hair, wincing as he did so. "God, I don't feel any better at all."

"Don't deflect my questions!" Vic exclaimed.

Ichi looked up at him. "I can do what I like. It's not like I forced myself on her. But...you knew that already," Ichi said, figuring out the truth for himself. He almost smiled. "Ah, that's why you're pissed. I'm not going to apologise because she didn't go running to you, Vic. Let her make her own damn decisions, even if you don't like them." Vic almost punched him.

"How can you act like what you did isn't wrong?! After everything you've done to her? Claire's a captive here – you're not giving her a chance to work out how she actually feels about anybody! And she can't work that out until she's free of –"

"And when will that be, Vic?" Ichi interrupted, a frown on his face. "Michael doesn't seem to be any closer to finding her parents than he was half a year ago. So unless you know something I don't, I'd say we should let Claire make whatever decisions she wants to make whilst she's here." Vic flinched. *He knows something he shouldn't.* Ichi was trying to stare Vic down, as if daring him to admit that there was more happening than Vic was letting on. But Vic couldn't afford to be baited into telling Ichi something he couldn't know.

"Just…leave her alone, Ichi. And I will too. What happens to Claire is nothing to do with us, much as we want it to be." It hurt Vic to say those words. Ichi looked away from him, frowning. Eventually, however, he nodded his head slowly in agreement.

"Fine." Vic felt his eyebrows rise in surprise. Ichi glared at him. "What, you don't expect me to be reasonable here?"

"Truthfully?" Vic replied. "Absolutely not." It was Ichi's turn to sigh.

"Well," Ichi began, "I don't need you to believe me for me to do it. So just let me sleep off this Godforsaken hangover." He glanced at Vic. "I suggest you do the same." Vic said nothing as he turned around and walked away.

Maybe I just imagined that he's on to me. Maybe my brain turned his words into what I was scared to hear. He looked at the door to Claire's room as he passed it, wondering whether he should simply ask her directly if she had told Ichi about the set-up of her kidnap. But as soon as he thought about it, he realised that it was a terrible idea. If Vic were to bring it up again then it would only confirm to Claire that it was a far more important element to what was going on than Vic wanted her, or Ichi for that matter, to know, and that was the last thing in the world that Vic wanted to deal with.

Claire

Claire was horrendously hungover. She couldn't remember ever having a hangover as bad as this, not even from her fresher's week when she started university. *But for all I know I've just forgotten them, like everything else.* She waved the thought away – she felt far too awful to indulge in any deep thinking.

Claire had no idea how many hours she had slept, only that it felt like a very long time. When she finally woke up, it took her several minutes to wrap her head around what she had done the night before, and once she realised she felt her face heat up. *Oh my God. Oh my God.* Claire crept around her room, looking to see if Ichi was somehow hiding out of sight. She spied his knife on the floor, the one she had tried to use against him, but all of his other possessions were gone, as well as the man himself. *Well, except for his leather jacket. But he doesn't know I have that.* Claire walked over to her wardrobe and took it out. She looked at it, not quite seeing anything.

"Shit," she mumbled, burying her face in Ichi's jacket. "That was definitely a mistake." And to make her feel even worse, Claire remembered *everything* that had occurred, so she couldn't hide behind the possibility that things weren't as bad as they seemed. She put Ichi's jacket back in her wardrobe and then walked over to her shower room to tentatively look in the mirror. Claire winced as she saw the state of her skin; it was covered in slowly developing bruises on her neck, shoulders, breasts...

"*Shit,*" she cursed. Claire turned her shower on, hoping the hot water would help alleviate both her hangover and her conscience, but she found that it didn't do much for the former and absolutely nothing for the latter. Instead, Claire mulled over everything that had happened as she inhaled the steam that surrounded her to clear her head. She felt her face grow red again as she remembered exactly how each and every one of the bruises on her skin had appeared, and how God damn amazing it had felt having Ichi's mouth all over her skin in the first place. It was as if he simply couldn't get enough of her. "Stop thinking about it, Claire," she muttered scornfully. *I'm supposed to regret what I've done, not revel in the memory of it.* But how could she feel bad about having sex with Ichi when it had felt so *good?* "It's not fair," she complained.

But then Claire thought of Vic, and her memory of the previous night was immediately sullied. Claire held her head in her hands, both because it ached and because she felt ashamed. She slid down on to the floor of her shower. "What the hell have I done?" And then she remembered what she had said to Ichi that had started everything between them the night before. Claire looked up from her hands and felt her face grow cold, despite the heat of the shower. "*What the hell have I done?*" she repeated, hating herself. *What if Ichi asks Vic why my assassination was never supposed to happen? What if he asks* Michael? *What if...*all of the hypothetical situations swirling around in Claire's head made her feel so nauseous that she promptly ran out of her shower, barely making it to the toilet before she threw up.

After putting some clothes on, drinking a glass of water and taking some painkillers before brushing her teeth, Claire crawled back into bed to try and sleep away more of her hangover. She knew she had to find Vic, but she couldn't face him in the state she was in now. And Ichi...*what do I say to him? What do I* do? Claire had no idea. It was only as she was drifting off to sleep that Claire realised that this was the first time since arriving at the complex that she had willingly gotten into her bed to sleep. *Last night doesn't count,* she thought sleepily, before her eyes drooped shut and she lost consciousness.

When she woke up again, Claire was immensely thankful that her hangover seemed to have abated somewhat, but it had been replaced with a sharp hunger that hurt her stomach almost as much as the nausea had. Claire wasn't surprised by this – she hadn't eaten since lunch time the previous day, and she figured it must be mid-afternoon at least by now. Suddenly, she heard a noise outside her door, and Claire spontaneously grabbed the blanket from her couch, draping it over herself to cover her bruised neck and shoulders to see who it was.

"Vic!" she called out hoarsely, realising as she spoke that her voice was rough from disuse. The blonde haired man turned around, not at all surprised by Claire's exclamation. He stopped where he stood, waiting for the elevator, but he didn't say a word. "Vic, I –"

"Save it, Claire," Vic interrupted, waving her words away with a hand. "I'm in no position to judge you. I just...don't want to see you right now, okay?" He turned his face away from Claire's. She gazed at the floor, ashamed and horrified at the realisation that Vic definitely knew what she had done. For half a moment, her brain wondered how he did.

"Okay," she replied, as the elevator doors pinged open and Vic got in without another word. Claire retreated back into her room. "Well I deserved that," she said to the air. Resigned to a day of self-resentment and guilt, Claire got changed into clothes that did a better job of hiding the bruises on her skin before heading down to the rec hall for some food. To Claire's relief, nobody was there when she gingerly opened the doors and entered the hall. When she reached the kitchen, Claire heard Roger whistling tunelessly to himself, spotting him by the freezer a moment later. "Hey, Roger," she said, trying to sound as if she didn't have a care in the world. Roger turned around at the sound of her voice and grinned.

"I hear you put someone in their place yesterday, Miss Danvers," he said. Claire's insides squirmed uncomfortably at the double entendre in his words that she wasn't entirely sure Roger had intended. *How could he possibly know what happened last night anyway? Unless Ichi or Vic said something...and why would they?* Roger eyed her up critically. "You look a little worse for wear," he commented.

Claire grimaced. "I feel it, too. I need food, and quickly. Please," she added on, remembering her manners.

Roger smiled at her. "Go have a seat and I'll fix you up something." Claire returned the smile and did as she was told, sitting down at the nearest table to the kitchen. She sat in silence for a while, head resting on her arms, when Ichi suddenly appeared, took one look at Claire and promptly turned tail and left. Claire sat up, frowning. *What the hell was that?* she wondered. *Maybe he's too hungover to deal with last night, like I am...* but Claire wasn't convinced. Ichi was definitely not the type of person to avoid what had happened between them. *Or is he?* Claire realised that, in reality, she knew nothing about Ichi at all.

When Roger handed her a bacon sandwich, Claire wolfed it down and forced herself not to think about Ichi or Vic or the situation she was in. She could hardly think about anything rationally when she still felt so bad. *Tomorrow I'll deal with my problems...today they don't exist.* And yet it appeared that the powers that be disagreed with Claire, because as she exited the rec hall she ran into Alexis who, for the first time in months, stopped to speak to her.

"I'd be careful if I were you, Claire. You know fine well that Ichi isn't just a normal guy," the other woman said, cutting straight to the point.

"Why the hell does everyone bloody *know?*" Claire protested, ignoring Alexis' warning.

Alexis narrowed her eyes at her. "Not everyone. But they all will sooner or later. Ichi's a terrible liar, after all."

"No he's not," Claire bit back almost immediately, knowing that she was correct. "He gets himself deliberately caught in a lie sometimes so nobody knows when he's lying about stuff that matters." *How do I know this?* Claire pushed the thought away.

Alexis smirked at her. "I didn't know you were such an expert on his behaviour," she replied sarcastically, before growing serious again. "Can't you just keep your head down and not attract attention to yourself until Michael finds your parents?"

Claire glared at her. "How dare you tell me what to do. *How dare you!*" she replied, anger colouring her voice. "You don't give a damn about me – you've made that perfectly clear. So don't pretend to start now." Alexis' expression turned sad, but only for a second; Claire almost thought that she had imagined it.

"You can think what you like, Claire," the other woman said as she started walking away from her towards the rec hall. "Just…don't be stupid. You're not here by choice, like any of us. You should wait until you have your life back before you make any reckless decisions, otherwise you might not have a life to go back to."

"But I *don't* have one to go back to. What do I have left?" Claire wondered aloud in a small voice once Alexis had closed the door behind her. She felt her eyes begin to sting as she thought of Olivia, and the fact that for all Claire knew, her sister could be dead. She shook her head violently. "Stop thinking like that, stop it!" But Claire couldn't help it. She ran up to her alcove under the fourth floor stairs and let herself cry, something that she hadn't allowed herself to do in months. She cried about Ichi and Vic and even about Alexis. She cried for Olivia. But most of all she cried for herself, because there was nothing else that she could do.

CHAPTER 21
Nothing Ever Happens

Claire

Claire hadn't spoken to Vic or Ichi for nearly a month. She had expected the silent treatment from Vic, but not four weeks of it. Claire didn't know what she was supposed to expect from Ichi. Paired with the fact that both Marie and Ryan had been sent away on undercover work two weeks prior and Imran had been in and out of the complex doing endless odd jobs for Michael, Claire was beginning to feel incredibly lonely and isolated.

Claire was getting ready to head down to the practice rooms to go over some taekwondo patterns by herself. It frustrated Claire that, with Vic not speaking to her, her training had also come to a stand-still. Michael had forbidden Claire from practicing with knives and guns unless she was supervised – Vic had informed her of this months ago, when he had begun teaching her. And Claire obviously couldn't practice self-defence without a partner. She sighed. It had been her only outlet, and now she had none. Running or swimming in the pool did nothing to alleviate Claire's boredom anymore, so she was consigned to try and perfect what she remembered of the various martial arts patterns that Vic had started to teach her before she ruined everything by sleeping with Ichi.

But it isn't fair, Claire complained as she waited on the elevator. Vic didn't have the right to be so angry at her for doing what she had done. It was hardly like she had made the decision to have sex with Ichi in a normal setting, whilst knowingly going out with Vic. Her life right now wasn't *normal,* so normal rules didn't apply. *Claire* was the one being held prisoner, not Vic. *Claire* was the one who was rightfully confused about how she felt about everything and everyone in the damn complex. *Claire* was the one who was subsequently vulnerable and in need of some kind of coping mechanism. So why had her actions resulted in Vic childishly ignoring her? Why couldn't Vic just take what Claire had done and accept it, given her circumstances? He had promised that he would be there for her, and now he wasn't. Claire couldn't help but wonder whether Vic had only ever said any of those wonderful things that had gotten her through her time in captivity because he had merely wanted to sleep with her. However, Claire balked at the idea immediately. Vic *had* been genuine to her without any ulterior motive, and there was still that overarching feeling Claire got when she was with him that she could trust him one hundred percent.

Which meant that Vic ignoring her was really just due to childish and unfair jealousy. Claire had nearly confronted him about it several times over the past few weeks, but she realised that in doing so she would be acting just as childish. So Claire resolved to let Vic have his tantrum until he realised he was acting horrendously like a fourteen-year-old boy.

As Claire stepped into the elevator, she wondered whether thinking that sleeping with Ichi had been a 'coping mechanism' was really just her lying to herself. *I'm weak-willed. I gave in to my stupid impulse to throw caution to the wind and literally screw the most dangerous person in my life.* And if that was a coping mechanism to help Claire deal with her situation, then maybe she needed to start questioning her sanity.

As the lift descended to the ground floor, Claire realised that Ichi was, in fact, *not* the most dangerous person in her life. That position was most definitely reserved for Michael. It disturbed Claire that she could go for days without thinking about the man who had had her kidnapped for use as a bargaining chip. *But I'm not just that. I'm the key to whatever it is he needs to know.* Claire couldn't help but wish that Michael would hurry up and find her parents, and not because of concern for them. She had forced herself to stop feeling anything for her parents months ago, so that she wouldn't mentally break down from worrying about them and Olivia and herself. No, what Claire couldn't stand, and was dying to resolve, were her lost memories. And she was sure that the only way to get her memories back would be for Michael to find her parents and for them to give her whatever password it was that Claire needed to unlock them. Thinking about her lack of memory made her head hurt, as it always did; it was like trying to read the most miniscule text through somebody else's glasses. And Claire hated that she could do nothing about it. She had to rely on her parents to show up, and Claire was beginning to increasingly believe with every passing day that they wouldn't.

Claire had planned on asking Michael about the progress of his man-hunt when she had been deliriously drunk, but after a few days of solid reflective thinking Claire had realised that it was a terrible idea. What if Michael told her nothing, but had her punished for asking in the first place? What if he told her something that she didn't want to hear? Claire didn't know enough about the man to work out what he would do. And by 'didn't know enough' she meant 'absolutely nothing at all', aside from the fact that Michael had clearly known Claire's mother well. Michael had told Claire, months ago, that they would discuss that at another time, but that conversation had never happened. In fact, Claire hadn't even seen Michael since she had first needed to see the doctor.

When the elevator reached the ground floor, Claire made a spur-of-the-moment decision to go bounding down the stairs to the sub-basement floor. Once she reached it, she wandered over to the glass doors that led to the laboratory that was so identical to that of her parents'. And then she just stood there, not quite sure what her plan had been in the first place. The uncanny resemblance between this lab and her parents' one did nothing to jog Claire's memory; all it did was make her feel incredibly sad. She glanced at the keypad and could feel the fingers on her right hand tingling. Claire knew that she shouldn't enter the code to open the door. *I shouldn't know the code in the first place,* she thought. And yet she did, her subconscious having written it to memory after watching both Michael and the doctor enter it. *It's sixteen characters long, how did I even manage to remember it?* Claire waved the worry away; too many strange things had happened in the past year of her life for her to worry about it. She returned her gaze to the lab, wishing that staring at it longingly enough would transform it into her parents' lab and return everything in her life back to normal. Claire sighed.

"So which of your numerous problems have you come all the way down here to mull over, Miss Danvers?" a male voice murmured softly to her left. Claire felt her heart thump painfully in her chest as she turned and realised it was Michael. *Oh shit.* Michael was standing a few feet away, his grey eyes watching her carefully, waiting for an answer.

Claire swallowed. "I don't know why I came down here," she replied, looking at the floor. "I'm sorry, I know I shouldn't be down here. I just…I don't know. I wanted to see something familiar." Claire was disgusted at her honesty. *Why can't I just lie to him?* She brought her head back up

201

sharply to look at Michael when she heard him laugh, his expression amused.

"I expected you to have come down here to look at the lab months ago. I'm surprised it took you so long."

Claire frowned. "So…you're not angry?"

Michael laughed again. "You haven't done anything for me to be angry about, Miss Danvers." He regarded her critically for a moment before continuing, "I'm also surprised you haven't demanded to know if I've tracked your parents down yet." Claire felt her cheeks grow red. *It's like he knew I was thinking about it. Though I suppose he* would *expect me to be curious about it.*

"I somehow doubt 'demanding' anything from you will get a response I want," Claire ventured, daring to be frank.

Michael grinned. "You're correct on that front." He waited patiently for Claire to continue.

"I didn't know if you would actually tell me anything," she eventually admitted, "Or you could lie. Or you could tell me the truth. Either way; I wouldn't know. Or you could be angry that I asked in the first place and punish me…" Claire felt her words trail away to nothing as she realised she was rambling.

Michael kept his expression mild as he replied, "All of your suggestions are plausible; I'll grant you that. But I will say this – when any information comes to me that is relevant to you, I will inform you…eventually." Claire was taken aback by his statement.

"Why would I believe that?" she asked.

Michael smiled slightly. "For the same reason that you believe that I'll let you go once I have everything I need from you. Because you have to." Claire forced herself to match Michael's stare. *I can't allow myself to feel inferior to him. I have the upper hand.*

"Then you better hope for your sake that you actually mean to let me go," she said.

Michael raised an eyebrow at her. "Is that so?"

"Yes," Claire continued, keeping her voice as level as possible, "Because if you have no intention of letting me go, then I have no intention of giving you what you want." She saw Michael's pale eyes darken, but she continued on anyway. "That's how a bargain works, right?"

"Indeed it is. Though I should warn you against making threats, Miss Danvers." Michael's jaw tightened as he spoke.

Claire kept up her brave front nonetheless. "It's not a threat at all if you mean to release me," she replied, smiling. "Unless there's something I don't know?" Michael let out a bark of humourless laughter.

"There's plenty you don't know." He took a step towards her; Claire forced herself to stay rooted to the spot. "You have guts, I'll grant you that," Michael conceded, and then: "So did Joanna."

The comment caused Claire's temper to flare. "Don't speak about my mother like that!" Claire bit back without thinking. Michael raised his eyebrows in surprise at her sudden outburst. *Crap. I think I may have crossed a line.* "I mean," Claire continued, attempting to climb out of the hole she had fallen into. "Don't talk about her if you're not going to actually tell me how you knew her, like you said you would…"

Michael smiled a shallow smile. "Then I guess this conversation is over. That subject is for another time. You should get going, Miss Danvers," he replied, gesturing up the stairs. The tone of his voice brooked no argument.

Claire inclined her head slightly. "Until next time, then," she said, forcing herself to turn her back on a man she absolutely didn't trust. *I guess I'm not as detached from my parents as I thought I was,* Claire mused as she rushed back up the stairs to the ground floor. *I don't want to hear Michael talking so familiarly about my mother. Not when he's probably the reason she's gone and I'm stuck here.* When Claire reached the main practice hall, she badly wished to have a sparring partner to vent her frustrations out on, but she knew that that wish was in vain. Instead, Claire slowed her breathing down and tried to recall the taekwondo patterns that Vic had been teaching her, starting from the simplest ones.

Claire would start the pattern from the beginning again every time she got a move wrong until she could do the whole thing perfectly. She would recite every move as she did it for the first few run-throughs, to engrain the pattern into her brain.

"Front stance, high block…mid punch…back stance, knife-hand guard…" Claire recited, until the transition from one move to the next was seamless and graceful.

"Not bad," she heard a male voice say after a while. Claire looked up, surprised; it was Imran. Claire had no idea how long he had been standing there. "Vic only ran through them with you a couple times, didn't he? Good memory."

"Weren't you meant to be out on a job for a few days?" Claire asked.

"I got back early," Imran replied. "I'll leave if you want, I was just wondering where everyone was." He made to turn for the door.

"No, wait!" Claire protested. *I wonder if he'll help me.* "I haven't had anyone to spar with for weeks. I'm rubbish at defending myself hand-to-hand, and I'm not going to get any better at it unless I can practice."

Imran looked puzzled. "What about Vic?"

Claire looked at the floor. "We're not exactly speaking right now, in case you hadn't noticed."

Imran laughed. "Oh, I noticed, I just wanted to see if you'd tell me why." Claire frowned at him and stayed silent. "Okay, okay, touchy subject," he continued, grinning, "You're going to have to be nicer to me if you want my help though."

Claire considered him for a moment. "I can play nice," she replied, finally. "I've not been in much of a talkative mood as of late, though."

Imran took his jacket off and walked towards her as he said, "Trust me, I'm not going to give you much time to talk if you want to train seriously."

Claire smiled. "That's *exactly* what I want," she remarked as they both got into ready stances, every nerve in Claire's body tingling with the urge to fight.

Ichi

Ignoring Claire for a solid month had been one of the hardest things Ichi had ever had to do since beginning to work for Michael. He had to ensure that he never ran into her in the corridors, the gym, the swimming pool, rec hall and practice rooms. To avoid her, Ichi essentially stayed holed up in his room for as long as possible, and timed his work outs for when Claire would return to her room to shower after having hers. That meant he couldn't watch said showers on his laptop as they happened if he wanted to exercise.

It left Ichi incredibly frustrated, having exercise as his only, disappointing outlet to let off some steam; he had only worked on two incredibly short jobs for Michael in the past month and he obviously wasn't going to sleep with Alexis anymore, so he was full of unused energy. And all he wanted was *Claire*.

Damn you, Vic. For it was Vic's fault that Ichi felt obliged to ignore Claire, even though he hated to. Or, rather, it was Ichi's fault for actually listening to Vic's request to leave her alone. *But what else can I do? I can't talk to Claire about what happened to her without raising Vic and Michael's suspicions. She's no doubt under their constant surveillance.* And that was the crux of the matter – to work out what exactly was going on, Ichi would need to speak to Claire, but to do so would alert Vic to what was going on. *And then what? Will Michael get rid of me? Will he hurt Claire? Would Vic allow that?* Ichi had been mulling over such questions constantly for the past four weeks. He figured that Vic would surely never allow something bad to happen to Claire if he cared about her so much, but what if his supposed feelings for her were part of a very clever act? It was what Vic was best at, after all. However, Ichi wasn't convinced by that in the slightest. Vic seemed to possess some very deep-rooted feelings for Claire, although Ichi wondered when that had occurred. It sometimes felt, to Ichi, that Vic had felt like that from the very beginning. But how could somebody feel so deeply for a person they had only just met? Ichi couldn't help but wonder whether Claire had known Vic before, and simply couldn't remember because of her memory loss. Ichi shook his head. *How could that be possible? Under what circumstances could she have met an assassin prior to her parents going missing? I don't understand.* That much was true: there were so many things Ichi couldn't possibly fathom right now.

But the most pressing issue was learning what Claire remembered, and what she didn't. And to figure that out Ichi had to speak to her.

"Oh for fuck's sake," Ichi cursed aloud. He couldn't stand his brain picking at the same problems over and over again, so he decided to head down to the practice rooms to let off some steam. Though the cameras in Claire's room showed him that she wasn't there, Claire had been gone for so long that Ichi couldn't stand to wait in his own room for any longer to stretch his muscles. *What would I even say to her?* Ichi wondered as he jogged down the twelve flights of stairs to the ground floor. *What if she doesn't want to speak to me, after I've ignored her for so long? What if she doesn't want to speak to me regardless of that? What if she completely regrets sleeping with me? What if she truly does hate me now?* The thoughts agonised Ichi far worse than thinking about anything else. He didn't know for how much longer he could stand to pretend that Claire didn't exist. *Even if I could just talk to her about things that didn't matter. That wouldn't raise suspicions...* Ichi paused on the second floor staircase as he realised that it actually would. He didn't *do* small talk; Michael would be on to him in a second. But Michael had never expressly told Ichi not to ask Claire about what was going on. Could he risk asking her, even just once, to see what Michael would do? Ichi wasn't sure, though he didn't entirely dismiss the idea. He continued jogging down the stairs.

Once he reached the viewing gallery by the largest practice room, Ichi stopped in surprise. Vic was there, watching two people sparring through the glass. It took Ichi only half a second to work out that those two people could only be Claire and Imran before he joined Vic to watch as well. "How long have they been practicing?" Ichi asked the other man. They hadn't spoken much since Vic had told him that they both needed to leave Claire alone.

Vic threw a quick sideways glance in Ichi's direction before replying. "Long enough. They haven't even realised I've been here for nearly twenty minutes." Vic paused, considering something. "Or if they have noticed, they're doing a great job of pretending they haven't. I wouldn't put it past Claire to be ignoring me watching. I'd deserve it." He sighed.

Ichi frowned at him. "Do we really need to keep ignoring her? You can't stand it...and neither can I," Ichi responded, truthfully. Vic's hands gripped the wooden frame underneath the glass a little too tightly.

"It's not about what we want. Claire needs her own space until she gets out of here. She should have had it from the beginning. But I – we – were too selfish. You can't say that you don't agree with that, Ichi."

It was Ichi's turn to sigh. "Fine. Whatever. You're right, again. Happy?" Vic laughed humourlessly.

"Not even close." They continued watching in silence as Imran and Claire fought. It took Ichi a few minutes observing them to realise something glaringly obvious.

"Vic," he said, once he worked it out.

Vic didn't bother looking at him as he replied, "What?"

"She's really good."

"I know."

"But that makes no sense. She was terrible against you."

"I know."

Ichi frowned. If Claire had no problem fighting against Imran, and was indeed very, very good at it, then that… "Then that means –"

"*I know*," Vic said for the third time. He shook his head, looking at the floor. "I know. It means that something was stopping her from fighting me properly. But that could have been because of a whole host of things." Ichi could feel the stirrings of what he assumed could only be jealousy at Vic's words.

"You know fine well it's because she cares for you," he replied tartly, suddenly incredibly pissed off.

Vic looked at Ichi, surprised. "You're actually acknowledging that?"

Ichi threw a glare at him. "Why do you keep acting like I don't notice anything? I'm not a fool."

Vic looked away. "That's not what I meant. I figured you were so intent on monopolising Claire that you'd ignore how she felt about me." It was Ichi's turn to release a bark of mirthless laughter.

"Not likely," he said. "I used her feelings for you against her, truth be told."

"You *what*?!" Vic demanded angrily.

Ichi held up his hands in protest. "Don't act like you wouldn't expect me to. I was trying to get a rise out of her. It never worked though," Ichi replied.

Vic eyed him suspiciously. "Why not?"

Ichi rolled his eyes. "Because somehow you're a freaking saint in her eyes. She's never doubted your sincerity for a second, which meant that nothing I said could twist her into thinking otherwise." They both turned their stares back to the sparring match in front of them, as Claire parried off an attack from Imran, grabbing his arm when he attempted a counterattack and twisting it down, simultaneously using her left leg to knock his feet out from underneath him, causing him to collapse to the floor. They were both laughing and breathing hard as Claire held out her hand to help Imran to his feet.

"You're still the one she slept with," Vic mumbled, almost to himself.

Ichi turned his head around to look at the other man. "Huh?" he asked.

Vic's face was blank as he replied, "You say she cares for me, so much so that you couldn't do anything to damage how she felt about me. But even then, the one Claire chose to sleep with that night was you."

Ichi looked at his feet, suddenly very uncomfortable. "It's probably just because I was there..." he replied, knowing that it was completely untrue.

"Ha!" Vic laughed. "Don't lie to me. It doesn't matter. I know she has some fucked up feelings for you."

Ichi scowled at him. "You're not allowed to be judgemental on that matter."

"I can be as judgemental as I want." Vic shook his head again. "I don't know why I bother with you sometimes, Ich."

Ichi shrugged his shoulders, choosing to take the sarcastic, petulant way out. "Then don't," he replied, leaving the viewing gallery before Vic could counter him. Ichi headed to the gym instead, kicking off his shoes and impulsively launching himself into the swimming pool fully clothed once he got there. He swam for a long time, vaulting off of the sides of the pool every time he reached them using all of his pent-up energy. Ichi knew the release it gave him wouldn't last long but, for now, it would do.

Eventually, however, Ichi's clothes started to feel heavy and his deft strokes through the water got slower and clumsier. "Guess it's time I stopped, then," he muttered as he dragged himself out of the water, wondering what he was supposed to do now. He wasn't hungry. He wasn't tired. Ichi sighed in resignation as he pulled his t-shirt off to wring it of excess water before slinging it over his shoulder, then grabbed his shoes and made for the lift. He didn't care about the fact that he was dripping water onto the corridor floor as he waited on it. Once it opened its doors to let him in, Ichi reluctantly pressed the twelfth floor button and rested his forehead against the mirrored wall. *I'm so bored. What did I actually do before I had Claire to fixate on? I don't even know.*

When the elevator reached the twelfth floor, Ichi thought he could hear a female voice singing. When the doors pinged open, he cautiously exited out onto the corridor to the sight of Claire sitting against the wall opposite her room, singing along to something on her laptop. Going by the sound blaring from her headphones, she was watching it at full volume. Claire was completely and utterly unaware that Ichi had just entered the corridor, and so continued to sing along with whatever it was that she was watching. Ichi cocked his head to one side, listening intently. *Is she singing in Japanese? Or attempting to, anyway,* he thought, smirking. He walked over to Claire with long, deliberate strides to make it obvious that he was there. However, when Claire noticed him she jumped in surprise regardless, her facing flushing a furious red as she gingerly removed her headphones.

"What are you doing out here?" Ichi asked her, curious. Claire looked down at her laptop, pausing whatever it was that she was watching. When she made no attempt to answer his question, Ichi chose to sit down next to her, despite the fact that he was soaking wet and only half-dressed. Or maybe it was *because* of that and he was hoping to get a reaction out of her; Ichi wasn't sure. "So," Ichi pressed on, "What are you doing out here?" Claire kept her gaze locked on her laptop screen. Ichi craned his neck over to see what she was watching. *Anime. Huh. Explains why she was singing in Japanese.*

Then Ichi looked straight out at the wall in front of him as he suddenly remembered something – an obscure reference made by both Claire and Marie that Ichi had had no understanding of. Hadn't Marie then been surprised that nobody at the table had deciphered the reference's meaning because they had never watched *anime?* "Claire," Ichi began, casually. "Who's Edward Elric?"

Claire flinched at his question, and her face grew even redder than it already was. "Why do you care? And why are you wet? And why are you –"

"Ah, so you *are* going to talk to me," Ichi interrupted, grinning. He pulled the laptop out of Claire's grasp and sat it on his knees.

"What are you doing?!" Claire protested. "You'll get it wet! And you're one to complain about me not talking, after you and Vic have pretended I don't exist for nearly a month now."

"So who's Edward in this show then? Who was the person Marie mentioned?" Ichi asked, ignoring Claire's previous statement entirely. He resumed the anime, eyeing up the characters critically as they flashed up on screen in time to the theme song. He paused it again as a character appeared with long, blonde hair kept tied back. "He kind of looks like…" Ichi started to say, but Claire interrupted the thought by grabbing the laptop back and slamming it shut, placing it on the floor to her left.

"Stop acting like we're friends, Ichi!" she bit out.

Ichi raised an eyebrow. "I'm not. I'm just bored." Claire seemed to splutter in anger, struggling to work out how to respond. Ichi smiled at her reaction as he raised his arms to place his hands behind his head. *This is much more satisfying than ignoring her,* he thought.

"I'm not your plaything! You can't just collude with Vic to leave me alone and then decide to talk to me because you're *bored.* No, I don't believe that at all." Claire's hair was loose around her face, all flyaway and messed up. She had clearly finished training with Imran and chose to watch anime straight away, forgoing a shower. Her expression was angry, but the pout to her lips as she spoke prevented Ichi from taking her seriously. The colour in her face had abated just enough for it to return with a fury as Ichi reached out to tuck some of the loose strands of her hair behind her ear. Claire made to swat his hand away, but he grabbed her wrist as she did so.

"What made you think Vic and I are 'colluding' with each other, as you put it?" he questioned, stroking the inside of her wrist slowly with his thumb. He could feel her pulse quickening.

Claire looked away from him quickly, pulling her wrist back as she did so. "You think I didn't notice the two of you speaking to each other when I was sparring with Imran? About me? Don't bother trying to lie, it was obvious," Claire muttered, bringing her knees up to her chest to rest her chin on top of them. Ichi almost chuckled at the put-out expression on her face.

"We have our reasons, none of which I have to relay to you," he replied, glancing up at the ceiling. There were two security cameras in the hallway, though Ichi was about eighty percent sure they were visual security measures only. *Can I risk asking her about her memory loss?*

"Well you can both just stop it," Claire said before Ichi had a chance to ask her anything.

"And why is that?" he replied, keeping his eyes on the ceiling.

"Because you're doing it for some stupid reason like giving me the space you think I need, aren't you?" Claire said, hitting the proverbial nail on the head. She continued: "Otherwise there's no way Vic would still be ignoring me. But in doing so you're taking the decision on who I get to speak to completely out of my hands, so you're actually doing the opposite of 'letting me work things out on my own'. Who knows if I'll ever get out of this place? I'd like to at least have some human interaction whilst I know I actually can."

Ichi forced himself to keep looking at the ceiling as he replied, "And what if we simply don't want to speak to you?" Ichi knew that he was being unnecessarily cruel, but hadn't he always been? Claire seemed to bristle at his words before slumping against the wall, stretching her legs back down across the floor.

"Fine. Go away then," she muttered. Instead, Ichi leaned over her legs to open up her laptop screen. "W-what are you doing, Ichi?!" Claire stammered, sitting up a little straighter to try and avoid him as he brushed past her chest.

"Is this guy who looks like Vic called Edward then?" Ichi pressed on, enjoying Claire's discomfort. Claire battered her fist against Ichi's bare back in protest.

"Why do you *care*? And get off me. I don't get what your angle is here." Ichi laughed, turning his head slightly to look at her but otherwise didn't move.

"I don't know what my angle is yet either. I haven't decided. So who is he?" Ichi asked again.

Claire sighed, blowing flyaway strands of hair out of her face as she did so. "Yes, that guy's Ed Elric. And yes, he reminds me and Marie of Vic a little bit. There. Happy? Now get off." But instead of moving away, Ichi swung one of his legs over so that he could sit in Claire's lap, much to her anger and surprise. "I should have known sitting out here was a terrible idea," she murmured under her breath. "Get off me before I hurt you, Ichi."

Ichi laughed again. "We both know that you're not going to. Why are you sitting out here if it's a terrible idea?" he asked, shaking his head slightly to remove his hair from his eyes. The movement sent droplets of water flying towards Claire, who closed her eyes for a second when one got caught in her eyelashes. When she opened them, she looked Ichi up and down before blushing and averting her eyes from his. Ichi felt like whooping in satisfaction at her reaction.

"I just…I wanted a change of scenery. Clearly this is the wrong scenery. Can't you go back to ignoring me?" Ichi turned Claire's head back around to look at him with his left hand.

"Nope. I don't like it." He stared at her for a few seconds, until his curiosity couldn't take not asking about Vic anymore, regardless of her answer. "Why *haven't* you slept with Vic, Claire? Why with me?"

Claire's eyes grew wide at the question. "Why would you ask me that?" she replied quietly, averting her eyes again as she did so. Ichi could feel the fingers on his right hand drawing circles against Claire's hip, as he always seemed to do when he had her pinned to something.

"Because I can. And because I want to know the answer. You know from experience that I won't leave until I get the answer."

Claire gulped and closed her eyes for a few seconds, as if considering how to reply. "He's a good man. And you're not." Ichi raised an eyebrow at the answer, waiting for her to elaborate. Claire took another deep breath before carrying on. "What I mean is, he's a decent enough guy that I don't want to make any important decisions regarding him whilst I'm here. I want

212

to be completely free so I can be sure of my feelings. And of *his*. And even though I know I might never be free of this place, I...I just have to hope Michael will hold up his end of our deal."

Ichi narrowed his eyes at her. "How do you know Vic's a good guy, truly? It really could all be an act."

Claire laughed mirthlessly. "Do you not think I haven't gone over that idea a thousand times already? I don't know how I know, but I do. It's just a feeling I have. I trusted him from the moment I saw him. And I'm definitely *not* the type of girl who trusts someone they've just met, so I don't really understand it." Claire frowned slightly. "But in a situation where I remember so little, I'm going to cling to anything that feels right. And it feels right to trust him, so I do." Ichi sat back a little from Claire, thinking about everything she had just said. She looked away from him again, her eyes downcast.

"Claire," Ichi said, eventually. She looked up through her eyelashes at him in such a way that made Ichi want to grab a hold of her and possessively never let her go.

"What?" she asked, almost in a whisper.

"Will you tell me everything that's going on? Everything that you remember? Not right this second," Ichi added on, when it looked like Claire might protest. "I don't even know whether there are any repercussions to me knowing anything. But I *want* to know; it's killing me not knowing what's going on. You must have known it would be like that for me, after you told me what you did before."

Claire's face paled a little at the very serious turn the conversation had taken. "Can I tell you in my own time? I...just...Ichi, you terrify me." Ichi flinched at her words. For months, he had made it his personal mission to frighten the woman in front of him, yet now that he knew he did, it left Ichi feeling empty. Claire looked him straight in the eye as she continued, "There's no use in me pretending that you don't for posterity's sake. You do. And I don't know the first thing about you. So how am I supposed to know how you'll react to anything I say?"

Ichi leaned back in towards her, running a hand through her hair as he did so. "So get to know me."

Claire blinked back up at him in response, her expression blank. "What…?"

"Get to know me," he repeated. "Get to know who I am, and then decide whether it's worth telling me anything."

"I literally just told you I think you're a bad person five minutes ago," Claire replied. "Why would you think I actually *want* to get to know you?"

Ichi smiled somewhat sadly at her question. "I *know* I'm a bad person. But it looks like your *good* person isn't telling you much, regardless of whether it's for your own wellbeing or not. So maybe a bad person is exactly what you need to work out what's going on around here."

Claire stared back at him, confused. "Once Michael finds my parents, I'll remember everything anyway. So what's the difference between working it out now and working it out then?"

"All the difference in the world," Ichi replied, seriously. And then he threw caution to the wind, risking that the security cameras truly did not pick up audio. "Don't you want to be the one in control, Claire? Why would you willingly go along with Michael's orders if you can do it your own way?"

Claire frowned at his words. "Wouldn't that be incredibly dangerous?" she asked.

Ichi smirked at her. "Haven't I told you I *love* dangerous?"

Claire half-smiled in return. "I may have inferred that by now." Ichi knew that his mind had stopped thinking about serious matters and had moved on to his physical proximity to Claire when he realised that all he wanted to do was have her remove what remained of his clothing and then her own. But that very notion brought another question to the forefront of his brain.

"Claire, if I'm such a terrible person, then why would you have sex with me?" Ichi was both relieved and excited to see all of the colour that had drained out of Claire's face return in the space of a second.

"Because I was drunk," she began. Ichi looked at her expectantly until Claire sighed. She elaborated, "And because…because I knew I'd regret it. Regardless of whether I slept with you in here or I met you out in the world somewhere and did the same thing, I'd ubiquitously regret it. And if the

214

final result was going to end up being the same regardless of where I was, then that meant it was a safe decision to make." Ichi brought his face closer to Claire's, dying to kiss her. Claire was growing more and more flustered as he got closer.

"And do you?" he asked.

"Do I what?" Claire replied, confused. She brought a hand up to Ichi's chest as if to push him away, but once she touched his bare skin her face flushed ever more scarlet and she immediately brought her hand back.

"Do you regret it?"

Claire held his gaze for a moment before looking away. "I should."

"But you don't."

"I'm still thinking about that."

Ichi chuckled at her response. "Good. I can work with that." And then, with all the self-restraint he could muster, Ichi stood up and walked away towards his room.

"Why are you going?" Claire called out after him.

Ichi turned to look at her. "To get changed into something dry. Why, are you disappointed?" he replied, smirking. Claire shook her head furiously. "Think about my request, Claire. I'll talk to you later."

"Later, then…" she mumbled, as Ichi entered his room and closed the door behind him, wishing that he could rush back out into the hallway and push Claire down onto the floor. But Ichi knew that his best course of action, this time, was to wait for her to come to him. And if their entire conversation was anything to go by, then Ichi wouldn't have to wait for long at all.

Vic

Vic was standing outside Michael's office, having been called there by Alexis who had just returned from an overseas job. Alexis was in the office too, and Vic couldn't help but hear what sounded like arguing coming through the door. *I wonder what's so important that Alexis would dare to disagree with Michael over it,* Vic thought. A minute or two later she came storming out of Michael's office, barely glancing at Vic as she by-passed him.

"You can come in now, Vic," he heard Michael say, the tone of his voice calm and even despite the clearly heated argument with Alexis.

"Is everything okay?" Vic asked as he closed the door to Michael's office behind him and sat down. Contrary to what Vic had expected, Michael looked almost *happy*, not angry.

He smiled at Vic. "Quite. Alexis simply had…issue…with something that she felt the need to vocalise. I'm calling you in here to discuss the subject matter that caused such an issue."

"Which is?" he asked. Michael laced his fingers together and rested his chin on top of them.

"There has been a development in the search for Miss Danvers' parents." Vic struggled to keep his face as placid as possible.

"And this development would be?"

Michael smiled again. "They know that I have their daughter. And they're willing to meet and give me everything I need if I let their daughter go. I must say, your little network of contacts has proven incredibly useful in this search. I give you my thanks."

Vic nodded his acknowledgement of the compliment before speaking. "That's exactly what you wanted to happen. So when are you meeting them?" Vic couldn't help but feel immensely guilty about ignoring Claire for the past month – what if she were gone tomorrow and Vic never saw her again? *I'm such a fool,* he admonished himself. *An immature, jealous fool. I told myself I was ignoring Claire for her sake but I know fine well that that's only half-true.*

"Something on your mind, Vic?" Michael asked with a tone of mild interest. *Get out of your head, Vic,* he cursed as he shook his head.

"Not particularly."

"I'd have thought you would be speaking to Miss Danvers again by now," Michael commented.

Vic raised his eyebrows. "Does it matter if I am or not?"

"Of course. I didn't keep you out of active duty to ignore her. You're supposed to be keeping tabs on our guest, to keep her busy and out of trouble. Why, only four hours ago I found her lingering outside the lab. That's not keeping her out of trouble, now is it?" Vic winced at his words.

"I suppose not. What was she doing?"

"I'm not entirely certain. She said she needed to see something familiar. I believe that to be a half-truth, though Miss Danvers would hardly tell me exactly what she was thinking if it would get her in trouble. That's why I need *you*."

Vic frowned. "But if you've found her parents, why do you need me to keep her out of trouble?" he asked.

Michael smiled. "Which brings us back to your original question. Her parents have demanded that their daughter appear at a safe, public event so that they can ensure that she is indeed alive and unharmed. They have chosen a biological sciences awards ball that takes place in London in June."

"June? But that's two months away!" Vic exclaimed.

"I am aware of that. Clearly they need the time to organise something. So *I'll* be using the time to figure out what that is. And *you*," he said, inclining his head at Vic, "You need to keep Miss Danvers distracted. She cannot know that any of this is going on in case she tries to do something…inadvisable."

"Such as…?" Vic ventured.

Michael smiled his blank, enigmatic smile again. "Oh, there are many 'inadvisable' things our guest could do, none of which I care to divulge. So you have to keep her distracted. Or…" Michael grinned somewhat maliciously, "I could ask Ichi to do so instead." Vic grimaced at the thought. *My feelings for Claire are allowing Michael to treat me like his puppet.*

"How do you propose I distract her?" he asked, keeping his thoughts entirely to himself.

Michael waved a dismissive hand at him. "Get creative. Do something unexpected. Just as long as it takes a while. I'm sure you can work

217

something out." Michael looked at him critically. "You may leave now. If you see Alexis, tell her to come to me once she has calmed down."

Vic stood up, but before he opened the door to leave his curiosity took a hold of him. "What was it that Alexis was so opposed to in all of this?"

Michael's features seemed to harden before he replied, "That is also something I don't care to divulge to you," he said, before turning his gaze away from Vic to rifle through a sheaf of notes he had on his desk.

Well that was incredibly suspicious, Vic mused as he waited on the elevator. *How am I going to distract Claire? She may not even want to speak to me.* Vic realised that he was just going to have to trust that she would forgive his behaviour. When the elevator reached the basement floor, Vic considered going to his own room first to work out how he was going to take up all of Claire's time, but decided against it at the last second and pushed the twelfth floor button instead. *I'll just wing it,* he thought resignedly. Vic hoped that Claire would be in her room – he didn't feel up for having a public confrontation with her in the gym or the rec hall.

He was in front of Claire's door and knocking against its surface before he knew it. *Don't slam the door in my face when you see me Claire, please,* Vic silently pleaded. When Claire answered the door, Vic couldn't help but smile at the sight of her in his t-shirt and those tiny blue shorts of hers. Claire's hair was wet and hung in a braid over her shoulder. She raised her eyebrows in surprise when she saw Vic.

"Oh God, not you too," Claire complained.

"Not me too what?" he asked.

Claire shook her head. "Never mind," she said, crossing her arms over her chest. "What do you want, Vic?"

"To apologise. I've been treating you pretty crappy this past month."

Claire let out a bark of laughter. "Ha! To treat me badly would imply that you weren't acting like I don't exist," she replied scathingly.

Vic sighed. "I know I don't deserve your forgiveness, but..." he grinned at Claire. "You're going to forgive me anyway." Claire tried to keep her expression serious but failed. She looked away.

"Don't try and joke your way out of this one, Vic."

"Aw, princess, don't be like that. I know you miss me. I'm sorry I was having an adolescent tantrum."

Claire frowned at him. "And that's the *only* reason you were ignoring me? Not anything else?" she asked suspiciously.

Ah, she's too sharp for her own good, Vic thought, hiding his alarm seamlessly as he replied, "Multiple reasons or not, I'm sorry. Now tell me you'll forgive me and we can go back to training." Claire's eyes lit up for a second at the mere mention of training again.

"Ah, but I have Imran to help me now, so why would I need you?" she remarked, but she was smiling as she spoke.

"But he can't teach you what I'm going to teach you," Vic said, pretending to be mysterious.

Claire laughed. "And what exactly is it that you can teach me that Imran can't? How to have beautiful hair? Because I'm sorry to tell you, but I rather like my hair."

Vic grinned. "I rather like it the way it is too," he said. "But no, that's not what I'll be teaching you."

Claire looked at him, confused. "Well then, what is it?" Vic stole a glance towards Ichi's door. *Let's see you compete with me at this, Ichi,* he thought.

"Have you ever learned to tango?"

CHAPTER 22
The Boy Does Nothing

Claire

"Have I ever learned to *what*?" Claire exclaimed, incredulous. Her head was only just getting around the fact that both Ichi and Vic had chosen the same day to stop ignoring her – and she couldn't work out if that was a coincidence or not – and now Vic was asking her, seemingly nonsensically, if she could dance. *What does that have to do with anything?*

"To tango. Don't look at me like that, princess," he replied when he saw the suspicious expression on her face. "Dancing's great for your balance and coordination. It's a fantastic way to build up muscle strength almost everywhere in your body. Everybody in here dances."

Claire raised a sceptical eyebrow. "If it's so great, why didn't you have me do it from the beginning?" Vic laughed. *Damn it, he's right. I've forgiven him for ignoring me already. Why does he have to laugh so endearingly like that?*

"I didn't know how long you'd actually be stuck in the complex for. And I doubt you would have agreed to dancing lessons a few months ago, when all you were focussed on was self-defence."

"Why do you think I'd even consider agreeing *now*?"

"Because you're bored out of your mind." Claire couldn't help but wince at his statement – it was completely true.

She let out an exaggerated sigh. "If I agree to this, will you also go back to teaching me self-defence?" she asked.

Vic shook his head slightly. "Not at first. Besides," Vic added on, when it looked like Claire would protest, "Imran seems to be a better sparring partner for you right now, anyway." *I can't really argue on that point, I suppose,* she thought. Claire narrowed her eyes at Vic, still not entirely convinced with his reasons for teaching her to dance. Vic laughed at her expression. "What's wrong now Miss Danvers?" he joked.

Claire crossed her arms over her chest. "Are you *sure* you don't have any ulterior motives with all of this? Or Michael?" she ventured. Claire almost thought she saw Vic recoil at her question, but in the space of half a second he had regained his composure.

"Of course I have an ulterior motive, princess," he replied, keeping his tone playful. "It's the best way for me to get up close and personal with you!" Vic grinned as Claire made to cuff him across his jaw.

"Don't think I've forgiven you *quite* that much yet, Mr Winters," Claire replied, but she was smiling as she said so. "When do we start?"

Vic looked up at the ceiling as he thought for a moment. "Tomorrow. After breakfast?" Claire was surprised that he didn't suggest beginning right that very moment, but on second thought she realised that it was probably too late in the day to start any kind of proper lesson. *Well, for Vic maybe. I'll be up hours and hours from now, still bored.*

"Okay then," she said. "Tomorrow." And with that, Vic bid her good bye and left. Claire stood in her doorframe, rooted to the spot for what felt like a very long time, wondering why Vic was lying to her.

There's another reason he's teaching me to dance that he's not telling me. Or maybe can't *tell me.* With a sigh, Claire closed the door behind her as she returned to her room and collapsed onto her bed. Ichi's leather jacket lay on her pillow – just before Vic had knocked on her door, she had brought it out of her wardrobe to look at whilst thinking about everything Ichi had said to her earlier that afternoon.

Should I tell Ichi about what Vic's doing? About how I think he's lying? Claire was so confused. Ichi had asked her to tell him about everything that was going on. He wanted to *help* her, if only to satisfy his own curiosity as to what was going on. Michael had used Ichi as a pawn in her kidnap, after all. *But do I* want *his help? And can I trust it? He admits to being a bad person...I can't trust him at all.*

And yet Claire found herself dying to knock on his door that very minute and tell Ichi everything. Everything that she could remember...and everything that she could not. *Maybe talking to somebody else will help me work out where the gaps in my memory are. Maybe Ichi can look at my problem in a whole different light from me and work something out.*

"Or maybe he can't do anything at all," Claire murmured, "Or worse…he *could* do something and chooses not to." After all, Ichi had never said that he wanted Claire to leave Michael's complex. Maybe he wanted to know everything Claire knew to ensure that she *couldn't* leave. Claire suppressed a shudder as she realised that it was an entirely plausible thing for Ichi to do. But then she thought about his excited face in the corridor as he asked her to tell him everything. Claire couldn't bring herself to believe that it had all been an act. *That doesn't mean I should go running to him for help, either.* No, Claire knew that she would have to spend many long, difficult hours weighing up the pros and cons of getting Ichi to help her. Claire glanced at the jacket lying by her head and felt her face flush as she remembered everything else Ichi had said and done in the corridor.

He was so close. And he didn't do anything. But he wanted to. It's as if… "It's as if he's waiting for *me* to make the next move," Claire finished out loud. She absent-mindedly twirled a strand of hair around a finger whilst she granted her brain permission to unashamedly think about Ichi. How the light in the corridor reflected oddly off of the tiny scars that littered Ichi's skin; how his dark, dark eyes were wide in earnest as he asked her to get to know him; how his wet hair was plastered to his forehead like a little kid's, but he didn't care; how his right hand drew continuous, soft circles against Claire's hip as he kept making her look at him. Ichi always wanted her to look at him. Claire shook her head. "Stop it, you idiot! You have bigger things to worry about". But Claire knew that she was getting nowhere on the matter of her lost memories and missing parents on her own; she needed another pair of eyes and ears to work through everything that she could remember.

I wish that person were Vic. Claire sighed heavily. She didn't understand how she could trust a man with so much and yet instinctively know that she shouldn't go to that very man for the help she needed. *He might be loyal to me, but he's also loyal to Michael. And I don't want to find out which of those loyalties is more important to him.* Ichi, on the other hand, was a loose cannon. He didn't seem to have any loyalties whatsoever; everything he did served his own interests and desires. And whilst that made him exactly the kind of person Claire knew she should never, ever trust, it also made him her best bet at actually getting any help against Michael.

"It sounds like I've already made up my mind," Claire murmured, rolling onto her side so that she didn't lie on her still-damp braided hair. *It's not like I can just march on over to Ichi's door tonight. I have to at least make it look like it took me longer to think about than one evening...* Claire's train of thought came to a rapid halt as she realised that there was no reason to delay getting Ichi's help if that was truly all that she wanted. *I'm only making him wait to show him that I don't want to jump his bones as soon as possible...but if I didn't actually want to do that then I'd have no problem going over and getting his help right this very second.*

"Damn it!" Claire cursed aloud. "Stupid, stupid girl. Get a grip." Forcing herself to think about something else, Claire's mind invariably wandered straight back over to Vic. She hadn't known that hearing somebody laugh when she hadn't heard them do so in what felt like an age could make her feel so at ease. It had made Claire feel almost at home, which considering her circumstances was a strange feeling indeed. *I missed him so much.* Claire was fairly certain that she still wanted Vic to pay for ignoring her for so long, but for now she was content to allow their relationship to go back to the way it had been before Claire had slept with Ichi. *Well, at least until I work out what these 'dance lessons' are a cover for.*

As Claire felt herself falling asleep earlier than she had ever done in the entirety of her eight months in Michael's complex, she made the final decision to wait a few days before telling Ichi anything. Her brain was eagerly trying to fool itself into believing that she would only delay getting his help until she had worked out what Vic's true 'ulterior motive' was. However, Claire knew that she would never be able to fool herself as she realised that she was clutching Ichi's jacket to her chest – she didn't even know when she had picked it up off of her pillow. But as she felt her eyelids growing heavy, Claire decided that, for tonight, she couldn't care less.

*

Claire awoke, hours later, dazed and disoriented. A white light was burning on the wall. *But there aren't any lights on the walls of my room,* Claire thought, confused. *They're all on the ceiling.* As she blinked focus back into her vision and gingerly sat up, Claire realised that she wasn't *in*

223

her room. Neither was she in Vic's, nor even down in the rec hall or the gym. A quick scan of her surroundings confirmed that she was under the fourth floor stairwell, in the alcove where she went to be alone. Ichi's leather jacket lay where her head had been; she had presumably been using it as a pillow.

"How in the world...?" Claire wondered, bringing her hand up to her forehead as she felt a massive migraine building up behind her eyes. "I think I might be sick," she said, knowing that she would never make it back up to her room in time to get to the toilet. But as she stood up, Claire felt her vision go black and she collapsed, unconscious, to the floor.

*

When Claire woke up again, the red-hot pain in her head had abated, but that left her feeling no less terrible. Dragging herself up from the floor, Claire stumbled her way out of the stairwell and numbly pressed the button for the elevator. When the doors to the lift pinged open, Claire saw her reflection in its mirrored walls as she pushed the twelfth floor button. She was white as a sheet; a thin trail of dried up blood ran down over her mouth and chin from her nose.

"What the hell happened to me?" Claire whispered, her voice hoarse. When the elevator reached the twelfth floor, it was all Claire could do to force herself back into her room rather than knock down Ichi's door for help, terrified of what had happened and the fact that she couldn't remember it. Claire poured herself a glass of water with shaking hands and forced it down in one go, before turning her shower on and hurriedly stripping off her clothes to sit on the floor of the cubicle, allowing the steaming hot water to burn away the chill in her bones.

Eventually Claire turned the shower off, dried herself and huddled under the duvet on her bed, pulling her Mp3 player out from the bedside cabinet to listen to Irish lullabies ever so quietly. It was a long time before Claire found herself eventually falling back into a third, unsteady slumber.

Vic

Something about Claire seemed slightly off when Vic met her in the mirrored practice hall, its long viewing gallery on the left hand wall empty of watchers. Which, considering Ichi was the only other assassin currently in the building, was not altogether unsurprising. Claire was very pale, the purple shadows under her eyes far darker than they normally were. For the first time in a long time, she looked decidedly frail. *When did she get that thin?* Vic wondered as he gave her a concerned once-over. *Is it just that I haven't looked at her properly in a month?*

Claire gave him a puzzled stare. "What are you looking at, Vic?" she asked.

Vic felt his eyebrows knit together. "Is something wrong, Claire? Are you eating okay?"

Claire waved his questions away with a hand and a smile. "I'm fine, Vic. I just didn't sleep very well last night. But when is that ever a new thing?"

"If you say so…" Vic replied, not at all convinced by Claire's response.

She cocked her head slightly to one side. "So, are we doing this tango or what?" she pressed on, clearly choosing to ignore Vic's worried expression. *I can't push her away by calling her out on this after we literally just made up,* he thought. *I'll have to wait a while before I ask her properly about what's going on.*

Vic smiled at her. "If you think I'm jumping right into teaching you that off-the-bat, you're sorely mistaken, princess," he remarked.

It was Claire's turn to frown. "Then what –"

"I need to teach you the basics, Little Miss Impatient," he scolded. Claire pouted at his admonishment, but made no verbal protest. *God, she's beautiful even when she looks like she just woke up from the dead,* Vic thought longingly. Determined not to get distracted by his own head, Vic pushed the thought away as he took a step towards Claire. When Claire followed suit, Vic laced the fingers of his right hand through Claire's left when they were close enough, placing his other hand on her waist.

Claire was clumsy. So clumsy, in fact, that Vic could scarcely believe it. He spent the next three days teaching her the absolute basics of ballroom dancing and, by the end of those three days, she was only marginally better than she had been in the beginning. Claire kept tripping up over her own feet, stepping on Vic's, spinning too quickly, over-balancing and subsequently falling over…by the end of the first week, Vic couldn't help but conclude that if there was ever something that Claire Danvers was inherently terrible at, it was dancing.

"Look, you're taking yourself too seriously. Stop being awkward and just relax!" Vic found himself telling her on the eighth day. Claire's cheeks were flushed and hot from three hours of practice, and they only grew redder at Vic's words.

"You can't just *tell* someone to be relaxed, you idiot. We can't all be perfect at everything," Claire replied scathingly. Vic let go of her hands for a moment to stare at her, nonplussed.

"Did you just call me an idiot?"

"What does it matter if I did?" Claire placed her hands on her hips, simply daring him to complain.

Vic laughed instead. "I can't believe you called me an idiot, is all. I was beginning to think you'd never realise it."

Claire raised an eyebrow at his statement, her lips curling up into the faintest of smiles. "Realise that you're an idiot?" Vic grabbed on to Claire's hand and twirled her around.

"Absolutely one hundred percent," he replied as Claire let out a laugh. "Only for you though," he added on slightly more quietly, as an afterthought. He glanced at Claire's face. She didn't look any better than she had done a week ago. If anything, she looked even worse.

Claire frowned at him. "Stop looking at me like that."

"Then eat something and get more than two hours' worth of sleep." There. He said it. There was no point tiptoeing around the subject now. Claire cringed at Vic's words and let go of his hand.

"I don't know why I'm like this right now," she replied honestly, looking at the floor. Vic felt his face break into a sympathetic smile.

He reached for Claire's hand again and she let him take it. "You know you can tell me what's up, princess. Or at least let me feed you." Claire smiled at him, but Vic felt like it was guarding some other feeling that he couldn't work out. *What are you thinking about, Claire? What's going on in your head that you feel like you can't share?* He gave her a searching look, which Claire eventually pulled her eyes away from.

"Stop it, Vic. You're embarrassing me," she mumbled, but her face had grown slightly paler as she said so. *I wonder...* Vic began to think.

"Claire, what's the largest glacier in the world?"

Claire flipped her head around to stare at him. "What the hell kind of bizarre question is that?!" she asked, all seriousness in her voice gone.

Vic chuckled. "Never mind, I just wanted to see what you said," he replied, fluffing her hair up as he did so. *Never mind, indeed. I was expecting too much, I suppose.* He gracefully pulled Claire back into his arms to continue practicing.

Claire raised her eyebrows in suspicion. "So now you're just going to gloss over how weird you're acting?"

"Yup."

Claire rolled her eyes. "Vic, what's going on? I thought you were supposed to be looking out for me," she said.

Vic gave her a look. "You know I am. And there *is* a lot going on...I just can't tell you yet," he replied, simultaneously going for the most truthful and dishonest answer. *Not that she'd be able to tell, if she doesn't know.*

Then Vic spied movement behind the glass of the viewing gallery out of the corner of his eye and turned his head to identify what it was; Claire followed suit. Vic felt his spirits drop as he realised that it was Ichi. When it became apparent that Ichi was making no attempt to interrupt them, Vic sighed and turned his attention back to Claire. She was still regarding Ichi, her expression contemplative.

"Claire?" Vic pressed, when she hadn't made any effort to get back into the lesson.

Claire shook her head slightly before looking at Vic. "Sorry, he just distracted me for a moment," she admitted honestly. Vic felt a flash of irritation. *Son of a bitch doesn't even have to do anything to steal her attention.* Inhaling deeply, Vic forced himself to ask a question he didn't necessarily want to know the answer to.

"Claire, do you two...talk at all now?" he asked, changing his words half way through when he realised that he couldn't face asking his actual question.

"Not at all," she replied, so quickly that Vic was taken aback for a second.

"Not...not at all?" he repeated back to her, feeling like a parrot.

Claire gave him a suspicious look. "Why? What does it matter? I only ever pass him on the twelfth floor and in the gym or rec hall sometimes." Vic felt his mouth turn into a grin. He spun Claire around as he had done only minutes before.

"You're so transparent, Vic," Claire laughed, as she struggled to keep her footing whilst Vic continued the spin.

"Well it's good you think so," he replied with a smile, sticking to his half-truthful answers for his own safety. Vic ignored the eyebrow Claire raised at his statement. "Should we continue where we left off?" Claire glanced to her right and saw that Ichi was no longer watching them. She broke away from Vic.

"Actually, I think I might go find Imran and do some sparring if that's okay. He got back this morning, right?"

"Right you are, princess. Well, same time tomorrow? I might even start teaching you to tango, if only to see how hilariously terrible you are at it." He moved out of Claire's reach as she attempted to swat him across the face.

"For all you know it's the one dance I'm capable of. Until tomorrow, it's Schrodinger's tango."

Vic laughed at her statement. "Only you could make a dance so passionate sound so...boring." She smiled at him, and Vic had to try his hardest to resist reaching out for her face and kissing her.

"It must be the scientist in me," she replied. "Though I must say in science's defence that it is entirely *un*-boring."

"Says the scientist," Vic rebuked, and he allowed Claire's playful fist to cuff him across the jaw. He brushed his fingers gently against her knuckles before she dropped her hand back down, blushing slightly.

"Careful, Vic," Claire warned him, though her words were soft.

Vic sighed. "I know, princess, I know. Okay, off to Imran with you. Have fun pummelling him for me."

"I'll try!" Claire called back, rushing out of the practice room a little faster than was strictly necessary.

"This ball can't come soon enough," Vic muttered aloud, running his fingers through his hair as he pondered for how much longer his self-control could possibly last.

Claire

Claire knew that Ichi had been watching her. She could *feel* it. He seemed to observe her every move, even when Claire thought that he couldn't possibly be anywhere near her. Even now, sitting in an empty rec hall, Claire couldn't shake the feeling that his eyes were on her. *He's waiting for my answer, which I foolishly don't want to give him yet.* Though as the first week of dance lessons with Vic passed by, Claire wondered whether waiting really was so foolish. Vic was clearly hiding something from her, though by the way he spoke Claire was beginning to wonder if he didn't perhaps want her to figure out what that something actually was. *Or maybe he's hiding multiple somethings.* But how was Claire to know? She had hoped that spending so much time together again would encourage Vic to tell her about whatever it was that he was keeping from her, thus restoring her absolute faith in him and absolving Claire of her requirement for Ichi's help.

Instead all she got were artfully dodged questions and enigmatic answers. *What does it matter which glacier is the largest? What was that, a trick question?* Claire couldn't work out the point of the question no matter how she thought about it, in much the same way that she couldn't work out how to actually *dance*. It had infuriated Claire at first, how her

229

solid sense of rhythm and timekeeping did nothing to improve her ability to move her feet and arms in such a way that could resemble a dance. And Vic was so *good* at it; effortlessly so. *Is there nothing he can't do?* Claire had thought on more than one occasion.

But Claire felt so incredibly tired. *Maybe I'd be better at all this dancing if I wasn't.* But she knew in her heart that that was untrue – her sparring sessions with Imran were going incredibly well, which meant that there couldn't possibly be any significant problems with her balance, coordination and concentration associated with a lack of sleep. *And appetite. And memory. And basically everything.* Claire had woken up under the fourth floor stairs twice more since the first time it had happened just over a week ago. *I wish I knew what I was doing. It must be the reason why I'm tired and don't want to eat, surely.* Claire sighed. *If none of those are the reasons I'm not improving at dancing, then…*

'Stop being awkward and just relax!' That's what Vic had said. But how could she, when Vic was hiding something from her? But it wasn't just that, Claire knew. The bizarre feeling of déjà-vu that Claire had felt on occasion around Vic in the months since she had met him had drastically increased in the past week. More than once, in the hazy area between wakefulness and sleep, Claire had felt like she had almost worked out why this was. But much to her chagrin, the answer she was grasping for frustratingly slipped out of her fingers as she invariably lost it to sleep. *Funny how at any other time sleep escapes me, but when I want to stay awake I'm asleep before I know it,* Claire thought, frustrated.

"Claire? Earth to Claire?" she vaguely heard someone call behind her. Claire turned her head and was pleasantly surprised to see Marie.

She smiled at the other woman. "Well, I haven't seen you in a while," she said.

Marie laughed. "I was half-hoping you'd be long gone by the time I finished this job," she remarked. Marie glanced up at the ceiling as if she was calculating something in her head. Then she hurriedly sat down on the table Claire was reading at. "I need to go report to Michael a.s.a.p., but I was wondering if you could clear something up for me."

Claire regarded the other woman curiously. "Which would be?" Claire reached for the glass of orange juice sitting in front of her that she was substituting for a dinner that she knew she had no appetite for.

"Did you sleep with Ichi just before Alexis and I left on our jobs a month or so ago?" Claire couldn't stop herself from spraying the juice she had gulped down all over the table in front of her in surprise.

"Excuse me?" she exclaimed between coughs and splutters.

Marie rolled her eyes. "Ah, I knew it," she remarked. "I knew that that had to be the reason for her super bitchy mood when we left. She always gets pissed when *he* shrugs her off," she explained to Claire, sparing a glance over her shoulder at the sound of the rec hall doors opening to let Ichi in and grinning as she realised who it was. "Hey, Ichi, over here!" Marie called.

Oh dear God no, Claire lamented as Ichi seemed to examine the situation in front of him before strolling over. *Just go away, I'm not prepared for this.* She felt herself flinch as Ichi casually sat down in the chair right next to hers, lounging in it seemingly without a care in the world.

Marie giggled softly. "Well, somebody seems happy for once," she remarked. Ichi gave her a half smile, not looking at Claire. But Claire could feel one of his boots against her leg, and she had to resist the urge to kick it away.

"Am I not allowed to be happy, Marie?" he asked, his voice all easy sarcasm. Claire could feel her ears going red just at the sound of his voice; she tilted her head down slightly to allow her hair to tumble over her face. *Idiot, idiot, idiot.*

"Why of course you can be," she vaguely heard Marie reply, but Claire's attention had almost completely diverted to watching Ichi through her curtain of hair. Had he edged his chair over just a little bit closer to hers? Had he curled his foot around her leg, just a little bit more than before? Claire wasn't sure if she was imagining it or not. "Although the two of you seem to have done something to make Alexis unhappy." *I hate you, Marie,* Claire thought as she felt her face flush at the other woman's goading. *I hate feeling like a silly schoolgirl.*

"Oh, have we now?" she heard Ichi chuckle in amusement. Claire thought that if her face grew any hotter than it already was then the man inching closer and closer to her would be sure to feel it. She recoiled in shock as Ichi tucked several strands of Claire's fallen hair behind her ear and grinned at her. "I don't suppose you're aware of what Marie is on about,

231

are you?" Ichi asked her, his eyes bright and mischievous. Claire kept her eyes on Marie, who was watching the two of them interact as if they were some kind of social television experiment.

"I'll leave you to it, then," she laughed. "You've pretty much confirmed everything for me anyway. Bye, Claire!" She waved and walked away from them, ignoring Claire's half-formed protests at her exit. After what felt like several excruciatingly slow minutes, during which Ichi made absolutely no move whatsoever, Claire forced herself to meet his gaze. Ichi's expression seemed to have grown slightly more serious since Marie's departure. She made to swat the hand that was still by her face away, but Ichi grabbed onto Claire's wrist instead. He raised his eyebrows as he did so before frowning at her wrist, and she felt his fingers wrap around it more tightly.

"Oh God, not you too," Claire complained, annoyance at Ichi's notice of her weight loss pulling her out of her inability to speak as she wrenched her wrist out of his grasp and stood up.

"I didn't say anything," Ichi remarked, and Claire heard him scrape his chair back as he stood up behind her. She had taken but a few steps towards the exit when she felt Ichi's arms wrap around her waist to stop her from leaving, pulling her close. Claire's breathing hitched as she felt Ichi's lips against her ear. "You can't ignore me forever," he murmured, and all Claire wanted to do was turn around and kiss him. Instead, she pulled out of his grasp and continued to walk away.

"Just watch me try!" she called over her shoulder, trying with all her might to sound confident.

"You don't sound like you want to," Claire heard Ichi say as she exited the hall. Choosing to run up the stairs as quickly as possible instead of waiting on the elevator, Claire struggled with the idea that it really was only a matter of time before her resolve ran out and she gave in to her desires – to tell Ichi everything, to get his help…and to have him.

CHAPTER 23
I Need to Know

Ichi

Ichi was cooking. And, for what felt like the first time in his life, not just for himself. He meticulously chopped onions and carrots, ginger and garlic, pak choi and chilli with deft hands before throwing the lot into a sizzling wok. Two duck breasts were cooking, fat side down, in an adjacent frying pan. All that was left to do was to cook the noodles in a mix of spices and then the whole lot would go into bowls.

Claire was entirely unaware that Ichi was cooking for her, and in reality Ichi had no idea how he was supposed to get her over to his room for dinner in the first place. *But she's getting too thin; she needs to eat.* Ichi had noticed that Claire wasn't eating over the past week – and was sleeping even less than usual – but he hadn't realised just how rapid her weight loss had become until he had grabbed her wrist the previous afternoon. *She'll end up collapsing sooner rather than later if she keeps this up,* Ichi thought as he held up the knife he had been chopping the vegetables with, considering its edge. Concluding that it needed sharpening, Ichi resolved to remember to fix up the whole set later on in the evening.

Ichi put on the noodles to cook over the hob and reduced the heat under each of the various pots and pans to a gentle flame in order to inspect himself in his bathroom mirror. He knew his hair could do with a trim as he swept the front of it out of his eyes, but Ichi wasn't about to go and attempt to cut it himself. He was wearing a long sleeved, smoke grey V-necked top that clung to his lean frame with navy slim-line jeans that were so dark they were the colour of midnight. It was as close to colour as Ichi ever got. He tugged at his hair as he wondered what Claire would think, then promptly rolled his eyes at his own reflection. *I shouldn't be caring about such things. I have to work out how to get her into my room first.*

Ichi walked out of his bathroom to glance at his laptop where it lay on his perfectly made bed. The camera feed in Claire's living space showed that she was lounging on her couch, listening to music and reading as she so often did. She was wearing a flowery dress Ichi had never seen on her before; for a moment he wondered why.

A check of the food on the hob confirmed that all of the components for dinner were ready. Ichi mixed the vegetables in with the noodles before grabbing two bowls from one of his kitchen cupboards and tossing the lot in to both of them. He placed the duck on top of each steaming bowl before examining the finished article. He was sure it was similar enough to something Roger had made for him before, which he had noticed Claire enjoying later that same day. Carrying both bowls over to his dining table, Ichi realised that he hadn't thought about what they were supposed to drink. *Do I go alcoholic? What does Claire even like outside of orange juice and rum?* Ichi shook his head at the trivial matter. To settle the problem, he took one of two bottles of white wine from his fridge that seemed to have been in there for forever and placed it on the table with two glasses. He added a jug of water as an afterthought.

And then Ichi knew he couldn't delay any longer – he had to actually get Claire to come into his room. He inhaled slowly, exhaled even more slowly and then made for his door. His laptop still lying open on the bed gave him pause, and he jogged over to it to close the camera feed to Claire's room, slamming the screen down too for good measure.

When he found himself outside the door to Claire's room Ichi paused again, the knuckles of his left hand millimetres from the wood. Just as he was about to knock on the door, however, he heard the handle click from the inside and the door swung open, bringing Claire face-to-face with him. She jumped in fright as she almost walked right into Ichi's still-raised hand. Taking an unsteady step backwards, Claire attempted to compose herself.

"Ichi? What are you doing?" she asked. Ichi's mind had gone blank; he didn't think he had ever felt so awkward in his entire life. When he still hadn't formed a response several seconds later, Claire frowned at him. "Ichi?" she repeated. In the spur of the moment, Ichi simply grabbed Claire's wrist and pulled her towards his room. "Hey! What the hell are you doing?!" she protested, trying to hold her ground and failing. Only once they had both entered Ichi's room did he let her go to close the door.

Claire stood on the spot, curiosity getting the better of her as she moved her head from side to side to take in her surroundings. When she spotted the food waiting on his dining table, Claire's frown deepened. "Ichi, what exactly is going on here?" Ichi went over and sat by his table and waited patiently for Claire to follow suit.

"You look like you're going to keel over at any given minute," he explained, his mind blank of anything else to say.

"Isn't that what you wanted from me in the first place?" Claire replied dryly as she cautiously sat down opposite Ichi. He made a noise at her response. "What?" she fired at him defensively.

"Nothing," he countered. "I just wasn't aware that you had such a dark sense of humour."

Claire laughed mirthlessly at his statement. "That's because you don't know anything about me." Ichi had to stop himself from smirking at her answer as he glanced at his closed laptop. He knew a lot more about Claire than he was going to willingly own up to. But Claire was still somewhat correct – there was a lot Ichi didn't know that he eagerly wished he did.

"Does that mean you've made a decision concerning my request last week?" Ichi asked casually, as he effortlessly unscrewed the cork from the wine without so much as a glance at the bottle. He poured them both a glass whilst Claire watched him do so, a confused expression on her face. "Eat, Claire," he said, gesturing at the steaming bowl sitting in front of her as he raised his glass to his lips. When Claire made no motion to either answer his question or to eat, Ichi put down his glass. "Doing nothing isn't going to get either of us anywhere."

"I don't have an appetite."

"Just eat anyway. Or drink. Wine has plenty of calories."

Claire couldn't help but laugh. "You sound like my sister."

Ichi raised an eyebrow as he took up his glass again. "Olivia?"

Claire flinched. "Of course you know her name," she said, half to herself.

"You sound surprised."

Claire shook her head. "I was being an idiot. Sometimes I forget who exactly it is you work for." Claire's mood had grown very dark very quickly. Ichi pushed her bowl closer towards her.

"*Eat.* And talk. Stop acting like you don't want to." Claire gave him a look Ichi couldn't quite figure out, before grabbing her glass and drinking several large gulps of wine.

"Don't think for even a second that I can have dinner with you sober," Claire said in response to the look Ichi threw her, as she flung her long hair over one shoulder and picked up her fork.

"A drunk Claire – my favourite kind," Ichi replied, grinning as he saw her splendid face grow red at the implication in his words.

"I hate you," she muttered.

Ichi's grin grew wider. "I know."

Claire

"I need a pen and some paper," Claire demanded once she and Ichi had finished eating. She had surprised herself by managing to eat more than half of the massive bowl of food Ichi had cooked for her. What surprised Claire even more was how delicious it had been. *Why is it that Vic and Ichi are so good at everything?* she grumbled. Claire was also pleasantly tipsy from the half bottle of wine that she had consumed along with dinner...and Ichi had now opened another.

"What do you need pen and paper for?" he asked her.

"I want to draw a timeline," Claire explained.

Ichi laughed. "You don't do things by half-measures, do you?" he joked, but he left the dining table to retrieve Claire's required supplies from a nearby chest of drawers nonetheless.

"I'd like to see you try and organise everything in your head when you don't even know exactly what it is you've forgotten," Claire muttered. Ichi gently cuffed her across the head with the newly opened bottle of wine as he walked past her.

"Come on, let's sit by the coffee table," he said, ignoring her previous comment. Ichi's couch, coffee table and rug were identical to the ones in Claire's room, as was the meticulously made bed, but his living area was almost double the size of that in Claire's room. Most of that space was taken up by the dining table and two chests of drawers, but other than that the extra space made his room look empty. Ichi didn't seem to have any personal items in his room, save for the laptop lying on his bed. Or if he did, they were well hidden away. Even his kitchen was deeply impersonal; Claire couldn't even see a hint that he had been cooking there less than an hour ago.

Ichi looked at her suspiciously when Claire made no attempt to move over to the couch. "What?" he demanded.

Claire shook her head slightly. "It's nothing. Just…you're very clean."

Ichi laughed again. "So are you." Claire smiled slightly at his observation, then slowly made her way over to the couch. But instead of sitting on it, she knelt on the floor in front of it in order to write over the coffee table.

"You don't have anything in here that belongs to you, except that," Claire continued, gesturing towards Ichi's laptop, "I mean, I'm a prisoner here and I have more of my own stuff in my room than you do." Claire organised the pieces of paper into a line, the better for her to work from as far back as she could remember to the present. She could feel Ichi sitting behind her.

"I didn't exactly come here with much," was all Ichi said as he handed Claire another glass of wine. She took it from his hand without looking at him, drank a swig of it then placed it on a coaster on the coffee table. *Of course he has coasters.* Claire held the pen Ichi had given her over the very left hand edge of the paper and paused.

She glanced over her shoulder at him. "What did you come here with?" she asked, curiosity getting the better of her. Ichi seemed amused by the question. He leaned forwards slightly, closing the gap between them. Claire internally cursed at the fact that she had trapped herself between the coffee table and Ichi's legs.

"I thought I was the one finding out about you tonight, not the other way around." Claire turned back to the paper in front of her and drew a long line from the left hand edge of the paper to the very right hand edge of the other sheet, as straight as she could manage freehand.

"Don't tell me then," she replied, trying to act as if she couldn't care less. There was a pause in the conversation as Claire started to annotate her line; she wrote the word 'now' at the far right and the phrase 'about four years ago' at the left end.

"A leather jacket," she heard Ichi say quietly behind her.

Claire struggled not to flinch. "What did you say?" she asked, though she had heard him perfectly well.

"A leather jacket," Ichi repeated. "That's all I brought with me when I started living here and working for Michael. Lord knows where it's disappeared to." There was a slight accusatory edge to Ichi's voice that Claire wasn't sure if her guilty conscience had imagined or not.

"Maybe Alexis has it," Claire replied, hiding her own guilt by turning it towards another person.

"Maybe," Ichi replied thoughtfully. Claire couldn't help but bristle at his acceptance of her suggestion. She felt Ichi's hand on her shoulder turning her around slightly. "Are you jealous?" he laughed, and Claire half felt like punching his stupid, smug face. Claire turned herself back around and grabbed her glass.

"Hardly," she countered, taking another long draught of wine. Ichi merely laughed again. "Look, I can go back to my room right this second and tell you nothing, you know," Claire retorted angrily, but her words trailed off as she felt Ichi rest his head against the back of hers, both of his hands on her shoulders. Claire struggled not to swat him off as Ichi's fingers started fiddling with the thin straps of her dress.

"You've never worn this before," he commented, before Claire could voice her irritation. Claire felt herself sober up ever-so-slightly.

"…it was my mum's," she explained eventually.

"It suits you. I like it."

"What does that matter?" Ichi brought his head down to the nape of her neck and kissed the skin there. It was the biggest physical interaction Claire had had with him since they had slept together, and it occurred to Claire that she had altogether forgotten what she was doing.

"I suppose it doesn't matter, but I like it nonetheless," Ichi murmured into her skin, before resting his chin on her shoulder. "So," he said, in a slightly louder voice, "Start talking. When did you start forgetting things?" It took Claire a second to realise that he wasn't referring to that very moment, and she struggled to return her thoughts to the matter of the last four years of her life instead of wishing she could rip Ichi's clingy top off of his gorgeous body.

"So...so," she began, her head swimming slightly from the wine and Ichi's proximity, "About four years ago – ah, I suppose it was nearer five now – in the summer before my first year of university, I started working properly in my parents' lab. I never knew the finer details of what their research was on before then because I lacked the knowledge to truly understand it, but I suppose I sort of knew what they were doing even for years before I started working for them. But that summer is my first full-on memory lapse...I think. I can't remember anything relating to working in their lab for four months, only that I did." Claire paused for a moment to annotate the beginning of her timeline. "I didn't work for my parents so much that year at the weekends because, you know, I was a first year university student and had other things to do." Claire could feel Ichi turn his head slightly to look at her from his position on her shoulder.

"Other things?" Claire rolled her eyes and finally found the willpower to shove Ichi off of her.

"Not relevant student things, like drinking and studying and boyfriends," she replied testily.

"Boyfriends *plural*?" Ichi put on a face of mock surprise.

"Not at the same time, Jesus. Do you even want to help me Ichi, or are you just using this as an excuse to find out stupid things about me?" Ichi waved a nonchalant hand her way as he lounged lazily into the back of his couch and sipped on his wine.

"Continue, then." Claire had some more wine herself, and then proceeded to write again on the paper.

"The summer before second year, and then third year was basically the same. I worked for my parents and I don't remember any of it. Keep in mind that it doesn't feel like I've forgotten much else out with anything pertaining to my parents' research, but for all I know I could be wrong. Third year...ah." Claire paused and giggled stupidly to herself. Ichi cocked his head to one side at the sound, an eyebrow raised.

"I take it something interesting happened?"

Claire nodded her head slightly, drinking more wine as she did so. "Zeke happened. He was an idiot. But I was an idiot too, for going out with him. But that was the second half of third year. I started working weekends in my parents' lab from the *beginning* of third year, if I remember correctly. My parents...I think they were getting close to whatever it was that they were trying to do, and I remember getting so excited. Not just for them, but for me as well, and everything it could mean. It's so strange," Claire sighed and looked up at the ceiling, as if doing so would somehow bring her memories back. "I hadn't thought about it before, but I can still recall how I felt about what was going on, but not what actually happened. Maybe it's because how I was feeling helped to decide what I did outside of the lab? Ah, I don't know."

Claire scribbled some more notes on her timeline, silent for a few minutes. Ichi had leaned forward again, but to Claire's side rather than over her head in order to properly see what she was writing. "So..." she continued, "Then I went out with Zeke, and that wasted half a year, and then I had another summer of working for my parents. I didn't do much in my final year of university but study and work in their lab, like a good little daughter. Olivia had just started uni that year though, so she pulled me out on some ridiculous nights out on occasion." Claire laughed, though she knew that Ichi could tell that it wasn't a happy sound. "But in general, I was in the library or at the lab. I had never been one for the library before – I had always studied at my parents' house – but there was a distinct reason I started going all the time. Ha, I really do owe John an apology."

"Who was John?" Ichi asked, curious.

Claire smiled sadly. "He...was a guy I really liked. He was in the library all of the time, working on his thesis. It took me months to work up the courage to talk to him."

"Did you go out with him?"

Claire paused to consider the question. *This is going in a direction that I don't want it to,* she thought. "No," she replied, "It never got to that." *Because of you and Vic and Michael.* "I had my own flat that year, I think originally so I was closer to campus for my classes but, now that I think about it, working for my parents was getting stressful. I don't think...I don't think things were going well." Claire held a hand up to her temple, rubbing into the area with her fingertips. Trying to recall this information that she couldn't reach was giving her a headache, as it always did. She pointed to part of her annotated timeline. "Um, this would be about May last year now. I was having my final exams. I...I wasn't going home at all now at this point. Funny, was it really just because of exams? I don't remember..." Claire realised that she was talking more to herself now than to Ichi, who her brain was barely acknowledging as it tried its hardest to work through her broken memories.

"Last summer is a complete blank," she continued, after a long pause. "I remember graduating, but I still went to the library even after that. I didn't want to go home, but I didn't want to stay holed up in my flat either. I can't even pinpoint when exactly my parents went missing, but it must have been some point near the end of June. Olivia went off to travel the world by herself. I couldn't bear to leave. I...I guess I should have left, huh." Claire knew she was beginning to cry; could feel the tears welling up in her eyes, but she couldn't stop her rambling train of thought. "At least Olivia got out of it all. She better be hanging out on a beach without a care in the world for the both of us. And I was...I was watching that damn house, hoping that our stupid parents would by some miracle return and make everything right again. I was so *angry* at them, I couldn't bear it! How dare they take up so much of my adult life with their Godforsaken research and then just *leave? How dare they!*"

Claire knew that she was starting to get hysterical, but because of the wine or the fact that she was finally talking out loud about what had happened she simply didn't care. She could see Ichi out of the corner of her eye, frozen to the spot, not knowing what to say or do. Claire turned on him. "And then *you,* you and Vic come along just as I was attempting to piece my life back together. You asked me if I ever went out with John," Claire said, heart hammering in her chest as she felt all of the anger and anguish she had kept deep inside her bubbling to the surface. "Have you never wondered what I had been so dressed up for, the day you came and hit me over the head with Vic's damn pistol?"

Ichi was watching her carefully, but his face was expressionless. Claire let out a laugh, but it was hollow and humourless. "I was going on a date with John, and I was so excited! *As I should have been!* And now he'll forever think I stood him up for absolutely no reason. My whole life has been ruined *and I can't even remember why.* I shouldn't have to be here! I-I-I'm leaving," Claire decided suddenly as she stood up and promptly ran for the door. Ichi didn't even try to stop her.

She was at Vic's door before she knew it.

CHAPTER 24
Beautiful Liar

Vic

Never in a million years could Vic have predicted that Claire would show up at his door near midnight, her face covered in tears. "Claire! What's wrong?" he asked, concern written all over his face as Claire barged past him into his living room. Vic closed the door gently behind him as he turned around to face her. Claire looked hysterical, eyes wild, cheeks red and wet; she didn't even seem to see the man standing in front of her. Vic couldn't recall having ever seen her this way since the day she had been kidnapped. "Claire?" he asked again, his voice uncertain. "What's got you into such a state?" His words seemed to bring Claire back to the present, and her face grew furious.

"You!" she shouted at him, "You and – and *him*. One minute you're looking out for me, wanting me to trust you, then you act like I don't exist and avoid all of my questions and hope I won't notice! And he – *he* acts like he wants me dead and then does a complete one-eighty flip and wants to make me dinner! What the fuck is wrong with you both?!" Claire was pulling at her hair, pacing back and forth and throwing venomous glares in Vic's general direction. Then she stopped in her tracks suddenly, staring at the ceiling. She laughed bitterly, bringing her gaze back down to stare at Vic.

"Claire...?"

"And do you know what the best part is?" she continued, not giving Vic an opportunity to speak. "None of that even fucking matters, because the two of you are the reason I'm here in the first place. *Neither of you should matter to me in the slightest!*" Claire began to walk towards Vic, and he didn't know what to do. Claire had a twisted grin on her face, and she laughed that horrible laugh again. "Oh, you should see your face, Vic, it

243

looks just like his. Do neither of you like me reminding you of what you did to me? You're both responsible for ruining my life!"

"Claire, *shut the hell up*," Vic found himself barking out before he could stop himself. Claire was right in front of him now. Her face turned ever more furious at his demand.

"Why should I? I'm right!"

"No you're not! Not completely. Your parents are at fault – we would never have had to come after you if they hadn't –"

"Do you think I don't know that?!" Claire interrupted, shoving her fingers into Vic's chest. He allowed the action to move him backwards slightly. "But what use is it for me to keep blaming them, when I don't even remember what they did that was bad enough that I had to be *kidnapped* for it?! I'm so fucking angry," Claire pushed Vic back a little more, "And there's nowhere for it to go! You-you-you –" Vic grabbed onto Claire's wrists when she made to push him again, forcing her to stop moving. Claire looked up at him, and in seconds all of her fury seemed to dissipate from her eyes.

"I what, Claire?" he asked, his voice quiet. Claire's eyes were glittering with fresh tears.

"How can you say you care for me so much? How can you possibly feel so much for me but still be responsible for tearing me away from my life? Damn it Vic, who are you to think you're allowed to do both?!" Vic almost flinched at her words, but brought Claire close to his chest and held her there instead. He could hear Claire sobbing into his shirt, and he started to stroke her hair.

Who am I? She asks me who I am. How can I possibly answer that?

"I'm just Vic," he answered eventually. "I'm *your* Vic, regardless of whether I make any sense or not." Claire glanced up at him through her eyelashes, and the expression on her face was heart breaking.

"That's not enough," she whispered.

"I know." He broke away from her slightly and used a thumb to gently wipe away her tears. "But it will have to be enough for now whether you think so or not."

Claire frowned slightly. "For...for now?"

Vic smiled slightly at her. "Sharp girl. So how much have you had to drink? And what was this about Ichi wanting to make you dinner?" *Changing the subject to* him *is better than where this current conversation is going,* Vic conceded.

Claire bristled slightly at his questions, then seemed to deflate again. "Most of a bottle of wine…I'm such a lightweight now," she laughed, but the sound was warped by the tears still in her throat.

"And the dinner invite?" Claire swallowed to clear her throat and ran her hands through her hair, pulling it away from her face.

"It wasn't so much an invite as a mandatory meal," she replied. Vic said nothing, waiting for her to elaborate. Claire swallowed again and turned away a fraction from him. "He…had noticed I wasn't eating. Just like you had. You're both such a nuisance, you know." She laughed again, and Vic was relieved to hear that it sounded more genuine. He smiled at her. "Anyway," she continued, "He made me dinner. He didn't even tell me he was doing it; he just knocked on my door and literally pulled me into his room and made me eat." *Bastard,* Vic thought, but his annoyance was directed more towards himself for not thinking of doing exactly what Ichi had done than at the man in question.

"Did it work?" Vic asked.

"Yes, I'm very full right now, thanks," Claire said, though the 'thanks' sounded distinctly sarcastic.

"Was that all you did?" Vic dared to ask. Risking another outbreak, he added an additional question: "Why did you get so upset?"

Claire gave him a look. "It doesn't matter," she replied after a long pause, making Vic entirely certain that it did. But Claire was evidently in no mood to be interrogated on her deception, and Vic was in no position to call her out on it without being named a hypocrite. Then Claire cocked her head to one side, frowning. "What are you listening to?" Vic sighed in relief at the drastic change in subject matter, and moved over to his speakers to turn the volume up.

"I was choosing some tango music. I only started teaching you the basic moves today…I figured we could have more fun with it tomorrow and actually put them into a dance. I was in the process of working it out when you knocked on my door."

"Show me." Vic turned from his speakers to look at Claire, who was leaning over the glass coffee table to use her reflection to fix her running mascara.

"Say that again?" he asked, confused.

Claire stood up properly and walked back over to Vic until she was mere inches from him. "Show me the dance. Or teach me it. Or whatever," she said, taking Vic's right hand and placing it on her waist.

"You should be going to sleep, princess," he replied, but he felt his right hand moving from Claire's waist to the small of her back nonetheless as Claire took his other hand in hers.

"We both know I won't sleep for hours," Claire argued. She smiled slightly. "So humour me." Vic pulled her in closer, and knew that *humouring* her was the last thing on his mind, even though a proper gentleman would insist that she went to bed that very second despite their despicable urges. *Well, I'm not a proper gentleman. I'm not even a proper man right now.*

"I won't go so easy on your mistakes now, Miss Danvers. You're the one that's come to me to dance this time, so you better be perfect."

Claire grinned devilishly at him. "I thought I already was perfect to you?"

Vic tightened his hold on Claire's back. "I wasn't aware I'd ever said as such. Now shut up and let me teach you this."

Claire raised an eyebrow at him. "You're so mean tonight," she complained, a pout on her lips.

"And you're mean always. And drunk right now – let's not forget that. Sure all this dancing won't make you sick?" Vic asked as he spun Claire around to emphasise his point.

"I'm not *that* much of a lightweight," Claire grumbled like a six-year-old child being scolded.

Vic let go of her hand to tilt her chin up. "Then keep your eyes on mine, princess. This dance is all about contact."

Claire

Claire never realised that she could dance. No, she *knew* that she couldn't dance, but she was dancing now, and dancing well. Or maybe she wasn't; Claire couldn't tell. All she knew was that so long as she let Vic lead and allowed him to move her where he wanted her to go, everything seemed to go the way it was supposed to. Vic's eyes never left hers and Claire's never left his – she didn't want to look away, not in the slightest.

She had instigated the tango as another opportunity for her to try and pull an honest answer out of Vic, but now that Claire was actually doing it all such ulterior motives had flown out of her head. For how could she think when Vic's hand was roaming up her leg, bringing her dress up with it? When he would spin her away with a fury she hadn't known possible for him, only to be pulled back in as close as he could physically get her? Or when Claire herself was touching Vic, feeling the material of his shirt underneath her fingertips and wishing it wasn't there? The fact that she had been thinking the very same about Ichi less than an hour ago flitted across her mind, but all Claire had to do was focus back on the moment at hand and the thought disappeared.

Claire didn't think it was possible for a man in incredibly tight jeans to be able to move with such speed and dexterity, but here was Vic, proving her wrong. Claire was *breathless* because of it, and she loved it. The warm glow of the lights in Vic's room had turned his pale blue eyes almost grey; she wondered what they had done to the colour of hers. His hair was in his eyes, but Vic didn't seem to care enough to do anything about it. And when Claire made to break from his grip to clear it herself, Vic only tightened his hold and brought her in closer. She wondered how they could possibly still be on the same song – it felt like they had been dancing for hours, when in reality it had been mere minutes. But eventually, the music drew to a close with the somewhat anguished cry of a Spanish guitar, and their dancing slowed to a halt. Vic made no move to break his hold on Claire, and only loosened his hand on hers when she, once again, moved her hand to clear the hair from his eyes.

And then he kissed her, and Claire had expected it, and she loved it. She kissed him back, one hand on the back of his neck pulling him in closer, and she felt herself walking backwards to fall onto Vic's couch. But when they both hit the cushions, Vic broke away from her lips. "We can't do this now," he murmured, his voice low and heavy.

Claire frowned slightly; she didn't understand. "Why?" she asked.

Vic kissed her again, but only lightly. "Because Lord help me, but you were right – I can't push my feelings on you when you're stuck in here." Claire could hear a new song begin to play over Vic's speakers, but it sounded more like classic rock than tango music; it abruptly broke the intoxicating spell that seemed to have been cast over the two of them.

Vic

"I'm pretty sure I'm being obvious about reciprocating those feelings," Claire replied, but she pushed Vic away an inch so that she could sit up nonetheless.

Vic sighed as he sat up fully. "Yes, but you reciprocated them months ago too and you *still* knew that the right thing to do was to give yourself the time to get out of here and sort your life out again before you thought about me seriously. Isn't that what you want to do still?"

Claire threw him a sideways glance. "What I should want and want I do want are two completely different things," she replied wryly, and Vic could see in her face that she had just thought about someone that Vic sincerely wished she hadn't.

He sighed again, heavier this time. "And you're still of two minds about a certain son of a bitch, even though –"

"That's not fair! I'm trying to avoid him!" Claire interrupted, outraged.

Vic messed her hair up. "Idiot. I never said that you weren't. But *he* isn't trying to avoid you, and he's getting to you whether you like it or not. Which is why your original decision to wait until you're free of everything here to sort your feelings out is the best thing to do." Vic paused. "Surely after everything you came storming in here to say you must believe that?"

Claire looked at the floor. "I know, but…getting out of here feels like a faraway dream that I'll never reach." Vic thought of the awards ball and how, if all went well, Claire would be gone in less than two months. But he knew that he couldn't tell her about that – not just because Michael had told him to stay silent on the matter, but because Vic genuinely thought that it wouldn't do Claire's current frame of mind any good to worry over it.

"You're also drunk," he said after a moment of thought. "Maybe I could be more convinced of your words if they were the product of sobriety."

Claire laughed. "Okay, fine, you win on that point." Claire looked at him, and Vic could practically see the cogs turning behind her eyes before she threw him a sly smile. "So what will you do if I come to you tomorrow, one hundred percent sober, and tell you I'd love nothing better than to rip your clothes off?" Vic had to stop himself from doing the same to Claire's dress.

"How about we deal with that tomorrow? And for the record, princess, I don't like girls who never eat or sleep."

Claire made a face at him. "I'm sure that between you and Ichi pestering me about it all of the time I'll be eating plenty from now on," she commented. "Can't promise anything about the sleep though."

Vic smiled at her. "I think I can work with that," he said, "But on the matter of sleep, you can at least pretend to try and get some tonight." Claire returned his smile as she slowly pulled herself up from the couch. Vic wished she would sit back down and insist on staying despite everything he had just told her.

"Okay, okay, I'll humour you, since you humoured me with the dancing." As Claire made for the door, Vic became aware of the song that was playing through his speakers. It was one of his favourites; he leaned back against the couch to enjoy it, tapping the drum beat out on his leg. But when he looked up to say a final goodbye to Claire, he saw that she was frozen to the spot.

"…I know you," she barely whispered, her eyes wide.

Oh shit.

Claire

Claire didn't understand. She looked at Vic, tapping out the beat of the song playing on his tightly-jeaned leg, and Claire saw somebody else. For just a second, she saw somebody completely different, and yet exactly the same. "I know you," she heard herself saying, though she was barely aware of doing so. Vic's muscles all seemed to tense at her words for a moment before he relaxed against the back of his couch again.

"What do you mean, princess? Of course you know me. You really need to go to bed."

Claire shook her head. "No! No, I don't mean now, I mean…" She shook her head again, before walking a few steps back over to Vic to stare at his face more directly. "I knew you before."

Vic raised his eyebrows. "No you didn't."

Claire felt herself frown. "Then why –"

"Look, Claire," Vic interjected, "You've barely slept or eaten for over a week. You're drunk. And we both just did something we probably shouldn't have. Your brain is likely half-remembering experiences you've had with someone else and putting them in the present. People experience déjà-vu all the time."

Claire's frown deepened. "Then answer me honestly, once and for all; until the day you came to kidnap me, had I ever met you before?"

Vic matched her stare as he replied, "No, you've never met Vic Winters before." Claire was somehow completely taken aback by Vic's answer, and her brain struggled to process it. *He's telling the truth. But…but it feels like he's not. How can that be?*

"I'll see you tomorrow then Vic, though I think laying off the tangos would be a good idea," Claire said finally, after a long pause in which she felt herself sober up entirely. And then she turned and left Vic's room, heart pounding in her chest as she felt the fear of her forgotten memories creep back up on her anew.

She should have expected Ichi to be waiting for her on the twelfth floor, but his presence in the corridor surprised her regardless. "…I'm not dealing with you right now," she said, making a beeline for her door.

250

Ichi blocked the way, as Claire also should have expected. "Where did you go?" he asked, his eyes sharp and intent upon hers. *Clearly I'm not the only one who did some super quick sobering up,* Claire thought.

She discovered that she didn't have the energy or the inclination to lie. "To Vic's. It was a mistake. A massive mistake." Claire could see a flash of irritation break Ichi's otherwise neutral expression. "Why, are you jealous?" she dared to ask, mimicking Ichi's very same question from earlier on in the evening.

"Yes," he replied unflinchingly, almost instantaneously. Ichi's willingness to admit it shocked Claire; she never thought in a million years that he would ever acknowledge any kind of weakness. "What did you do that was a mistake?" he asked her.

"Something that you definitely don't want to know," she said, and Claire knew that she had said it simply to get a reaction out of him. She could see the tendons in Ichi's left hand tighten as he made a fist against the wall he was leaning on. "Though not nearly as bad as you think," she added on, and with a bitter smirk on her face: "Not as bad as you and Alexis."

Ichi threw her against her door. "Why are you doing this to me?" he growled, his face mere millimetres from her own.

"I think, for various reasons that I seem to recall pointing out in my outburst earlier, you don't really get to be pissed at me 'doing things to you', after what you've done to me," Claire bit out, and she could see in Ichi's eyes that he knew she was right.

He lowered his head slightly and laughed quietly. "You're as fucked up as I am," he muttered.

"The only difference is that *you* did this to me, and I didn't do it to you. No," Claire continued on scathingly, as Ichi's dark eyes bored into her own, waiting to see what other insults she could throw his way, "You fucked yourself up all on your own."

Ichi slammed a fist above her head. "Damn it, Claire!"

"Damn me *what*, Ichi?" she countered. "If you want to screw me, just do it! You know fine well that I won't say no." *Why am I baiting him like this?* Claire wondered, but it gave her a kind of bitter enjoyment nevertheless. It was thrilling, not knowing exactly how Ichi was going to react. But at least his responses were honest, and Claire considered whether that was what she was yearning for. She felt Ichi's right hand roam up her thigh, much like Vic had done in their tango not so long ago. But when his fingers reached her hip bone, Ichi paused.

"No."

"No?" Claire echoed.

"No," Ichi repeated, "I'm not instigating it this time. *You* are."

Claire frowned at him. "Why?" He stared at her until it made Claire feel so uncomfortable that she struggled not to look away.

"Because that's the way it is," he answered simply.

Claire almost laughed. "That's incredibly childish."

"I'd call it obstinate. Either way, that's the rule of the game."

Claire narrowed her eyes at him. "I'm not playing your game."

"Yes you are. You have been since the start." Claire didn't want to think about what that meant.

She pushed him away. "I'm going to bed, Ichi. But I'll come by tomorrow." Ichi raised his eyebrows in genuine surprise. He gave Claire enough space to turn around and open her door. "You said it yourself," she explained, in response to his confusion, "I need a bad guy for this. My good guy is lying; tonight confirmed that more than ever." She felt Ichi's hands on her waist attempting to turn her around, but Claire resisted. She put her hands over his and gently removed them.

"Tomorrow then," she heard Ichi murmur behind her.

Claire threw him a half smile over her shoulder. "Yes, tomorrow. And I promise there will be no more outbursts. Heaven forbid you learn any more about how to push my buttons than you already have." Ichi moved in closer to her again, and she could feel his breath on her neck.

"Some of those buttons are enjoyable, though."

"Good*bye*, Ichi," Claire announced a little too loudly, as she whirled around and slammed the door in his face to hide the flush that had swept up over her cheeks. She could hear him chuckling through the wood before he walked back to his own room.

Claire flung herself onto her bed, wondering how it could possibly make evolutionary sense for a woman to simultaneously want to screw a man and punch him in the face...*or two men,* she added on as a guilty afterthought.

Vic

I can't possibly get away with this for much longer, Vic thought as he turned his music off.

"No, Claire, you've never met 'Vic Winters' before," he muttered, hating himself.

CHAPTER 25
Up

Ichi

Ichi was leaning against the glass that separated the viewing gallery from the practice hall. Vic and Claire weren't there yet, which struck him as odd. *They're always here by now,* Ichi thought, suspicious. Claire had also been absent from her usual early-morning swim, so for a moment Ichi entertained the idea that she was having a rare morning lie-in. However, Ichi knew better than to believe that.

What the hell happened between Claire and Vic last night? he wondered for the hundredth time. In reality, Ichi didn't even know why he was waiting for them to show up in the practice hall in the first place. *Maybe I was hoping I could work out what went on by watching them.* Ichi sighed, running a hand over his face. He hadn't slept much, having ran back to his laptop to religiously watch the camera feeds in Claire's room as soon as she had bid him good bye in the corridor the previous night. Claire had seemed incredibly agitated, to say the least. Ichi supposed he couldn't blame her.

Thinking back to everything Claire had said to him after dinner made Ichi feel more uncomfortable than he had thought possible. However, rather than that feeling stemming from any kind of guilt towards kidnapping Claire, Ichi realised that it was a product of the fact that he simply didn't care. He hadn't felt a thing during Claire's outburst. Ichi had never spared his lack of sympathy or empathy a thought before, but now that he was…he didn't know what to think. If he was being completely honest with himself, the only thing Ichi had felt when Claire was crying her eyes out had been *satisfaction,* because he never would have met Claire if he hadn't ruined her life. Her outburst also demonstrated to Ichi that Claire had been keeping the strongest of her emotions regarding him to herself. How could Claire expect Ichi to not feel like he had won against her on some level after everything she had said?

But Ichi knew that he couldn't voice any of these thoughts to Claire, even though the sick part of his brain badly wanted to do so. Instead, Ichi had simply kept his face blank until Claire had, admittedly unexpectedly, stormed out of his room to go to Vic's. Vic's. And Ichi had known this, and couldn't help but confront her about it upon her return. *But then all she did was deliberately throw me off by saying things that would infuriate me. She's hiding something.* Ichi was beginning to believe that, rather than himself or Vic or maybe even Michael, *Claire* was the one most capable of keeping things hidden from other people.

"I'll get it out of her somehow," Ichi mumbled aloud as his body slowly slid down the glass panelling to the floor. He knew fine well that, above all else, he was wanting to observe Claire and Vic's dance lesson so that Vic couldn't be alone with her. *I'm the one she's gone to for help, after all. Why should Vic still get to monopolise her?* Ichi knew that he was steadily losing his already weak self-control when it came to Claire. He didn't want her to touch anybody else; Ichi felt like he might die if he didn't get to have his way with her again soon. He chuckled darkly at the exaggeration, knowing that it certainly didn't feel like one. But he also knew that waiting for Claire to come to him for *everything* was definitely the correct way to go about things...he just hated the actual waiting. Ichi was reassured by the fact that Claire had said she would continue speaking to him about her past that evening; he wondered excitedly whether he could get the same reactions out of her sober as he did when she was drunk. Ichi promptly banged the back of his head against the wall to knock some sense into himself.

I should be thinking about getting her memories back, not about the various ways in which I can get her to have sex with me.

"What are you doing here, Ichi?" an all-too-familiar female voice asked him, startling Ichi out of his own thoughts.

"Well *you're* late, Claire," he replied smoothly, as if he hadn't just been thinking about how it would feel to take her clothes off again.

Claire frowned at him. "That absolutely didn't answer my question."

"Does it matter why I'm here?" Claire sighed before entering the practice hall, speakers and Mp3 player in tow. Ichi felt a smug sense of satisfaction when he made Claire jump by following her straight through the door.

"Ichi, what are you –"

"Where's Vic? It's not like either of you to be late," he interrupted, standing over her as Claire knelt down to plug the speakers into a socket and began flicking through her music.

"How should I know? Maybe he's doing something for Michael. I can just practice by myself," she mumbled over her shoulder.

Ichi scoffed at her. "Practice dancing? By yourself? I can't see how that could possibly fail."

Claire whipped her head around, eyebrows knitted together. "Unless you have a better idea?!" But even as Claire said it, her frown disappeared and her cheeks started to go red as she saw Ichi smirking at her. She stood up slowly and started to walk back towards the viewing gallery door, but Ichi put out his right arm to stop her. "No way. Absolutely not. Get lost, Ichi," Claire threw at him.

Ichi merely laughed. "Have you never thought about the reason why you're so awful at self-defence and dancing with Vic?" he asked her. Claire ducked under Ichi's outstretched arm in an attempt to escape, but he grabbed onto her hand with his left and spun her back around to stand in front of him.

Claire raised an eyebrow. "That is literally the most frivolous action you have ever taken."

"Don't ignore me," Ichi ordered.

Claire glanced at the hand that Ichi was holding onto before replying. "He's too tall for me to spar against properly and I'm terrible at dancing."

It was Ichi's turn to raise an eyebrow as he said, "Stop lying." Ichi felt himself loosen his grip on Claire's hand to slowly interlace his fingers with hers, and was pleased to see her face flush even brighter than before. "What's the common denominator between the two things that you're bad at? And don't even think about saying yourself, because your sparring skills against Imran are excellent." He saw Claire's mouth upturn slightly at the back-handed compliment before schooling her expression back to neutral once more.

"Fine, whatever," Claire responded, trying to sound casual. "It's Vic. That's nothing new, though. I worked it out ages ago."

Ichi smiled. "Good, then you're not stupid. So let's dance," he said, and was amused to see Claire's expression go from one of annoyance to one of worry.

"B-but you can't be serious?" she stammered. Ichi chuckled as he let go of her hand to crouch in front of the speakers.

"You don't have anything to lose. And this is hardly the worst thing we've ever done," he added on as an afterthought as he located Claire's folk music on her Mp3 player.

"Yeah, but it's definitely the strangest," Claire muttered.

Ichi selected a song and turned around to face Claire. "Maybe so," he conceded as music began to play out of the speakers. Claire's eyes grew wide as she recognised the melody.

"Um, this isn't...this isn't ballroom music, Ichi..." she mumbled as she shifted uncomfortably on her feet, looking at the floor. Ichi closed the gap between them and raised Claire's chin up with a finger. He stared at her intently.

"No, it isn't. But so long as it has the same rhythm as something you've already been taught, it doesn't really matter, right?"

Claire looked at him suspiciously. "It's not a coincidence that you picked this kind of music."

"Nope," Ichi replied. "I spy on you; haven't you noticed?" It seemed as if Claire couldn't help but laugh at his outrageous confession. Then Ichi placed a hand on her hip, took her hand in the other and then took a step forwards, but the action caused Claire to look at him with a confused expression on her face. "What?" Ichi asked, defensive. Claire frowned.

"...you started on the wrong foot," she answered, her voice uncertain. Ichi pulled Claire in closer and tilted his head down to look at her.

"I'm left handed; I do everything the opposite way. Or hadn't you noticed that either?" he murmured. Claire glanced up at him through her eyelashes, a sly smile growing on her lips. The look on her face caused Ichi to almost forget about dancing entirely.

"I may have had a notion," Claire replied. "Though I'm pretty certain that dancing the opposite way from what I'm used to will screw me over entirely." Ichi took a step forward, and then another; Claire responded by following the movement backwards.

"One can only hope," he commented, knowing entirely how filthy it sounded. Claire bit down on her lip slightly before replying as Ichi spun her slowly under his arm.

"Trying to woo me with words and dancing won't make me do what you want." Ichi brought his forehead down to rest on Claire's as he let go of her hand to clear stray strands of hair away from her face. Ichi's eyes never left hers.

"I know. You were already doing what I wanted beforehand," he grinned, breaking the atmosphere with his quip. But Claire wasn't looking at him anymore; her eyes were focused on some point behind Ichi's head. He turned around to see what she was looking at. *Ah...*

"No need to say anything, princess. I get it," Vic said, a somewhat forced smile upon his face. Ichi had to turn away again to hide his glee at what was transpiring. *This couldn't have gone any better if I had planned it myself.*

Vic

He could see the pained expression blossom on Claire's face as he spoke, but Vic knew he had to keep up a somewhat more closed front to prevent Claire from working out more than she already had done the previous night.

"Vic, you weren't here yet, so Ichi –"

"No, it's honestly fine, Claire," he interjected, holding a hand up to silence her. "Sorry I was late; I had some stuff to think about. And after last night…" Vic paused, casting an obvious glance at Ichi, who had quickly turned around again at the mere mention of the previous night, a suspicious look on his face. Claire looked worried. "After last night," he repeated, "I decided it's probably for the best that we stop dancing altogether. We can't have what happened before repeat itself, can we?" Vic laughed, and was pleased to hear that it actually sounded genuine. Claire gave him a sheepish smile; Ichi glared at him.

"No...I suppose not. Not right now, anyway," Claire replied, her tone flirtatious by the end of the sentence. Vic could see Ichi's grip on her waist grow slightly tighter. *Yes, be confused whilst Claire and I pretend everything's all okay, you prick,* Vic thought. He took a couple of steps towards the pair of them, and Claire broke away from Ichi's arms to meet him. Vic was entirely satisfied to see a look of furious disbelief plastered all over Ichi's face. "But then you won't be teaching me anything at all," Claire pouted, bringing Vic out of his own head. He smiled down at her before mussing her hair up.

"Don't be ridiculous. I'll go back to teaching you self-defence, but you're absolutely not getting away with being terrible at it anymore. I've seen how good you are against Imran," he replied. The look he gave Claire as he spoke was a little sharper than Vic had intended, and she flinched a little before responding.

"Okay, no more being rubbish. I promise." Claire grinned up at him as if she hadn't just recoiled at the expression on his face.

Vic sighed, ruffled her hair once more and chuckled. "I'll see you tomorrow then, princess. I have a meeting with Michael soon that I probably shouldn't be late for," he said, giving Claire a final smile before walking back towards the viewing gallery. When he reached the door, he spared Ichi a glance over his shoulder, and was surprised to see that he no longer appeared to be angry at all. Instead, the other man had a distinctly quizzical look upon his face, as if he were trying to figure something out. Vic promptly turned tail and left in case the 'something' that Ichi was trying to work out was Vic himself.

As he walked down the staircase to Michael's office, Vic wondered what exactly Ichi was privy to, and what he wasn't. *But I can't ask him about it without making it glaringly obvious that something's going on.* Lamenting the situation he had put himself in, Vic knocked softly on Michael's door and let himself in when he heard the other man usher him inside.

"You called?" Vic asked casually whilst he took a seat. Michael regarded him with a stony expression on his face; Vic was surprised at the absence of his usual bland smile. "What have I done?" Vic inquired, as he thought of the thousand things he had done that he rather wished Michael would never find out about.

There was a pause before Michael replied, "It's not something you have done, per se. It's your contacts." Vic waited patiently for Michael to elaborate. "As you know, I have been trying to identify what Miss Danvers' parents need two months to do before their daughter shows up in public, and your contacts have been crucial in finding out just what exactly that is." Michael waited for Vic to nod his head in agreement at the statement. "They have been more than willing to pass information over to me directly. Until now." His gaze sharpened; Vic kept his expression blank and unreadable in return. *And here we go.*

"Until now?" he parroted back.

Michael narrowed his eyes at Vic. "Yes. Now they have informed me that they have some critical information regarding what Joanna and Mark have been up to, but they are only willing to pass it on *directly to you and in person.*"

Vic regarded Michael carefully for a moment before replying, "That's not really that unusual, Michael."

"Maybe not if that was how they *always* relayed information to me," Michael countered, "Or if this was the first time they were giving me information and were being careful. So why have they decided that this particular piece of information must go through you first?" *Because I need to filter it before it reaches your ears, obviously,* Vic thought. *And I only had them feed you information directly before so I could gain your trust enough to direct this damn investigation. I can't exactly go out and say that though.*

"It's probably just the nature of the information," Vic reasoned, choosing to tell a half-truth, as he had done so often in the past. "My contacts are used to just tracking the people I ask them about. What said people are getting up to is another matter entirely. Maybe they don't know what you're planning on doing with the information, and don't expect you to tell the truth about what you would do even if they asked. But they would trust me to tell them the truth about you, so it's a safer bet for them."

Vic was relieved to see Michael's face relax into an amused chuckle. "And if I asked you to lie on my behalf?"

Vic grinned back at his boss. "Then I'd make it sound like the truth, as always."

Michael stared at him for a long moment before breaking away from it, sighing. "Then so be it. Go and meet them. Confirm the information they give you if you can. You have a week."

Vic's eyebrows raised in surprise. "Why so long?" The smirk that played across Michael's lips looked distinctly devilish to Vic, and he instinctively knew that he wouldn't like what the other man was about to say.

"I need Miss Danvers to spend some more time with Ichi." *Oh yes, I didn't like that at all.*

"I thought you wanted him to be keeping her in line, not keeping her company," Vic replied, attempting to hide his annoyance and failing.

Michael's smile grew wider. "Let's just say that I've changed tactic slightly, but my goal of keeping Miss Danvers compliant is still the same. You can go," Michael said, waving a hand towards the door as an abrupt signal that the conversation was over.

As Vic made his way back up to his room, he considered the situation he was in. He felt like there was a net slowly closing in on him from all sides, waiting to trap him in one of his many deceptions. But whether that deception would end up being one aimed at Michael or Claire or even Ichi, Vic didn't know. He could only hope that he could keep up his front for long enough to complete what he was doing.

Vic shook his long hair out of his eyes and attempted to clear such thoughts from his head as he opened the door to his room. He considered writing Claire a note to tell her that he'd be gone for a while, but realised with a grimace that in doing so he may raise suspicions that he could certainly do without dealing with, since he had never left a note to explain his absence to her before. *She's gonna be pissed if I don't tell her I'm leaving though.* But Vic couldn't help but feel somewhat relieved; by being absent, Claire couldn't continue to work out whatever it was that she was so close to remembering. *And she absolutely cannot remember anything right now,* Vic thought solemnly. Sighing, he resigned himself to the fact that leaving Claire in Ichi's hands for the moment was the best long-term plan that Vic could see working. *If only Michael hadn't said that that's what he wanted.* Vic couldn't work out what Michael's angle was; he could only hope that whatever it was wouldn't leave Claire so broken that she was beyond Vic's help when he returned.

Claire

Claire was swinging her legs back and forth over the edge of Ichi's dining table. He wasn't there, and indeed Claire shouldn't have been there either. But curiosity had gotten the better of her and Claire had finally relented to her desire to scope out her neighbour's room. Claire had expected that she would have had to make an attempt at picking the lock on Ichi's door (a skill she was, in fact, adept at, as she and her sister used to pick the locks on each other's bedroom doors frequently as teenagers). But to her surprise, Ichi's door had actually been unlocked. *How careless,* she thought. *Or maybe he's simply arrogant and assumes that I wouldn't dare go near his room.*

Claire had been incredibly disappointed at what she had found once she was inside, insomuch as what Claire found was next to nothing. She had felt a spark of hope when she realised Ichi had a clock in his kitchen that she hadn't noticed before, but that spark was quickly extinguished when it became apparent that it no longer worked. Ichi's wardrobe was filled with dark-coloured clothes, and his chests of drawers were barely used at all. Claire had found Ichi's laptop charger on the coffee table, but could see no sign of the laptop itself. She didn't even find anything under the bed. Both the kitchen and shower room were just as impersonal.

Damn it, I thought for sure he'd have some stuff somewhere, Claire thought, irritated. She sighed as she continued to swing her legs from her perch. Claire knew that she should have left Ichi's room already so as not to be caught, but something was preventing her from leaving. She sighed again, this time from exhaustion. Claire had woken up under the fourth floor stairs again at some obscure point that morning, her chin and mouth caked in dried-up blood that had spewed from her nostrils.

"Maybe I *want* him to find me here," Claire mused aloud, disgusted by herself. But she knew that she needed the distraction to prevent her from dwelling on her mysterious late-night sleep walks for too long. And with Vic having disappeared several days prior without so much as a word to Claire about where he was going or how long he'd be (which Claire couldn't help but think was awfully convenient, considering how their last proper conversation had gone), Claire had found herself spending ever more time with Ichi, though she wasn't entirely sure how that had transpired. *He said that I was the one that had to initiate things, but all he seems to do is try and push me to do so when* he *wants me to.* Claire laughed quietly as she realised that Ichi *always* seemed to want her to 'initiate' things at any given second, so perhaps he figured that that meant he wasn't breaking the rules of his own game.

Claire couldn't help but admit that it was getting harder and harder to ignore her desire to do exactly as Ichi wished. He had spent the last five days listening intently to her past and all of the minute things Claire could remember, only occasionally interrupting her to pass some sarcastic comment that he clearly couldn't hold back. There had been no more wine. No more dancing. Only Ichi, sitting beside her at all times, looking at her out of the corner of his eye and smirking as she invariably blushed every time he touched her. And he did so on such a frequent basis that Claire had considered wearing more clothes than was strictly necessary just to avoid any skin-on-skin contact.

And yet here Claire was, wearing Olivia's beautiful white sundress for the first time in months, which exposed as much of her skin as possible. *I really hate myself sometimes,* she thought. And yet the gesture also made Claire fiercely proud; wearing the dress meant that she had gotten over what Ichi had done to her, in much the same way as wearing her lilac one again had helped her get over the trauma of her kidnap. *But when I wore that I ended up having sex with Ichi…oh crap. What is my subconscious doing to me?!* Claire shook her head in self-directed fury. For how was it possible that she wanted that to happen again? Claire had sworn to herself that sleeping with Ichi had been a mistake. A terrible, stupid, alcohol-induced mistake. Claire closed her eyes, as if doing so would make the world disappear.

"And yet here I am," she finally muttered.

"Yes, here you are. May I ask why?" Claire flinched at the sound of Ichi's voice and opened her eyes. *How did I not hear him come in?!* Claire thought, unnerved. Ichi seemed both surprised and amused at her sitting there on the table. With his face flushed and wearing a black tank top and dark grey jogging pants, Claire could only conclude that Ichi had just been in the gym. Claire looked away, her face reddening.

"Your door was unlocked," she mumbled in response to Ichi's question.

"I know."

Claire whipped her head back around to stare at him. "Why would you leave it unlocked? It doesn't seem like you at all." Ichi smirked at her the way he always did, and Claire had to struggle not to blush again.

"It was an experiment. It's been unlocked since the night you drunkenly thought you could snoop around in my room. I can't believe it took you this long to try again." Ichi's smirk widened into a grin at the appalled look on Claire's face.

"Is that all I am to you – an experiment? Because I've had just about enough of being an experiment," Claire replied in a low voice, thinking of her parents. And for half a second, Claire almost thought she saw a flash of sympathy cross Ichi's face, but it was gone before she could be sure it had ever been there. Having put herself into an altogether much darker mood, Claire pushed off of Ichi's dining table, intending to leave. However, the man himself had crossed over to Claire in the moment it had taken her to decide to do so.

"And where do you think you're going, dressed like that?" Ichi murmured into Claire's ear. He had pinned her against the table, reminding Claire of him doing the exact same thing to her all those months ago in the classroom she still couldn't bear to go into. *I knew I shouldn't have worn this dress. I'm not over it at all.* Claire couldn't stop her body from shivering slightly at the memory. *How can I be so terrified of what happened and* still *want to have sex with him? I don't even make sense to myself any more.*

And now Ichi's hands were on Claire's waist, but as soon as Claire glanced down at them Ichi began to move them slowly upwards, lingering over the skin of her cleavage before bringing them up to her face, forcing her head upwards to look at him.

Claire was scared of what she might find in Ichi's eyes, but when she finally looked into them Claire discovered that Ichi looked confused. "…what?" she half-whispered.

Ichi took a moment to reply. "I don't understand what you're doing," he said.

"What do you mean?"

Ichi frowned. "Why are you here, wearing that? What are you looking for from me? An apology? You're not going to get one," he replied frankly. Claire pulled Ichi's hands away from her face, half-horrified by his response and half-furious.

"As if I'd ever expect that from you!" Claire attempted to storm away but Ichi followed her, and when she reached the couch he pulled her onto it. "Ichi, what are you doing?! Let me go!" Claire cried out in protest, as Ichi lay down on the couch and dragged Claire on top of him, holding onto her wrists to prevent her from leaving.

Ichi raised an eyebrow at her. "I thought you weren't going to have any more emotional outbursts, lest I take advantage of them?" he commented wryly. Claire leant down and viciously bit down into the bottom of Ichi's neck in anger. She had expected the action to loosen his grip on her wrists but, to Claire's surprise, it caused him to tighten his hold on her instead.

"Oh God, do that again please," Ichi groaned, eyes closed, a serene look upon his face. All of Claire's fury abruptly left her as she stared down at Ichi in shock. She could taste his blood on her tongue; little red beads were slowly welling up on his skin from where her teeth had punctured it.

"W-what?" Claire stammered, incredibly confused by what had just transpired. She could feel Ichi rapidly growing hard against her knee as his grip on her wrists grew even tighter.

"Do that to me again. Do it *anywhere,* I don't care." He opened his eyes slightly to look at Claire, and she realised that Ichi was being completely serious.

"…I had you down as a sadist," Claire ended up blurting out.

Ichi let out a chuckle. "How could I be a sadist and spend months enduring countless attempts to monopolise you? That's a pain all on its own. No," Ichi replied, almost to himself, "I'm far more complicated a person to merely be a sadist. You just hadn't worked that out yet."

Claire collapsed against Ichi's chest, exasperated. "It's exhausting trying to understand you," she mumbled into his bloodied neck.

"Well then it seems we share the same sentiment towards each other," Ichi replied. Claire felt him let go of her wrists in order to put an arm around her back. He shuffled over on the couch an inch or two, allowing Claire to sink into it right next to him. She didn't even try to protest; Claire discovered that she had lost all of the will and energy to do so. "Although I rather think your exhaustion stems from not sleeping at all last night," Ichi added on, his voice quiet.

Claire glanced up at him, immediately suspicious. "How could you know that?" Ichi turned his head to face hers, and they were so close that Claire was certain that Ichi was going to kiss her.

"Because you look half-dead again. It's not actually a bad look on you, with your skin as pale as it is and my blood running down your chin," he joked. Claire was halfway towards a retort when she felt Ichi's lips brush against her own as he cleared away the blood with the tip of his tongue. Claire's heart was battering against her ribcage; she knew Ichi must be able to feel it too. And then, when Claire was seconds away from giving in to her incessant desire to kiss the deplorable man at her side, Ichi spoke again. "Try and sleep, Claire. You can't possibly function without any. I would know."

Claire glanced at Ichi through her eyelashes and realised, to her surprise, that he also looked exhausted. *Why hadn't I noticed earlier? Was it because he made me so angry?* Ichi pulled down a blanket that was draped over the top of his couch to cover the two of them.

"How could you possibly expect me to sleep in this situation?" she complained, but Claire felt herself moulding to the side of Ichi's body nonetheless. His arm tightened around her slightly.

"Just shut up and sleep," he said, and eventually she did.

Ichi

Ichi woke up hours later to discover that Claire had disappeared. He glanced over at the clock in his kitchen only to remember that the batteries in it had run dry months ago. He stretched over the edge of the couch and nimbly extracted his laptop from underneath a loose floorboard that was hidden underneath it, then lay on his back as its system booted up. When it had, Ichi saw that it was close to four in the morning. *I can't believe we slept for nearly seven hours.* Or, at least, *he* had slept for seven hours; Ichi couldn't be sure when Claire had actually left his room. It irked him somewhat that Claire had left without waking him up.

Ichi swung himself up into a sitting position and promptly flinched at a sharp pain between his neck and right shoulder as he did so. When he brought his hand up to soothe the pain away, Ichi remembered what had happened to cause the pain in the first place and couldn't help but curse aloud. *If I hadn't been so damn tired there's no way I could have stopped myself from screwing her on the spot after she did that.* Ichi had been extremely surprised to discover that he drew immense pleasure from Claire biting him, and he wondered whether it was because he liked pain or merely enjoyed it because Claire had inflicted it. He vaguely recalled being excited when she had stabbed his face with his own knife several weeks prior. *I'll have to investigate this…it's not like anybody else has ever managed to harm me.* Alexis had never attempted anything that resembled violence against him, no matter how often Ichi had bitten into her.

Ichi brushed the idea of Alexis away as he scanned the camera feeds from Claire's room, but he couldn't find her anywhere. *Odd,* he thought. *It's just like last night, and several other nights before that.* Ichi had assumed that Claire had headed over to Vic's on those initial nights, regardless of how pissed off the idea made him, but Vic had been gone from the complex for several days, leaving Claire's location the previous night and at present as mysteries.

"So where are you off to, Claire?" Ichi mumbled aloud. Ichi glanced at his door and spontaneously decided to investigate. He jogged easily down the stairs, checking underneath every staircase (taking extra care in exploring the alcove under the fourth floor) as he passed them. But Claire was nowhere to be found on the stairs, so Ichi checked the rec hall; the gym and swimming pool; the large practice hall and, finally, each classroom in turn. Ichi somehow doubted that she would be in any of them but he lingered in the one he had attacked her in regardless. *She was in an odd mood and wearing that white dress, after all.* And yet Claire was not there, and it left Ichi feeling confused. He wondered if she had broken into another one of the rooms in the complex. *I suppose she could be speaking to Michael, but that doesn't feel right,* Ichi thought.

Resigned to having failed to satisfy his curiosity, Ichi walked over to the elevator and pressed the button to call it. When he realised that it was currently on the sub-basement floor, Ichi frowned. *I don't recall the doctor ever working so late before. Maybe it's Michael?* But Ichi's question was answered when the elevator arrived and its doors pinged open to reveal Claire.

"Claire, what the hell were you –" Ichi started to ask as he got into the lift and pressed the twelfth floor button, but the question caught in his throat as Claire turned around and Ichi saw her face. Claire's nose was beginning to bleed; her eyes seemed glassy and lifeless. "Claire?" he ventured, and was caught by surprise as Claire grabbed onto his shoulders and threw him against the mirrored wall of the elevator, kissing him furiously. Ichi pushed her away a few inches in order to look at her face. "Claire, what's up with you? Why are you bleeding?" he asked as he brought a hand up to wipe the blood from her face.

But Claire didn't answer any of his questions, instead proceeding to press her body back up against his. Clare bit into his neck in the same location as before, opening up the puncture wounds afresh. "Claire, if you do that, I –" Ichi began, but Claire's mouth was back on his before he could finish his warning. When the lift doors opened to let them on to the twelfth floor, Claire pushed Ichi out into the corridor and against the opposite wall. Ichi could feel his common sense rapidly leaving him as he struggled not to reciprocate Claire's advances. But when she reached down to tug at his trousers, Ichi snapped, threw Claire to the floor and was on her in a second. He barely felt his hand untie the straps of her dress as he kissed her so violently that he thought he must surely have bruised both of their lips.

And then something changed. Ichi felt Claire stiffen underneath him, and he opened his eyes to see Claire looking lost and confused. "Ichi, what are you…what happened?" Ichi had to use all of his willpower to not continue with what he was doing regardless of Claire's questions, but he dragged himself back to reality nonetheless.

"I woke up and you were gone," Ichi replied honestly, "Then I went looking for you and eventually found you in the elevator. I swear to God, you were completely out of it and your nose was bleeding. And then you basically jumped me. I *did* protest...at first." Claire pushed up on Ichi's chest slightly and he took the hint to sit up. Claire followed suit, grabbing at her untied dress straps as they began to fall away. But instead of growing red from embarrassment as Ichi had expected, Claire's face was pale as a ghost. She stared at Ichi with terrified eyes. Ichi couldn't help but feel what he assumed was concern, though he reasoned that it could also simply be his morbid curiosity. "This has happened more than once, hasn't it?" he asked.

Claire suddenly looked away. "I don't want to talk about it." Ichi made to grab for her shoulder but Claire stood up and began to walk towards her room, so Ichi stood up and followed after her.

"You'll have to, if you want my help," he countered.

Claire glanced over her shoulder at him as she opened her door. "Then I guess I don't want you tonight," she replied, closing the door behind her.

"And what the hell is that supposed to mean?!" Ichi ended up shouting at Claire's door despite himself. He stood on the spot for a minute or two, furious and confused, knowing that at least half of his anger came from the fact that he was currently thinking with his dick and not his brain. "You can't just do that and walk away," Ichi muttered as he stalked back to his room, turning on the shower when he got there.

Yet even after tending to his own needs in the shower, Ichi still felt antsy and incredibly unsatisfied. He paced around his room for close to thirty minutes, wondering what he could do. Eventually he decided that he couldn't take it anymore and walked over to his door. *Screw my rules; I'm fed up waiting for her to make the next move.* But when he roughly threw open his door, body full of adrenaline and testosterone, Ichi was abruptly taken aback by the presence of Claire, her hand in a fist as if she were about to knock on the door. She looked up at him, and her expression was both fiery and vulnerable at the same time. Ichi wondered how that was possible.

"Claire?" he said questioningly, entirely confused by her presence at his door.

"I lied," was all Claire said as she threw her arms around Ichi's neck and kissed him.

CHAPTER 26
Down Down Down

Vic

"Hey you, sleepyhead! Time to get up. You're not going to sleep all morning, are you?" Vic murmured into Claire's ear. He had been shocked to discover that she was still asleep at eleven in the morning upon his return to the complex, after checking all of the places Claire would normally be.

Vic was supposed to have headed directly to Michael's office when he returned, but after everything he had discovered during his week away he couldn't help but see Claire first. And so here Vic was, sitting on the edge of Claire's bed and revelling in how relaxed and carefree her face looked as she clung on to sleep. Vic thought that he couldn't possibly love anybody more than he loved Claire in that moment, when she looked so much like her old self that he couldn't bear it. Not for the first time, Vic wished that Claire had her memories back. *Well, some of them at least.* But Vic knew that that desire was selfish and would put Claire in an even more dangerous situation than she was already in.

This may be the final time I ever get to see her so...so happy, Vic thought, smiling sadly at the content look plastered across Claire's face. He nudged Claire's shoulder, trying to rouse her from her unusually deep sleep. He wondered what had happened in the seven days that he was gone that would cause Claire to sleep so well.

"Not right now, Ichi, give me a chance to sleep..." Vic heard Claire mutter, and suddenly his question received the worst possible answer. He felt a surge of anger course right through him, but Vic forced it away in an attempt to think rationally. *You knew this would happen, Vic,* he reminded himself. He shook his head slightly. *What's more important is why* Michael *wanted Ichi to get his hands on Claire like this.* Vic felt himself frown. Trying to work out why Michael wanted to do anything was like attempting to untie an impossibly tight knot; it made Vic either want to give up trying entirely or to simply walk up to the man and demand an explanation. *But I can't do that,* Vic sighed. *Michael's been playing Ichi like a fiddle from the beginning, and all simply to control Claire. I wasn't here to try and stop Claire from doing whatever it is Ichi's doing with her, which means...which means my being here* would *have prevented it, and Michael knew it,* Vic realised with a grimace. *Which is why he sent me out for so long on an ordinarily short job. Why the hell is Ichi sleeping with Claire so important to Michael's game plan?*

He continued to watch Claire sleep for several, long minutes. *Do you even know that you're surrounded by a pack of wolves, princess? And some of them should have been sheep.* Vic hovered his fingers over Claire's shoulder as he wondered whether to attempt to wake her up again, but just as he decided against it Claire opened her eyes slightly and spied him sitting there. When she realised who was beside her, Claire opened her eyes wider and made to sit up. When she did, Vic suddenly pulled her into a fierce hug. *This better work, for your sake,* he thought. *And mine, too.*

"Vic, what –"

"Shh, don't say anything," he interrupted. Keeping his voice quiet, Vic continued to speak: "Please don't ask me where I was; I can't tell you. Just...give me some more time. I know you have a million questions, but you have to be patient." He felt Claire wriggle against his chest slightly to glance up at him, through a tangle of hair that had been slept on for far too long. *Just give me enough time to save you,* he added on silently.

"You said that last time, Vic." Claire also kept her voice quiet, and for that Vic was grateful.

Vic looked down at her, his face grave. "Yes, and that was a horrendously dangerous conversation to have in this complex. Do you know how lucky you are that there are no cameras in my room?" Vic's voice was barely a whisper.

Claire bit her lip. "Vic, what's going on?"

He pulled her in even closer to his chest. "All you need to do is wait a little longer, I swear. In a few weeks this will all be over. Now hug me back or something, otherwise this'll look incredibly suspicious."

"Wait, Michael has cameras in here?"

"Of course he does, princess. Surely you knew he'd be keeping tabs on you in here?"

"I suppose I knew," Claire replied, though she sounded infinitely more unnerved than she had done just seconds before. She brought her arms up to wrap them around Vic's neck. "It's just…such an invasion of privacy," Claire added on.

Vic chuckled down at her as he let her go to stand up. "Why would you have expected anything less? Now come on," he said, raising his voice back up to an ordinary speaking volume. "I'm not having you sleep all day. Go get changed and we can head down to the practice hall." Claire grinned at him, and Vic couldn't help but be impressed by how genuine she made it look.

"I'll floor you this time, I hope you know that," she said slyly.

Vic laughed at the statement. "We'll see, we'll see."

But when the pair of them reached the practice hall, Vic heard the sound of hurried footsteps behind them and turned to see Marie. When the woman reached them, Vic smiled at her and Claire voiced a hello. Marie returned their greeting with a frown directed entirely at Vic.

"Are you really going to keep Michael waiting all morning for a status update, you fool? He's getting pretty antsy about you seemingly ignoring him," Marie scolded.

"Ah, shit, I almost forgot about that," Vic replied, with a chuckle that belied his reluctance to talk to Michael. He turned to Claire. "Sorry, princess, can you take care of yourself for the next half hour or so? I won't be too long, I promise."

"Claire! There you are," came Imran's voice suddenly from behind Vic.

"Hey Imran," Claire said with a smile on her face. "I may have slept in and missed practice," she added on sheepishly.

Imran cuffed her over the head. "Yeah, today and yesterday and the day before that too. You're getting lazy!" Vic felt a twinge of jealousy in the back of his mind at the idea of what Claire had been doing to sleep in for three days straight.

Claire's face flushed a furious red before turning to face Vic. "I'll practice with Imran until you get back, Vic."

Imran grinned up at him. "Oh, are you finally going to let her fight against you again?" Imran asked. "Because I think you'll find she's a hell of a lot better now than she was before. I'm going to have to get Ryan down so we can watch how you do against her!" Vic felt Marie elbow him in the ribs.

"You can chat later. Go see Michael first, you idiot." So Vic waved them all a good bye and headed towards the stairs but was surprised when he realised that Marie had followed him. When the two of them reached the door to the basement, Marie put out a hand to stop Vic from going through it.

"What's up, Marie?" he asked her, trying to sound nonchalant.

"Cut the crap, Vic. I've known you for far too long for you to act like something's not up," Marie scolded. "I know we haven't been able to talk properly for a while, and you don't have to apologise for that," she said, when it became apparent that Vic was going to attempt to do just that. Marie softened up her serious expression with a small smile. "Whatever it is that's going on is obviously important to you, and Claire even more so. And I don't want to know what those things are besides what you told me months ago, because I don't want to get involved in anything that would complicate my job. But I will warn you, Vic: be careful. I don't think you're fooling as many people as you think with that carefree act, okay?"

Vic raised his eyebrows in surprise at his closest, and likely only genuine, friend. "Thanks for the heads up," he replied, then he smiled at her. "I'm sorry for making you worry. There's just so much going on right now. Too much, possibly. And I can't tell *her* any of it."

Marie gave him a sympathetic look. "Trust me, she might be pissed at you for keeping her in the dark, but from where I'm standing your princess definitely wouldn't be able to handle all of the shit you want to drop on her right now."

"How eloquently put," Vic chuckled as he made to ruffle Marie's hair, but she dodged his hand.

"Hey, I'm not a kid, you fool. Do you do that to Claire?"

"…all the time," Vic admitted.

Marie rolled her eyes. "God, no wonder Ichi got to her. And don't give me that look," she admonished when she saw the outraged expression on

273

Vic's face. "You don't consistently treat her seriously. You baby her. Ichi absolutely doesn't. I mean, I don't think he could do so if his life depended on it, but...my point is, he's always serious about Claire. And he doesn't have anything to hide. I think she likes that. Ahh, but what girl wouldn't?" Marie added on as an afterthought. She glanced at Vic. "I know you can't help that you're hiding things from her, so there's nothing you can do on that front. But you can at least treat her like a full grown woman rather than a kid sister." Marie stared at the door that connected the stairwell to the basement. "You really should go speak to Michael now."

Vic gave Marie a long, searching look. "You're my best friend, you know."

Marie smiled, and it was sad. "Yes, and more fool me for it. Now go!" So Vic left through the door, thinking about everything Marie had said. *But where's the line between treating Claire like a kid and making her laugh and feel comfortable?* Vic thought about their tango from just over a week ago and sighed. *Whenever I act seriously I end up getting carried away. I don't know what I should do anymore.* When Vic reached Michael's office, he shook his head several times to try and clear it. *If Claire only knew how seriously I took her, and the lengths I've been going to just for her...*

"Stop lingering by the doorway and come in, Vic," he suddenly heard Michael call through the door. Vic took a deep breath, exhaled, and then entered the office. Michael had a frown on his face. "Are you going to let me know what was so important to you that you blatantly disregarded my orders to come straight to me upon your return to the complex?" his boss asked as Vic sat down. *At least for this meeting, I can tell Michael around eighty percent of the truth. That's better than usual.*

"I went to see Claire. Don't bother having a go at me about it," he added on when he saw how visibly irked Michael was at his answer. "You know how I feel about her. And after what I found out, I just wanted to see her first."

"Which is?"

Vic took another deep breath. "Claire's parents intend to have her assassinated at the awards ceremony if it looks like there's even a chance that she has her memories back."

Michael's frowned deepened. "But she hasn't. Or if she has, then she's doing a damn fine job of keeping what she's remembered to herself," Michael replied. "So what is their point in seeing —"

"Because they want to make sure she hasn't told you anything," Vic said, daring to interrupt his boss.

Michael's eyes narrowed even further. "Then that means…"

"Yes. They don't plan on saving her at all. Getting her to the ceremony is simply a way for them to ensure that they can get rid of her if she's remembered anything."

Michael was silent for a moment. "Why would they only kill her if it appears that she remembers something?" he pondered quietly, almost to himself. "If she hasn't, then Miss Danvers would be returned to the complex. Where, if their concern is correct that she could remember something on her own, she may be able to recall part of her parents' research at some point in the future and relay that information to me?"

"My sources tell me that her parents strongly believe it to be impossible for Claire to remember anything about their research without their buzzword. Apparently they plan on having her hear it at the event to see if it triggers anything."

Michael looked up at Vic sharply. "But that would mean that they plan for their daughter to definitely remember everything and then kill her for it."

Vic shook his head at the statement. "No, not so. If I remember correctly from when you had me guard over their lab in the months before they disappeared, the buzzword is only supposed to work if her *father* says it, so if Claire were to hear it said in somebody else's voice then it shouldn't trigger anything. And that's what they want to confirm…apparently their cold-heartedness stops at assassinating their own bloody daughter if she definitely cannot recall anything. But that then condemns her to a life in captivity, or death at your hands for being useless." Vic paused for long enough to glare at his boss, deciding that the best way to hide his upcoming deception was to push his emotions to the front of the conversation. "You told me in the beginning that Claire's parents would definitely give themselves up for their daughter, Michael! But I was right all along. The fuckers —"

"Calm down, Vic," Michael interrupted. "You absolutely must stop prioritising your feelings for the girl over your job, or there will be consequences."

"In this instance, both priorities line up perfectly."

"Not if I intend to kill her for being 'useless', as you only just suggested."

"But you won't."

Michael raised an eyebrow. "And why do you suppose that?"

"Because I don't believe for a second that you think Claire Danvers is useless." Michael smirked, and it reminded Vic terribly of Ichi when he was up to something unspeakable.

"And on that front you would be correct," Michael said. "I'm assuming you have already begun preparing countermeasures for whatever assassins her parents will be putting in place at the awards ceremony?"

Vic rolled his eyes. "As if you needed to ask. I took the liberty of contacting Misao and Ray in Beijing and told them to get their asses back over here to help out with that."

"How audacious of you, ordering my own agents around like that."

Vic grinned. "I had a feeling you'd forgive me, given how damn important this research seems to be to you."

Michael returned the grin with an altogether more devilish one. "And I have the feeling you can keep Miss Danvers alive and well for me, given how damn important she seems to be to you." The remark caused Vic to grow serious once more. He hesitated, wondering if it was worth voicing his thoughts. Michael raised an eyebrow at him. "What is it?"

Vic sighed. "I don't suppose we could simply…not take her to the event? Since we know it won't do anything other than put her life at risk, I mean."

Michael considered Vic for a long moment. "No," he eventually said. And then: "I have a theory I want to test out for myself, so Miss Danvers will have to be the belle of the ball and you will have to protect her. I entirely trust that I can rely on you to do that." Michael glanced at the laptop he had open on the desk in front of him and smiled. "You should be getting to the main practice hall, Vic. It appears Miss Danvers is defending herself against two assailants, and I don't imagine you want to miss that."

Vic inclined his head at Michael as he stood up. After he left the office and headed back up the stairs to the practice hall, he wondered what on earth Michael's 'theory' could possibly be about. *But if I get my way, he'll never get to test it,* Vic thought. *If all goes well, Claire and I will be long gone before Michael or Claire's parents can do anything about it.*

CHAPTER 27
Fighter

Vic

Claire was enthralling to watch. She had both Ryan and Imran attacking her, yet she was managing to hold her own against them both. Claire was dodging their kicks and parrying their fists before they got too close to her, replying in kind with lightning quick reflexes that Vic had never seen her use before. Even from behind the glass of the viewing gallery, he could see the sweat beading up on Claire's forehead, her chest heaving from the struggle to bring oxygen back into her lungs, but Claire didn't seem like she had any intention of giving up the fight.

Vic glanced to his right; Ichi and Marie were watching Claire fend of Ryan and Imran with two completely different expressions. Marie had a grin spread across her face that only grew wider every time Claire landed a blow against her assailants, but Ichi...Ichi had a rather calculative look about him, as if he were analysing every detail of the fight happening before his eyes and hadn't yet reached a conclusion about it.

"If she fights like that against you, Vic, you might actually be in trouble," Marie commented without looking away from Claire. Ichi said nothing, so engrossed in whatever he was thinking about that Vic wasn't even sure if the other man knew he was there. Vic watched the fight continue for another couple of minutes, until it looked like Claire would collapse from exhaustion for sure. Then he entered the hall, calling out to Ryan and Imran as he did so.

"I think that's enough, guys. You've gotta leave Claire enough energy to fight *me*, remember?" The two men stopped what they were doing to look at Vic. He was satisfied to see that both of them were also breathing heavily. *Looks like Claire was a bigger challenge that they had anticipated,* Vic thought, a feeling of pride swelling through him at the notion.

"Who are you to tell us to stop – the big, bad, final boss?" Ryan asked sarcastically.

Vic smirked at him. "Something like that." He spied Claire out of the corner of his eye using the temporary respite to guzzle down as much water as she possibly could from the bottle she had brought with her. "You ready for round two, princess?" he asked.

Claire wiped the sweat away from her forehead and took several, long breaths before replying, "Almost."

Imran walked over to Claire and punched her gently on the arm. "If you ever feel like changing career, you should seriously consider our line of work," he joked.

Claire rolled her eyes. "I'll keep that in mind." Vic saw her shift her focus over to the viewing gallery to wave at Marie. She seemed to completely ignore Ichi. *Weird,* Vic thought. *I expected them to be acting...differently, somehow. But they're exactly the same with each other as they were a week ago. Maybe I read Claire all wrong this morning; maybe nothing's happened between them.* Vic knew it was a desperate thought to cling on to, yet he felt himself clinging to it nonetheless, despite Marie's words from earlier. "Vic? Are you there?" he heard Claire say to him, so he forced himself out of his own head to smile down at her.

"Sorry, I was thinking about something. You ready now?" Claire frowned slightly for half a moment, but it was just as quickly replaced with a grin.

"As ready as I'll ever be."

"Okay, then punch me in the face."

Claire took a step back from Vic, confused "What...?"

"You heard me," Vic replied, his tone serious. "Punch me as hard as you can. You never seemed to want to when fighting me before, and I don't want you to hold back in the slightest. So you're going to get one in now. I'm not going to go easy on you, and I'll be damned if you try and hold back again after I just witnessed first-hand what you're capable of. So don't patronise me, and hit me with all you've got."

Claire

Claire still hadn't quite recovered from the onslaught Ryan and Imran had brought down upon her, but despite that Claire felt like her body had never been more ready for a fight against Vic than it was right now. *Or maybe it's* because *of them,* she mused. But to punch Vic in the face before they even got started? Claire wasn't sure she could do it. She closed her eyes for a moment whilst she breathed in deeply through her nose, letting the air out in a low whistle after a few seconds. She looked up at Vic; his face was deadly serious.

Claire realised that the last time she had seen him look so serious was the night he had found her lying in that classroom, covered in white paint and bruises. The thought made Claire involuntarily look over at Ichi, and she immediately regretted it. Claire had discovered from the past few days that it didn't do her any good to think about the terrible things Ichi had done to her whilst she was currently engaged in a consensual relationship with the man. *Is 'relationship' even the correct word for it?* Claire mused. *That doesn't feel right at all.*

"Oh for fuck's sake Claire, look at *me!*" she heard Vic complain in a tone that belied his normally, extremely composed self. And hearing him say that one phrase, that one order that Ichi was always giving her, caused Claire to abruptly snap. She remembered that she was furious with Vic for all of his deceptions, and that he absolutely had no prerogative to tell her to do *anything*, and Claire felt her fist connect with the right hand side of Vic's face before she knew it. Vic staggered backwards half an inch at the attack, surprise written all over his features despite the fact that it was he who had ordered Claire to hit him. But before Vic had the opportunity to regain his composure, Claire hit him again, this time with a backhanded strike that left a blazing red mark across his cheek.

He didn't let the third strike hit. Vic parried it with his left arm, and tried to use the momentum of Claire's attempted punch against her. But Claire had expected that, and she ducked under his arm before he could do so before snapping out a roundhouse kick that barely hit the back of his head. Vic swiftly turned around to face Claire, sweeping his leg out as he did so in an attempt to kick Claire's feet out from under her. But Claire gracefully avoided the attack, and responded with an identical leg sweep whilst all of Vic's weight was on one foot, and that was all she needed; Vic was unbalanced just long enough for Claire to throw a ferocious side kick at his gut, spinning around to aim another at his head when he recoiled, and then he was down. Claire leapt on top of him, driven by nothing but sheer fury and the desire to see Vic's blood on the floor, and punched him in the face, again and again and again.

"Claire, what – what's wrong?! Stop it!" Vic barely managed to spit out between punches. Claire could feel his hands on her waist, trying to pull her off, but Claire seemed to have drawn some new-found strength from somewhere and she kept her ground.

"You don't…get to tell me…what to do! You don't! *None of you do!*" Claire screamed at Vic, as she continued to ruin his beautiful face. When she hit his nose, a spray of blood exploded across her knuckles. Claire vaguely heard somebody shouting at her in the background, but she didn't hear what they were saying. Her vision had gone red, red, red and black, and she couldn't feel anything but rage. In the back of her mind, a very small part of Claire's brain was protesting against what she was doing to Vic, telling her that he didn't deserve this, but it was too easily washed away by her primal desire to knock the life out of him.

Eventually, she felt somebody remove her from her position on top of Vic, and Claire, furious, turned her head around to see that it was Ichi. "Let me go!" she raged, not quite seeing him as she struggled against his iron grip on her arms, but Ichi turned Claire fully around to face him and forcibly kissed her, biting into her lip until it bled. And the pain brought Claire back, just a little. She looked down at her hands, curled up into bloody fists, and she looked at Vic, who wasn't conscious. She swept her head from side to side, and saw Marie run towards them and then crouch down to help Vic, Imran and Ryan only feet away with shocked expressions on their faces…and Alexis. Alexis was by the door, looking straight at Claire, and she was horrified.

"Claire, what have you –" she heard Alexis say, but Claire thrust herself out of Ichi's grasp without looking at him and bolted past the other woman before she could finish her sentence. Claire ran up the stairs to her fourth floor alcove and collapsed onto her knees. She could feel herself beginning to hyperventilate.

"What have I done what have I done what have I done?" Claire kept repeating, over and over again, until the words no longer held any meaning to her ears. Claire stared at her hands without seeing them; all she could see was red. And the rage was still there – it wouldn't go away. Claire could feel her eyes beginning to well up, and couldn't stop the tears when they began to stream unchecked down her face. But even the tears didn't wash away the unexplainable anger Claire was experiencing, and she felt her entire body begin to shake with it.

"Claire. Claire!" she heard a female voice call out to her. Claire blinked enough focus back into her eyes to realise that Alexis was kneeling in front of her.

"What are you –" Claire began, but Alexis interrupted her.

"Long breaths. Take long breaths, Claire, and close your eyes. Think of the sea. Think of grass. Think of God damn bunny rabbits if it helps, but don't think of red. It needs to go away; you need to get back in *control*. And you hate not being in control." Alexis was forcing Claire to hold her gaze, and in the back of her mind Claire acknowledged that Alexis looked incredibly distraught. *Strange,* she thought. *How strange.* "Come on," Alexis continued, "You can try harder than that! You know you can!"

Claire felt the other woman's fingers grip tightly into her arms, and the pain worked in much the same way as when Ichi had bitten her. It brought Claire back, just a little bit more, and then a little bit more. She forced herself to slow her breathing, keeping her eyes on Alexis. And, by what felt like a miracle, Claire felt the rage starting to dissipate as more of her own self began to permeate back through.

"Al-Alexis?" Claire finally stuttered, in a small, small voice. "What have I done?" As the fiery emotions left her, Claire felt more vulnerable than she had ever done in her entire life, and it was in that one moment when she needed another person the most that Alexis pulled away from her.

The other woman stood up. "You *cannot* let this happen again," she said. Claire looked up at her through a fresh wave of tears.

"What am I supposed to do?" she cried out pleadingly, but Alexis' expression was cold and indifferent, as it had been for most of the time Claire had known her.

Alexis regarded her for a moment. "You cope. You deal with it. Do whatever it takes, but deal with it." And with that, Alexis turned tail for her room through the fourth floor door. Claire stared down at her hands again, dumbfounded, before she felt the tears break down her face again as she allowed herself to cry hysterically, regardless of who could see or hear her.

*

Claire had barely spoken a word to anybody days later, and she hadn't seen Vic at all. The guilt Claire felt for what she had done to him had gotten so unbearable that, every night, she numbed the feeling away by allowing Ichi to screw her senseless until she could almost forget about it all. She could tell that her behaviour was infuriating him, but in typical Ichi fashion he was clearly loathe to bring up the subject of Vic, so he avoided it altogether and continued to sleep with Claire regardless of her reasons for wanting him to do so. Claire knew it made her a despicable person.

I'll just add it to the ever-growing list of things that are wrong with me, she thought humourlessly. Claire had expected that her violent outburst would have demanded at least a warning or two from Michael, but there seemed to have been no repercussions to her actions whatsoever. *Apart from the fact that nobody will speak to me now.* Claire supposed it was because she was avoiding everybody, but she couldn't help but feel like the other residents in Michael's complex had grown somewhat wary of her.

"Ha!" she barked from her solitary position in the corner of the rec hall, where she had sat looking at the same page of her Kindle for the past half an hour. "Assassins being wary of Claire Danvers. Who'd have ever thought it?"

"Who indeed?" Claire heard Ichi murmur into her ear, startling her out of her own head. Claire turned around slightly to look at him, unnerved that she hadn't heard him enter the rec hall at all. Ichi gave her a half-grin as he took the seat beside her. He was carrying what Claire could only describe as some kind of large leather folder; for a moment she wondered what was in it.

"What do you want, Ichi?" Claire sighed, running a hand absent-mindedly through her hair. She rarely spoke to Ichi during the day; it helped

Claire avoid thinking about what she was doing with him when the sun went down. Not that she had seen the sun rise or fall for months now, but the sentiment was there. And to keep Ichi even more at a distance, Claire never slept with him in her own room – it was always on his bed, on his couch, on his floor…and then Claire would leave. In the middle of the night, when Ichi was fast asleep, Claire would leave, though not always consciously. On at least half of the occasions, she had woken up under the fourth floor stairs, or in the rec hall, or on the floor of her own room, with no memory of having gotten there. But Ichi hadn't complained about her leaving in the small hours of the morning, nor indeed had he asked *why*. Claire was grateful for this, even if his not asking was out of sheer apathy rather than any kind of respect for Claire's privacy, of which Claire suspected Ichi had none.

"I want you back," Ichi said, so matter-of-factly that Claire laughed.

"Excuse me?"

Ichi brought his seat in closer to Claire's, and she felt a familiar heat creep up over her cheeks. "You've not been yourself since you pummelled Vic half to death," Ichi explained, and Claire flinched at his words.

She looked at the floor. "I'd say that that's a pretty fair reason for not acting like myself," Claire mumbled as she struggled not to think about how Vic had looked after Ichi had pulled her off of him. Ichi lifted her chin up with a finger, forcing Claire to look at him.

"Do you not think it strange?"

Claire frowned at him. "You'll have to be more specific, Ichi. Everything is strange now."

Ichi stared at her, and it made Claire feel uncomfortable. "Vic was being strange," he eventually explained. "He could have thrown you off of him, but he didn't. Yes, I know it *looks* like he tried," Ichi added on, when it appeared that Claire would argue the point, "But trust me, I know Vic's full strength. He could *definitely* have stopped you. Which leads me to suspect that he probably allowed you to beat him up to let out all of your anger against him. Though perhaps he didn't expect you to knock him unconscious." Ichi laughed, sounding genuinely amused by the notion.

Claire was speechless for a moment. It hadn't occurred to her that Vic had actually allowed her to attack him, but now that she thought about it, it made perfect sense, given Vic's personality. Claire stood up suddenly. "I need to see him," she announced, more to the empty rec hall than to Ichi, and she rushed out of the double doors. It took her a second to realise that Ichi had followed directly behind her, strange black folder in tow.

When Claire reached the hallway, Ichi wrapped an arm around her waist and easily dragged her into the nearest classroom before locking it behind him. Claire spun around to face him, annoyed. "Ichi, I don't have the time for this," she said, but Ichi ignored her protest. He turned from her in order to open up his leather folder, and when Claire caught a flash of silver she felt her face grow cold. "Ichi, what are you doing?" she asked. Ichi glanced up at her, and there was a calculative edge to his expression that Claire had seen on his face before – whilst he had watched her fight against Ryan and Imran and then against Vic.

Ichi extricated a knife from the collection he had brought with him, and Claire realised with horror that it was the very same one he had intended to use to kill her, all those months ago. Claire backed away slowly, and could feel a drop of cold sweat run down the back of her spine. Ichi took a step towards her, and then another, his eyes all curious intent.

"I wonder," he said, slowly. "If you could have done so well in those fights if your attacker had been armed. If Ryan or Imran had had a knife, would you have stood a chance? They'd have had them if they went after you on a job, mark my words." Claire glanced behind her and realised that there was nothing behind her but a chair and the wall.

"What's your point, Ichi?" Claire asked, trying desperately to mask the fear in her voice. She could feel her pulse starting to catch in her throat; her breathing was getting shallower and shallower. Flashes of her kidnap flew before her eyes, and they were terrifying.

"None of your punches or side kicks will mean a damn thing if you can't deflect against *this,*" Ichi said, throwing his knife into the air and easily catching it by the handle as it fell. "So I wonder," he muttered, almost to himself, "Can you fight against an armed man?"

Claire felt her eyes go wide with a fear that she could no longer suppress. "I-I can't, Ichi, I can't!" she cried, and all she could see was the knife and how it could so easily cut into her skin as it had before. Ichi took another step towards her, and Claire felt the back of her knees hit the chair behind her. Then Ichi closed the gap between them, and his knife was at Claire's throat. Claire could see the gleam of the blade reflected in Ichi's bright, excited eyes. Claire felt her breathing hitch and she collapsed into the chair behind her. "Put it away!" Claire begged, looking up at Ichi through a flood of tears. "I can't do this, don't do this to me…just…please…I can't…just kill me!" Claire found herself begging, not understanding how the words had appeared on her lips.

And then Ichi leant over her and pulled her head back by her hair, a furious expression on his face. Claire heard his knife clatter to the floor. "Where has all your fire gone?" he demanded, outraged. "Do you realise how *wonderful* it was? Even if I had come at you with *this*," Ichi said, picking up his knife again to place the edge of the blade against Claire's cheek, "It wouldn't have stopped you. You were invincible! When I pulled you off of Vic, I didn't do it to stop you." Ichi dropped his voice down to a murmur, as if what he was about to say was for Claire's ears alone. Claire couldn't tear her eyes from Ichi's fervent, earnest face, both terrified and in awe of it. "I did it because I have never wanted you more than when I saw you fight like that. But your reaction to it all was to sit under the stairs and cry!" Ichi sounded entirely appalled. "When I found you there, I wanted nothing more than to congratulate you, but you were hysterical, like you are now. Where does acting like that get you? That's a serious question, Claire. And you know the answer." Claire was acutely aware of the cold steel resting against her face, completely at odds with the burning in Ichi's eyes. And Claire did know the answer; of course she did.

"It will kill me," she replied, and the words were barely audible. Ichi held the knife against her cheek for a moment longer before allowing it to drop to the floor once again. He lowered himself onto his knees, sighing. Then he placed his hands on the chair's arm rests and looked up at her.

"Kiss me." And Claire didn't question the order; she tilted her head down and softly kissed him. She felt Ichi smirk underneath her mouth. Suddenly, he grabbed on to the back of Claire's head and kissed her back, harder. "It looks like you listen to my orders, after all. What happened to that 'nobody tells me what to do' speech to Vic?" Ichi inquired after Claire pulled away from his lips. Claire brought a hand up to brush the tears away that had yet to dry on her skin.

"You never give me a choice," she answered, and Claire knew that what she had said was only half true. Ichi chuckled at her answer as he stood up to walk back over to his leather folder. When he returned, he was holding

286

onto two small knives, the handles of which had leather bands attached. Claire eyed them up warily as Ichi closed the distance between them.

"Let's run on the assumption that, from this point onwards, you're always armed. Which would be a sensible thing for you to do, by the way." He turned the knives around to proffer the handles to Claire. After a moment she hesitantly took them, and Ichi slipped the leather bands surprisingly gently around her wrists. Claire knew he would be able to feel her pulse still hammering away in fear against his fingertips, so Claire swallowed and tried to force her heartbeat to calm down. Ichi kissed her again before reaching down to pick up his original knife. "Would you be up for trying to defend yourself against me *now*?"

Claire swallowed again and met Ichi's gaze. What had all of her training with Vic been for, if not to be able to defend herself in this exact situation? If she turned away from this opportunity she would be a fool. And a disappointment, Claire acknowledged, not just to herself but also to Ichi, whom Claire was only just beginning to realise she valued the opinion of, perhaps more than anybody else. She allowed herself a few seconds to breathe slowly before smiling very slightly.

"I don't see why I can't try."

Ichi

Ichi never thought a knife fight where there was no intention of killing the opponent could be so exciting. Not that either of them were unscathed, however. Claire was bleeding from a shallow cut to her left hip, and her right arm was also bleeding from a cut that Ichi hadn't intended to go as deep as it had actually gone. But Claire had responded in kind – Ichi's t-shirt was torn from his chest down to his navel by a large backslash Claire had managed to get in. He could feel the blood trickling down his front, intermingled with the sweat from all of the physical exertion.

Claire had danced around most of Ichi's attacks against her, her entire person completely transformed from the cowering mess she had been over the past six days. But Ichi had her in a chokehold now, his blade pressed against the inside of her thigh.

"Give up yet?" he panted. Claire only just managed to look up at him from the stranglehold Ichi had her in, and he could see that Claire was just as excited as he was. She grinned, breathing heavily.

"Never," she protested, but then Ichi's gaze swept over Claire's bleeding right arm. He frowned, and let her go. Claire whipped around to face him, confused. "Why did you let go?" she asked.

Ichi looked at her arm pointedly. "That's bleeding too much. We need to stop, since I'm not *actually* trying to kill you right now."

"…right now. Huh," was Claire's reply, and she turned away from Ichi before he could see the expression on her face. And then, in one deft movement, she pulled the thin top she was wearing over her head and wrapped it around her bleeding arm. Ichi clucked his tongue at her, trying desperately to ignore his desire to fling Claire on to the nearest table, despite her injuries.

"You know fine well that that won't do."

"Of course I know that. I'm going to have Roger look at it. Or maybe I should see the doctor," Claire commented as she inspected how deep the cut was. Ichi walked over and unlocked the classroom door.

"Don't be ridiculous. I can do it up for you," he said, opening the door and gesturing through it to allow Claire to exit first. Claire raised an eyebrow at him.

"Ichi the gentleman. It doesn't suit you at all," she chided. "And I think I'd be better off going to the doctor for this." Ichi laughed softly at her as they waited on the elevator.

"You think I can't stitch up a wound properly? Give me some credit, woman."

Claire looked up at him, appalled. "This *woman* has a name," she complained, but Ichi merely laughed again. When the elevator doors opened, he pushed Claire in and barely gave the doors a chance to close before he started kissing her. Claire used her hands to push his face away after a couple of seconds. "If stitching me up is just a ploy to get me into your room…" Ichi chuckled, then took Claire's hands and placed them on his bloodied chest.

"I need stitched up too. But there's no reason why we can't have sex first." Claire let out a mock sigh of exasperation at his statement. Ichi kissed her once more, then picked her up and bodily carried her out of the lift when the doors opened out onto the twelfth floor.

"Hey, Ichi! You're not giving me much of a choice here," Claire exclaimed, and he felt her pound a fist into his back.

He grinned. "I thought I *never* gave you a choice?" When they reached his door, Ichi kicked it open and closed it behind them, before dropping Claire unceremoniously to the floor.

"You're not being very gentle towards your injured patient," she remarked, as the top she had roughly tied around her arm came loose. Ichi smirked, kneeling down in front of Claire as she sat up.

"Being gentle's for later," he replied, kissing Claire again. Ichi made to push Claire back down onto the floor but was surprised when, instead, she pushed *him* down and began to take off his belt. "Well someone's up for it," he laughed, as Claire undid the buttons of his jeans before taking off her shorts. Then she crept over him and kissed him lightly.

"You're so transparent, Ichi." Ichi made to reply, but the words were caught in his throat as Claire pulled the rest of his clothes off and took him easily inside of her. It was Claire's turn to laugh at the shocked look on Ichi's face. "I didn't say I *wasn't* up for it," she murmured into his ear, grinding into him slowly as she did so. "Only that you were transparent." Ichi felt her bite his neck, and part of him wondered where this ridiculously forward version of Claire had been hiding all this time whilst the rest of him struggled to hold coherent thought at all.

"H-how so?" he managed to get out as Claire sat up in order to build a faster rhythm. Ichi realised she still had her bra on, and he attempted to sit up to claw it off, but Claire pushed him back down.

"Stay where you are," she ordered, and it made Ichi feel more turned on than he thought possible. Ichi grabbed into the sides of Claire's thighs, aching for her hips to move faster. "You're so…obvious…when you want something," Claire said, beginning to answer Ichi's question as she obliged his body's demand for her to move faster. "But you never ask for it…you just keep pestering me, expecting me to say 'yes' eventually." Ichi moaned

289

as Claire dug into his bleeding chest, keeping a grip on his skin as he was doing to her.

"You always do," he replied with difficulty through staggered breaths. The fight in the classroom had left him so excited that Ichi knew he wasn't going to last for much longer, especially not with Claire acting so domineering. Claire shook her long, dishevelled hair out of her face; Ichi didn't think she had ever looked so beautiful, with blood and sweat covering her body whilst she gave *him* her total attention. *More. I want more.* But just as Ichi thought this, Claire changed how she was grinding into him, and he groaned both in pleasure and annoyance as he felt himself come. He frowned up at Claire. "What did you do that for?" he complained, breathless and annoyed. Claire tossed her hair over her shoulder as she stood up, leaving Ichi in a mess on the floor.

"Stop thinking of fighting as foreplay and that won't happen again," she replied wryly as she walked into the bathroom to turn the shower on.

Ichi propped himself up on his elbows. "But what about you? You didn't –" Claire glanced at him over her shoulder and smiled at him in a somewhat superior manner.

"If you think I need you for that, you're sadly mistaken. I don't care right now anyway; all I want is a shower." Ichi gave her a few minutes in the shower by herself, his endorphin-filled brain struggling to process what Claire had just said. Then he got up and entered the shower himself, and Claire didn't look at all surprised. He grabbed a hold of her from behind, and brought his hands around to touch her.

"*I* care though," he murmured into Claire's ear as he felt her breathing hitch. She rolled her eyes at him through strands of soaking wet hair.

"Your ego does, not you."

Ichi bit into her shoulder. "That's the same thing." He was satisfied when he felt Claire shudder against him, and she put her hands up against the tiled wall to keep herself steady. Ichi noticed that her arm hadn't yet stopped bleeding, but he continued with what he was doing nonetheless.

"Ichi, stop it, it-it's too hot in here…" Ichi kissed Claire's neck as he pushed her against the wall, and his fingers began to move faster in response to her body's involuntary tremors. Claire turned her head slightly to look at him, and her eyes were slightly unfocused. "You have to…stop…"

290

"Ah, shit," Ichi muttered aloud as Claire fainted against him.

*

Claire woke up half an hour later. Ichi had carried her over to his bed and stitched her arm and hip up as she lay unconscious. Claire groaned as she came to, flinching against the light in the room. "What happened?" she muttered, bringing a hand up to her temple. Ichi climbed on top of her and kissed her.

"You fainted...was I *that* good?" he joked, deftly moving out of the way when Claire made to hit him across the head.

Claire glanced at her freshly stitched up arm. "I obviously lost too much blood."

"Obviously," Ichi replied, as he began to place gentle kisses down Claire's neck, along her shoulder and down her injured arm to her fingers. When he reached back up to kiss Claire on her lips again, he paused millimetres from them when he saw that she wore an odd expression upon her face. "What is it?" Ichi asked, frowning. *And just when I thought she'd finally gotten out of her head after what happened with Vic.* Claire looked at him, then tried to sit up. Ichi moved off of her so that she could do so, then promptly sat her in his lap, facing him, so he could continue kissing her skin. Claire raised an eyebrow at him, but didn't protest.

"What's the date, Ichi?" she asked, and the question was so unexpected that Ichi found himself immediately answering.

"May the first, why?" And then: "Ahh, but you're not supposed to know that, if you've lost track. Whatever, I don't care."

"Huh." Claire's face was blank and unreadable.

"Why?"

"I turned twenty-three last week. Funny, I don't feel twenty-three at all." Ichi ran his left hand through Claire's still-damp hair to try and tilt her head to look at him.

"And what does twenty-three feel like?"

291

"I've no clue," Claire replied, expressionless. Then she glanced at Ichi, and her eyes seemed to come back to life. "How old are you?"

Ichi frowned again. "Are we seriously having this kind of ridiculous conversation?" he asked.

Claire kept her gaze level with his own. "Yes," she replied, serious.

Ichi sighed, looking up at the ceiling as he thought about it. "In all honesty, I don't know. I think I'm twenty-four or -five. Could be wrong though."

Claire looked almost horrified at his response. "That's so sad." Ichi said nothing, knowing where the conversation was headed. He continued to kiss Claire absent-mindedly.

"Did you not know your parents or something?" Claire eventually asked.

Ichi's frown deepened. "What's with all the sudden interest?"

It was Claire's turn to frown. "*You're* the one who told me to get to know you before I told you anything about *me*. I'm just doing things the opposite way."

Ichi almost laughed. "I suppose I *did* say that." Claire looked at him, waiting patiently for him to elaborate. "I knew my parents," Ichi eventually said. "Well, my dad left when I was very young. Or maybe he died. Either way, it doesn't matter. It made my mother go a little…insane. Oh, nobody knew of course, no one but me, but that's how it always is, isn't it?" He paused, glancing down at his chest. "She gave me all of these scars, but was careful to never give me any on my arms or legs where people might see. Don't act like that's not what you wanted to know about most of all," Ichi added on in response to the shocked look on Claire's face. "She gave me one for every week my dad wasn't there. When I was around twelve or thirteen, I had enough and left. The next however many years are an indistinct blur in my head." Ichi cocked his head to one side to regard Claire. "Until I met you."

Claire gave him the smallest of smiles. "That sounded almost romantic."

But Claire didn't say anything else, prompting Ichi to speak again. "That's all there is, really," he said somewhat flatly.

292

"Both of your parents weren't Japanese, were they?"

Ichi shook his head. "My dad was English; my mum was Japanese. I thought you knew that much."

Claire raised an eyebrow. "Why would I know that? I had a notion, though."

"I thought Vic would have told you. We were almost friends, you know, before you showed up. I don't for the life of me remember *why*, though." Ichi immediately regretted bringing up Vic, but Claire smiled at his statement.

"He was never one for talking about you much. Guess you both have that in common." Claire was silent for a moment. "I'll go and see him tomorrow and make up with him. It's the least I can do." Ichi pulled her in against his chest.

"You don't have to do anything for him. He's obviously keeping you in the dark about basically everything."

He could feel Claire sigh heavily against his chest. "He has his reasons. Genuine, good-for-*me* reasons. I just got so frustrated at him." Claire looked up at Ichi. "But that's not part of this conversation. Did you ever live in Japan?" Ichi glanced at her, surprised. It was the first time Ichi had seen Claire willingly put Vic aside for him for anything other than sex. Ichi didn't know what to think about that, so he abandoned the thought altogether.

"Yes, when I was young. My dad may or may not have been around at the time; I don't remember."

"But you speak Japanese?"

"Fluently. Where is this going...?" Ichi asked, knowing entirely where it was headed.

"Say something in Japanese for me."

Ichi groaned. "No. Absolutely not. Do you realise how demeaning it is to be asked to do that? And I'm certainly not doing it for a Japanophile like you," he added on, thinking of Claire's love of anime.

Claire pouted; Ichi responded by biting her lip. "Surely that'd be a reason to speak in Japanese for me, since I would love it so much?" Claire

293

argued. And then she smiled slyly. "You never know, it might turn me on." Ichi pushed her back down on to the bed and lay down beside her.

"As if I needed to work out how to do that." But after a few moments, Ichi did as was asked of him. He spoke mostly nonsense for a minute or two, and then found himself softly singing an old lullaby to her, one that he thought he had long since forgotten. Claire nestled herself into the crook of his arm. He felt her making little circles against his skin with her fingers, carefully avoiding the long cut on his chest that had only just stopped bleeding.

Ichi felt utterly content, and wondered how it was possible that this was the first time he was experiencing such a feeling. Eventually he stopped singing, and Claire brought her head up to kiss him. "Thank you," she said, very quietly.

"For what?" Ichi asked, kissing her back.

"For speaking in Japanese. For telling me about your parents. For almost cutting my arm off." Claire laughed quietly for a second. "For all of today. I needed it." Claire yawned, so Ichi pulled the duvet over both of them. "I won't sleep tonight if I fall asleep now," Claire complained half-heartedly.

"I'm not going to let you, so you may as well get as much sleep as you can now," Ichi replied, his expression wicked. Claire bit into his collarbone slightly, and Ichi felt her laugh against his skin before she brought her head up to look at him. And Claire looked *happy*.

Funny, Ichi thought. *I don't think I've ever seen her happy when she's with me.* But Ichi realised that he liked it; he liked it a lot. *If I can make her happy then she won't need Vic at all.* He kissed her forehead, then allowed her to settle against his chest to sleep, pondering how he had ever lived before he met Claire Danvers.

CHAPTER 28
You Drive Me Crazy

Ichi

It was the final week of May. Ichi was mindlessly playing a game of pool against Ryan, a habit the two of them had somehow picked up in the last three weeks despite Ichi's dislike of the other man. Claire was lying on her back on one of the long tables close by, reading her Kindle, whilst Marie braided her hair. Imran and Vic were sitting with them. They were all chatting contentedly about one inane topic after another, as if they were university students on their lunch break rather than a hostage with a group of hired assassins.

From where Ichi stood, it appeared as if Claire had done a stellar job of making up with Vic and integrating herself back into the group. Perhaps it helped that Vic was healing up well – all that remained of Claire's assault on his face were a few small scratches and the yellowed remains of several bruises. Ichi supposed that Vic was lucky; he had thought for sure that Claire had broken the taller man's nose, but after the blood had been cleared away it had transpired that it was actually okay. Ichi couldn't help but wish that it hadn't been. *It would serve him right for letting Claire do that to him in the first place,* Ichi thought. He hadn't spoken to Vic on his own since the fight, even though Ichi had half a hundred questions that he wished to vocalise. *Not that Vic would answer my questions though, if he isn't answering Claire's.*

He glanced over at Claire lying on the table, her hair fanning out behind her for the benefit of Marie playing with it. She clearly wasn't paying attention to the book she was reading, but hadn't given up on it enough to simply put it away. Claire had been looking slightly better over the course of the past month; Ichi wondered if being on good terms with Vic was so important to Claire that it would affect her health if she wasn't. Ichi shook his head slightly at the thought. *It's just a coincidence that she looks like crap when they're not speaking…there's no way he can affect her that much.* And yet Ichi felt jealous nonetheless, because as much as he wanted to, he couldn't eliminate the notion completely. *She might only be looking better because she actually gets some sleep now,* his brain countered. *And she's only sleeping better now because of* me.

That one thought was all it took to spread a grin over Ichi's face. He kept his head down to hide it from Ryan, but the other man noticed it nonetheless. "What's got you smiling like that, Ich? You're actually *losing* this time round," Ryan said as he potted a ball. Ichi had to struggle to reign his thoughts back in to focus on the present.

"That's none of your concern," he replied. And, still smiling: "You've made your next shot essentially impossible, by the way." Ryan considered the layout of the balls on the pool table with a slight frown upon his face. Ichi saw the frown deepen as Ryan realised that he was correct, but it was quickly replaced with an easy smile.

"I'll be the one to see if it's impossible," he said. But Ryan's shot failed, as Ichi knew it would, and so he took the cue and began to clear the table to the pleasant sound of Ryan cursing at him. In under three minutes, Ichi won the game.

"You're an idiot," he told Ryan. "I've said before that you're careless about planning ahead for your next shot." Ryan grumbled something that sounded incredibly offensive, but Ichi merely laughed at him. "One more game?"

Ryan shook his head. "I've had enough of you beating me for one day, man. Think I might join them for a while," he said, gesturing to Claire and the others with a thumb. He seemed to hesitate for a moment before continuing. "Wanna join too? You can't possibly keep yourself entertained with just Claire for company…" Ryan glanced over his shoulder to look at Claire, just as she dropped her Kindle to the floor. She rolled over onto her front and leant precariously over the edge of the table to retrieve it, giving both Ryan and Ichi an almost full view down the top of her dress. "On second thoughts, I bet you can," Ryan added on, and Ichi thought he could almost detect a hint of jealousy in his voice.

Ichi didn't respond as he watched Imran grab Claire around her waist to stop her falling to the floor, but Imran pulled her back so quickly that they both ended up falling over the other side of the table instead. The sight of them sprawled out on the floor, limbs completely entwined, pissed Ichi off to no end. And then he heard Claire giggle. *She giggled,* he thought. *She actually* giggled. *Claire doesn't do that.*

"Do you know what?" he said to Ryan, "I think I will join for a while. It's not as if I have much else to do." Ryan glanced at the mess that was Claire and Imran still lying on the floor, then at Ichi. A lazy grin slowly spread across his face. Ichi scowled at him. "Don't give me that look."

Ryan raised his hands up in surrender. "You'll work out why it's so funny eventually. I just hope for my enjoyment that it's not *too* soon," he chuckled as the two of them walked over to join the others at their long table. Ryan melted into the seat beside Marie's as if he had always been there, leaving Ichi to choose between sitting by Vic or Imran, if Claire chose to reclaim her position on top of the table. He hesitated for half a second, wondering why he was even bothering with pretending to socialise. Then he saw Imran wrap his arms around Claire's waist to haul her upright, so Ichi reluctantly threw himself down into the seat next to Vic's with a grimace. Vic gave him a look like he knew exactly why Ichi had chosen to grace the group with his presence.

Marie smiled at him. "Hey, loner. Breaking your emo persona to talk to us lowly humans? Or are you just jealous?" Claire and Imran didn't hear Marie's comment over the sound of their own laughter. Imran started spinning Claire around on the spot, causing her laughter to increase in volume.

"Sing me a song, beautiful," Imran requested, as he spun Claire away from him only to pull her back in. "Something to dance to."

Ichi rolled his eyes at Marie. "I hardly think I need to answer that question." Marie and Ryan laughed at him; even Vic had the shadow of a smile on his lips. Ichi couldn't for the life of him understand what was so funny. All he knew was that the sound of incessant laughter was beginning to irritate him immensely. He glared at nobody in particular as Claire began to sing something that sounded awfully like Britney Spears or some other teen nineties idol might have sung it originally. Marie joined in tunefully when Claire reached the chorus, who continued to dance clumsily with Imran as she did so. Ichi couldn't help but flinch at the lyrics she was singing: *you drive me crazy.* It summarised how Ichi felt about everything pertaining to Claire perfectly.

Ichi was still silently fuming when Claire and Imran finally sat down, the two of them breathless with laughter still firmly on their lips. They sat together, opposite everybody else. Claire was literally sitting as far away from both Ichi and Vic as she could whilst still being within the confines of the group; Ichi wondered if it had been deliberate. *Stop over-analysing everything, you jealous fool.* Ichi shook his head slightly, as if doing so would get rid of his unwanted, entirely adolescent thoughts.

"You have no taste in music, Claire," Vic said to the group, and Claire made a noise in complaint.

"I find her taste in music impeccable," Imran countered, and Claire kissed him on the cheek in thanks.

"Well, *you* would, Imran," Vic replied, smiling. Ichi could feel both Vic and Marie's eyes on him, looking at him with an air of superiority.

Then Marie's eyes turned mischievous before she turned her gaze to Claire. "As I was saying before you fell over, what *is* your type exactly, Claire? I can't work it out at all." Ichi felt his ears prick up at the question as he wondered how he hadn't heard Marie ask it the first time round. Ichi figured that he really needed to stop getting stuck in his own head for so long, if he was missing important questions such as *what Claire's type was* and *why she would be with Ichi if he wasn't that type.* Once again, Ichi felt entirely like a teenage boy and not a twenty-four (or twenty-five) year old man. But despite acknowledging that, Ichi knew he wanted to hear the answer to Marie's question nonetheless.

Claire laughed before responding. "Blonde," she said without hesitation or thought. Ichi didn't have to look up to know that Vic was grinning at Claire's answer. "Green eyes. Sorry, Vic," Claire added on when she heard Vic's protest. She looked up at the ceiling as she pondered her answer. "Think young Simon Baker and you get the idea, Marie. Or maybe just Simon Baker full stop." She laughed again, and Marie echoed the sound. "Yeah, that's definitely my type. Or Daniel Henney, who looks nothing like him. Or Matt Bomer."

"That last one's gay," Imran chimed in with a grin.

Claire sighed a melodramatic sigh. "Doesn't stop him being so bloody beautiful though, does it?" Claire replied.

Marie frowned at her. "Claire, you're useless at this; you just listed three guys who could cover like two-thirds of all the types there are. The only things they have in common are that they're all actors and practically old enough to be your dad!" Claire gave her a nonchalant shrug, as if she didn't care about the age of them at all. Then Ichi noticed that Marie was looking at him and grinning. "Aw, Ichi, you look confused. You don't know who any of them are, do you?" And then, without giving him time to answer, Marie turned to Ryan. "What about you? Other than 'female' and 'breathing', what are your physical criteria?" but Ichi wasn't really listening any more. Marie had been right, of course, and that meant that Ichi couldn't process Claire's answer. He knew he was staring at her, waiting for her to look back at him, but Claire either remained blissfully unaware of his eyes on her or was simply ignoring him. Ichi couldn't stand it either way.

"Blonde," Ichi vaguely heard Ryan reply, echoing Claire's answer. There was a collective sigh at his response, as if everybody in the room had expected that answer. "And smart. But not too smart. I'd like her to think she was smarter than me but not actually be."

"Not leaving yourself many options then, mate!" Imran chided, to a round of appreciative laughter.

Ryan waved it off. "And hot," he continued, as if he'd never been interrupted. "Yeah, definitely hot. Actually, scrap the 'blonde' thing. She just has to be 'ready to screw out of the shower' hot." He threw a pointed look in Claire's direction, and she blushed a little before laughing at something Imran whispered into her ear.

Ichi couldn't stand it anymore; he turned to Vic and murmured under his breath, "When the hell did they get so close?" Vic looked at him for a second, a slight frown furrowing his brow that cast his extremely pale blue eyes into shadow.

Then he rolled his eyes as if Ichi's confusion was something to be pitied. "Imran," Vic began, "What about *your* type?" Marie pouted at Vic as if he had just spoiled something for her, which only served to infuriate Ichi more.

Imran pointed to Claire, and Ichi felt his insides coil up like a snake. "Her older brother," Imran said.

Claire knocked his hand away, smiling. "I don't have any brothers, older or otherwise."

"That's a terrible shame. I'd have to go with Matt Bomer as well then, since he's basically what your older brother would look like." Imran chuckled, and Claire joined in with an easy, chime-like laugh of her own at Imran's somewhat absurd answer. Ichi let out a breath he hadn't known he was holding in, and the action caused everyone to look at him.

Ryan threw him a wolfish grin. "Told you you'd find it funny once you worked it out," he said. He watched as Ichi's face continued to appear blank and unamused. "Or maybe not," Ryan added on with a laugh. Ichi felt entirely like he had become the bottom member of the pack; the one that everyone ridiculed, rather than the lone wolf that everybody was rightfully wary of.

He abruptly stood up. "Claire, come with me for a minute," he said quietly, but the tone of his voice meant that the words spread across the group despite their lack of volume. And, finally, she looked at him, one eyebrow raised in amusement.

"And why would I do that?" Claire replied off-handedly, as if Ichi's request was not something that had ever crossed her mind to oblige. On impulse, Ichi vaulted himself gracefully over the table, closed the distance between himself and Claire in two strides and picked her up out of her chair, slinging her over his shoulder as he turned around to leave the rec hall. He saw Marie's eyes glitter with amusement, Imran's lips curl into a smile full of laughter, Ryan's face light up with respect and approval. And Vic...Vic looked like he wished he could pick Claire up and carry her off just as easily as Ichi had done.

"Ichi, what the hell are you doing?" he heard Claire mutter into his ear. Her breath tickled his skin as she spoke.

He didn't spare her a glance as he replied, "I'm going to take you into the nearest classroom and screw you senseless." He felt Claire's eyelashes flutter across his cheek as her eyes widened slightly in surprise, but then she clucked her tongue as if she was annoyed at the statement.

"Don't forget I'm coming around later, princess!" Ichi heard Vic call out behind their backs, and Ichi was sure that the other man had said it so that Ichi would feel inferior to him. Ichi knew that Claire was grinning back at Vic without having to see it; he quickened his pace out of the rec hall.

Claire had an annoyed expression plastered across her face when Ichi locked the door behind them in the classroom that they had had their knife fight in. He carried her over to the nearest table, kicking a chair roughly out of the way in order to drop her down onto it. After he did, Ichi made to remove Claire's delicate little summer dress, realising that it was the one her mother had given her as he did so. But Claire put her hands on Ichi's, stopping him.

She looked up at him, a rebellious expression on her face. "And who decided that you were allowed to screw me senseless right at this very moment?" Claire murmured, though she had removed her hands from Ichi's to undo his belt. He glanced down at the movement for a second before looking at Claire again. With deft fingers she began to undo the buttons of his jeans, one by one.

"*I* decided that I could," Ichi replied, running his hands through Claire's hair to pull her face closer to his. But Claire surprised him by jerking his jeans and underwear down before pushing him away from her with enough force to knock him back into the chair he had kicked out of the way only moments before.

"Sit down," Claire ordered, and Ichi was shocked enough to do as he was told.

"Claire, what are you –" Ichi began, but his question was answered when Claire slid off of the table to kneel down in front of him. And even though it then became glaringly obvious as to what Claire intended to do, Ichi found himself accidentally biting his lip so hard that it bled when she *did*. He felt Claire's fingers press into his waist; his thighs; his hips as she worked out how best to keep her balance as her head moved slowly up and down. "I don't understand how this is supposed to – oh." Ichi found his train of thought and therefore ability to vocalise such thoughts come to a sudden halt as he felt pleasure course through his brain. He ran a somewhat shaky hand through Claire's hair, feeling it fall to tickle his bare skin as it dropped between his fingers.

Ichi felt like both several minutes and no time at all had passed before he felt that achingly familiar tug in his groin that meant he was going to come, and it occurred to him too late that that was what Claire had been waiting for. He groaned, both in pleasure and in understanding. "No, Claire, don't do that," he said between gritted teeth, and Claire glanced up at him for just long enough to relay to Ichi that she absolutely would. Ichi knew he should stop her now before it got even more frustrating for him, but part of his brain desperately thought that he might be able to get Claire to finish him off despite her intentions.

Of course he was wrong. Claire merely waited until the last possible moment, when Ichi was all but bucking his hips into her, to break away from him. She stood up and walked swiftly to the door before Ichi thought to grab her. "Stop telling me what to do," Claire said, her voice commanding and unbelievably sexy because of it. She looked Ichi up and down then, allowing a smug smile to play across her face. "Have fun thinking about me for the rest of the day," she laughed, unlocking the door as she did so.

Ichi thought back to the song Claire had been singing what felt like an age ago. *You drive me crazy. You drive me crazy.*

"You're going to pay for that," he muttered, but the classroom was empty.

*

Hours later, Claire still hadn't appeared at Ichi's door, so he took it upon himself to go over to her room and demand her attention. Ichi was aware of the fact that Claire may not let him in – after all, not once had they slept or even socialised together in her room since they had both gotten horrendously drunk months before. *I could just force myself in,* Ichi reasoned. *Though I gather that that wouldn't put Claire in the mood I'd want her to be in.*

So he knocked on the door instead, quietly at first and then louder when Claire didn't respond. It took Claire a full two minutes to answer her door, and she started speaking before it was fully open. "Vic, I didn't expect you round so – oh. Ichi. What are you doing here?" Claire asked, a puzzled expression on her face. Her hair was sodden; Ichi figured that she must have just gotten out of the shower, explaining her delay in opening the door.

302

Ichi frowned slightly. "What do you mean what am I doing here? You're normally in my room by now." Ichi realised that he sounded like a petulant child, but he didn't care. He crossed his arms and leant against the door frame, looking Claire up and down. He wished that Claire hadn't bothered to put any clothes on after her shower.

Claire frowned back at him. "Don't you remember? Vic's coming around tonight. We're going to watch countless eighties movies until God knows what hour in the morning and eat our body weight in popcorn." Claire looked genuinely excited by the prospect.

"Sounds fascinating," Ichi replied scathingly. He paused for a second. "Is there any ulterior motive to your having a night in with Vic?"

Claire rolled her eyes. "Do you think I'd tell you if I was? And whether I am or not, it's better for me to get back to the way things were with him before…" She let the sentence trail off.

"Before you beat him half to death," Ichi finished for her.

Claire scowled. "Thanks for reminding me, Ichi." Neither of them said anything for a minute, and just when it looked like Claire might bid him goodbye, Ichi was struck by a sudden revelation.

"You *knew* I wasn't paying attention when Vic said he was coming around tonight. So you did all that in the classroom knowing full well you weren't going to have sex with me later on!" Claire let out a chuckle as she wrung the excess water out of her hair onto the floor.

"What? Did you not expect me to do something like that? You're just pissed I outsmarted you." Ichi grabbed onto Claire's wrist and pulled her closer to him.

"Let me in for ten minutes."

Claire laughed again as she pushed Ichi away slightly. "As if I'd do that. Just deal with it, Ichi. Go toss yourself off in the shower or something." Claire's words caused Ichi to stand perfectly still, and he struggled to maintain a neutral expression on his face.

"…what?"

Claire gave him a look as she stepped back into her room. "Oh, like you wouldn't expect me to notice the water going through the pipes to your room after almost every single one of our encounters in the hallway? As you've already gathered, I'm not an idiot. I can put two and two together." Ichi ran a hand through his hair and turned his gaze away from Claire. He felt his face grow just a little bit warmer. To his disgust, he saw Claire's smile grow even wider at his involuntary response to her observation.

"Just…shut up," he muttered.

Claire reached up and kissed him lightly. "It's flattering, I suppose," she said, "But also incredibly creepy. Now go do something else tonight, and maybe you'll think twice about telling me to do things or carrying me off on a whim from now on." But as she closed to door, Ichi suddenly thrust out his arm to keep it open.

"What's gotten into you over the past few weeks? You're much more…assertive," he said.

Claire raised an eyebrow at him. "I was always assertive, before. It just took me a while to be myself again after I was brought here. I guess it's not like you could have known that though." Now Claire's face was contemplative; Ichi wondered why. After a moment, she put a hand on Ichi's arm to remove it from her door. "I'll see you tomorrow. I'm serious – go do something else tonight."

"I want to do *you* tonight," Ichi replied almost immediately. Claire smiled as if she had already known that Ichi was going to reply with something of that ilk.

"I know," Claire said, and then she closed the door in his face.

*

It was close to eleven when Ichi finally relented and opened up the camera feeds in Claire's room to see what she was up to with Vic. Though he knew that the two of them truly could spend hours watching films together without saying anything interesting, Ichi couldn't help but think that they were whispering about important things behind his back that he wanted to know. *Although talking about such things in Claire's room is stupid if they don't want Michael to hear,* he thought.

Even though Ichi was fairly certain that Claire only discussed trying to make sense of her past with him, he just couldn't shake the feeling that she

304

wasn't telling him everything she knew about Vic. Not for the first time, Ichi considered the idea that Claire knew Vic from before her memory loss.

"Could've been undercover," he mumbled aloud to his laptop screen. But that made little to no sense – if Michael hadn't known about Claire being the key to obtaining her parents' research prior to her kidnap, then why would he have ever had Vic slip into her life to watch her? Ichi felt his stomach grumble, so he wandered over to his kitchen and poured himself a bowl of cereal. When he returned to his bed, he propped up his laptop on a pillow and plugged in his headphones in order to hear Claire and Vic's conversation properly.

Ichi couldn't tell what the film was that they were watching on Claire's laptop, but Vic was providing a running commentary of extra information about it that caused Claire to either laugh, scoff in disbelief or roll her eyes depending on what the information was. The pair of them continued on like this for another half an hour (Ichi realised that the film was Edward Scissorhands by this point, and wondered for a moment if it was actually from the eighties), then quietened as the film reached its climax. When it was over, Claire sighed contentedly and sunk into Vic's side. He smiled fondly at her; Ichi felt the vein in his temple twitch.

Just as Ichi was beginning to think that he wasn't going to hear anything interesting enough to warrant having just pissed himself off by watching the pair of them, Claire's expression sobered, and Ichi saw her swallow before she spoke.

"Vic…" she said, her voice trailing off into an infuriatingly silent question. Vic's smile turned tired.

"Soon, I promise. Soon. Super soon. Just hold on for a little longer, okay?" Claire tilted her head back to stare up at him.

"You keep telling me that. I hate non-specific measurements like *soon* and *later*. When do I get a quantifiable answer?"

Vic laughed, and it was sad. "Ever the scientist, princess. I thought you punching my lights out gave me a little bit of a time respite, anyway?" Claire's looked at him, horrified, so Vic ruffled her hair up for a half a second, before looking at the hand doing the ruffling and pulling it away quickly. *Odd,* Ichi thought. "Don't look at me that way, Claire. I deserved it. You really think I'd have let you get in all of those punches at the end if

305

I thought I didn't? I just…never expected you to knock me unconscious and then keep going." He laughed again, and it didn't sound as sad anymore. He gently pushed Claire off of him and stood up, stretching his arms into the air as he did so.

Claire jumped up after him. "You can't be going now, surely? It's not even that late yet!" she protested.

"It is for me; I have to get away early to check something out. If I'm not back tomorrow evening then I'll definitely be back the following morning, okay?"

Claire pouted. "Fine. But you can make me breakfast when you come back." Vic chuckled; Ichi was beginning to get fed up with just how frequently the other man laughed. *I suppose he laughed a lot with me before we brought Claire in…then he stopped altogether.* Ichi knew he couldn't blame Vic for not enjoying or wanting his company over the last few months. Then he rolled his eyes for nobody to see, thinking about how stupid it was to be bothered by such a thing when he had no desire to be friends with Vic.

"I'll translate that as 'make me croissants please'," Ichi heard Vic say to Claire. She grinned, then threw her arms around his neck. He slid his arms around her waist and held her tight in return. And then…Ichi saw that they were whispering something to each other, but Ichi couldn't hear it. And if Ichi couldn't hear it then neither could Michael, which was obviously precisely their intention.

Vic left a minute or two later, and Ichi saw Claire collapse back onto her couch with a deflated sigh. Ichi watched her do nothing but browse through something on her laptop restlessly for nearly half an hour, but her attention was clearly elsewhere. *I shouldn't go over there,* Ichi thought. *I need to show that I have at least* some *self-restraint. And yet…*

With a noise of disgust directed entirely at himself, Ichi closed his laptop and swung himself over the edge of his bed. The infernal song that Claire had been singing hours before was still ringing in Ichi's ears, but since he wasn't sure how the original went, it was Claire's version that he heard. *You drive me crazy,* in Claire's voice, over and over again. It was all Ichi could think about as he left his room to knock on Claire's door.

She didn't look all that surprised by Ichi's presence at her door, only a little bemused.

"1990," Ichi said before she could say anything.

"Say what?" Claire replied, a frown on her face.

"1990," he repeated. "That's when Edward Scissorhands came out, so it falls out with your eighties film theme."

Claire's frown turned into something much darker. "Ichi, how would you know that we were watching that? There's no way you could have heard it through the door," she said. Ichi glanced up at the ceiling, considering his next words. *You drive me crazy, but it feels alright,* he recited, thinking of the song. *To hell with it.*

He let his mouth fall into a smirk. "As if you hadn't considered that I had cameras in your room, Claire. Now let me in and I'll recount all of the other terrible things I've done to you that you didn't know about."

CHAPTER 29
Love Fool

Claire

She didn't know why she let him in, but before Claire could think of anything to say to the contrary Ichi had slid past her in the doorway to fall lazily onto her couch. Claire turned around to face him, momentarily stunned by Ichi's easy confession of guilt. *Well he's* guilty, *but he doesn't feel even the least bit bad about it,* she corrected. Then it hit Claire just what exactly it was that Ichi had confessed to, and she turned from him to walk around her room whilst scouring the corners of the ceiling for the cameras that he had hidden.

"How many are there?" Claire demanded, jumping onto her bed to get a better look at the ceiling.

"Hell if I remember," Ichi replied off-handedly, as if he knew exactly how many there were.

"How many, Ichi?" Claire repeated, trying her best to keep her voice level and calm. "Where are they all?" She heard Ichi laugh softly behind her, so she turned to face him from her position on the bed.

"What? And ruin all the fun?" But Claire saw his gaze shift almost imperceptively towards her shower room. Claire felt her mouth open in surprise even though, in all honesty, she shouldn't have been surprised at all. She vaulted off of the bed and wrenched open the shower room door, desperately searching the small room for Ichi's camera. But Claire had no idea what it would look like, or how small it could be. Ichi was continuing to laugh at her endeavours, so Claire paused to think. *If I were an emotionally repressed pervert with absolutely no conscience, where would I put a camera in a girl's bathroom?*

Claire glanced up at the extractor fan unit, a feature that had seemed so innocuous to her before. So normal. Now it was suspicious, because it could hide a camera angled directly over the top of the shower perfectly. And then Claire saw it, too high above her head to reach. Soundlessly, she marched back through to her bedroom to haul the small chest of drawers that she used as a bedside table over to the extractor fan, throwing the lamp that lay on top of it unceremoniously to the floor as she did so.

Ichi's laughter had dropped to a quiet chuckle as Claire stepped on top of the drawers to rip the camera away from the fan, and it stopped altogether when Claire flung it to the floor with enough strength to break it into pieces.

"That was expensive," he muttered as Claire made her way back to the bed to sit down on the very edge of it, face furious.

"Good."

"Are you done now?"

"Where are the rest of them?"

Ichi turned his head away to gaze sightlessly at Claire's non-functional kitchen. "Work it out yourself. Just don't damage any of Michael's; he wouldn't be too happy."

Claire sighed and threw herself onto her back. *Don't ask,* she thought. *Just don't ask.* "What else have you done?" she asked anyway.

Ichi clucked his tongue at the question. "Are you sure you want to know?"

"Yes," Claire replied immediately. And then: "No." *You can't be that surprised that Ichi would do things like this to you, Claire,* she thought, silently weighing up the pros and cons of having Ichi confess to everything. *It's* Ichi. *You knew what you were getting into.* Claire wondered what exactly it was that she was allowing herself to 'get into', and frowned. *I'm not getting into anything. Ichi's just an escape so I don't have to think about anything. That's all he is. Definitely...*

Ichi continued to stare at nothing as he waited patiently for Claire to make up her mind. She watched as he casually rolled up the sleeves of his dark top, before deciding against it and unrolling them. He tapped the long fingers of his left hand against the couch, again and again and again.

You're fooling yourself if you say you feel nothing for him. You need to know exactly what it is he's done to you up to this point so that you can either accept it or decide that that's the final straw. Claire stared up at the ceiling from her place on the bed, watching the shadows that the bedside lamp now lying on the floor made. Then she closed her eyes, thinking hard. *Besides, what could he have done to you that's any worse than what you already knew he'd done to you? And you're sleeping with him despite all of that.* Claire shook her head as she opened her eyes, thinking sadly about how screwed up she had become.

"Yes," she said, finally. Ichi turned his head around slightly to look at her, face blank and unreadable. "Yes. Tell me what exactly it is that you've done." Ichi raised an eyebrow, and then grinned widely. Claire narrowed her eyes. "You don't have to look so bloody pleased with yourself."

Ichi stretched out on the couch like a cat, arms raised high above his head. "You'd be pleased too, if you had managed to do everything I've done and gotten away with it." Claire closed her eyes momentarily as she swung back up into a sitting position again, willing any kind of deity to give her strength.

She breathed in deeply, already regretting the question she was about to ask. "When did you install the cameras in my room?"

"As soon as you weren't locked in your room anymore, so the fourth day you were here," Ichi replied, in a manner that suggested he was telling Claire what the weather was like. He sat up to lean over the top of the back of the couch, resting his chin on his arms to watch Claire. He looked incredibly smug; Claire wanted to punch him in the face, but thought better of it. She curled and uncurled her fists, taking another deep breath before she asked another question. "Actually, that's only half-true," Ichi added on before she had opened her mouth. He was looking thoughtfully towards the shower room, and gestured towards it as he spoke. "The one by your shower was installed after I came back from that two-month job for Michael. I didn't have a waterproof camera before then."

"And you don't have one now either!" Claire replied testily. Then a memory struck her, and she frowned suspiciously at Ichi. "Did you install it the night I caught you in my room?" Ichi laughed, then leapt over the back of the couch to perch on top of it. His slow journey towards Claire's position on the bed was not lost on her, and she followed every one of his body movements with calculating eyes.

"Do you seriously think that I'd let you 'catch' me in your room? I sat in front of you until you woke up. I had a rather important question that needed answered, after all." Claire couldn't get over how blasé Ichi was being about every despicable thing that he had done to her. Ichi was wandering around her room now, looking mildly interested in his entirely uninteresting surroundings. Claire wished she could break his cool and calm exterior, but she couldn't work out how.

When it became apparent that Ichi wasn't going to continue regaling her with more of his triumphs, Claire asked him another question. "What was the point of the cameras, other than watching me in the bloody shower?" Claire had a notion about the answer, but she wanted to hear it confirmed by Ichi himself.

Ichi didn't stop walking about her room as he replied, "I wanted to learn your routine – when you got up, when you left your room, when you got back, when you went to sleep, what you did in your spare time...you knew that already though." Ichi spared Claire a glance before he knelt down in the shower room to pick up the shattered remains of his camera.

"I knew you were watching me around the complex, even when it felt like you couldn't possibly be anywhere. I just didn't realise that your obsession with what I did went so far." Ichi walked over to the bin in the kitchen to dispose of his broken camera, then he came straight back over to Claire and sat on the bed beside her. Claire made a noise in protest. "I didn't say you could sit here!"

Ichi chuckled and ran a hand through his hair, only for it to fall back into his eyes as soon as he took his hand away. "When have I ever needed your say-so? You have no idea how many times I crept into your room and sat on that coffee table whilst you slept on the couch. Surely it's preferable for you to be conscious when I sit beside you now?"

Claire looked at him, horrified. "How can you be so – so *casual* about all of this?! You're absolutely insane!"

Ichi flashed a grin at her. "You know that that's a lie. I'm perfectly lucid when I make those 'insane' decisions. I just have no conscience. There's a difference."

311

Claire rolled her eyes at the distinction. "Is there anything else I ought to know about?" she asked, thinking that Ichi had pretty much already covered everything he could do. "I mean, you've attacked me, stalked me, had me on twenty-four-hour watch, broken into my room…" Claire listed everything Ichi had done on her fingers, attempting to be as casual as he was. "What else could possibly be left?" She stole a glance at the man beside her and saw that he was staring at her intently. Claire edged back onto the bed a little, suddenly very sure that whatever it was that Ichi was about to tell her was something that she didn't want to know.

And then he pinned her to the bed in one quick, fluid motion. The light from the lamp, still lying forgotten on the floor, gave Ichi's eyes a shine that only accentuated how crazed he currently looked to Claire. He snaked a hand under the top of her skirt to pull out the hem of the shirt that was tucked into it, allowing his fingers to continue roving up Claire's skin unimpeded.

"I drugged you," he said, and Claire stiffened under his fingertips.

"…when?" she asked.

"Work it out." Claire pulled up her hand as if to hit Ichi across the face, but he caught it mid-flight and kissed each of her fingertips instead, watching Claire intently as he did so. "Do you know how many nights I spent watching you on those damn cameras, desperately trying to work out what you were thinking and why you acted the way you did around me? You consistently made no sense. I was so confused, and not being able to read you made it even worse." He dropped Claire's hand back down on to the bed and kissed her neck just above the collar of her shirt. "So many nights, waiting for you to fall asleep so that I could too, like some kind of OCD tic that I just couldn't shake. And every time I could only conclude that you genuinely didn't think about me at all, Ryan or Marie or Imran would say something completely to the contrary, and I thought that they were just messing with me, but then you – *you* – would do something that would make me think that maybe they were speaking the truth." Ichi paused for a moment, then let his mouth fall into a smirk. "You say I'm insane. Well you're the one who drove me there." He bit down into her neck with his canines, just enough for Claire to shudder beneath him. When Claire brought her eyes up to look into his face, she didn't know what she was going to see, and she didn't know what she was supposed to say in the first place. Ichi held her gaze with bright, frantic eyes. "I didn't know what to do, so I drugged you."

And then his expression seemed to break, and he rolled off of Claire to collapse beside her. Claire propped herself up onto her elbows to look over at him. Ichi pulled a hand over his face and sighed. "I honestly didn't know what I was supposed to do," he murmured, "and the first solution I came to was to drug you to find out how you felt." He let out a bark of humourless laughter. "I guess that *is* insane." Then there was a long pause as Claire considered whether to ask her next question or wait for Ichi to continue.

Eventually, she couldn't take the silence. "Did you do anything to me?" Ichi looked at her, but Claire rather felt like he was looking through her instead. He didn't seem to be listening.

"Huh?" Ichi said. Then he seemed to come out of his reverie, and he shook his head. "No, I didn't do anything to you. I was very, very drunk, and apparently when I'm drunk I possess some kind of moral compass that I quite obviously lack when I'm sober."

Understanding finally dawned on Claire. "This was the night of the blackjack game, wasn't it?"

"Bingo. Guess what I drugged?"

Claire let out a bitter laugh. "My orange juice. You knew fine well I'd definitely drink it." Ichi gave her a sarcastic thumbs up as he gazed at the ceiling. There was another pause as Claire continued to look at Ichi not looking at her. "What happened then?" Claire finally asked. "I feel like perhaps I should be allowed to know that."

Still not looking at her, Ichi replied, "You were in the shower. Because I was drunk it seemed to make perfect sense for me to join you with my jeans on. I asked you questions. You answered them. Then I put you to bed."

Claire raised an eyebrow at him. "That seems like an extremely summarised version of events," she said. "You can't possibly expect me to believe that nothing happened when I was entirely naked in a shower." Ichi looked at Claire then, and he curled a finger around the neck of her shirt and tugged, opening some of the popper-style buttons keeping it closed. He smirked when Claire's face reddened slightly.

"I may have felt you up a little. You were the one who was incredibly eager to get me out of my jeans, though." His smirk widened into a grin as Claire spluttered in her attempt to find a retort.

"I did *not*," she finally managed to childishly reply.

"And how would you know, Miss Memory Loss? Besides, nothing actually happened except for that – I genuinely put you to bed instead of doing what I actually wanted to do." He looked pointedly at Claire, and she realised that he was telling the truth. Then he looked back up at the ceiling, his expression contemplative. "I figured I could use the information I got out of you against you the following day, but you…you know what happened. Suddenly I didn't understand you anymore, and everything you had told me in the shower was overwritten by what you screamed at me in the rec hall. You know the rest." Claire edged herself a little closer to Ichi on the bed, which seemed to startle him.

"Yes, I do know the rest – I slept with you. Even though I definitely shouldn't have."

Ichi still looked surprised as he replied, "Aren't you supposed to be angry?"

Claire sighed. "Didn't you hear what I just said, Ichi? Yes, of course I'm angry, but it doesn't actually change anything. I definitely shouldn't be doing this, but I am. I don't know why." *Yes you do.*

"You can't possibly forgive me that easily for being a violent, arrogant, compulsive sham of a human being." It sounded incredibly strange to hear Ichi being self-reflective, for admitting exactly what he was. *He's always honest though, even when he's being despicable, and I never am, even when I'm being kind.*

"Did I say I had forgiven you?" *Because I have.* Claire didn't know if she had forgiven Ichi out of desperation for human contact with someone who wasn't hiding anything from her or whether she was merely screwed up. *Either way, Vic, I'm sorry.*

Ichi shifted slightly so that he could put an arm around Claire, and they were silent for a while. Claire's mind was spinning round and round with a mountain of questions that she needed to ask Ichi, Vic, Michael, her parents, and herself. But as more time passed, one question loomed above them all, even though it was entirely hypothetical.

"Ichi," she said.

He glanced down at her, eyes very slightly sleepy. "What now?"

Claire closed her eyes, not wanting to see Ichi's face as she asked her question. "What would you have done, back then, had I actually been pregnant?"

There was a pause, and then: "I don't know how to answer that."

Claire opened her eyes to look up at him. "You really need to think about the consequences of your actions a little more, you know."

Ichi frowned slightly, and Claire saw what almost looked like worry flash across his face. "You're not –"

"Oh my God, no!" Claire exclaimed, working out what Ichi was about to say from his face alone. "Ichi, you might be careless but I'm most definitely not. Which is lucky for you, I guess."

Ichi sighed in relief, then chuckled softly. "What are you laughing at?" Claire asked, suspicious. Ichi bent down to kiss her, then bit into her lower lip instead.

"I can't think of a child who could possibly be more messed up than one who's the product of the two of us."

Claire swatted his face away from hers. "Shut up Ichi, that's not funny at all," she said, but she was laughing.

Ichi

Claire's room was too hot for Ichi, but she seemed to be used to it. Before Ichi knew it, the heat was sending Claire to sleep, curled up in the crook of his arm. Ichi pushed her slightly. "Hey, hey! You're not allowed to fall asleep yet," he complained, but Claire didn't seem to hear him. Or maybe she was ignoring him; Ichi couldn't tell. He nudged her again.

"Just for a minute, Ich…" she mumbled, and the name caught Ichi off-guard. Had Claire ever called him that before? He didn't think so. Ichi didn't know how he felt about Claire using what was basically a nickname to refer to him. A nickname was essentially a term of endearment, after all, and this one had been forced upon him by Vic and Alexis and, later, stolen by Ryan. But Claire? Claire using anything that might imply some kind of actual affection towards him was a different thing entirely. Ichi sighed.

I'm completely over-analysing this. Maybe she just didn't get out my full name before she fell back asleep. He turned his head to look at Claire, her face nuzzled against his chest. Everything about her, from the way her lips curved into the slightest of smiles to the way her skirt had risen up over her thighs, screamed *defenceless* to Ichi. *You fool,* he thought. *If you look like that I'll take advantage of you,* and he ran his hand under the hem of Claire's skirt to do precisely that. He slipped it down over her legs, and Claire didn't so much as breathe as he did so. He finished unbuttoning the shirt she was wearing, trailing his fingers down from her collarbone to her navel after he had done so. No reaction. Ichi slowly climbed on top of Claire to nibble at her ear, and then followed the path his fingers had taken with his mouth. Claire seemed to shudder a little underneath him at that.

"This is payback for earlier," he murmured into her skin, thinking of how Claire had left him in the classroom – excited and intoxicated and desperate beyond measure. That desperation had clung on to him all day with a vice-like grip; he *had* to have Claire now, otherwise he'd go insane. But he wanted to make her suffer first, so Ichi continued to toy with her, planting kisses all over her body as his hand went to work between her thighs.

It didn't take long for Claire's shuddering to grow more frequent, and Ichi was incredibly satisfied when he heard a low moan escape from her lips. But Claire still wasn't awake. Ichi paused what he was doing to remove his clothes with shaking hands that could barely contain his urge to hold Claire down and screw her senseless even if she was unconscious. *But there's no point in that,* Ichi had to remind himself, not thinking for a second about how morally reprehensible the action was in the first place. *I want her to know how I felt earlier, and she has to be awake for that.*

So he let Claire feel how hard he was, grinding into her as he moved his face up to hers and smothered her unbearably sexy moans with his mouth. Claire wasn't asleep for long after that, and when she half opened her eyes, heavy-lidded from sleep, she didn't look shocked or appalled. Her expression made it appear as if she wanted Ichi just as much as he wanted her, and that was what he needed to see. Ichi felt Claire hook one of her ankles around the back of his calves. Her other leg she brought up over his back, trying to push him down towards her body.

"I'm awake," Claire murmured, grazing her teeth against Ichi's lips. "What else are you waiting for?" Ichi allowed his body to be pushed closer to Claire's, but he used all of the self-control he had left in him to do nothing more, even though he ached to be inside of her. Claire frowned at him slightly, her head clearly still thick with sleep, before a light of understanding seemed to turn on behind her eyes. She chuckled. "If you're doing this to me because of what I did to you, then you're going to fail." Ichi kissed her again as he brought his left hand back down between her thighs, and was satisfied to see Claire bite her lip and roll her eyes back slightly in response.

"Why would you say that?" he asked, his voice rough and unsteady. Claire managed to laugh again despite what Ichi was doing to her.

"You...don't have the self-control," she replied, her voice low and melodic against his ear. Ichi couldn't stand it. He thrust his fingers up into her, and it was his turn to laugh at the cry of shock that escaped Claire's lips at the action.

"You have no idea how much self-control I have," Ichi growled, as he continued his altogether more violent onslaught against Claire's body. But it was working; he could feel Claire's legs shaking, could see her fingers dig into the bed harder and harder with every passing second. But then Claire seemed to have an idea, and she grabbed onto Ichi's hip with jittery fingers.

"I can d-do things to you too," she managed to utter, her voice breathless but determined. He felt her fingers trail over his skin to his penis, and Ichi lost the ability to think rationally after she started to tug on it insistently. He felt his breath catch in his throat for a second.

"Fuck you, Claire!" Ichi exclaimed angrily, as he tossed her hand aside and thrust inside of her in one deft movement. Claire ran her hands through Ichi's hair and pulled him back towards her lips.

"Please do," she half-laughed into his mouth, and Ichi couldn't help but grin back at the comment despite his earlier anger, which was lost entirely the moment Claire uttered those words. It was only after they had both finished, spent and exhausted, that Ichi, too, managed to fall asleep in Claire's unbearably hot room.

*

He woke up an indeterminate amount of time later, the duvet damp with sweat and twisted around his legs. *Why did I wake up?* Ichi thought groggily, then he glanced to his right and realised that Claire wasn't there. He sat up and scanned the dark room for her, and eventually spied her, fully clothed, near the front door.

"Claire?" he called, but she didn't look around. Instead, she finished walking towards the door and reached out for the handle, but Ichi leapt out of bed, ran over and stopped her. He turned on the lights and saw that Claire didn't seem to be conscious. *She's in some kind of trance again, like the one I found her in a month ago.* "Claire," he repeated, shaking her shoulder slightly, "Claire, wake up."

But Claire didn't hear him. She stood on the spot, swaying slightly, and she wore the saddest expression that Ichi thought he had even seen in his entire life upon her face. When Claire eventually spoke, Ichi had to strain to hear what she was saying. "...ve him," she murmured. Ichi frowned as Claire continued, "You can't send him away. Where did you send him to? Bring him back. I love..." Claire's voice, wavering and insubstantial, trailed away to nothing. Ichi could see her lovely blue eyes shining with tears for some other person that wasn't him.

Ichi shook Claire's shoulder, harder this time. "Claire, stop it! Wake up!" he exclaimed, raising his voice to try and get through to her. But it didn't work; Claire continued to silently cry for an unknown man. Ichi's brain worked furiously through his memories of the last time he had found Claire in a trance – she had kissed him in the elevator, pushed him against the wall, all whilst having no recollection of it. And then...and then Ichi had thrown her to the floor, and the force had startled her awake. Ichi breathed in, mumbled an apology to Claire under his breath, then slapped her hard across the face.

And it worked. Claire blinked several times, bringing her hand up slowly to touch her reddening cheek, eyes never leaving Ichi's face. Her

318

eyebrows were knitted together in fear and confusion. "Ichi, why did you hit me?" she asked softly. Ichi realised he felt incredibly angry, but he didn't know why, and he found himself shouting at Claire as a result.

"To snap you out of it! How often does this fucking happen Claire? And don't lie to me!" The edge and volume of his voice made Claire flinch, but her only reply was a small, sad shake of her head. Ichi took a step forward and grabbed Claire by her shoulders, causing her to gasp in surprise.

"Ichi, I don't –"

"Stop lying!" Ichi raged into her face. "You think I'm going to believe that this has only happened to you twice, and I just so happened to be there on both occasions?! What do you think I am, some kind of fool?" And then Ichi realised that something about his words didn't ring true. "No…" he continued, quieter now. "No, not twice…three times. There was that time in the corridor months ago, when you asked me about the windows." Ichi looked at the floor, thinking. Then he brought his face back up to glare at the woman in front of him who was keeping so much to herself. "Claire, have you been wandering around the complex like this, not knowing what you've been doing, since *January*?" Claire could only look up at him, the tears in her eyes beginning to fall down her face. She tried to shake Ichi's hands off of her shoulders, but he kept his grip tight.

"I don't know. No, honestly, I don't!" she added on when she noticed the furious expression on Ichi's face. "Maybe. It could have been before – "

"Before?!"

"Or it could have been after! I don't know! But I…I know it's been happening far more frequently since March. Sometimes I wake up in my room; sometimes I wake up under the fourth floor stairs. I can't remember what I've been doing during the time I've blacked out, no matter how hard I try to." Claire was looking at the floor; at the walls; anywhere but at Ichi. He grabbed onto her chin to force her to look at him.

Claire closed her eyes in frustration. "Ichi, don't do that!" she cried.

"How frequent is frequent?" Ichi demanded to know, ignoring Claire's complaint entirely.

"Ichi, I don't –"

"*Stop lying!*"

"Fine!" Claire screamed back at him. "Almost every night! I lose hours of time and wake up with a fucking bleeding nose and a migraine that feels like it might kill me *almost every night.* Are you happy now?" Claire's breathing was frantic, her chest heaving from the ferocity with which she had just exploded at Ichi. In those few moments of silence, she seemed to try her hardest to compose herself, but it didn't work. Ichi kept his face blank as his brain processed everything Claire had said. *This is all too much. What the hell is going on? Just what did her parents do to her to result in this?*

Ichi took a deep breath. Exhaled. "Claire. Do you know who it was you were just talking about? The man who was being sent away?" Claire's gaze seemed to sharpen for a second, only for it to crumple a moment later.

"No, I don't." She paused, a frown on her face. "It feels like I almost know if I don't think about it, but the moment I concentrate on anything from my past it just…disappears. Like it was never meant to be there." They were both quiet for a few seconds.

Ichi let go of Claire and turned away. "You seemed to care about him a lot, whoever he was." *What if it was Vic?* Suddenly, Ichi straightened up and stared at the wall, seeing nothing. *I can't believe I'm jealous of a lost memory. But when she gets these memories back, Claire will know who that man is. And what if it's Vic? What if it's Vic? What if –*

"I need to see Vic," Claire said, as if reading Ichi's thoughts. He spun back around and grabbed her arm again.

"No! Why? Why does it have to be *him*?" Ichi demanded, and Claire seemed to be shocked at how vehement he sounded. Even Ichi himself was.

Claire took a step away from him. "You don't know how to deal with anybody who's upset, or fragile, or angry, Ichi. You don't *want* to deal with it. You don't care. Vic does. I'm ashamed of myself for needing *anybody* when I'm like this, but I do. And he's all I have."

Ichi took a step towards her, backing her against the door. "Then why are you here with me, every night? Surely the novelty of screwing me instead of him was over weeks ago, right? So why are you still here with me, if I'm as fucking deplorable as you say?" Ichi kept his voice quiet, because he was so furious and confused that he felt no amount of screaming at Claire could vocalise those feelings. He leant against the door, containing Claire in the space between his body and the wood. He could feel her heart hammering in her chest, but until she said anything, Ichi couldn't be sure why it was. He knew *his* was beating manically for a whole host of reasons, all of which were related to the damnable woman in front of him.

Claire looked at him with a fury all her own. "You don't get to ask me why! It's my decision, isn't it?"

Ichi banged his fist against the door. "Hell *yes* I get to ask you why, Claire! If it's me you're with, then I get to ask why!" And then, suddenly, Claire wrapped her arms around Ichi's neck and pulled him in until there were mere millimetres between their lips. Ichi looked into her eyes and tried desperately to work out what was going on behind them. "Why do you drive me insane, Claire? Why do you get to?" Ichi asked, and all of the anger had drained from his voice, leaving only confusion.

"Because I lo –" Claire began, only to stop herself, and Ichi saw the horror creep up over her face. She let go of Ichi's neck to push him away slightly. "No," she said, closing her eyes and shaking her head violently as she did so. "I can't, I can't! What kind of a fool does that?! I can't..." It took Ichi a few seconds of dumbfounded silence to work out what Claire was saying. And then, even when he knew, he didn't know what to say or do. So instead of responding to Claire's non-confession, he kissed her, softly, and rested his chin on top of her head.

He sighed. "Just stay with me in here tonight. Don't go to Vic. For the love of God, don't go to Vic," he muttered into her hair. He felt Claire slowly bring her hands up to rest them on his bare chest; it was only in that moment that Ichi remembered that he had no clothes on. *What a conversation to be having stark naked,* he thought wryly.

He heard Claire let out a shallow, uneven breath. "Okay."

After Ichi led her back to bed, he gently removed Claire's clothes, Claire blushing slightly every time she felt Ichi's fingers brush her skin. After she crawled under the duvet and Ichi followed suit, they were silent for a while. Ichi thought, more than once, that Claire had fallen asleep, but upon listening to her breathing properly he realised that she wasn't. Eventually, Claire mumbled, "Can you...just forget I said anything?" But her voice was resigned, as if she already knew the answer to her own question.

Ichi didn't reply immediately, his mind too absorbed with committing every word Claire had and hadn't said to memory. "Absolutely no fucking way," he replied after a few seconds, chuckling slightly at the way Claire took his response. She rolled away from him, but Ichi kept a hand on her wrist. Claire turned her head back to raise a questioning eyebrow in his general direction. Ichi kept his face serious. "I won't let you go anywhere, so just fall back asleep," he explained, and Claire's entire expression softened; she almost smiled.

She rolled back in and kissed him. "Thank you," Claire whispered, and it sounded like she meant it.

A long time later, when Claire had finally fallen asleep again, Ichi lay there looking at her, wondering. Wondering how it was possible for her to have fallen in love with him, and wondering if every furious, intense emotion he felt when he looked at her meant that he loved her too.

CHAPTER 30
Crazy

Claire

Claire woke up abruptly the next morning when she felt Ichi's breath on the back of her neck. Her body tensed against his as a result and was startled even further when he snaked an arm around her waist to pull her in closer. "Stay where you are," Ichi murmured. Claire wriggled around within the confines of his arm to turn and face him; Ichi opened his sleep-heavy eyes when she did so to add: "Be asleep again."

Claire gave him a small smile. "I'm too awake to be asleep. I want to go for a swim." Ichi seemed to regard Claire for a moment, then he let her go to sit up and stretch both arms up above his head, yawning as he did so.

"Fine, so we're awake then. Are we going to spend the next twelve hours pretending we don't speak to each other as usual?"

Claire rolled off of the bed to fish for her swimming costume out of her chest of drawers, but spared Ichi a glance before replying, "You just don't know how to speak to me when there are other people around. I have no problem with it."

Ichi let out a bark of laughter as he pulled on his clothes that had lain forgotten on the floor all night. "That's a lie, and you know it." Claire cringed slightly at being caught out.

"Okay, whatever," she said as she pulled on her swimming costume, "But it's only because you don't 'do' casual conversation."

"Yes I do. Just not with you."

"And why is that? Pray tell," Claire called out from the shower room, where she was busy brushing her hair up into a ponytail. Ichi walked over and pulled out the band Claire had only just tied her hair up with in order to tug her head back to look at him. Claire clucked out a noise of disapproval at the action.

"There are far more interesting things to do with you than to have casual conversation." He trailed a finger down Claire's spine, making her shiver.

"Don't do that, Ichi, it's creepy as hell."

He chuckled into her ear. "I know; that's why I did it." Claire turned around for a second to push him away before redoing her hair, and was vaguely aware of Ichi then walking away to wander about the rest of her room. Claire allowed him to do so whilst she brushed her teeth. When she was done, she popped her head out of the doorway to see what Ichi was doing, and frowned when she saw that he was riffling through her wardrobe.

Claire marched over to him. "I'm aware that you have no respect whatsoever for my privacy, but there must be a limit even for you," she complained. Ichi took something out of the wardrobe, and it occurred to Claire that the item of clothing could only be one thing a second before she saw it.

"I haven't seen this in a while," Ichi said nonchalantly, inspecting his leather jacket before putting it on. Claire felt her cheeks growing red.

"H-how did you know I –"

"Are you seriously asking me that after everything we discussed last night, Claire?" Ichi interrupted, a questioning eyebrow raised at her supposed lapse in intelligence. Claire swept her gaze about the room and cursed.

"Why did you let me blame it on Alexis then?"

Ichi chuckled. "It was interesting to see you jealous over something that you had made up entirely. You can be incredibly childish, you know." Ichi walked over to the shower room before Claire could form a retort. "I'm going to use your toothbrush!" he called, raising his voice slightly to make sure that Claire heard him. She was by his side in a second, pulling the toothbrush out of his hand.

"The hell you are! Just go back to your own room and get ready there like a normal person." Ichi let her push him all the way to the main door before turning around to face her.

"Do you want to do some target practice later?" he asked.

Claire thought about it for a moment, then shook her head. "I'm doing some sparring with Imran later, so no." If Ichi was disappointed with her answer, he didn't show it on his face. Claire was surprised to realise that she had almost wished that he was. She sighed. "I'll see you tonight, I guess."

"I guess?"

"I could decide that there's something or someone else more deserving of my evening for all you know," Claire threw back, just to see what Ichi would say. He laughed, running a hand through his hair to take it out of his eyes.

"We both know that that won't happen." Claire watched as Ichi's hair fell back into his eyes as soon as he took his hand away.

"You need a haircut," she commented. Ichi glanced upwards at the strands of hair caught in between his eyelashes.

"I know."

"Then go get one." Ichi looked at her for a long moment, and Claire wondered what it was that he was thinking about.

Eventually he grinned. "Then I think I will. The forecast's really good for today as well, so I might just go lounge in the sun for a while whilst I'm at it." Claire almost slapped him; her hand had found its way halfway up to Ichi's face before she stopped it. It had been such a reflex reaction that Claire didn't know what to say or do about it. She looked at the floor. "Michael's going to take advantage of you if you act like that," Ichi muttered after a while.

"You didn't need to flaunt your freedom in front of me," Claire replied, very quietly. Ichi curled a finger underneath her chin to lift her head up. He kissed her gently, an act that occurred very rarely.

"It's because I'm cruel," he said, and Claire, knowing it to be entirely true, didn't say anything in return.

And then Ichi opened her door and left for his own room, leaving Claire to live out another day trapped inside Michael's complex, dreaming longingly of the sun.

Ah, shit, Claire thought as she woke up with a terrible headache, her body cramped and sore from lying underneath the fourth floor stairs for however long she had been unconscious for this time. For a moment she wondered why Ichi had let her wander off in the middle of the night, and then Claire remembered that he had never returned from his day trip, so she had fallen asleep on her own.

"So much for your help, Ichi," she muttered aloud, rubbing her temple as she eased her body out of the alcove. She licked the skin above her lips and then felt it with her fingertips, surprised. "No nosebleed this time, huh? Is that a good thing?" Claire stood up on slightly shaky legs, testing them out on the landing before braving the stairs. *I'll just get some painkillers for my head from the kitchen and then go to bed,* she thought as she made her slow descent towards the rec hall.

Claire wondered if she should be proud of herself for dealing with her memory lapses so efficiently, or if she should be worried that her way of coping was to be as apathetic as possible. *It basically means that I'm acting like Ichi. Though I suppose* acting *like him and being like him are entirely different things.*

Claire didn't even attempt to remember what it was that she had been doing before falling unconscious under the stairs. But she did think about how upset she had gotten when Ichi had caught her in one of her trances the previous night, and wondered whether the reason she had gotten so upset was because she had been dragged out of said trance whilst talking about something traumatic, or whether it had been because *Ichi* had been the one who had found her in such a state.

"I'd have felt better if it were Vic," Claire said quietly, knowing it to be true. Vic always knew what to say; Ichi had resorted to losing his temper entirely. Claire sighed when she realised that she had deserved it. *It just felt weird having Ichi take what was essentially a moral high ground. Can a person with no morals even do that?*

Claire was broken out of her reverie by the sound of voices through the rec hall doors. As silently as she could, she pushed open one of the swing doors by a few millimetres in an attempt to hear them more clearly.

"…amazing what they'll talk about when they think I'm not there," Claire heard a man's voice say. She frowned, concentrating hard on who it might be. *Is that…Roger?*

"Such as?" came a voice that was undoubtedly Michael's. Claire held a hand up to her mouth to stifle the gasp that she had half-emitted. *What are Roger and Michael talking about at God knows what time in the morning?!*

She heard Roger laugh. "Let's just say that there have been one or two 'private' investigations you may want to investigate yourself. And then of course there's Little Miss Sleepwalker, who's currently lurking by the door over there." Claire flinched. *What am I supposed to do now?*

"Yes, I'm well aware of that," Michael replied. And then, much louder: "Won't you join us, Miss Danvers?" Claire let out a shaky breath, wished that she could be anywhere else, then opened the door and cautiously walked over to Michael and Roger, who were leaning over opposite sides of the kitchen's breakfast bar. Michael was dressed in a sharp grey suit that he no doubt knew matched his eyes, as he had been on the three other occasions that Claire had met him. It made Claire feel entirely inappropriate in her oversized blue jumper and tiny shorts, though by all accounts she was the one more suitably dressed for the current time of night. Michael straightened up when Claire reached them, raising an inquiring eyebrow as he did so; it reminded Claire of Ichi. "Did you know that your nose is bleeding?" he asked off-handedly.

Claire's hand jolted immediately to her nose where she felt warm, wet blood underneath her fingertips. *I guess the nosebleed was merely delayed this time,* she thought, repressing a sigh. "I just came down to get some painkillers," Claire said, knowing that it was a completely insubstantial reason for loitering outside the rec hall door in the dead of night.

Roger laughed. "I told you that she never tells me what's actually happened to her, even when Ichi had clearly half-bashed her skull open. Do you still have his knife, by the way?"

Claire looked at the pair of them, eyes wide. "You didn't honestly believe that I wasn't aware of everything that occurred inside my own building, Miss Danvers?" Michael asked, amused. Claire thought of what Ichi had said earlier – that Michael could take advantage of her if she got emotional – and so opted to stand her ground.

"So what if I do have his knife?" she replied, crossing her arms as she did so. "I haven't tried to attack anyone with it, have I? I haven't tried to break through one of your cleverly boarded up windows to escape, either. And I certainly haven't said anything in the months I've been here that you would care to know about." Michael smiled slightly at that final sentence, as if to say that Claire was wrong.

Roger laughed again. "Oh, she really is like her mother, isn't she? You picked a winner here, Michael." Claire stared at Roger, knowing that surprise was written all over her face.

"You knew my…"

Roger smiled at her, creasing up his crow foot eyes in the process. "Yes my dear, I knew your mother. Didn't know your dad, though, but according to Michael I didn't really miss much there." Claire bristled at his answer, but she forced herself to remain calm.

She turned to Michael. "Is there a reason you called me over here? Other than to flaunt your apparent omnipresence, I mean." Michael looked at her, silent, all traces of amusement gone from his face. Claire felt as though he might have been searching her face for some answer that she was withholding from him – it unnerved her to no end. And then Michael shocked Claire by reaching out for her, grabbing the back of her head to prevent her from backing away. "What are you –" Claire spluttered out, but Michael answered the question by cleaning the blood away from her face with the edge of his hand. Claire didn't know what to do; she felt altogether like a deer caught in headlights, much like she had done on the day she was kidnapped. And Michael just kept looking at her with his distinctive non-expression, telling Claire nothing of his intentions.

"Come see me in my office tomorrow," he said eventually. "I have something important to discuss with you." Michael continued to bore through Claire's blue eyes with his grey ones, until Claire thought that she would surely go insane before another word was uttered, and even then she felt as if she wouldn't have heard it in the first place. But then Michael said, "You may go," and with that he released her and turned to face Roger. Claire backed away slowly for a few steps, then turned around and had to stop herself from all but running out of the rec hall.

When Claire reached the twelfth floor she banged on Ichi's door repeatedly, not knowing what it was that she was there for but desperately

328

needing to see him nonetheless. But Ichi didn't answer, so Claire, resigned, went back to her own room and collapsed on top of the bed.

If Vic's not here and Ichi's not here, who am I supposed to go to? she thought despairingly, ashamed to feel tears welling up in her eyes. *How am I supposed to go through all of this alone?* She glanced at her bedside lamp, hating how it would continue to function as a normal bedside lamp even though Claire felt like her whole perspective on the life she had now had been irreversibly altered. *In the grand scheme of things, my life means nothing. What does the world care if Michael watches over every little thing I do and limits what I can do in the first place?*

Frustrated, Claire swept her arm out to knock the lamp over and was satisfied to hear the ceramic crack against the floor. Then she sat up, surveying her room for anything else breakable. Claire felt a dangerous grin spread across her face as her gaze locked on the glass coffee table. *Maybe I'm finally going mad,* Claire thought as she walked over to the table, but she didn't care.

CHAPTER 31
Bad Things

Vic

Claire was acting strangely when Vic showed up in front of her door with the promised breakfast croissants, though it was closer to lunch time by the time he finally got around to it. *She seems reluctant to even let me past the front door, for one,* he thought. *And she looks like she hasn't slept at all.* Claire's hair was in disarray, eyes furtive and almost guilty-looking. She couldn't seem to be able to stand still; she kept tugging at the bottom of her camisole top or shifting her weight from one foot to the other, all whilst blocking the entrance to her room.

"Claire," Vic said, suspicious. "What are you hiding?" Claire looked up at him with pleading blue eyes, and Vic almost let her off without further questioning. Almost. He deliberately let go of the tray of food he had brought up with him, forcing Claire to catch it before it fell to the floor, then used the momentary distraction to slam open her door.

"Vic, don't –" Claire began, but Vic silenced her with a hand.

"Claire, what the hell?"

"I second that," came Ichi's voice from behind him, surprising both Vic and Claire in the process.

"Where did you come from?" Vic asked, turning to face Ichi.

The other man shrugged. "The stairs. Just got back from an overdue haircut," Ichi explained. He ran a hand through his now-shorter hair to prove his point.

"In what, America?!" Claire exclaimed, Ichi's presence having drawn her attention away from the actual topic of conversation.

Ichi smirked at her. "Yes, actually. Ryan recommended a guy who would actually cut my hair the way I wanted it. He wasn't wrong." There were a few seconds of silence where Vic and Ichi continued to stare into Claire's room and she continued to flick her gaze from Ichi to Vic and then back again. "But Jesus Christ, Claire," Ichi finally said, "Is this what happens when Vic and I are both gone for a night?"

"I had a...rough time," Claire mumbled, looking abashed. Vic pushed her gently to the side so that he could walk past her into the room. The place was a wreck – it appeared as if anything Claire could bodily destroy and throw to the floor had been dutifully destroyed and thrown to the floor. The drawers in the non-functional kitchen had all been ripped away from the units they belonged to; the fridge toppled over onto its side; the mattress had been cut to pieces and several wooden slats of the bed had been broken. The glass coffee table had been shattered, the rug beneath it transformed into a mess of clear and, most worryingly to Vic, red glass shards. He spun around quickly to look at Claire; he couldn't see any obvious injuries. But then she slowly picked up her feet one at a time, and Vic saw that they were covered in raw, angry cuts.

"Claire, what the hell happened to you? Why did you do *that*?!" Vic demanded, pointing at her feet before grabbing the tray of food from her and placing it on one of the less-damaged kitchen countertops. Claire ran both of her hands through her hair, looking at the ceiling. But she didn't say anything; Vic wondered if she even knew what to say in the first place.

"You've done a number on the shower," Vic heard Ichi call over to them. He turned to see Ichi holding several tiles from the shower as well as the shower unit itself. "Mind telling us what this was all for?" Ichi threw himself onto the couch; it alone had remained undamaged. But Claire still refused to answer, proceeding to pick through the bomb site that was her room to retrieve her favourite, dark blue jumper from the floor, wincing every time she took a step. But as she pulled the jumper on over her head, Vic marched over and grabbed her, carrying her over to the hallway before letting her go.

"For fuck's sake Claire, don't do any more damage to yourself than you've already done!" Vic snapped. He saw Ichi look up at him in surprise out of the corner of his eye. *I guess he's not used to seeing me lose my temper with her. Hell,* I'm *not used to it either.* But Vic knew he had to keep pressing Claire to get an answer even if he had to be forceful about it, because otherwise she would just keep it to herself. He stared at her until she finally looked him in the eye. Behind him, Vic heard Ichi get up from the couch and join them.

Claire's face was completely blank; Vic was taken aback by how dead her eyes appeared to be. "What's the point?" Claire muttered, her voice monotonous. "What's the point in anything? What's the point in you talking to me in whispers so nobody hears, Vic?" She shifted her dead eyes to Ichi. "What's the point in you trying to trigger my memories behind everybody's back?" Vic turned his head to look at the man behind him, then back to Claire.

"Ah," he said, finally understanding why Claire seemed to have stopped discussing anything to do with her past entirely with him. *She was speaking about it with Ichi. Always Ichi! I've made her distrust me so much that she's ended up running to him for* everything. Vic almost felt as though his heart were breaking, and he thought that he might have let it happen if Claire didn't seem to be physically and mentally breaking in front of him.

"Claire, stop being crazy," Ichi said simply. "What happened?"

Claire's gaze had returned to the floor. "Michael happened," she replied, before turning from the two of them to limp towards the elevator; Vic realised that she had a large bruise beginning to flower on the back of her right leg.

"Claire, where are you going?!" Vic called out after her as both he and Ichi followed her down the corridor.

"Claire, where are you going?" Claire chimed back as she pressed the button for the elevator. "Claire, what are you doing? Claire, what are you hiding? What's the point to any of those questions? I'm in Michael's building – I can't go anywhere else. I can only do things that are limited to Michael's building. And I can't hide anything from Michael's building." She brought her sleeve up to wipe her eye. "And now Michael's building will see me cry, and Michael will know. That's just great."

Vic glanced at Ichi to see if he was going to do anything, but Ichi returned the look with indifference. Vic struggled not to punch him. *There is something inherently wrong with him. Seriously, seriously wrong.* So Vic took it upon himself to turn Claire around to face him, using a thumb to brush away the rest of her tears before hugging her fiercely.

"I'm so sorry, Claire. I'm so sorry."

"For what?" she mumbled into his chest.

"For everything." He let her go just as the elevator door pinged open. "But can you please tell me where you're going with your feet like that?" Claire looked at him pointedly, as if he should have worked it out already.

"Michael wants to see me."

Vic frowned at her. "How did you know that?" he asked. "I was supposed to tell you that this morning. He wants to see you, too," Vic added, throwing a glance at Ichi. Ichi didn't respond.

"Michael told me at about four this morning," Claire replied, her voice hollow.

"Ah," Ichi said, mimicking Vic's noise of understanding from earlier, "So your mental breakdown wasn't entirely unwarranted." Vic turned from Claire to shove him against the wall.

"What the *hell* is wrong with you?!" he shouted, but then he felt Claire tug him away.

"Vic, don't do that!" she protested. "He's just saying what you won't. And it's not like it isn't a valid point."

Vic shook his head furiously. "Why do you defend him, Claire? I don't understand."

She walked into the lift, waiting for both Vic and Ichi to follow suit before replying. "That's definitely the only time I've ever defended him. He doesn't need it." And then the three of them said nothing until they reached the basement floor.

As they exited the elevator, Vic saw Ichi knock Claire gently on the head with his knuckles, just barely hearing him mutter, "You didn't listen to a word I said yesterday morning."

"I did listen," Claire replied quietly. "It was just very hard advice to follow through on." Vic was left wondering what the two of them were discussing, in the world that they had somehow managed to create for themselves in which nobody else seemed to exist, until Michael answered his knock on the door. As they entered his office, Vic noted that his boss was dressed impeccably, as if he were expecting to be called away to give

333

an important speech at any given second. *But he's always dressed like that,* Vic thought. *It's just weird to see him in a sharp suit against Claire in a bloody mess.*

Michael was also wearing the same bland, vaguely amused smile he always wore as he looked Claire up and down. "Well that was certainly interesting to watch, Miss Danvers," he said, "Though I do hope you've gotten it all out of your system; I'm not moving you to another room after all. The doctor's expecting you after this, I'm sure you'll be thrilled to hear. Please, take a seat." Claire reluctantly sat down in one of the chairs in front of Michael's desk, never taking her eyes off of the man in front of her. Both Ichi and Vic opted to stand. Ichi leant casually against the back wall, the shadows in the room half-hiding him from view.

"So what do you need to see all three of us about?" Ichi asked.

Michael chuckled. "As blunt as ever. I'll get to the point, then." His gaze sharpened on Claire; to Claire's credit, she never flinched nor gave away any sign of discomfort on her face as he did so. *How are you managing that after what you've just been through, Claire?* Vic wondered, feeling his chest swelling with pride at his ever-complicated princess. "Miss Danvers, there's a biological awards ball being held in two weeks and you need to be at it."

Claire stared at him blankly. "This is to do with my parents?"

"As it usually is."

"So why are Vic and Ichi here?"

Michael grinned. "Ichi's your 'date'. Vic's your bodyguard."

"Wait, what?" Ichi exclaimed from his position at the back of the room. "I wasn't told about any of this before!"

"And justly so; it wasn't any of your business until now," Michael replied. "The only one who needed to know anything before now was Vic." Ichi and Claire both turned their heads to stare at Vic.

"Of course," the two of them said in unison, though whilst Ichi was sarcastic Claire was merely resigned.

"I'd have thought you would be more excited, Miss Danvers," Michael said. "You finally get to leave…for a night."

Claire swung her head back around to look at him. "Yes, *for a night*. I'll be excited when I get to leave permanently."

"Somebody certainly seems to be doing their hardest to act like they don't care," Michael chided. Then he fixed her with a hard stare and said nothing, as if he was waiting for Claire to reply. Both Vic and Ichi watched the exchange, and Vic could tell that Ichi was just as confused about it as he was.

"Is there anything else you're actually going to tell me about all of this right now?" Claire finally asked. "Because otherwise, I should probably get my feet stitched up if I want to be able to dance in – ah…" And then Claire was looking at Vic. "I get it now. Everything you do really is premeditated, isn't it?" Vic didn't know what to say, because Claire was right.

"But of course it is," Michael answered for him. Then: "And you're correct. You'll get more information as and when you need it. Vic, take her to the doctor's; Ichi, stay back. I have a quick job I need doing that I think you'll rather like." Ichi's eyes flashed with interest then, and Vic knew that the 'job' couldn't be anything pleasant. *There's something wrong with you,* Vic thought again. *And there's something horribly wrong with me,* he added on, looking at Claire as he did so and thinking of all of the things he was hiding from her.

Claire stood up and made for the door without another word; Vic followed suit. As they opened the door, Vic said, "I'll come up later and clean your room, okay? Don't think for a second that you're doing it."

"What's the point?" Claire replied, repeating her horrifically nihilistic words from earlier.

And behind them, just as Vic closed the door, Michael answered her rhetorical question. "The point is for you to give me what I want, Miss Danvers."

Vic didn't think he had ever seen a person look as terrified as Claire did in that moment.

Ichi

"So how quick is quick?" Ichi asked Michael as soon as Vic and Claire had vacated the man's office.

Michael gave him a benign smile. "Oh, *very* quick, Ichi," he replied. "In fact, your target is only just about to leave this base."

Ichi frowned at him, confused. "So who are they?" Michael's expression changed from genial to something much more dangerous.

"Somebody who thought I wouldn't work out that they had been giving me false information."

Ichi regarded his boss carefully. "Is this to do with Claire's parents?"

"Does that change anything?" Ichi shook his head in response to the question. Michael smiled again. "Good. I'm sending them back to the mainland on a helicopter. The pilot knows to expect you upstairs in ten minutes."

"Any particular requests for cause of death?" Ichi asked casually, as if he were asking Michael what the weather forecast was for the coming week.

Michael considered his question for a moment before responding. "Ah, you simply need to ensure that this man's death is…memorable." Michael's last words piqued Ichi's interest.

"Memorable? For whom?"

Michael's smile grew wider. "For the woman he's travelling with. They both gave me false information. Let the man act as a warning for the woman to relay back to the people they work for."

Ichi matched Michael's grin. "I've never killed someone in the air before."

Michael chuckled softly at Ichi's obvious excitement. "Then I suppose this one will be memorable for you too."

*

Less than three hours later, Ichi was back on the landing pad on the top of Michael's complex. It was pouring with rain; Ichi allowed it to soak through his clothes and skin and hair. He knew he was covered in blood. *Well, Michael did say to make it memorable.* The look of terror on the face of his victim when he knew he was going to die had been exceptionally satisfying for Ichi; the fear in his companion's face even more so. Ichi had nearly lost complete control and killed her too, but he knew Michael would have been furious with him if he had. So he had left the sobbing, shaking woman with the butchered corpse of the man she had worked with and told the pilot to carry on back to the mainland.

And now here Ichi was, back at Michael's complex as if he had never left in the first place. *Except now I'm drenched in blood and rain.* Ichi tried to recall the last time he had assassinated someone for Michael. *Early March, maybe?* he thought. *It's June now.* He couldn't quite believe that he had gone for so long without killing anyone. The adrenaline coursing through his veins as he looked at the blood slowly falling onto the ground from his hands felt dizzyingly good. He felt ecstatic. He felt *free.*

The very thought of freedom caused Ichi to suddenly remember something Claire had said to him, months ago. She hadn't known she had said it, of course, and Ichi still wasn't completely convinced that she had meant for it to be about him. *'You miss your freedom almost as much as I do,'* she had said. *'You just don't know it yet...'* The feeling of freedom Ichi got from mindlessly killing another human being could not possibly have been the same freedom Claire had been referring to. *But if not that, then what? I've never experienced anything else that makes me feel this way.* For the past few months, he had thought that sleeping with Claire elicited the same reaction as he got from a kill. Now Ichi realised that he was wrong. Yes, it *satisfied* his urge to kill, and it felt unbelievable, but it didn't make him feel free.

If anything, it left Ichi trapped – there was nothing else he wanted to do more than to have sex with Claire; to be with Claire; to monopolise her entire person; so when he *wasn't* he couldn't bear it. It felt like an addiction. *Not one that I want to break out of, but...*Ichi knew now that Claire wouldn't be enough to satisfy his bloodlust. *No,* he thought, glancing at the dark red stains on his clothes. *The only thing that can satisfy bloodlust is* blood.

Finally, Ichi left the landing pad and the rain in favour of a roof over his head, a shower and some dry clothes. He knew that he was supposed to talk to Michael first about the job's completion, but in his current frame of mind Ichi didn't care. He walked down the stairs, heading to the twelfth floor and his own room instead. But just as he reached his door, he heard the sound of another one opening behind him.

"Vic, is that – oh. Ichi," he heard Claire say to his back. *Even now, after all this time, she wants the person walking down the corridor to be Vic, not me,* he thought. Ichi knew that he was in a dangerous mood, and such thoughts certainly didn't help that frame of mind. *But what do I care? I* am *dangerous.*

"Ichi, why are you wet?" Claire asked.

Ichi took half a moment to reply. "Because it's raining outside," he answered, stating the obvious. He didn't turn around, even when he heard Claire walking towards him. It was only when he felt her hand on his leather jacket that Ichi spun around to face her. Her feet were wrapped in clean white bandages; it took Ichi a few moments to remember that she had cut her feet that morning. Claire had a look of confusion on her beautiful face that quickly turned to horror as she took in Ichi's bloody appearance. In a second, Claire managed to school her expression to something far more neutral, but there was nothing she could do to hide the fact that her cheeks had grown pale.

"What was this job for Michael then?" she mumbled, keeping her eyes averted from Ichi's. Ichi kept his face blank.

"What you're asking is if I killed someone," he corrected. Claire kept her gaze on the floor, choosing not to respond. Just as it looked as if she was planning on leaving for her own room, Ichi pinned her against his door and brought his forehead down to rest against hers, his sodden hair slowly dripping pink water down Claire's cheeks. She brought her eyes up to look at him and they were wide with surprise and…was that fear Ichi could see? He hadn't seen any fear directed at him for months; he had forgotten that that expression was all part of his brain longed for. "Killing people is what I do, Claire. It's my entire purpose. I shouldn't have to remind *you* of this," he murmured in a soft, low voice. He ran his hand through her hair, leaving droplets of water and blood in its wake.

"You *don't* need to remind me of that," Claire replied, though her voice was small and her words were almost lost as Ichi kissed her with such a ferocity that Claire gasped at his actions. Ichi opened his door without deviating from her mouth.

"Ichi, what are you –" Claire began, as he pushed her into his room and closed the door behind him in one smooth motion. Ignoring her protests, Ichi grabbed her around the waist and threw her onto his bed. Claire frowned at him. "We are not doing this now," she insisted, trying to sound confident. Ichi could hear the waver in her voice nonetheless. He took his jacket off in a slow, deliberate motion.

"And why not? If I didn't need to remind you of what I do, then that means you have no problem with it. Which makes this time no different than any other," Ichi replied. In that moment as he made to remove her clothes, Ichi decided to channel the adrenaline from his kill into dominating Claire once and for all.

Claire

Claire was scared. She hadn't had an encounter with Ichi that had been anything other than mutual for months, and now he seemed to have reverted to who he had been the night he had raped her. *Had he really ever changed? Or was I just fooling myself?* It was easy to forget exactly what Ichi was when he hadn't left the complex on one of Michael's jobs for nearly three months now, and he always ensured that he had Claire's consent before doing anything. *Surely asking for my consent means he changed though...right? It can't all have been an act!*

Claire was growing frantic; Ichi was removing her clothes and his logic behind Claire not having a problem with him doing so meant that Claire knew she couldn't argue her way out of the situation. But one look at Ichi's expression told Claire another story – he *knew* what he was doing was wrong. There was a challenge in his bright, excited eyes, as if a fight was exactly what he was hoping for. *He wants me to fight him so he can win.* Even now, after two months of feeling like they were actually getting to know one another, Ichi was still a child. A psychotic, violent, sadistic child. And Claire had forgotten that. She *had* needed reminding of his desire to kill. *There's so much I don't remember from my past and here I am, willingly forgetting pieces of information just because I wish they weren't true.*

When Ichi moved his hand behind her back to undo her bra, Claire snapped back to life and tried to push him away. "Stop it, Ichi! Stop it! You know I don't want this!" Ichi chuckled at her protests before leaning in to nibble at her ear.

"You know, Claire, killing is just about the only thing I get any kind of rush from. Screwing you is the other; I'm sure you worked that out for yourself. So you're going to let me do this." He kissed her, his eyes never leaving her own. Claire stared back at him, aghast. She couldn't keep the fear from her face, which was made all the worse when she saw Ichi's reaction to it. He *enjoyed* it.

Claire attempted to roll over to her left and escape, but Ichi grabbed onto her and rolled off the bed with her, leaving her trapped underneath him in the narrow space between his bed and the wall. "That was incredibly stupid," he commented, so casually that Claire couldn't quite believe he had said it. And with nowhere else to run, Claire realised that she would have no choice but to be Ichi's human plaything until he got it out of his system.

She had thought that it wouldn't last long, hoping that whatever high Ichi was riding on would dissipate quickly, but she could not have been more wrong. Whenever it felt like Ichi was close to finishing, he slowed himself down and focussed solely on Claire, and whenever she came close he stopped altogether.

"What are you doing?" Claire eventually asked him, breathless from his extended onslaught of her nerve endings. Ichi bodily picked Claire up and flung her back onto the bed, his hungry mouth back on hers before her head hit the pillow. He bit into her lower lip before pulling away ever so slightly.

"I want you to beg me to finish you," he demanded of her, his expression fervent and alive and crazed. And beautiful, though Claire hated herself for thinking so. But she knew it to be true; Ichi was enthralling when he was like this. She couldn't look away, could *never* look away, not even in the beginning. She suddenly remembered that Ichi had said he was going to take everything from her. Claire couldn't believe that it was only now, months later, that she realised that he had. *The last two months weren't all an act,* she thought again, desperately. *They can't be.*

340

"I won't," she replied to this man who she didn't understand at all, who seemed to be two completely different people. Ichi ran his left hand through Claire's hair, using it to pin her head to the pillow. Claire thought back to a worry she had had at the beginning of those two months, back when she was deciding whether to tell Ichi everything that she could remember. *What if he has no intention of letting me go when Michael finds my parents?*

"You will," Ichi said, his voice confident and authoritative. Claire felt her eyes beginning to grow wet, and she wrapped her arms around Ichi's neck to hide her face against his shoulder. Ichi forced her back down against the bed. "Don't think I'll let you get away with hiding from me like you did the first time," he grinned, as he continued to drive her body insane.

Eventually, Claire couldn't take any more. Despite the stubborn part of her brain screaming at her not to do it, her body felt like it might die if she remained silent. "Do it," she whispered, her voice barely audible against Ichi's mouth. She felt his lips curl into a smile.

"Do what?" he asked, his breathing rapid and unsteady. Claire felt her fingernails dig into his arm.

"God damn it Ichi, you've won! Please, please, just end it," she begged, desperate and terrified.

And he did. In the space of thirty seconds he finished them both, and Claire felt no pleasure, only relief. Ichi collapsed on top of her, his hands in her hair, twirling it around and around his fingers. "Do you get it now?" he murmured into her ear. He was exhausted; Claire could hear it in his voice, could feel it in the blood-tinged sweat that had no doubt soaked into her skin from his. *All this to prove a point.*

"...yes," Claire replied after a long moment, and she could hear the tears in her voice. *There, you won.*

When Ichi fell asleep, Claire didn't move from his bed for a while, her mind blank with shock and fear. Eventually, however, she gingerly stood up, found her clothes and made a silent escape for her own room. Claire sat in the bottom of her destroyed shower – as she had so often done when she had first been taken from her parent's house – and cried. She didn't care whether she could be heard or not. Claire couldn't believe that she had forgotten the very first thing that Ichi had promised her.

I was a fool for thinking he'd let me go.

341

CHAPTER 32
For Your Entertainment

Claire

It was only in waking up that Claire realised she had actually slept at all. She was lying on her couch, the bed too destroyed to be slept in. As Claire glanced around her room, however, she realised that much of the destruction she had wrought on the place had been cleared away and repaired. *Vic, when did you do all of this?* Claire thought. In reality, the only things that were still broken were her bed and the shower, although she was now missing a coffee table. Claire sat up slowly, mildly relieved that she didn't appear to have left her room in the middle of the night in a trance, when she realised that it could actually be the middle of the night *now,* or two in the afternoon for all she knew. But then Claire noticed a piece of paper on one of the kitchen countertops and she forgot about working out the time.

The dull pain in her feet as she walked over to retrieve the paper reminded Claire of just how stupid she had been in destroying the room around her. *All I managed to do was amuse Michael...I really am completely powerless.* She picked up the paper and recognised Vic's slanted handwriting immediately.

Didn't want to wake you up from your early evening nap (what's all that about, anyway? Are you a cat now?) so I cleaned up as best I could around you. Your table and mattress are ruined; you'll get new ones soon. Looks like you're back to sleeping on your beloved couch for a little while! Let me make you dinner tonight?

I'm so sorry for everything.

Vic

Claire almost laughed at the note. "You do have things to be sorry for, but definitely not everything," she muttered aloud. And then Claire remembered that everything she said and did in her room could be documented by both Michael and Ichi; she cursed silently. Claire found the large blue jumper she had been wearing the day before and a pair of shorts from her chest of drawers and threw them both on, not bothering with a bra.

Now where do I go? Ichi doesn't have any cameras in his room – he told me he destroyed them – but that's the last place on earth I want to be right now. And Ichi knows I hide under the fourth floor stairs. There are cameras literally everywhere else. So where...? And then Claire remembered that the fourth floor stairs weren't the only stairs that had an alcove underneath them. Forgoing shoes because they wouldn't fit properly over her bandaged feet, Claire crept down the twelfth floor corridor and opened the door to the stairwell as quietly as possible, hoping against hope that Ichi was somewhere else in the building and not watching her from his room. Closing the door just as quietly behind her, Claire proceeded to gingerly walk down two flights of stairs to the tenth floor on feet heavily protesting against being walked upon.

She inspected the space underneath the stairs – it wasn't as large as the one underneath the fourth floor, but it did go further back, almost like a triangular tunnel. Claire swept her gaze around the walls and ceiling surrounding her to confirm that none of the cameras could see her once she was underneath the stairs. Satisfied, she crawled through the space until she could lean against the back wall, stretched her legs out in front of her and sighed.

Claire felt a wave of relief wash over her once she knew that she wasn't being watched. It wasn't that she hadn't realised that Michael's cameras had been on her since the moment she was brought to the building; it was simply that Claire had never actively thought about it. She had had so many other things to worry over, after all, but now all Claire could think about was that working out how to deal with the cameras trained on her person should have been her first priority. *I've been so naïve,* she admonished. And then there were Ichi's cameras; Claire suppressed a shudder at the thought. She couldn't think about Ichi – not right now, not after what he had done. *If I think about him I'll scream, or cry, or...I don't know. Whatever it is I do, it won't make a difference to my situation anyway, except make it worse.*

In reality, Claire knew that she couldn't *not* think about Ichi, because she was sure that there was absolutely no way he'd allow Claire to avoid him for the next two weeks. *And then he'll be my 'date' at the awards ball, which is Michael's way of saying he's making sure I don't go anywhere alone.* Claire wondered why Michael had set up Vic as her bodyguard rather than her date and resolved to ask Vic about it later. She decided that she would let him make her dinner after all, if only so that she could stay away from Ichi. *Now I know that he was hiding this ball from me, maybe I can work out if there's anything else he's hiding.* Claire knew that Vic had to be hiding at least one or two other, clearly important, pieces of information from her, and now she was more determined than ever to try and work out what they might be.

Suddenly, Claire remembered that Vic didn't have any cameras in his room, and she considered going to find him now to discuss things with him, when she heard footsteps above her head. Knowing that in all likelihood it could only be Ichi, Claire silently pulled her legs back in against her chest and willed herself to disappear into the shadows of the alcove. She heard the footsteps get louder and louder as they reached the tenth floor; Claire realised that she was holding her breath. And then the footsteps started to head down the stairs to the ninth floor landing, and Claire felt immense relief wash over her. But then the footsteps stopped, and Claire went cold. "That would have worked, you know," Ichi called up to her, "if it wasn't for the fact that from the very beginning I always expected you to go to the tenth floor rather than the fourth." Then he walked back up the stairs to where Claire was hiding, crouching in front of the alcove when he got there. Claire hoped that the darkness under the stairs would hide the fact that her hands were shaking uncontrollably, but then Ichi crept into the space after her. Claire resorted to squeezing her hands between her chest and thighs to force them to stay still, but all that did was send the shaking up through her arms into her entire body.

How can I be in love with him? Claire despaired as she watched Ichi steadily grow closer to her, his eyes bright and alert but otherwise expressionless. *How could I end up letting him know that? And how am I getting out of here?* But whether she was referring to the situation at hand or the now futile concept of finally leaving Michael's complex unscathed, Claire didn't know.

Ichi

Ichi felt hungover. He had been running on such an adrenaline high and used up so much energy the previous day that, even though he had fallen asleep at around six in the evening and stayed asleep for close to twelve hours, he now felt low and drained.

It was coincidence that he had come across Claire on the tenth floor, though by the look on her face she didn't seem to think so. Ichi supposed he couldn't blame her, considering what he had done and said to her the previous day. *It was her own fault for ignoring who I actually was for her own convenience or conscience or whatever,* Ichi thought. It was then he noticed that Claire seemed to be a bit unsteady.

"Why are you shaking?" he asked, his tone devoid of anything but mild curiosity. He reached out a hand towards Claire's face, which she quickly turned away from. Ichi frowned, creeping in closer towards her until the space between them was almost obsolete. But Claire had her legs pressed up against her chest which prevented Ichi from getting as close as he might have liked. "Claire," he said, "Look at me." She gave the tiniest shake of her head in response, so Ichi leant in and kissed her, putting a hand on the wall behind her to stop her from moving away. When Claire tried to recoil anyway, Ichi kissed her harder until she relaxed her legs enough to extricate her hands from behind them in order to push him away. Ichi used the action as an opportunity to grab onto her wrists, preventing Claire from pulling her hands back.

But she still wasn't looking at him. Frustrated, Ichi pulled on her wrists until Claire fell forwards onto her knees, then again to pull her against his chest. He let go of her wrists to snake his arms around her waist; Claire didn't even attempt to struggle against him. "That's better," Ichi said. "You've stopped shaking now, anyway. Is this about yesterday? Or are you hiding under here because it's a camera-free zone?"

Claire kept her eyes downcast. "Both," she replied after a long pause. "I wanted to get away from everything. Obviously you have other plans." Ichi felt himself roll his eyes at Claire's answer, so he tugged on her hair to force her head up.

"I was riding an extreme adrenaline high yesterday, if you hadn't noticed."

Claire scowled. "That doesn't mean anything, Ichi! That doesn't give you permission to act like you did."

"I know that, but I did it anyway." Claire looked at him then; holding his gaze as if she were trying to force a less flippant answer out of him.

"And you don't regret it in the slightest."

"I know that too."

There was a pause as Claire continued to watch him with an expressionless face. "You meant everything you said."

Ichi raised an eyebrow at her, tightening his grip around her waist ever so slightly as he did so. "I know," he said for the third time, "I always do. Incidentally, I don't see why what I did yesterday is any worse than the things I did to you before." Claire gaped at him for a second, as if she couldn't believe what she was hearing.

Then she closed her eyes and sighed. "I'm not going to explain it to you if you're incapable of working it out for yourself. You wouldn't care for the answer anyway. And I was stupid to think that you'd know it in the first place."

Ichi frowned. "You knew who I was when you got involved with me. You can't expect me to just suddenly change. And I don't see why what I did yesterday changes anything."

Claire looked up at him sadly. "I know," she said, repeating his own words, but it sounded odd to Ichi's ears having Claire confess to knowing exactly what Ichi was like – knowing that it wouldn't change anything, but sounding so resigned about it. *No, that's not the right word,* Ichi thought. *But it's something like that.* There was another long pause.

"So," Ichi finally said to break the silence, "What are you going to do now? If nothing's changed?"

Ichi didn't know what to think when he saw that Claire's eyes had filled with tears. "Everything's changed," she said. "The reason for everything has changed. I don't know what to do, because nothing I can do will make any difference." Ichi realised that she wasn't just talking about the two of them, though that had been what his question was about. And without the rush of adrenaline in his system, Ichi realised that he had regained the capacity to understand that Claire had so much more going on in her life that was probably more important to her than him. Ichi didn't like that at all, but he knew that that was never going to change whilst Claire was still stuck in Michael's complex.

"Don't cry," he muttered, bringing a hand up from her waist to run it through her hair. Claire looked at him through her tear-heavy eyes, surprise written all over her face. "Crying isn't going to change anything, after all," Ichi continued, confused by Claire's expression. "What's the point in it?"

Claire let out a bark of humourless laughter. "I can't believe I thought for a second that you were actually being nice. I don't know why I keep getting my hopes up."

"If you want nice, go and find Vic," Ichi replied, annoyed. "I've never been nice to you."

"You made dinner for me once," Claire remarked pointedly.

"So you wouldn't keel over and die; I wouldn't necessarily say that that was me being nice…just practical." Claire sighed, but it looked to Ichi as if her mood had lifted just a little bit. Then Ichi heard footsteps below them and the murmur of voices, and his ears automatically pricked up to catch the conversation that was occurring.

"Ichi, why are you –"

"Shh," Ichi murmured, holding a hand over Claire's mouth to quieten her. She bit into his hand in protest, but remained silent once he had pulled it away with a voiceless curse.

"…losing it, Marie. Properly losing it. I don't know what to do to help her." Ichi recognised Vic's voice immediately; one glance at Claire confirmed that she did too.

"You can't do any more than you're already doing, Vic," they heard Marie reply. "She's been here for months now – surely you knew it'd get to her eventually? At least if this awards thing goes well she'll be gone soon."

"I know! I know, but…I don't think it's just being here that's freaked her out. Michael…"

"Michael is capable of creeping out any normal person, Vic. We're just immune to it 'cause we've worked with him for so long."

"I just wish…" Ichi heard Vic sigh heavily. "I wish I could do more for her."

"Well unless you're going to tell her about *before* then I honestly don't think there's anything you can do…and you already told me you think she's worked it out anyway. Would it really be so bad to tell her before she gets her memory back?" Ichi felt Claire's fingernails grip into his arm, and when he looked at her face her skin was deathly pale.

"Claire…?" he ventured, very quietly, but she didn't seem to hear him. Vic and Marie's voices trailed away to nothing as they descended the stairs. Ichi shook Claire's head slightly with the hand he still had entwined in her hair. "Claire, they're gone. Snap out of it."

"He told me I didn't know him."

"Huh?"

Claire stared sightlessly out of the alcove. "Vic. I asked him a couple of months ago if I knew him from before my memory loss. He said – no, *did* something – that made me think he was somebody else for a moment. But I couldn't work out who it was that he reminded me of as soon as I thought about it. It's so…so frustrating." She looked at Ichi. "He promised me I'd never met him prior to the day you two kidnapped me! And I – foolishly – believed him! But he…he wasn't lying. I can always tell when he's lying, and he wasn't. He just wasn't telling me the whole story. Ichi, how can somebody be lying and telling the truth at the same time?"

"Hell if I know," Ichi replied, keeping as calm and collected on the surface as he could be, but in truth he was deathly curious. And he couldn't help but be impressed with how many layers there seemed to be to Vic. *I wonder if the Vic we know resembles who he really is in the slightest.* But then that very thought gave Ichi an idea. "Claire," he began, "What *exactly* was it that Vic said to you, when you asked if you had ever met him before?"

Claire frowned at the floor as she tried to remember. "He…he said 'No, you've never met Vic Wint'-*he said I'd never met Vic Winters before!* Crap, I – let me past, Ichi, I can't believe how stupid I've been," Claire said, and she pushed Ichi back slightly. He didn't budge. "Ichi," Claire repeated, "Move out of the way."

Ichi grabbed onto her waist again to stop her. "Think about this for a minute, Claire," he said. "What can you actually do here? Vic might just lie to you again. Or he could tell you the truth, and it will do absolutely nothing to change your situation." Ichi trailed one of his hands up underneath Claire's massive jumper, fingers trailing up her spine until – "Claire, are you – you're not wearing a bra."

Claire looked up at him, nonplussed. "And?"

Ichi raised an eyebrow in surprise. "And nothing. I'm just regretting not getting under your jumper earlier," he replied, sliding his other hand easily underneath the fabric. Claire squirmed slightly at his touch.

"It's not the time for this, Ichi," she reprimanded. "I need to work out what to do." Ichi pulled Claire back against him so that he could nibble her ear.

"It's always the time for this." He heard Claire sigh, and he knew he had almost won. "Besides," he continued, "The logical thing to do is to wait and see what Vic does over the next two weeks leading up to this awards ball. You know Michael's only going to give you more information when he thinks you need it. Which means that until you get said information, every conclusion you reach will be mere speculation."

"Your point being…?" Claire asked, her voice low.

"Do nothing. Wait both Vic and Michael out. Let them put their cards on the table but keep yours back. Stop letting them play you and start playing *them*." Ichi lifted his head up from Claire's neck to look at her, the tips of their noses just barely touching.

"So start acting like you," Claire said.

Ichi grinned. "Could have saved yourself a lot of hassle if you'd listened to me two days ago, so how about you start listening now?" Claire smiled slightly in return, and Ichi crept his hands up her back just a little bit more.

"I have one request."

"Which is?" He grazed Claire's lips with his teeth, and he felt her breathing accelerate to match his own. *And there's the adrenaline again. Hello, old friend, I was wondering where you were.*

"Can I use your shower? Mine's broken." Ichi chuckled, then hauled Claire out of the alcove and threw her over his shoulder.

"Deal. But I'm getting in it too."

Vic

Vic was sitting in the rec hall, browsing a website full of dresses on his laptop. *How did it fall down to me to pick Claire's dress?* he wondered. *Surely she can dress herself?* Yet here Vic was, completely clueless about what the difference between a fishtail and a waterfall dress was and the colours teal and turquoise. He looked up when the rec hall doors opened, letting Ichi in. Vic repressed a scowl.

"What are you doing?" Ichi called over when he noticed Vic.

"You don't actually care, so just go back to being silent, Ichi," Vic replied. Ichi closed the gap between them and sat in the seat next to Vic's despite the warning.

"Information-gathering is interesting, though," he countered. Ichi glanced at Vic's laptop screen, a slight frown creasing his brow. "Is this for Claire?"

Vic nodded reluctantly in assent. "She doesn't have anything here or in her flat that would work for the awards ball."

Ichi raised an eyebrow in surprise. "When did you go snooping around in her flat?"

"Days ago, but it's none of your business. I need to pick something today so that it can get made in time; there's only a week left until this damn ball." Vic glared pointedly at Ichi. "So leave me alone."

"Then stop looking at blue dresses," Ichi replied, decidedly not leaving Vic alone. He frowned at the laptop screen again, then raised a hand to point at one of the dresses on it. "Can you get that in purple?"

"But blue matches her eyes," Vic complained.

Ichi was silent for a moment, then replied, quietly, "Not at night."

350

Vic couldn't help but be surprised by Ichi's answer. "That almost sounds like you admitting you like her, you know."

"Just look at it in purple, Vic." Vic sighed, but complied anyway. Then he sighed again when he realised that Ichi was correct; Vic could practically see Claire in the dress on his laptop screen already.

Ichi grinned at the look on his face. "Told you it was her colour."

"What colour is whose colour?" came a female voice – Alexis, walking over to join them. Ichi barely glanced at her as she came over to inspect what they were doing. "Ahh," she said once she saw the laptop screen. "For Claire? Go with purple for sure."

"I get Ichi thinking that, but how did you come to that conclusion, Alexis?" Vic asked, irritated and confused. "You're never around her." The look on Alexis' face reminded Vic of how she had looked the night he had told her Ichi had attacked Claire; suddenly Vic wanted very much to punch the other man in the face.

"Why are you looking at me like you want to punch me in the face?" Ichi murmured, reading Vic's thoughts.

"I always want to."

"That's a lie…you didn't *always* want to."

"That's enough, boys!" Alexis exclaimed, cutting the conversation short before it could become an argument. Vic shot a glare over at Ichi, which he responded in kind. Alexis rolled her eyes, running a hand through her hair to move it away from her face. Something about the action reminded Vic of Claire, but he didn't know why. "Oh for God's sake, there's no helping you two, is there? Vic, I'm a girl – we kind of all know what colour would go well on someone else. But the actual dress choice here is pretty smart too."

"Why?" both Vic and Ichi asked in unison. Alexis laughed as they scowled at each other.

"You two are idiots." She pointed to the dress on the laptop screen. "This is strapless –"

"Oh, Claire wouldn't like that, actually," Vic interjected. "Because she –"

"Has massive boobs, yeah, I get that," Alexis said, interrupting Vic in turn. "But that's the point. What do you think a strapless dress means she has to wear underneath it?"

"A corset," Ichi replied immediately. Vic threw a sidelong glance his way and could see that the other man was clearly imagining Claire with a corset on and very little else. And now that Vic had thought about it, it was all he could see too.

"Now if you could both take your mind out of the gutter, what advantage do we have to putting her in a corset?" Alexis asked them, in a tone that altogether made Vic feel like a five-year-old child.

"Hmm?" Ichi murmured, clearly struggling to get his mind out of the proverbial gutter Alexis had mentioned.

"You're both useless," she chided. "Have you ever seen a girl run anywhere fast in a *corset?* No you haven't, because it's pretty damn hard to do. Even someone as flighty as Claire won't be able to run off from the two of you at the awards ball if I tie her into one."

"*You* will?" Vic asked, surprised for what felt like the umpteenth time in the past hour.

Alexis grinned. "Trust me, I'll have lots of fun cutting off most of her air supply. But I'll make her look beautiful too, don't worry."

"She already is," Vic complained, looking at Ichi to see that his mouth was open as if to make the same retort.

"Then just wait until you see her once I'm done with her."

"I don't get whether you want to kill her or help her here," Vic said.

Alexis raised an eyebrow at him. "Who said I wanted to kill her? That was *your* job," Alexis replied, inclining her head towards the two of them. Before either Ichi or Vic could respond to her jibe, however, she continued, "No, I don't want to kill her, I just want to…piss her off a little."

"Why?" Ichi asked, looking at Alexis as if she made absolutely no sense, which was precisely how Vic felt about her too.

Alexis gave them both a wry smile. "Wouldn't the two of you like to know?" And then she left the rec hall, shouting back as she got to the doors, "You order the dress, Vic, and I'll get everything else!"

Vic and Ichi said nothing for a while, both momentarily stunned. Then Ichi turned to Vic. "Why does it feel like she's had her own agenda from the beginning?"

"Because she has."

Ichi stared sightlessly at the rec hall doors for a moment; Vic couldn't work out what he was contemplating. "I wonder…" Ichi said eventually, but he didn't finish the thought. Then he got up and made to leave.

"Ich," Vic ended up calling out after him.

Ichi turned slightly, surprised. "What?"

Vic hesitated for a second. "When Claire finally gets to leave, what do you plan on doing?"

Ichi took a moment to answer, before murmuring, "I don't know." And then he left, leaving Vic sitting there to consider what he had said.

"You and me both," he muttered under his breath, ordering the dress that Claire would wear for what could very possibly be the second assassination attempt against her in her life, hoping against hope that his small window of opportunity in which to help her escape during said attempt would be enough to do so.

CHAPTER 33
Ambiguous

Claire

The day of the awards ball was upon Claire before she knew it. She had spent the last two weeks constantly training, trying to get herself into the best physical shape possible as the soles of her feet healed. She couldn't shake the sense of foreboding that chased her everywhere she went, telling her that the awards ball was not going to be what she thought it would be. *Something terrible is going to happen,* Claire thought again and again, even though she had no reason to think as such.

Michael hadn't given Claire any further information on why she was going to the ball, or what she was supposed to do, or essentially anything else useful that she would have liked to know. But Claire had kept stoic and calm about it; there had been no more breakdowns, no more destroying inanimate objects, no more crying. And Vic seemed to believe that Claire had genuinely stopped heading towards a full-on meltdown, so she supposed that she was doing a good job of pretending that everything was fine. It was the most in control that Claire had felt for a long time, even if she was faking it.

But the only one who knows that *is Ichi.* Claire had reached an uneasy alliance with him – not willing to forget what he had done to her two weeks prior but also not letting herself think about it. At the very least, Ichi prevented her from wandering about in the middle of the night, having woken up and stopped her a dozen times over the past two weeks. It made Claire feel altogether like she was floating in limbo, waiting for the catalyst that would spark the next horrendous thing that would happen to her.

And it's going to be this damn ball, I know it. Claire was pacing her room impatiently; when Ichi had told her that Alexis was going to help her get ready, Claire couldn't quite believe it. She also felt just the slightest bit indignant at the idea that nobody thought she could get ready for a fancy event by herself. *I was all dressed up the day I was kidnapped, after all.* But despite her misgivings, Claire was dutifully waiting for Alexis before beginning her make up, though the other woman was definitely taking her time in showing up.

And then, as if on cue, Claire heard a knock on her door, followed by the sound of Alexis' voice announcing her presence. *Well,* Claire thought as she headed over to the front door, *let's see how bizarre a meeting this is.*

"Alexis," Claire said upon opening the front door. The other woman nodded at her, then made her way into Claire's room with her arms full of various bags and cases. "Are you sure you don't want some –" Claire began, but Alexis dumped most of it on the couch before Claire could finish the sentence. She hung the longest bag on the back of the shower room door, which Claire presumed was protecting the dress she was supposed to wear.

There was an awkward silence as Alexis looked Claire up and down, giving Claire the disturbing feeling of being sized up. *That's what she did the first time I met her,* Claire suddenly remembered. "You're going to have to sit down for me to do your hair and make-up," Alexis pointed out, startling Claire out of her own head.

"Do I not get to see what I'm wearing first?" Claire asked, moving some of the bags Alexis had thrown onto the couch so that she could sit down nonetheless.

Alexis laughed. "Oh, God no. Where's the fun in that?" Claire made a face as Alexis began to pull out a make-up kit from one of the bags, and she got to work without another word. However, after ten minutes or so Alexis clucked her tongue in annoyance.

"What?" Claire asked, certain that Alexis was about to criticise her.

"You're so bloody pale," Alexis replied, and Claire couldn't help but laugh derisively in return.

"Try being trapped indoors for God knows how long and see how tanned that leaves you." Claire was suddenly aware of the fact that Alexis was *very* tanned, though she knew that that hadn't always been the case. "Where was your last job?"

Alexis raised an eyebrow. "California."

"Well that explains *your* tan then." Alexis smiled at her, then frowned slightly as if she were thinking about something very difficult.

Finally, she said, "How about we call a temporary truce, just for this evening?"

"I never knew what your problem was with me anyway," Claire fired back. But upon seeing the look Alexis gave her, she added: "Okay, okay, fine. The silence was deafening anyway."

Alexis seemed to transform after that, and she giggled and chatted away easily with Claire as she worked on her make-up and then her hair. They discussed the music they liked (Alexis was as critical about Claire's music tastes as Vic was), television shows that they both enjoyed (X-Files, Lost and Pride and Prejudice in particular) and then they invariably moved on to discussing the people around them. Alexis laughed as Claire recounted how frequently she had had to deal with Ryan being a dick, and Alexis told her about the job she had completed with Marie a few months ago, making Claire jealous of the many places in the world the two of them got to travel to. Alexis never brought up Vic or Ichi, and that suited Claire just fine. When it finally came to seeing the dress that she was supposed to be wearing, Claire found herself feeling more relaxed and like her old self than she had ever felt in the entirety of her captivity, and she relished it.

But then Alexis grinned at Claire in such a way that convinced Claire that she was going to see something she didn't like. "Don't get mad, okay?" Alexis said, before unzipping the bag. The dress itself was beautiful, all dark purple material with a low back, cinched in waist and sweeping tail. And then Claire looked at the top of the dress properly and spluttered in protest.

"But this is strapless!" she complained. "I can't wear that, and you know it."

"Not unless you're wearing a corset," Alexis replied, unzipping a smaller bag on the couch to bring one out. Claire baulked at her for a moment, then closed her eyes and sighed as she realised what wearing a corset meant.

"This is so I can't run away," she said, voice flat, all enthusiasm gone. Alexis looked at her with what appeared to be genuine sympathy.

"You weren't honestly considering doing so, surely?"

356

Claire glanced around her room, knowing that Michael and most likely Ichi were watching her. "Maybe if I managed to smash a champagne glass into Ichi's face," she replied boldly.

Alexis laughed. "It would almost be worth you trying that simply so I could see it. Now, come on, clothes off." Claire just looked at her, and Alexis rolled her eyes. "What does it matter if you undress in front of me? You have eyes on you all the time. At least you look gorgeous as hell."

So Claire reluctantly stripped and allowed Alexis to lace her into what was admittedly the nicest corset she had ever seen, made up of panels of silk in a darker purple than the dress, with delicate black lace running along the bones as well as at the top and bottom of the material. But as Alexis pulled on the ribbons ever tighter, Claire gasped.

"Is this bloody steel-boned or something? I can barely breathe," she bit out, indignant.

"That's supposed to be the point," Alexis replied wryly. "And it's whale bone – Michael would have no expenses spared for his favourite captive."

"I'm his *only* captive."

"Maybe so, but even if there were others you'd still be his favourite." There was something in the tone of Alexis' voice as she spoke that caused the hairs on the back of Claire's neck to stand on end, and she shuddered. "You can't possibly be cold, Claire, your room is roasting!" Alexis said, apparently not noticing Claire's sudden apprehension, and then: "That's you all laced up now anyway." Then she took the dress from its hanger and helped Claire into it, before putting some delicate silver heels on her feet. They reminded Claire of the pair she had considered wearing the day she was kidnapped, and she felt her heart twist painfully.

"Alexis, I...I don't know what I'm supposed to be doing tonight," Claire found herself admitting to the other woman, tugging nervously on a strand of hair as she did so. "I don't know what the point of me going to this ball is. And even if I knew, what if I mess up? What if...what if my parents really don't care, and I'm stuck here forever? Alexis, I can't, I can't!" Alexis grabbed on to her hand, pulling it gently away from her hair; Claire could see the terror she felt reflected back at her in Alexis' dark brown eyes. "If I have to stay here for much longer, I'll kill myself." Claire knew that she meant it as she said it, and felt oddly calm about it. It was

357

somehow comforting to remember that she had a permanent way out of her situation that she could choose for herself.

Alexis held Claire's gaze, her face furious. "Don't *ever* talk about your life like that, Claire! Do you not remember what I told you the first night you were here?"

Claire had to think for a moment to bring back the memory. "You told me not to think of myself as a dead girl walking. You told me that I saved my own life."

"And does a person who managed to save their own life in an impossible situation strike you as the kind of person who thinks taking their own life is the solution to their problems?" Claire had to struggle not to say that she *hadn't* saved her own life, since taking it had never been Michael's intention. She let out a shaky breath and forced a small smile onto her face.

"You're right, of course. I'm just…sorry. This is all really hard," Claire replied, and Alexis' face softened.

"Of course it is. And I'm certain that if you were going to kill yourself, you'd have done it already. You just have to be careful tonight, okay?" She paused for a moment, glancing up as if she could see through the ceiling of Claire's room. "And on that incredibly positive note, it's time we headed upstairs."

Claire looked at her, surprised. "*Up*stairs?"

Alexis laughed. "Yes, upstairs. You're travelling by air, Claire Danvers. I hope you're okay with heights."

Ichi

When Claire arrived on the thirteenth floor of Michael's complex, Ichi couldn't quite believe his eyes. Claire had always been beautiful, but now…

"Oh God. Wow. *Wow*. You really look like a princess…princess," he heard Vic remark, sparing the other man a glance to see the grin spread across his face as he took in the sight of Claire. Claire returned his smile with a radiant one of her own, her cheeks flushing at the compliment. The dark purple dress looked better on Claire than Ichi could have imagined, with her hair all loosely curled and mostly thrown over one shoulder. Her eye make-up was reminiscent of how she had done it for her date on the day of her kidnap, but it was darker, bolder and more striking than it had been then. Ichi didn't think he had ever seen a person look so stunning.

But the moment had passed for him to comment on it, and even if it hadn't Ichi wasn't sure what he was supposed to have said. He saw Alexis standing behind Claire, her mouth turned upwards into a smug smile as she took in Vic and Ichi's reaction to her handiwork.

"You look pleased with yourself," Ichi ended up saying. Alexis' smile only grew wider.

"Have you seen how kick-ass she looks?" Alexis said, waving a hand in Claire's general direction. Claire laughed at the other woman's comment, giving her hand a slight squeeze before walking over to Vic. Ichi frowned, wondering how Claire and Alexis could possibly have become close in the space of three hours, after months of not speaking to each other.

"A suit suits you, Vic," he heard Claire giggle. Ichi supposed that she was correct; Vic cut quite a sharp figure in his dark suit and tie with his hair tied away from his face. His height also made him look intimidating, which was precisely the point in him acting as Claire's bodyguard. Ichi hooked a finger under the collar of his shirt to tug on it slightly; he felt as uncomfortable in a suit as Vic looked good in one. "And you even tied your hair up!" Claire gushed, pushing a stray strand of hair out of Vic's eyes as she did so, a warm smile on her face. "Very bodyguard-like." Ichi felt his skin prickle at the compliments Claire was drowning Vic in.

"You should see me with the matching sunglasses on," Vic replied, taking Claire's hand and spinning her underneath his arm to test her balance in the heels she was wearing.

"No way," Claire said in disbelief as she stumbled a little. "There's no way you actually have bodyguard sunglasses!"

"That's not a real term," Ichi cut in scathingly, because Vic and Claire's closeness was irritating him far too much. He couldn't tell if Claire was pretending to be close to the other man anymore, or whether it had become genuine again. Claire gave Ichi an uncertain smile before staring at the floor.

"I know that," she mumbled.

Vic flashed him a warning look. "Ichi, stop being a dick. You're not going to make a very believable date if you don't," the other man said. Ichi had to bite back a retort that he knew would probably result in Vic punching him in the face.

"Play nice, boys," Alexis said, walking over to intervene before things could escalate. She turned to Ichi. "Just because you're uncomfortable with wearing a bloody suit doesn't mean you get to spoil everybody else's fun, Ich. And Vic, try not to punch Ichi just because he's Ichi."

"No promises," Vic replied, but he softened the harshness of his words with a smile in Alexis' direction. Ichi looked at Claire again and saw that she had moved a step or two away from Vic. She was still staring at the floor.

Ichi rolled his eyes and walked over to her, tilting his head down to murmur into her ear. "Everything will be fine," he told her, then added on as an afterthought: "And even if it's not we'll deal with it." Claire glanced up at him through thick eyelashes, her dark blue eyes slightly too bright.

"And what happens after tonight?" she whispered, and Ichi could see the genuine fear playing across her face. He knew that in this kind of situation any decent man would say something comforting. *Vic would know exactly what to say,* Ichi found himself thinking. But he wasn't Vic, and he couldn't be considered decent in any sense of the word. So he turned Claire away a little more from Vic and Alexis and kissed her, running a hand up the exposed part of her spine as he did so.

"What happens after tonight is that I take your dress off and see what that corset looks like on you for real," he said, his voice low. "I'd wager you look even better in it than in the dress, which is saying something." Claire bit into his lower lip slightly.

"That sounded like a compliment."

"Is it a compliment if it's the truth?" Claire blushed slightly, then brought her hands up to play with Ichi's dark purple bowtie. That had been Alexis' idea, to colour match him to Claire's dress. *'You're meant to be her date, after all,'* she had said, *'So you better look the part.'* Ichi wondered if him *looking* the part was because nobody believed he could actually *be* the part. Suddenly, he was filled with the desire to prove them all wrong.

360

"You look pretty damn good yourself," Claire told him, and he flashed her the lazy smile he knew she loved, though she'd never admit it. He pulled Claire in closer, despite the audience of Vic and Alexis, the two people least likely to be happy about him doing so.

"There might be enough time yet to run back down to the twelfth floor, you know," he told her.

She grinned back at him, a wicked, rebellious look on her face. "That might be exactly what I –"

"I see you're all here," came Michael's voice, both announcing his arrival and interrupting Claire and Ichi's murmured conversation. Ichi felt Claire stiffen in his arms slightly, so he tightened his grip on her.

"Boss," Alexis said. "She's all ready to go."

"Ichi," Michael began, "I don't need to have heard what you were saying to know exactly what your intentions were before I arrived. You're already behind schedule as it is, so don't even think about disappearing."

"Ah, sorry," Alexis chimed in, sounding abashed. "That's all my fault. Claire and I got…carried away, as it were." Michael's smile then was full of amusement as he turned his gaze on Claire. She still hadn't turned around to face him, and Ichi had half a notion to prevent her from having to, since it was clearly the last thing on earth that she wanted to do.

"So I heard. Miss Danvers, a moment please, if you will," Michael requested. Claire looked at Ichi for a moment, flicked her gaze quickly over to Vic and then closed her eyes, as if she were bracing herself. Then she extricated herself from Ichi's arms and waltzed over to Michael.

"Do I get to know what I'm doing yet?" she asked.

Michael maintained his amused smile as he replied, "All you need to do is go to the awards ball, thus proving that you are indeed alive and well. You might want to try and look like you're having a good time for posterity's sake, too. After all, the world doesn't know you've been kidnapped. You may want to steer conversation away from the topic of your parents' disappearance, as well." Claire didn't break away from Michael's unwavering gaze, apparently completely unintimidated by the man.

"Sure," she replied, her tone casual but her eyes hard. "Easy. I'll just act like everything's fine, no problem at all. It's not like anything terrible has happened."

Michael let out a humourless laugh. "You don't know what terrible *is* yet, Miss Danvers; not truly. I could educate you on the matter upon your return if you want."

"The only thing I want you to educate me on is how both yourself and Roger knew my parents."

Ichi sidled over to Vic and Alexis, a frown on his face. "Do they always talk to each other like this?" he asked in an undertone. They returned his frown with looks of confusion.

"I don't know…" Vic mumbled back, and Ichi saw that he looked incredibly worried. *Worried about what?* Ichi wondered. *Or maybe it's who.*

"She's got balls, I'll give her that," Alexis said. The three of them continued to watch Claire and Michael from the side lines, their existence seemingly forgotten. Something about the way Michael was looking at Claire was beginning to make Ichi feel uncomfortable, but he couldn't work out why.

"A subject for another time, Miss Danvers, as I keep reminding you," Michael told Claire.

"You're going to run out of time to tell me, eventually."

"Something tells me that I won't." Michael's reply seemed to take Claire aback, so much so that she literally took a step away from him. Ichi spied Vic curl and uncurl his fists behind his back.

"If that in any way implies that you won't let me go…then you know I won't give you any of the research, even if my parents *do* show up…or did *you* need reminding of that?" Ichi stared at Claire, eyes wide. *Why the hell is she threatening Michael at a time like this?* He saw Vic react in a similar fashion out of the corner of his eye; only Alexis, it seemed, remained impassive.

"Come here, Miss Danvers," Michael demanded, but Claire shook her head and took another step backwards. Michael grabbed onto her wrist and pulled her closer to him anyway, then he took a thin box out of his suit jacket and opened it, revealing an incredibly expensive looking silver and diamond necklace. Ichi heard Alexis let out a low whistle. Michael let go of Claire's wrist to stand behind her, then he swept all of her hair over one shoulder. Very slowly and deliberately, he put the necklace on her, Claire rooted to the spot as he did so with a fear Ichi was all too familiar with seeing on her face. "There," Michael said. "Now you look perfect." Then he tilted his head down slightly to whisper something into Claire's ear, and Ichi felt himself taking a step forward at the same time Vic did. Michael glanced up at them as they did so and grinned.

"I thought you said we were running late, boss," Alexis said, breaking the tension between them all.

Michael looked at Claire one last time before heading for the elevator doors. "Blindfold her," he said once he had reached them, waving a hand dismissively at Claire. "Vic, Ichi, don't forget to do your job. Especially *you*, Vic. Misao and Ray will be on scene, but if all goes well you won't even know that they're there. Alexis, come with me." And with that, Ichi was left alone with Vic and with Claire, who was frozen to the spot. He got to her a moment before Vic did.

"For fuck's sake Claire, what were you thinking, antagonising Michael like that?!" he almost shouted at her, shaking her shoulders roughly. Vic put out his arm to stop him.

"Ichi, cut it out."

"He was looking at her like he was going to fucking devour her, and her solution was to talk back to him like that! Vic, if that doesn't call for shaking sense into her, then I don't know what does."

Vic sighed. "Let's just go up to the roof and get on the helicopter. I'm sorry, princess, but orders are orders. I'm going to have to blindfold you." Claire let Vic do so, her face devoid of any emotion, allowing him to then take her hand and lead her up the short staircase to the roof. It was only once they got onto the helicopter that Ichi realised that he should have been the one holding her hand.

After a while in the air, during which time nobody said anything, Ichi slowly put a hand over Claire's, venturing to bring her back to reality. When he felt Claire shaking underneath his fingertips, he gripped onto her hand as tightly as he dared, and eventually she squeezed his hand back. Vic looked on with an unreadable expression on his face from the seat opposite, but he nodded in understanding when Ichi caught him staring.

I'm not a decent man; I don't make people feel better, he thought. Yet even so, he found himself saying, "It'll be okay; you'll get out of here before you know it." Vic looked at him sharply then, and Ichi was suddenly reminded of something the other man had asked him only a week earlier. *"When Claire finally gets to leave, what do you plan on doing?"* He looked at Claire again, her face a blank slate with her eyes covered as they were, her beautiful mouth devoid of anything to say. *If she gets to leave,* Ichi thought, *will she want nothing more to do with me? Will she just disappear? And if that's the case…* Ichi squeezed Claire's hand just a little tighter than he meant to, causing her to sightlessly look down at their entwined fingers.

If that's the case, do I want her to leave at all?

364

CHAPTER 34
Mystery

Claire

Claire had recovered from her encounter with Michael by the time the helicopter landed. Or, rather, she had decided to put her fear aside to focus on what she had to do – pretend that everything was normal. She had absolutely no doubt now that much more was going on behind the scenes than she could possibly fathom, so Claire resolved to think about it later when she had the time.

"I haven't been to London since I turned twenty-one," Claire said as Ichi untied her blindfold, marking the first words she had uttered since leaving Michael's complex. She saw both Vic and Ichi look at her in surprise, and felt a grim sense of satisfaction. "What, you didn't expect me to know where we were going?"

"How could you possibly know?" Vic asked her, incredulous.

Claire smiled at him. "Oh, Vic, did nobody seriously think about the fact that I *know* when these events are, and where?" Claire replied, her smile growing wider. "Come on, super famous geneticist parents and all that. Also, I've been to it before."

Ichi laughed at her reply. Claire felt him squeeze her hand again; he hadn't let go of it since he had taken it in the helicopter, around three hours ago. It had been reassuring, a word Claire never thought she would have associated with Ichi. Yet now that she could see again, Claire realised that there was something slightly off about Ichi's expression, but Claire couldn't work out what it was. She squeezed his hand gently in return, then let go to walk over to Vic.

"Keep me safe, Mr Bodyguard," she said, trying to sound nonchalant.

"Always," Vic replied, and Claire knew that he meant it, despite everything he was hiding from her.

"We should probably head downstairs to the event and, you know, prove that Claire is alive before the night is done," Ichi interjected, proffering an arm for Claire to take. She took it rather suspiciously, not knowing how to handle Ichi acting like this.

"What's wrong with you?" Claire asked. Ichi smiled easily at her; it transformed his ordinarily serious face into something wonderful.

"I'm your date, aren't I? Or so they keep telling me."

Claire glanced at Vic. "You'll stay close?" she asked him, not knowing why it felt so imperative for that to be the case, but knowing it nonetheless.

Vic gave her a salute. "Of course, princess."

Claire let out a sigh and gripped Ichi's arm. "Then let's go."

*

The next couple of hours passed in a blur of polite conversation and glasses of champagne. Claire had found it awkward and daunting at first to talk to so many people that she didn't know, especially after months and months of being stuck with the same, small group of people. But after the first couple of glasses of champagne, Claire found herself relaxing into her role as the concerned but most definitely not kidnapped daughter of the famous Mark and Joanna Danvers, lying easily to anybody who asked her how the past year had been for her with them gone.

"You truly are a fantastic liar," Ichi murmured into her ear at one point, and Claire had giggled tipsily at the remark. She knew she shouldn't be drinking in order to keep her head clear, but she couldn't bring herself to refuse every fresh glass offered up to her. When she was handed her sixth, however, Ichi took it from her. "Remember why you're here, Claire. And you don't want to fly back on a helicopter when you're drunk, trust me." Claire rolled her eyes but didn't complain.

When the music being played by the house band changed, both Claire and Ichi's ears pricked up as they recognised the tune. "If I'm not mistaken,

Vic taught you a dance to this," Ichi said. Claire caught Vic's eye over Ichi's shoulder, and he waved a hand towards the dance floor with a smile.

"I don't suppose people dance with their bodyguards at fancy balls," Claire replied, still looking at Vic.

"No, but you can dance with your date." Ichi held a hand out to her. Claire looked at it for a moment before taking it, allowing Ichi to lead her over to the dance floor.

"Your acting's a little too good, you know," Claire remarked as Ichi put a hand on her waist.

He pulled her in closer. "Then maybe it's not an act," he said, kissing her quickly before they started to dance. And, for a while, there was nothing for Claire but the music playing in her ears and being in Ichi's arms. She couldn't quite believe that he was the one who had intimidated her so much two weeks prior. *Maybe it really was just an overload of adrenaline that made him act that way,* Claire's tipsy brain thought. *If I could only get him to stop killing people, maybe he...* Claire sighed, knowing that that was a very big 'if' indeed. Ichi raised an eyebrow at her, and Claire let out a shaky laugh.

"It's just...very hard to breathe properly right now," Claire said, which wasn't a lie. Ichi spun her around.

"You wouldn't be thinking of smashing a champagne flute into my face and running off, would you?"

Claire flinched slightly. "So you *did* hear me say that. I was wondering," she replied. Ichi tightened his grip slightly on her waist, pulling her in a little closer.

"Let's say you managed to do so – what would you do next?" he murmured into her ear. Claire's brain seemed to freeze; she wasn't sure where Ichi was going with his line of questioning.

She turned her gaze away from his. "That's not funny, Ichi," she mumbled.

"I'm not being funny. It's a serious question." Claire could feel Ichi's eyes boring into her until she finally looked back at him, and she saw that his expression had turned dark. "Let's say you get away from me – who's to say Vic will let you go? He might, for argument's sake, but what then?

Jump into a taxi on the street? You have no money. Ask somebody for help? You'd sooner be attacked on the street before someone helped you out. Try and find a police station? You have no identification and you can be certain that Michael has people working for him in the force, especially in London."

"Ichi, stop it," Claire protested. "You're scaring me."

Ichi didn't smile. "Good; I should be. Don't forget that you're a prisoner, and whether you like it or not you aren't the one who gets to call the shots. Clearly trying to regain your memories without the help of your parents hasn't worked, so you have absolutely no leverage."

Claire stared at him, eyes wide. "I don't understand where all of this is coming from. Why...why do you keep flipping between the good guy and the bad guy?"

"I was never the good guy, Claire. You just saw what you needed to see to ease your own conscience about screwing me."

Claire slapped him then, hard and furious. "You do *not* get to say that," she growled at him, voice low. Then she ripped away from Ichi's grasp and headed for one of several large, ornate staircases, not entirely knowing where she was headed. When she had reached the second floor of the grand building that she was in, Claire glanced behind her and saw that Ichi hadn't followed her. "Idiot. I'm an *idiot*," she mumbled as she walked, feeling a wave of hot tears beginning to well up in her eyes. But before long her corset-restricted breathing began to burn her lungs, so Claire stopped by what appeared to be a bar set up in an alcove separated from the rest of the hallway by several stone pillars. *A bar in an alcove...how ideal,* she thought.

"What're you drinking, beautiful?" asked the barman, a kindly looking man who appeared to be in his fifties. Claire closed her eyes for a moment, taking a few seconds to breathe deeply and will away her unshed tears.

"Rum. A double."

"Any mixer?"

Claire laughed at him. "This hasn't been a mixer kind of night." He smiled at her almost knowingly, then free-poured a measure of rum that was definitely more than a double should have been. Claire thanked him as he handed her the glass.

368

"You're the Danvers girl, aren't you?" the barman asked suddenly, causing Claire to almost drop her glass.

"Excuse me?" *How does he know? Does he work for Michael? Oh my God how many people does he have here?!*

"Ah, my apologies," he replied bashfully. "That was rude of me. People had been talking about how one of the Danvers girls was here after staying out of the public eye for most of the year. Everyone knows your whole family is blessed with good genes, so I figured that a beautiful but very sad-looking young woman asking for straight rum at the most isolated bar possible within this event would probably be said Danvers girl."

Claire eyed him suspiciously. "You're in the wrong profession, Mr Barman." She took a tentative sip of her rum, then threw caution to the wind and swallowed the whole lot in one go. The way it burned the back of her throat felt wonderful.

"Call me Dave," Dave said, smiling. He held out his hand. Claire hesitated for a second, then shook it.

"Claire Danvers."

"So what'll it be, Claire? Another rum?" Claire looked at her empty glass. *I wish my head was empty too. Well, at least alcohol can help with that.*

"Oh yes," she replied. Claire took her time with the second lot of rum, knowing that she'd probably regret it if she drank it in one go and then ended up being hit by around six units of alcohol at the same time. *And on top of all of that champagne too. This is a terrible, fantastic idea.*

"You know," Dave said, dragging Claire back to the present, "I work a lot of these big science-type events – and boy do you scientists like your parties – and the word on the street at a lot of them was that you had actually gone missing, just like your parents."

Claire struggled to remain calm and collected as she replied, "Well, I'm here, aren't I? I just needed some time alone to deal with their disappearance."

Dave gave her a sympathetic smile. "I'm sorry; there's me being rude again. I'm not so good with small talk, you see. Maybe I *am* in the wrong profession." He laughed, and Claire joined in simply because she didn't trust her voice to say anything. "Do you mind if I turn the radio on a little, dear? Just for background noise…might make my little bar feel less awkward." Claire nodded her head in agreement.

As Dave busied himself with tuning the radio he had behind the bar, Claire stared sightlessly into her drink as her mind ended up wandering back to what Michael had whispered into her ear earlier that evening. *'You're quite something to see, Miss Danvers,'* he had said, *'But keep in mind that all of this is mine; don't think for even a second that your life is yours to take.'* Claire fiddled nervously with her hair as she tried to blank Michael's voice out, but she couldn't. *I've been so obsessed with Ichi and Vic that I couldn't see what exactly was going on with* Michael. *He's acting like he knows something I don't.* Claire frowned at that thought, for she had always known that Michael knew a whole lot more about the situation Claire was in than she knew herself. *But ever since I ran into him and Roger in the rec hall two weeks ago, it feels like he knows something specifically about* me *relating to* him *that I don't. And how is that possible?*

Claire was brought out of her reverie by the music playing out of Dave's little radio. She recognised the song, and the band. "That's Del Amitri!" she exclaimed, and Dave looked up at her, surprised.

"A little old for you to recognise, surely?"

"No, I – my parents – love them. They played them all the time as I grew up. I guess I ended up loving them too. Strange, I haven't listened to them in…months."

Dave nodded at her appraisingly. "You have good taste in music, for a twenty-something."

"Twenty-two," Claire said, and then: "Oh. Twenty-three, actually. Forgot about that."

"You forgot your own birthday?"

"It's been a tough year." Suddenly, Claire was filled with an overwhelming desire to spill all of her secrets to this unknown barman, just so that she could have somebody normal to discuss them with. But then the chorus to the Del Amitri song rolled in, and she forgot all about telling Dave anything.

Vic

"Why would you let Claire run off like that?!" Vic demanded of Ichi, when he reached the other man on the dance floor. Together, the two of them headed up the staircase they had seen Claire run up, Vic frantically searching left and right for where she could have gone.

"She slapped me; I was caught off-guard," Ichi replied, shrugging slightly.

Vic glared at him. "Something tells me that you completely deserved it, and should therefore not have caught you off-guard."

Ichi gave him a look. "She knew who I was right from the beginning – if I offended her then it's her own fault."

"If we weren't in a public place I'd slap you too, you fucker," Vic said in an undertone as he concluded that Claire was nowhere to be found on the first floor.

"I don't know what you're so worried about, Vic…it's not like she could have gone anywhere." Vic turned around to face Ichi abruptly when they reached the top of the second floor staircase, grabbing on to the other man's shirt to haul him over to the nearest wall.

"Look, don't make this sham of a mission any more fucked up than it already is," he muttered. He looked at Ichi seriously. "Now listen to me very clearly, and know that every word I say stems from wanting to keep Claire alive, not because of some stupid rivalry with you: *we cannot let her out of our sight.*"

Ichi looked at him suspiciously. "What exactly is going on here, aside from proving to Claire's parents that she's alive?" Vic frowned, glancing around to see if he could spot Misao or Ray even though Michael had told him that he was unlikely to even know that they were there. After confirming that they were nowhere in sight, he removed his earpiece that was Michael's window into what was going on and held it tightly in his hand. Vic looked back at Ichi, seriously considering whether he should simply give up on him entirely. Then he sighed, gave in and told him.

"This whole event is a trap set by Claire's parents to see if her memories will be triggered just by hearing her buzzword, without it being in her father's voice. If they are, they plan to have her killed. Tonight."

Ichi stared at Vic, shell shocked. "Then…what was the point in bringing her here?" Vic impulsively punched the wall behind Ichi's head, drawing several curious stares.

"I don't know!" he exclaimed. "I don't know. I think Michael's hoping Claire's memories *will* be triggered, but that we'll be able to get her away safely before anything else happens. But I don't understand why Michael thinks it'll happen in the first place…there's something he's not been telling me, I'm sure of it."

Ichi laughed cynically. "I'm fairly certain that the moral of this entire story is that everyone involved in this hasn't been telling everyone everything."

"You can be a dick about it later, Ich. We need to find Claire first."

Ichi rolled his eyes. "I've known where she was from the moment she ran off. She's about ten feet to my right, drinking rum like it's nobody's business in that half-hidden bar behind the pillars." Vic spared a quick glance to his left and sure enough there Claire was, hands pressed against the bar as if she couldn't stand up straight.

Vic narrowed his eyes at Ichi. "If you knew where she was, why didn't you follow after her immediately?"

"Because if I had done, we would have caused a scene, and I didn't imagine Michael wanted a situation in which a drunken Claire blurts out that she's, oh, I don't know, been kidnapped or anything. Of course, this was all *before* I knew about the attempt on her life, so thanks for keeping me in the loop."

Vic dragged a hand over his face, wishing the night to be over. "This is so fucked up," he muttered. Ichi looked at him pointedly, as if telling him that he was stating the obvious was too much effort for him. Vic looked over at Claire again, still clutching onto the bar, and frowned. "Something's wrong with her." In the background, Vic vaguely heard a song playing from behind the bar that he didn't recognise; a mournful, acoustic guitar-fuelled song that he thought somehow suited the mood perfectly.

Ichi let out a bark of mirthless laughter. "She's drunk, Vic. We should take her back; the night's a bust. I'm definitely not okay with risking her life on some slim chance that she might remember something, anyway."

"Me neither," Vic heard himself reply, but he wasn't listening to his conversation with Ichi anymore. Claire had her head in her hands, and Vic was distinctly certain that her current condition had nothing to do with alcohol. Reluctantly, he put his earpiece back in place. "Michael," he muttered slowly, "I think a whole lot of shit is about to go down."

Claire

Claire couldn't see. All she could hear was the song playing on the radio; Del Amitri telling her about driving with the brakes on. But it was those very words – driving with the brakes on – that felt like they were splitting her skull in two. Suddenly, her brain was being bombarded with image after confusing image of her working in the lab, then playing with her parents in the park as a child, then back to the lab again, then watching a man in the library, running a hand through his golden hair as he pored over his thesis…

"Claire!" she vaguely heard somebody shout to her right, and she forced her head out of her hands to turn and see who it was. It was Vic, but to Claire he wasn't Vic. He was the man she had just seen sitting in the library, tapping out the beat of his favourite song on his legs. Claire kept staring at him, struggling to see what was in front of her eyes. She stumbled, reaching out a hand to support herself on the bar. She heard Ichi mutter something about her being too drunk. And there was that song playing in her ears, telling her over and over again about driving with the brakes on.

"It's hard to say you love someone," she found herself mumbling, barely getting the words out. Through her blurry vision, she saw the man that was and wasn't Vic walk towards her.

"What did you say, Claire?" he asked, his voice full of concern.

"And it's hard to say you don't," Claire said, finishing the chorus to the song. And then she looked at Vic in a moment of perfect clarity.

"Claire? It's me, Vic," Vic said, uncertain.

"But you're John," Claire replied, certain. And then her hand slipped from the bar, and she came crashing to the floor.

CHAPTER 35
Don't Speak

Vic

Oh shit, was all Vic thought as he came running over to grab Claire before she hit her head against the hardwood floor. *Oh shit oh shit oh shit.* He frantically swept Claire's hair out of her face to see if she was still conscious, but she was out cold.

"Claire, wake up – *oh shit!*" Vic exclaimed as he saw that the barman had pulled out a gun, aiming it at Claire. But the man was dead before he could pull the trigger, a knife lodged firmly in his throat.

"Get her the hell out of here, Vic!" Ichi yelled as he extricated more knives out of his jacket. From somewhere behind them a gun went off, and then another. "I've got this, just *go!*"

Vic didn't have to be told twice; he picked Claire up and cradled her in his arms, calling back as he ran off, "If you're not on the roof in three minutes, I'm leaving without you!" He glanced back for a half a second and had never been more relieved to see that horrifically wicked grin begin to spread across Ichi's face as he spied who had fired off the gunshots.

"Vic, we've got you covered to the roof, so just use the main staircases!" came a woman's voice to Vic's left as he bolted down the hallway.

"Thanks Misao!" he yelled back, knowing that it could only be her. He heard her return fire, and was glad that he had called in the only people who were a true match for him with a gun. He knew that Ray had to be hidden up high somewhere with his sniper rifle, with a good vantage point and an excellent aim. And, sure enough, a shot was fired off from above him, but it was followed by another from a different direction, and then another. *My*

God, how many people do Claire's parents have here?! he thought frantically as he ran up the stairs.

Ichi

Ichi wasn't thinking anymore, only acting. The knife he had lodged into the barman's throat had been thrown on reflex when he had spied the glimmer of gunmetal in the man's hand, but now he had to actively look for anyone else targeting Claire. To his left, he saw Vic shouting to a woman with a gun, then saw that same woman shoot down another would-be assassin behind his back. But there was another one about to take their place, so Ichi launched himself at the man and slit his throat.

The woman looked at him appraisingly, then shouted, "Behind you!" Ichi turned just in time to parry off an attack from another man, slashing him clean up the chest before ramming the blade into the side of the man's neck. The resultant spray of blood soaked through Ichi's white shirt in seconds, but he revelled in it. He twisted his head up at the sound of gunshots above him and cursed. And everywhere there were screaming, frantic people, trying desperately to escape the building.

Ichi's eyes found a sniper high up to his right, but just as he made to run up the stairs towards him, there was another gunshot and the same man fell. "Who was —" he began, but the woman from earlier interrupted him.

"Back-up for my back-up," she grinned. She waved a hand towards the stairs. "You need to get out of here. You're not part of clean-up." Ichi gave her one final look, then bounded down the stairs instead of up, knowing that there was a fire escape ladder on the side of the building. When he reached the first floor, another assailant fired his gun at him, but it hit a terrified woman to his right instead. Ichi pulled out his own gun and shot the man square in the face to the sound of a hundred horrified shrieks. Then he shot the window to his right several times, shattering the glass before he threw himself through the resultant hole in the wall. Adrenaline making him immune to the pain of hitting the pavement, Ichi bolted for the fire escape ladder and nimbly climbed up it, despite the blood on his hands making his grip slippery and unreliable.

He reached the roof before Vic did, giving Ichi an opportunity to get his breath back and kick-start his brain into operating as a tool for thinking again. When Vic finally appeared on the roof with Claire in tow, Ichi came to the realisation that he had more questions for the other man than he had ever had for one person before in his entire life.

Vic

When Vic finally reached the roof, he realised that Ichi was already there.

"I took a quicker route," Ichi explained before Vic could ask. The other man had a spray of blood across his shirt and his face; for a moment Vic wondered whose it was. But he shook his head slightly to chase the thought away and ran over to the helicopter, Ichi close behind. It was off the ground before the two of them had even sat down.

Ichi

Who are you to Claire?

    What's your real name?

Vic

"Where to?" the pilot asked Vic once they were safely in the air.

"A hospital, of course!" he replied, knowing that this was his final chance to escape with Claire. Then Vic heard the altogether foreboding sound of static in his earpiece.

"Take her back here," Michael's voice said into his ear.

"Are you kidding?!" Vic protested. "She needs a hospital and a doctor – a proper one!" Vic was getting frantic, knowing that his final chance was rapidly slipping away.

Ichi

Why didn't you tell Michael about what happened to Claire before she passed out?

Are you John?

Are you trying to escape with Claire?

Do you really work for Michael?

Vic

"She *is* breathing, I take it?" Michael asked, just as Vic decided to check Claire's pulse of his own accord.

"Yes," he replied after a moment.

"Then just make sure she *stays* breathing," Michael said. "Bring her back here, Vic. No more arguments." And then Michael's voice was gone, leaving Vic to stare despairingly at the girl in his arms who he loved so much, knowing he could do no more to help her.

After a while, it occurred to Vic that Ichi hadn't said anything since they escaped, and he looked up at the other man. Ichi was staring at Claire, an unreadable expression on his face. Vic knew that that meant Ichi was analysing every little thing that had happened in the past hour, and he gritted his teeth to wait for the inevitable onslaught of questions about what Claire had said before she fell unconscious.

Ichi

If you're not working for Michael, then who are you working for?

Were the two people who helped us out back there working for Michael, or working for you?

Vic

Instead, the first question Ichi vocalised was, "Who were the two that were helping us out?"

Vic blinked, surprised. "Misao and Ray, from Michael's Beijing office," Vic replied, slowly.

"Why them?"

"These kinds of situations are their forte." And then there was another long silence in which the two men did nothing, until Ichi finally broke it by leaving his seat to kneel in front of Claire. He put a hand on her stomach, and Vic watched as it barely rose and fall with her breathing.

Ichi

Okay, say I believe that those two work for Michael. Then does Vic really work for Michael too, or perhaps genuinely worked for him in the past?

Did he go rogue, then?

Or is he a double agent?

Is Vic even good enough to deceive that many people? Oh, scrap that, of course he is.

Claire's barely breathing. What can we do to help with that?

Vic

"We need to loosen that damn corset," Ichi murmured, and Vic couldn't believe that it wasn't the first thing he had thought of doing when he got onto the helicopter. Nodding at Ichi in assent, he gently turned Claire over onto her front and unzipped her dress.

"Sorry for being indecent, princess," Vic muttered in an undertone, before proceeding to unlace the corset.

Ichi

This is not what I meant when I said I wanted to see you with just your corset on, Claire.

Damn it, Vic's taking too long being a bloody gentleman. You're stripping her; there's nothing 'gentlemanly' about that…does that mean you really, truly love her?

Vic

"Just take the whole damn thing off, Vic," Ichi finally said, clearly impatient at how slowly Vic was working. Vic gave him a look, but did as he was told, taking his jacket off to drape it over Claire's shoulders when he was done. He attempted to remove the heavy necklace that Michael had put on her, but Vic simply couldn't work out how to operate the clasp with his mind all over the place, so he left it on. Ichi helped him prop Claire up into a sitting position, resting her head against Vic's shoulder to hear that her breathing had noticeably relaxed. Vic tried not to look down, knowing that he'd see far too much of Claire than she'd be comfortable with had she been conscious.

"Button my jacket up, Ich," he ended up saying, and Ichi rolled his eyes. But he complied anyway, which Vic was grateful for. Then Ichi moved back to his own seat opposite Vic and stayed silent, never taking his eyes off of Claire.

Why aren't you asking me about anything? Vic wondered once more. *You're supposed to ask me what she meant by 'but you're John'. You're supposed to have a million questions.* He stared at Ichi until the other man finally tore his eyes away from Claire. Then they just looked at each other for a while, saying nothing. *Why aren't you asking me anything?* Vic thought again.

Ichi

When did you fall in love with her?

How long have you been in love with her?

If she has her memories back, will she remember she loves you too?

Or did she ever love you in the first place?

For fuck's sake, I can't ask about any of this with Michael listening in.

Vic

"It's not the time for that," Ichi said quietly, as if he were reading Vic's thoughts. Then he glanced pointedly at the pilot, then at Vic's earpiece, and Vic realised ashamedly that, of the two of them, the only one who was keeping their head in the game right now was Ichi. Ichi returned to looking at Claire, a frown on his face. "I just hope she wakes up."

Vic let out a heavy sigh before turning his gaze to the unconscious girl by his side. Claire almost looked as if she were having a nightmare, with her brow creased and her mouth open very slightly. Vic thought of all of the horrible things that had happened to her, wondering which one was going through her head.

"I hope so too," he replied very quietly, almost to himself. *More than anything, you have to wake up, Claire.*

Ichi

When they reached the roof of Michael's complex, the man himself was waiting for them. Ichi didn't think he had ever seen his boss look so furious.

"You cut that far too closely for my liking," he told them sharply. Ichi kept quiet.

"We need to get her down to the lab!" Vic exclaimed, ignoring Michael entirely. He had Claire huddled protectively against his chest again, as if he didn't intend to let her go.

"I'm well aware of that," Michael replied, firing Vic a look of pure impatience. They made their way down to the lab in relative silence; Ichi spent the journey listening to Claire's breathing as it seemed to grow more and more fitful. Vic kept his head down to look at her, and Ichi didn't think he'd ever seen anyone so worried.

Just what exactly is she to you, Vic? Ichi thought, feeling as if his own curiosity might drive him mad. It was only then that Ichi realised that Michael was also looking at Claire, an intent expression on his face that Ichi knew all too well. *And just what is it exactly that* he *wants with her?*

When they reached the lab, the female doctor who resided there ushered them all in quickly, indicating to a bed for Vic to put Claire down. He did so reluctantly, and even after he put Claire down he didn't let go of her hand.

Michael looked at Ichi, and then at Vic. "Out, the two of you," he said. "Meet me in my office in two hours."

Vic finally tore his eyes away from Claire, aghast. "I'm not leaving her side!"

"You will, if you want to see her again," Michael warned. Vic seemed to flinch at Michael's words, then his face hardened. Michael looked at Ichi again. "Any similar protests from you?" Ichi shrugged. *Remain impassive, and they'll never know your true intentions.*

When Ichi made for the stairs instead of the elevator after leaving the lab, he was surprised to find Vic following him.

"Ich," the taller man said, his voice quiet. Ichi continued to walk up the stairs.

"What?"

He heard Vic sigh. "Out of the thousand questions in your head, which one do you feel needs answered the most?"

Ichi turned his head slightly to look at him. "What exactly Michael wants from Claire, of course." Ichi was surprised when Vic let out a short burst of laughter. "What?" he asked again, testily this time.

Vic gave him a bitter smile. "Nothing. I just can't believe that, of everything you want to know, what you feel is most important is the same question I want answered."

Ichi turned away from Vic before replying. "Every other question doesn't matter next to that one."

"You might be my only ally on this front," Vic said.

"Just so long as you don't get in my way."

"Your way to what?" The two of them continued to ascend the stairs in silence for a while. When they reached the fifth floor, Ichi turned to face Vic properly.

"I don't know," was all he said, before heading up the rest of the stairs. After he got to his room, Ichi collapsed onto his bed and thought of nothing but Claire for a long time, hoping that when she finally woke up all of his questions would be answered. But the more he thought about it, the more he realised just how dangerous some of those answers could be.

Just what does Michael want from Claire? And what does that mean for her…and me?

Vic

"I should pick my bosses better," Vic muttered once he reached his room, feeling like he could weep. *I've run out of time.*

Claire

"Is there any physical damage?" Claire just barely heard somebody ask. Her head was in agony; she knew it was the most pain she had ever felt in her entire life. But Claire couldn't open her eyes, and she couldn't move her body, stuck in some excruciating limbo between consciousness and sleep. And she *couldn't* fall asleep – more than anything, Claire knew that she couldn't fall asleep.

"No," came a female voice. "Vic got her out unharmed, as you knew he would, Michael." Claire vaguely recognised the voice as the doctor who worked in the perfect imitation of her parents' lab, but that information meant nothing to her now.

"Good," Michael replied. Claire felt the man's hand on her forehead. "She has a fever though."

"That's to be expected. She's had an on-and-off fever for months now, which considering the stuff she's been injecting herself with is hardly surprising." Claire struggled to hold coherent thought for long enough to process what the doctor was saying.

"Just so long as she remembers everything and wakes up to tell the tale," she heard Michael murmur. He was far too close to Claire's face; she found herself somehow making a small noise in protest. To her relief, Michael moved away from her, but with her eyes closed Claire couldn't tell how far. "Should she be regaining consciousness now?"

"I don't think it would be wise until her fever's broken, if you want to make sure she remembers anything."

"Then give her a sedative until it has." *No,* Claire thought frantically. *No, no, no. I can't go to sleep, I can't!*

"No…" she managed to moan aloud.

Michael chuckled. "I'm sorry Miss Danvers, but you don't get a say in the matter." *No, don't do this, please don't do this. I don't want to know!* But all of her protests were in her head, and even if she had been able to vocalise them Claire knew that Michael wouldn't care. When Claire felt a needle prick her skin, her hand reflexively grabbed onto the object closest to it. But by the time she realised that that object was Michael's arm, Claire felt her consciousness and her hand slip away, and then there was nothing.

CHAPTER 36
Comatose

Claire

Claire was dreaming. Or was she remembering? She couldn't work it out. Her brain was being flooded with image after image and sound after sound of things that she used to know but had forgotten. And nothing seemed to be missed out, from the moment Claire was old enough to have coherent thought to the moment she collapsed at the awards ball. *I'll go with remembering, then,* Claire decided. But none of the memories were in order; everything was spinning round and round in her head until Claire was forced to admit that she didn't know how she was supposed to sort through and make sense of any of it.

But then she caught a glimpse of golden hair and Claire's brain latched onto the memory with all of the willpower she could muster. It was John, worrying over his thesis as he had always done, but now Claire knew better; the man was definitely Vic. *And just what is that supposed to mean, that Michael had me tailed for months?* Claire thought, frustrated at how little she knew. *But I was fawning over John before my parents even disappeared, so...how was Michael to know that I was important? Was he just keeping tabs on any leverage he could use against my parents?*

Claire knew that at least some of the answers she had been craving over the past year had to be inside her head, so she allowed the flood of memories to wash over her again until something promising showed up. Eventually she saw a flash of her parents' lab, so Claire concentrated on that and nothing else. She saw herself – which Claire felt oddly disconcerted about – feeding the mice in the lab. And there were her parents at the back of the lab, looking haggard and harassed and talking to a tall man in a beanie hat whose back was turned from the Claire in the past.

"Is my princess safe?" asked the man, and then Claire knew that she didn't need to see the man's face to know that it was Vic. *Does this fall before or after me beginning to watch him in the library? I didn't pluck up the courage to talk to him for ages, so...*

"Never mind that, what can you tell us about how up-to-date Michael is on what we've actually been doing in here?" Claire's mother replied.

"'Never mind that', you say? What's wrong with you?!" Vic exclaimed, voicing the outrage Claire was now feeling. "Your children should be your top priority here!" *Did I just blank this conversation out when it was happening?* she wondered, confused. *Because the past me doesn't seem bothered at all. Do I suddenly have better hearing or something? Or is it just that I know which part of my surroundings to properly concentrate on, whereas the past me was only focused on feeding the damn mice?*

Claire heard her father sigh. "Of course they're our top priority," he said to Vic. "And yes, they're safe. Claire's over there just now, you know. She can't possibly be safer than right under our noses."

It was Vic's turn to sigh. "Okay, okay, Mark. Sorry for blowing up at you. Michael doesn't know about your little side project, but if you truly mean to pursue it as your sole focus then it's only a matter of time before he knows. And no, Joanna, you know I don't want to know anything about what you're actually doing, so stop looking at me all excited like that just because you wanna boast to someone." That sentence piqued Claire's interest immensely. *So Vic had an opportunity to know exactly what they were doing but he didn't want to know? But by the sounds of it, he was the one making sure* Michael *didn't know. Is that because my parents' research wasn't finished yet, or because they had reason to never want him to know?*

"I'm sorry Vic, I'm just...excited, as you said." Claire heard her mother let out her beautiful laugh, the one she knew won hearts over to her cause, and she could just imagine Vic's face softening at the sound. *After all, it's what I do to him too,* Claire thought guiltily.

"It's okay, Joanna. But please don't lose sight of your original goal. If what you're doing on the side is so dangerous, is it really worth doing? You're convinced that Michael must never know, so...is it worth putting your whole family at risk?"

"Absolutely," answered both of her parents at the same time.

"This research is ground-breaking," her father continued. "It will change the world. It just cannot fall into the wrong hands, especially *Michael's*." Claire was shocked at the malice in her father's voice as he uttered Michael's name – she had never heard him sound so hateful.

"...I thought your *main* research was ground-breaking," Vic muttered. Claire saw her parents shift on the spot uncomfortably.

"It is, but..." her mother began, then she sighed. "We're at a bit of an impasse." Then her eyes went wide. "But you can't let Michael know that either! Just...just tell him everything is going as well as it ever was."

Strange, Claire thought. *Was my mother ever this terrified of anything? Who was Michael to my parents to make them end up hating and fearing him so much?*

"You know that I can't do that for forever," Vic replied. "But until the day that I can't, you have to promise to continue to keep your daughters safe. Especially..." Claire saw her mother glance pointedly at her past self, cleaning glassware now that the mice had been dutifully fed.

"What is it about her that you're so drawn to, Vic?" her mother asked, and Claire felt a bit affronted. *She practically just said that she doesn't think there's anything about me for him to like.*

Vic seemed to be thinking the same thing, for he said, "What you're insinuating is incredibly bitchy, even for you Joanna. Luckily, your daughter isn't like that at all." Claire felt a fresh wave of affection for Vic wash over her. *He was defending me before I even knew him. My God, I have so much to ask him.*

"Don't take her question like that, Vic," her father interjected. "Everything we say sounds a bit...bitchy, as you'd say. It's the damn stress we're under. I *am* curious about why you're so interested in my daughter though, you know." Her father's gaze fell on her cleaning the glassware, and his face almost seemed to glow. "I'm not supposed to have a favourite, but it's definitely Claire for me. She's my pride and joy."

"Yes, and she'll end up outshining us both if she doesn't stop getting more brilliant," her mother muttered.

"Oh, Joanna, stop it," Claire's father snapped. "You're just bitter that she's the only one coming up with plausible new ideas these days. Don't forget that, twenty years ago, that was you. And still is you; don't give me that look. We're both just…in a rut right now. A fresh pair of eyes is what we need. Ah, sorry Vic, you didn't need to hear any of that."

"I'll leave my answer to your question to myself then," Vic replied. Then he left the lab without so much as a glance in the past Claire's direction. *Damn it, why couldn't he just turn around?* Claire lamented.

Then her brain was abruptly bombarded with image upon image of random lab work, days turned into nights staying up late to help her parents with their research. But this was their 'main research' – the work that both the public and Michael knew about, the research that had been making Claire's parents so famous in the first place. They had been working on the restoration of forgotten memories in long-term amnesia and Alzheimer cases, and they had made significant progress in mouse models. Watching everything as it happened again filled Claire with an immense feeling of excitement, because her parents' research truly *was* ground-breaking. But then another research group released a paper about the implanting of false memories into mice, and her parents had grabbed onto the idea with their life. For what if they could reprogramme the brains of mice to teach them how to perform tasks that they had never encountered in real life before, but to a much larger extent than the other group? What if they could go beyond simply making a mouse believe that it had gone through a particular maze before? And what if they could scale it up to humans? Claire recalled the research going incredibly well, and being just as excited about it as she was for the memory-restoration research, for how could she not?

Claire had always loved her father's way of explaining the research in popular terms: "It's like the Matrix for mice," he had said. "Just pop in a memory and boom! The mouse knows how to escape from its cage, just like that. Can you imagine, Claire? Can you imagine this working for *people*? We could all be fluent in fifty different languages, experts in taekwondo, masterminds in physics…think how much mankind could achieve! It wouldn't be the Matrix any more, it'd be real life." Claire had been more than a little upset when they had all but abandoned their main research, but she knew that the best way to get back to it was to help her parents iron out the kinks in the new stuff.

Iron out the kinks, huh? Just like that. Easy. But everything *had* felt easy, because everything was working. But then…Claire's brain clung onto a memory that, in her current state of euphoria, she didn't want to see. But there it was – all of their perfect little Neo-from-the-Matrix mice going mad, violently attacking each other until the other mice were dead. And then they'd be reclusive on their own, engaging in repetitive and isolated behaviours. The only social interaction the mice seemed to have with each other that didn't involve their deaths was mating, which they did far more frequently than the control group. Claire saw how upset her parents were at this unexpected side effect, and how they desperately tried to figure out how to counteract it. They tried everything from diet control to drugs and then far more complicated genetics-based methods, such as lentiviral vectors aimed at specific neuronal pathway genes. However, nothing seemed to be working, and morale in the lab got low. Claire suddenly remembered how palpable the fear had been between her parents, and they started to become secretive and quiet around Claire. *How didn't I notice? Did I just think they were taking the bad turn in their research too much to heart?*

Claire didn't know how to answer that question, so she allowed her brain to skip ahead through more memories, watching her parents get steadily more erratic and less like themselves on fast-forward. *I wonder if I would have noticed it earlier if I had gotten to see their decline as rapidly as this, rather than over months and months.*

Then Claire focussed on one memory in particular and felt her heart stop. *My parents were working on human subjects,* Claire thought numbly as she watched the Claire in the past stumble upon the subjects herself, and the horrifying moment when she realised that one of the subjects was her sister. But it wasn't Olivia; it was Alexis. *But that can't be! How is that even possible?!* Yet even as Claire thought on it, a flurry of emotions and memories began flooding into her brain; memories of her childhood with Alexis and Olivia, growing up together as an inseparable trio. But then she watched as Alexis grew more and more distant from Claire as they grew up, resenting her younger sister for being the star daughter who had taken up their parents' mantle. Claire could not understand why Alexis was being experimented on, until her sister admitted that she willingly agreed to it, driven by a desire to be better than her sister that Claire had failed to fully comprehend in their teenage years. *And now it's too late.* And their parents...their parents were so blinded by their desperation for their research to be successful that they had allowed their eldest daughter to be treated like a lab rat. A horrific wave of guilt at herself and hatred for her parents washed over Claire, and she thought that surely nothing could get worse than this.

But then Claire paid proper attention to the other test subject lying on a bed opposite Alexis', and she thought that her brain must have truly been making everything up from the very beginning, because it was Ichi. That first memory of discovering that the pair of them were being experimented on didn't linger on Ichi, however, as the Claire in the past was too caught up in her older sister. And Alexis wouldn't even speak to her after that one brief, explanatory sentence about why she was there in the first place, not even when Claire stood in front of her, pleading and sobbing and begging her to stop. And Ichi…past Claire didn't even know where her parents had found this darkly handsome, Japanese man, but he acted just as aloof towards Claire as Alexis was being.

Claire felt her own anguish all over again as she worried over what she was supposed to do. She couldn't inform the authorities of what her parents were doing; she didn't want them to go to prison, regardless of how much she currently hated them. Claire didn't want her sister and the strange man named Ichi to be quarantined and subject to experimentation for the rest of their lives in order to identify just how her parents had altered them. And then there was the ever increasing threat of Michael, who at this point even Claire was terrified of, simply because of her parents. It was absolutely imperative that Michael never found out what her parents were doing – it was the one coherent, sane thought that both of her parents still seemed to possess.

So Claire watched herself continue to watch Alexis and Ichi, wishing she could do something to help them. She saw past Claire resolved to at least make sure that the two of them were taken care of, since in her parents' neglect both Alexis and Ichi began looking more ragged with every passing day. And she continued to work with the Matrix mice, making desperate attempts at combating the disastrous side effects that Claire dreaded seeing in her sister and in Ichi.

Then Claire watched in awe as the pair of them suddenly became adept at self-defence, weapons use, speaking in foreign languages, mathematics, physics…*This is unbelievable!* Claire thought. *Everything my father was hoping for and more. I can hate them all I want but my parents truly* are *geniuses.* Claire felt herself getting excited despite herself at the prospect of her parents' research actually working, only for the inevitable side effects to eventually occur. It was like a punch to the gut for Claire; a heart-wrenching, unbearable feeling since all she could do was look on as Alexis and Ichi became excessively violent. The two of them ended up becoming permanently constrained to their beds to prevent them from hurting other people, in a constant state of sedation.

So Claire continued to feed them, keep them hydrated and, in the rare moments when they seemed to be more like themselves, attempt to talk to them. But Alexis continued to dutifully ignore Claire, which broke her heart a little more every day. *I can't take this,* the present Claire thought as she watched herself try and deal with Alexis' silence. *I can't just take on everything I had felt over months and months in a matter of seconds…it's too much.*

But then something happened that was like a singular ray of sunshine breaking through the gloom of the Claire in the past's life – Ichi began to talk to her. He slowly opened up about his life between moments of murderous rage, for which Claire was truly grateful. The present Claire honed in on one particular conversation between herself and Ichi, simply to listen to his voice.

"I haven't done much with my life, not really," Ichi said. Claire saw that he was clinging on to the railings on either side of the bed; he was clearly suppressing a lot of anger to engage in the conversation, which surprised Claire because the Ichi she knew now would never have done so. "I mean," he continued, "if I had been going somewhere, do you think I'd have signed up for this?" He laughed bitterly, and Claire watched herself give him a sad smile.

"So why *did* you sign up?" she ventured. Ichi looked at her critically, as if deciding whether Claire was worthy of the answer or not.

"Because your parents told me they could transform my life. The whole 'roof over my head and three meals a day' thing helped too. Don't feel so great about the transformation they promised now, though…but then how was I to know that your parents were worse monsters than mine?" The Claire in the past looked at him with confusion in her eyes, because she was yet to find out what Ichi's mother had done to him.

"…what did your parents do?" Claire heard herself ask timidly. "Is it…is it to do with the scars on your chest?"

"Well aren't you observant," Ichi replied off-handedly. *God, Ichi's such a dick,* Claire found herself thinking.

Claire in the past looked at the floor, abashed. "They're pretty obvious," she mumbled. Then she looked at Ichi for a second before standing up to leave. "You know what? This was a mistake. I haven't been trying to speak to you for weeks just so you can look at me with that haughty expression of yours, like it would be too much of your time and effort to give me anything but sarcastic answers. Just go back to ignoring me." *Oh, go me!* Claire thought. *I almost forgot that I didn't take crap from anyone in the past.*

"Wait!" Ichi called out after Claire as she began to walk away. She turned around to look at him, and he was frowning. "Just…wait. I'm sorry. I'm not exactly myself right now." Claire took a few steps back towards him and waited patiently for an actual answer from him. Ichi sighed. "My mother, Mikasa, gave me the scars. They're not just on my chest, but you haven't seen the rest of them so you wouldn't know. I didn't really know my dad, but I think he died or left or something when I was young. He might have been called Roy. Or maybe Robert, I don't really care." He paused, as if he was thinking about what to say next. "My mother was pretty mental, so I left home when I was thirteen. That was…eleven years ago."

"When's your birthday?" Claire from the past asked. Present Claire almost laughed at the ridiculous question. Ichi raised an eyebrow at her; it was so familiar an action that Claire felt her heart ache.

"Seriously? That's your question?"

"Well, you managed to establish that your mother is indeed a monster, but that my parents are definitely worse. I can't do anything about that except maybe cry to myself about it later on, but that's such a stupid thing to do that I'll try my best to *not* think about it." Claire gave Ichi a small smile. "So, yeah, the only thing I want to ask you about based on what you told me is when your birthday is."

Ichi gave her a searching look that neither past nor present Claire understood. "December twenty-third," he finally replied, and then he added, "When's yours?" Claire watched her own face light up in response to Ichi finally asking her for information about herself.

"April twenty-fourth. I'll be twenty-two. Your birthday is on a terrible date."

Ichi let out a bark of laughter. "As if I ever got to celebrate Christmas, you moron. My mother was Japanese."

"There's no need to be such a dick, you know," Claire replied, but Ichi just rolled his eyes in response. She saw that his grip on the bedside railing had loosened just a little bit, so Claire kept him talking. "Was your dad Japanese as well?"

"Nope," Ichi said. "He was English. I don't look anything like him, as you can probably imagine. He was way tall though, and I luckily inherited some of that, so…guess he wasn't all bad."

"You said you grew up in England, so how did you end up in Scotland?"

Ichi wrinkled his nose slightly as he tried to remember; Claire thought it was the most adorable thing she had even seen. *I've never seen him do that before,* she thought. *But then again, he's like a completely different person now.* "I walked here, believe it or not. No, seriously," Ichi added on when Claire laughed in disbelief, "I walked everywhere. It's not like I had much money or a passport or anything, so walking was usually my only form of transport." Claire saw herself look puzzled at his answer.

"How did you manage for so long with no identification or money?" Hearing herself ask Ichi that suddenly reminded Claire that Ichi had essentially asked her the same question at the awards ball. *Well, he figured I wouldn't last two minutes on the street without either, so how did he manage it?*

"Sob stories," Ichi replied bluntly. "If you work out who the suckers are, you can get pretty much anything from anyone." He was quiet for a minute. "I stole a lot. When I was old enough I got myself a bar job with someone who paid in cash. And then…I don't know, really. I just survived."

Claire made a face at him. "Your life sounds unbearably dreary."

"So you can see exactly how I ended up here." Claire watched herself smile at his response, then saw Ichi return the smile with an oh-so-familiar side smirk. And that was when Claire realised that she was watching herself fall in love with Ichi all over again. Her memories flashed in front of her eyes, showing Claire how frequently the two of them would talk after that initial conversation; how Claire moved from standing beside Ichi's bed to sitting beside it to sitting on it. She watched as Ichi laced his fingers together with Claire's for the first time, and how she had blushed a furious red in response and he had laughed at her reaction.

Claire's brain abruptly changed the focus of her memories from Ichi to mice then, and she saw that the Claire in the past had made a miraculous discovery regarding the origin of the Matrix mice side effects. "They're X linked, they're bloody X linked, dad!" Claire watched herself tell her father excitedly, all hatred for the man temporarily forgotten. Her father just looked at her, as if he couldn't believe his daughter until she explained it further, so Claire did. "You know how in Rett Syndrome patients, the severity of their condition depends on how many affected versus unaffected X chromosomes are inactivated?" Her father nodded, and Claire could see in his face that he was beginning to grasp what she was getting at. "Well," Claire continued, "I noticed that, with the female Matrix mice, most of them exhibited less pronounced bouts of rage and their periods of isolation weren't as long compared to the male mice, so I thought it was worth exploring that you and mum had messed up with the X chromosome somehow, and..." Claire laughed at her past self, because she had paused for dramatic effect.

"And? *And*?!" her father prompted, excitement glittering in his eyes for once instead of mad desperation.

Claire grinned at him. "And I was right. The side effects are X linked, and I know how to fix them, without taking away the Matrix ability. I know I can!"

"But what about the male mice?" Claire's mother interrupted; Claire hadn't even noticed when she had joined the conversation.

She frowned at her mother. "Well, since there *are* male mice at all, that tells us that the side effects aren't lethal. But it means we can't use targeted X inactivation to fix them...we'll need to work out something else." Claire let out a noise of surprise as her father picked her up and spun her around.

"Ah, Claire, I love you so much!" her father burst out, delight written all over his face. He let Claire down to look at his wife, who had a much more measured expression on her face. "Joanna, we can fix this. *We can fix this!* And then Michael won't get his hands on it, and –"

"The two aren't mutually exclusive, Mark," Claire's mother interrupted. "Remember what Vic keeps telling us – he can't keep all of this hidden from Michael for ever. And what do you propose we do once we've fixed everything? Go into protective custody?"

"Well why the hell not?!" he exploded back at her. Claire abruptly felt side-lined, and she realised that this was not the first time her parents had had this argument. "Seriously Joanna," her father continued, "The only reason we're not right now is because we can't let anybody know that we experimented on people in the first place! But if we can fix Lexi and Ichi, then we don't have that problem anymore! We can –"

"*Michael will find us.* You know he will! If we go into protective custody we're dead. We need to destroy everything and go off the grid completely, or let Michael know what we're doing and allow him to do God knows what with the research. And you know I'll never accept the latter decision, Mark." Claire's father looked at his wife coldly then, and in that moment Claire knew what her mother was talking about.

"You can't...*you can't kill them*!" Claire screamed at her mother. "Alexis is your *daughter,* and Ichi..."

"Yes, I've seen how you are with him; there's no need to provide an explanation for why you're attached to him," her mother interjected, her voice devoid of any emotion.

Claire looked at her, aghast. "What's wrong with you, mum? Why do you not seem to know how wrong this is?!"

Her mother turned on her then, and Claire saw tears in her eyes. "You think I don't know, Claire?!" she yelled. "Of course I do! I know more than any of you! Do you have any idea what Michael will do if he gets his hands on this research? *Do you*?"

"N-no," Claire stammered, "I don't –"

"Then you don't understand! Neither of you do! Michael *cannot* gain access or knowledge of this research. It's for the greater good for all evidence of our research to be destroyed, even if..." Her mother's voice trailed away to nothing.

"You can't even say it, mum! So how can you expect to do it? You can't kill Ichi or my sister!"

"Then fix them!" her mother screamed, and Claire backed away slightly. "Use your bloody brilliant theory and fix them, and then we all have to disappear! And I don't just mean your dad and me, Claire."

"Wait, what?" Claire's father said, suddenly part of the mother-daughter argument again. "Joanna, we never discussed Claire having to disappear with us. Vic said he'd keep our daughters safe."

Joanna laughed bitterly. "Liv, definitely. Claire? No way. She knows too much! And Michael knows that she does!"

"Wait, how...?" Claire in the past asked, and she found herself wondering the same thing in the present.

"It's your own damn fault!" her mother replied, but before Claire could hear an explanation her brain skipped forward in time. And Claire realised that she had indeed managed to fix the side effects in the female mice, and Alexis was to be tested on that day.

Their father injected Alexis with the treatment, because Claire's hands wouldn't stop shaking. But when it became obvious that the treatment was working, the shaking was replaced with sobs of relief as their father untied Alexis from the bed that she had been stuck in for months, and their mother moved forward to hold her hand. Present Claire knew what would happen next without having to see it, because she knew her sister better than her parents did. Alexis knocked the two of them out, then turned to briefly face Claire.

Her eyes were intense and serious as she said, "Fix him, and then get the two of you the hell out of here." Alexis glanced over at Ichi, who was sedated out of his mind to keep him calm, then looked back at Claire. "Can you do that?"

Claire's sobs, only moments before the product of joy, turned to cries of agony in her throat as she forced herself to reply, "Y-yes. Yes. I can do it, I'll work it out. Alexis, please, don't –"

"Don't tell me to stay," her sister cut in. "Our parents are monsters. Don't think I haven't heard everything they've said in here. So promise me you'll do what I asked!"

"I promise!" Claire exclaimed, and then Alexis was gone. When their parents came to, they seemed to, finally, be wracked with guilt for what they had done. But their fear was stronger.

"Claire, if you can't fix Ichi in the next couple of weeks, we're going to have to kill him," her mother told her, and that was when Claire knew that she had definitely lost the woman who had brought her up.

"They're going to kill you, they're going to kill you if I can't fix you, and I don't think I can!" Claire watched herself confess to Ichi in a later memory. She was crying into his shoulder, and Ichi rested his forehead on top of her hair.

"It's okay, Claire. Don't cry. Don't cry. Hey – look at me," he said, so Claire looked at him.

"Let's run away," she whispered, and present Claire thought it to be a superb idea, but Ichi shook his head sadly.

"I can't deal with this, Claire. This – rage – or whatever it is. I want to kill everyone I see. Even now, knowing how I feel about you, I still want to rip your throat out. Good thing I'm restrained, right?" He laughed bitterly. "No. If I'm out there in the world it won't be long before I truly become something that I don't want to be."

"Then I want to die, too."

Ichi smiled at her, and it broke Claire's heart to see it. "No you don't," he said. "It's not in your nature. You'll keep on living for me, okay? And you sisters. Olivia's still oblivious, right? Keep her that way. You can do that, can't you? Keep her away from your parents' utter poison? Promise me you will."

Claire let out a broken sob. "So many promises. How am I supposed to keep them all?" Ichi leaned towards her and kissed her chastely. It was like nothing Claire had ever seen from the present Ichi, which made it all the more difficult to watch.

"Because you're Claire Elizabeth Danvers, that's why." Then Claire heard footsteps behind her, and there was her father, looking ragged and half-dead.

"I might have another solution," he said. Claire and Ichi looked at him in silence until he elaborated. "Well," her father began, "Our problem is with anybody finding out what Ichi is capable of, and how. But if he doesn't *remember* why he can do everything that he can do, then he can't tell anyone, and nobody will ever know what happened to him."

"But…what about the rage? And the other behavioural side effects?" Claire asked, not daring to feel hope.

Claire's father scratched his head. "I'm hoping that, by not knowing how the anger came about, Ichi will be able to somewhat control it. I mean, there are people who can be excessively violent everywhere, right? But they know that it's not normal, so they try their best to control it." He turned to Ichi. "As you are now, you know that the rage you're feeling is merely the side effect to an experiment. But if you were to believe that you had always felt this way, yet had somehow reached twenty-four years of age without anything disastrous happening, would that not in a way teach you to keep it to yourself? Your memories could be activated again with a buzzword, like they use in hypnotism and other psychological tricks. We could ensure it only works when a specific person says it, to reduce the risk of you remembering anything by mistake. I know it's not a true solution, but…" Claire's father turned to face his daughter. "But I can't take away the life of someone you care about, sweetheart. With what humanity I have left, I want to save your world, if I can."

Claire didn't expect Ichi to agree to it, but he nodded his assent. "Okay," he said. He turned his gaze to Claire. "It would give you more time to fix me, right? And you could be in charge of my…buzzword, so I'd only hear it when you were ready to fix me. And then, maybe…" Claire felt tears spring into her eyes anew.

"Okay. Okay. Let's do this."

And so Ichi forgot everything, but Claire clung onto the belief that, at some point in the near future, he would remember her again. What Claire wasn't expecting was to have Ichi removed from her life entirely with no idea of where he had been taken, which was precisely what her parents did.

"How am I supposed to fix him if I don't know where he is?!" Claire saw herself scream at her parents.

"You don't!" her mother replied. "What we did to Ichi was the best your father and I could come up with, but it's as far as any of us can help him. If you were to continue with the research in order to fix him them Michael would find out, and we'd all be ruined. Claire, now that Ichi and Alexis are out, we need to destroy everything." Claire looked at her father then, and the only word she could find to describe him was desolate, because that was precisely how she felt too.

"I can't deal with this," the Claire in the past uttered, just as present Claire thought the exact same thing.

"Joanna, we can't just lose everything…it could still do so much good," her father said sadly.

"But we can't leave any physical or computer evidence of what we did, Mark! We can't!"

"You keep saying it's for the greater good that we make sure Michael never gets it, but surely the risk that he *might* for the sake of the greater good benefitting from our research in the end is worth it?!" he countered, the desperation in his voice palpable. Claire's mother ran her hands through her long, dark hair, the way that Claire herself always did when she was stressed.

"There's nothing we can do, Mark. There's nothing "

"There is."

Claire's parents both stopped their argument to stare at their daughter. "Excuse me?" her mother said. Her father said nothing.

"There *is* a way you can keep the research," Claire said, and her voice was blank. "Use it on me. Turn me into a Matrix mouse. Put all of the research into my head…then block my memories. Dad can be in charge of my buzzword." *Let me keep a hold of the way I can save Ichi, even if I can't do it right now.*

"Claire, you're a genius," her father said.

Her mother let out a bark of laughter. "I can't believe, after all of this, you're going to save us."

Claire gave her a hard stare. "Just do it, and be done with it." And so they did, and Claire's buzzword became the title of her father's favourite Del Amitri song, Driving with the Brakes On. And then…Claire watched as, for the following month, things were normal. Claire stopped working in her parents' lab in favour of studying and sitting her final exams, and she started fawning over John in the library. *That sorts out the timeline, then, but not Vic's motive for watching me,* Claire thought, forcing her brain to be productive rather than fulfilling her desire to break down and cry over Ichi and Alexis. Claire didn't see much of Olivia either, which would perhaps explain why Alexis had never been brought up, since it became apparent that Claire had no memory of her older sister by this point.

When Claire's parents inevitably disappeared, she had to relive the disbelief, anger and sadness all over again as she graduated from the university that her parents had gone to without her parents in tow. *I did it all for the two of you, you fuckers,* Claire thought angrily. Olivia had come along, of course, but then she had run off abroad to deal with their parents' disappearance in the only way she knew how. Olivia had asked Claire to go, too, but she had stayed behind to look after their family home which she had loved so much. *And I know what a big mistake that was now, of course.*

The very thought of her kidnap caused Claire to wonder how she had been able to remember Michael's name at all, thus enabling her to save her life that day whilst simultaneously being unable to recognise Vic, despite him being the man that she had been getting ready to go on a date with that very evening. *Perhaps hearing him as 'Vic' rather than 'John' caused me to forget him, since he was like a totally different person,* Claire reasoned, desperately trying to make sense of everything. *And maybe all of the fear and adrenaline caused me to remember just enough of my blocked memories to save my life. But of all the people to remember, why did I remember* Michael, *who I hadn't even met yet?*

But that thought in turn caused Claire to remember something else – a memory seemingly entirely unrelated to everything she had seen so far. She was getting ready in her bathroom at her parents' house to go out, still wrapped in a towel as she finished off her make-up and moved through to her bedroom to dry her hair, when Claire heard her mother call up the stairs.

"Claire, can you come down here for a second?" she said.

Claire frowned at her reflection in the full length mirrors. "Give me a couple of minutes, mum!" she shouted down through the open door. Present Claire looked at her past self suspiciously, inspecting the length of her hair and the potential outfit choices lying on the bed. *I remember this,* Claire thought. *I'm eighteen here. I was getting ready to go on my first 'legal' night out with Alexis, after waiting for weeks for her to be free.*

"Just come down now, please!" she heard her mother say, and the Claire in the past let out a heavy sigh as she abandoned her hair dryer to head downstairs. She used the secret, rickety staircase hidden behind the hallway panelling to get downstairs, because Claire had always preferred the old relics in the house rather than the modern approach her mother had taken when restructuring the main part of the house. *Plus it continually gave her a fright when Alexis or Olivia or I came crashing through the wall,* Claire thought, almost giggling at the memory. *She always regretted giving into dad's request to keep that staircase.*

So Claire went pelting down the stairs three at a time, grabbing onto her towel to prevent it from falling off, shoving open the downstairs panelling with her shoulder when she reached it. But instead of hitting empty air, Claire walked straight into a person, and she yelped in fright. The stranger took a few steps away from her before turning around, allowing Claire access out onto the hallway, but she didn't move as she took in the appearance of the man in front of her. He looked to be a fair bit younger than Claire's mother; his dark blonde hair was swept away from his face and he wore a sharp grey suit that matched his eyes. Past Claire noted that he had excellent cheekbones and was pretty good-looking, and that he was taller than her father. Present Claire couldn't believe what she was seeing.

Oh my God it's Michael, Claire finally managed to acknowledge, though she didn't want to. Then, in the past, Claire froze internally as she looked at him, as if even then she knew that something was off about him after taking in his appearance. Michael gave her a smile that the present Claire knew hid everything he was thinking about, then turned to glance at Claire's mother over his shoulder.

"So which Miss Danvers is this, Joanna?" he asked, in a liquid honey tone that Claire had never heard him use before.

Joanna laughed. "Oh, this is Claire, though we seem to have caught her at a bad time." The Claire in the past seemed to come to her senses then, and her face flushed a bright red when she realised she was still staring at Michael.

"Jesus *Christ,* mum!" she complained, "Next time tell me someone has come over so I'm not basically naked!" Then she slammed the panelling closed to run back up the stairs, heart hammering in her chest. When she reached her room again, Claire took her time drying her hair before deliberating between a green and a blue dress for far longer than was warranted, simply to delay going back downstairs. Eventually, she decided on the beautiful white sundress that she had stolen from Olivia, since the late-May weather had left the evenings positively balmy for Scotland. She left her naturally wavy hair down to tumble over her shoulders and checked herself out in the mirror, secretly hoping that she could upstage her gorgeous big sister on their first proper night out together. Claire remembered hoping that, in having a night out, she could begin to get closer to Alexis again, since the two of them had been growing ever more distant from each other and Claire didn't really understand why.

*If only I had known back then, maybe I could have...*Claire began to think, then forced the train of thought to stop since she could do nothing about it now. The Claire in the past put on a pair of strappy sandals to complete her outfit, then grabbed her mobile phone before heading down the stairs, much more slowly this time than on her first descent. Knowing that she'd have to apologise for being rude to her mother's guest (even though she didn't particularly want to), Claire reluctantly made her way to the kitchen, knowing that she'd find both of her parents in there with several bottles of wine. *It was a Saturday, after all,* Claire thought wryly.

When she sheepishly opened the kitchen door, Claire heard her mother cluck her tongue at her. "Claire Elizabeth Danvers, you are not leaving the house dressed like that!"

"Oh, leave her alone Joanna," her father cut in with an easy smile and a wave of a hand. "You're only eighteen once, and she's only got a couple more months before she'll have to get her head stuck into uni work!"

"I do recall that you didn't get stuck into uni work until *final* year, Mark," Claire's mother replied, taking a sip of wine as she did so.

Her father laughed at the comment. "Let's hope Claire takes after you then!"

"Well it's good to see that you're both drunk and arguing already," Claire commented, before making herself look at the man her mother had let in. She put on a radiant smile akin to her mother's to hide the fact that he made her uncomfortable, and flipped all of her hair over her left shoulder in one smooth motion. "I'm sorry for being rude earlier," she said. "I'm Claire, the second Danvers daughter, but I'm already late as it is so I won't be hanging around."

Michael smiled at her again, but both present and past Claire could tell that he was using it to hide the fact that he was sizing her up. "I'm Michael, one of your parents'...associates."

"Oh don't be ridiculous, Michael!" Claire's mother protested, smiling beautifully for him. She turned to her daughter. "Claire, Michael's one of my old friends. One of his companies privately funds some of our research."

"*One* of his companies?" Claire echoed back, suspicious. She glanced at her father then, and realised that he didn't much care for how close his wife seemed to be to this younger man, if the rate at which he was drinking a bottle of wine was anything to go by.

Michael laughed lightly. "Yes, one of them. I'm very rich."

"And very arrogant," Claire bit out before she could stop herself, then put a hand over her mouth in horror. She heard her father let out a bark of laughter at the comment, but her mother frowned at her.

"Claire, that's a terrible thing to say."

"In all fairness, it's true, so I guess I can let it slide," Michael said, and Claire noted out of the corner of her eye that the way he looked at her had changed very slightly. She was saved from thinking about it any further when she felt her phone buzz in her hand, so she looked to see who had sent her a text. Claire's heart sank when she realised what it was about.

"What's up, sweetheart?" her father asked, and Claire pouted at him.

"Lexi cancelled on me."

"*Again?* Do you want me to call her? That's one time too many for my liking."

"No, dad, it's okay, it's fine," Claire mumbled. "I'm used to it. She'll drink with me when she wants to." She laughed in an attempt to lighten her mood. "Guess I'll just head back upstairs and watch some TV, then."

"No you're not!" her father announced to her already-turned back. "You're drinking with us. Here, have a seat." He gestured to the seat on his right, the only one left at the small, circular table, and Claire realised that she would have to sit beside the stranger named Michael on *her* right.

"Yes, won't you join us, Miss Danvers?" Michael chimed in pleasantly.

Claire ignored him and gave her dad a smile. "No, it's okay, I don't want to interrupt your night. I have some results from the lab I wanna go over anyway."

"Mark, just let her do what she wants," her mother said, and Claire could tell that she couldn't care less what her daughter did, only that she was gone for the evening.

"Oh don't be ridiculous, Joanna. Claire, go get what you were working on and bring it down here. We can go over it together – it's about time you learned the joys of drunken collaboration!" It was then that Claire realised that her father was desperate for somebody else's company in the kitchen, so Claire decided to ignore her seemingly unfounded discomfort towards Michael (who she had dutifully avoided eye contact with since introducing herself) to help her father out.

"Be right back, dad," she grinned, before running back upstairs to get the data she had been poring over earlier in the day. When she returned, her dad had poured her a glass of wine, which Claire happily took. She sat down and turned her chair ever so slightly to face her father, but Michael didn't seem to notice as he was deep in conversation with her mother.

And so Claire whiled a couple of hours away discussing the pros and cons of targeting various gene pathways of potential benefit to her parents' research, going from sober to tipsy to rather drunk as time passed on. She entirely forgot about Michael or her mother, which seemed to suit the pair of them just fine.

"I really don't see why you're so averse to testing some of these in flies," Claire found herself saying to her father eventually. "The Drosophila lab in –"

"I don't know what your obsession with Drosophila is, Claire, but it would be completely backwards for us to conduct our research in a non-mammalian model organism," her father countered, voice slightly louder than the conversation warranted due to the wine he had consumed.

Present Claire found herself almost laughing; she had had this argument with her father before. "But it's so much quicker!" she complained. "And there's been some really good research on Huntington's and other neurological-based human disorders in flies recently, and the gamma secretase complex has been reconstituted in flies too. *And* they're so much cheaper –"

"Oh, money isn't a problem," a male voice to Claire's right interjected, and she flipped her head around to look at Michael before she had a chance

405

to remember why she had been avoiding her right hand side in the first place.

"Says who?" Claire found herself saying, the alcohol in her system making her bold despite her discomfort.

Michael raised an eyebrow at her. "Says me, of course. I'm very rich, or have you forgotten that already?"

Claire waved a dismissive hand at him before turning back to her father. "You should stop being so blinded by your mouse models, is all I'm saying," Claire told him, then her mother touched his arm to grab his attention, and her father started a new conversation with her. Claire turned to look down at the notes she had brought down with her and finished her glass of wine as she shuffled through them, trying to appear as if she were looking for something in them. Then she felt Michael lean over her shoulder, and Claire struggled not to jump.

"So what's an eighteen-year-old girl doing with such advanced research notes?" he murmured into her ear, as he hooked a foot around the bottom of one of Claire's chair legs to bring her closer to him. Her drunken parents didn't notice the action; they were too engrossed in their own conversation.

Claire carefully swept her hair over her right shoulder to help provide a barrier between herself and Michael before replying, "You really think I could get away with not knowing any of this stuff with parents like *them*?" She gestured to her parents as she did so, hoping that the action would make them take notice of her, but it failed. Claire struggled not to flinch as Michael reached over her slightly to pick up the bottle of wine at her father's side of the table; he refilled Claire's glass before tending to his own.

"You have some good ideas, you know," Michael told her.

Claire kept her eyes on her notes. "They won't budge from mouse models though," she mumbled, because she didn't know what else to say.

"It might be worth having the Beijing lab look into it," Michael replied. That made Claire look at him, because she didn't know that there *was* an associate lab.

"You fund another lab?" Claire couldn't help but ask. "Just how interested in research are you?"

Michael laughed. "Let's just say I'm very interested in one area of research in particular. And I don't just fund another lab; I *own* it, Miss Danvers."

"What do you mean, 'own another lab'? You don't own my parents' lab," Claire replied, suspicious.

Michael glanced at his watch then, and Claire saw a grin slowly spread across his face. "As of precisely two minutes ago, I do," he informed her, throwing her a sidelong glance as he did so. "Didn't your parents tell you about it?" Claire hid behind her hair again to prevent Michael from seeing her looking both annoyed and confused.

"Obviously not," she muttered, then she felt Michael's hand tuck her hair behind her ear.

"Stop hiding from me," he ordered, and Claire was shocked to hear how easily Michael had transitioned from casual conversationalist to full-on authoritarian. Claire made herself match the hard stare he was giving her, willing herself to stand her ground. *Come on, Claire, just tell him to fuck off*, present Claire thought, then abruptly regretted it, for she realised that saying as much would definitely come back to haunt her present. *If I wake up, that is.*

"I can do what I like in my own home," she told Michael, and she felt his hand brush past her own on the table. *How are you not seeing this, you useless parents!* present Claire thought angrily. The Claire in the past edged her hand back slightly, suddenly very nervous about what was going on, but Michael's hand followed it.

He grinned at her, his eyes bright with interest. "Maybe I should get you out of your own home, then." *Oh Jesus fucking Christ Michael did not say that to me. How am I supposed to wake up and pretend that he didn't say that to me?!*

"That's an entirely inappropriate thing to say," past Claire said, and present Claire couldn't be prouder of herself. *I think current me would have ended up punching him in the face.*

"You're very, very good-looking, you know."

"And so are you. Doesn't make what you said any less inappropriate." *Oh no, please tell me I did not just say that,* Claire thought despairingly, though she knew that her past self had said it simply to make a drunken point. *But my God, that was a stupid thing to say.*

Michael's grin only got wider as he continued to look at Claire, and it was all she could do not to turn away.

Eventually Michael broke the silence, but he took his time finishing his glass of wine first, never taking his eyes off of Claire's. "Yes, you're definitely interesting," he said, almost to himself. And then, "Joanna, it's been a pleasure as always, but I really should be getting back to my hotel. I have a very early flight in the morning." It was only when Michael spoke to her that Claire's mother turned her attention to the two of them, and she frowned slightly. *A bit late now, mother,* Claire thought bitterly. Michael stood up and Claire's parents followed suit. Because she didn't want to get into a fight about manners with her mother at one in the morning, Claire reluctantly did so as well.

"Are you sure you wouldn't rather stay here for the night, Michael?" her mother asked him as they made their way through the hall. "I could drive you to the airport in the morning." Michael smiled a flawless smile at her; one which he hadn't bothered using on Claire because she would never have fallen for it.

"I'm sure I would love that," Michael replied, and he threw an almost imperceptible glance at Claire that neither of her parents noticed. "But you'll still be over the limit in four hours Joanna, and my driver is waiting for me outside already." Joanna pouted at him, then gave him a hug. Claire watched her father begrudgingly shake Michael's hand, and then Michael turned to Claire, which she had been dreading with a passion ever since they had entered the hallway. "It's been a pleasure, Miss Danvers," he told her, and he leant in and kissed her on the cheek. Claire flinched, but Michael put a hand on her back to prevent her from leaning away. "I'm quite certain I'll be seeing you again," he murmured into Claire's ear, for nobody to hear but her, and then he was gone.

When her mother had left the hallway, Claire muttered, "I hate him," just to hear herself say it out loud.

"I hate him too, sweetheart," her father replied from behind her, giving her a hug before sending her to bed.

And now Claire could feel her consciousness beginning to stir, just as she decided that she would quite happily never wake up again, because her head was full of things that her mother had, quite rightly, told her should never fall into the hands of the one person definitely waiting for her to wake up.

I don't want to wake up, I don't want to wake up, I don't want to – but then, because she didn't want to, Claire woke up.

CHAPTER 37
Time Is Running Out

Ichi

Ichi was the only one by Claire's bedside when she woke up, three days after she had collapsed in the first place. She was dazed and disoriented at first, eyes barely open as she rolled her head from side to side; Ichi wondered whether she was simply going to fall unconscious again. But then Claire sat up suddenly, eyes wide as she finally noticed Ichi sitting on the side of her bed.

"Claire, you're naked, don't do that," Ichi told her, pulling the covers up for Claire's sake as he did so. "Well, except for that damn necklace; the catch is caught in your hair." But Claire didn't seem to care; her eyes had filled with tears as she looked at Ichi, and then she threw her arms around his neck. "Claire, what the –"

"I'm sorry!" Claire interrupted, sobbing onto his shoulder. "I'm sorry, Ichi, I'm so sorry, I'm sorry –"

"Okay, I get it," Ichi said, though he was fairly certain that he didn't. "You're sorry. What for?" But Claire didn't reply, choosing instead to kiss him with trembling lips. Ichi realised that she was shaking all over. Frowning, he gently pulled Claire away. He tilted her head up with a finger under her chin and said, "Claire, what's wrong? What happened?" Claire shook her head sadly, but then she closed her eyes and took several deep breaths to try and calm herself.

When she eventually opened her eyes again, Claire had stopped crying and seemed altogether more like herself. "I'm not...I'm not okay, Ichi," she finally said, her voice quiet and cracked from disuse. Ichi left her bedside for a moment to pour her a glass of water, which Claire gratefully took. When she was finished drinking it, she asked, "What's the time?"

Ichi frowned at her. "About ten in the morning. Why?"

Ignoring his question, Claire asked another of her own. "Do you have a pen and some paper?"

Ichi raised his eyebrows at the absurd question. "I'm sure there's some in this lab." And then, again: "Why?"

"Please just get some, Ichi. Please." So Ichi did as he was told, more confused than ever as to what was happening in Claire's head. He riffled through several drawers in the lab, then kicked open the door to the doctor's office to retrieve a pen and paper from her desk. When he returned, Claire said, "That was overly dramatic." Ichi was relieved to see a very faint smile play across her lips.

"I got impatient," he replied off-handedly. Claire was silent for a while as she wrote several things down on the paper, then ripped off some of what she had written and put it into the pocket of Ichi's leather jacket. Then she hugged him tightly again.

"That's the code for the lab," she whispered into his ear.

"And why do I need that?" he asked, keeping his voice as low as Claire's was.

"I need you to come back in here when the doctor or Michael aren't around to let you in. When are they both normally away from the lab for the night?"

Ichi frowned slightly at the question. "The doctor tends to be gone by nine or ten in the evening. Michael's usually in his office or his rooms, so…Claire, what are you wanting me to do?" Claire kissed him again; Ichi could taste the salt from her tears on her lips.

"K-kill me," she stammered, and Ichi couldn't believe what he was hearing. "Kill me," Claire repeated, a little stronger this time, "Or get me the hell out of here." Ichi pulled Claire away from him very slightly to look at her again.

"Why are you asking me to do this?"

Ichi didn't think he had ever seen Claire look as vulnerable as she did now as she replied, "Because I'm not strong enough to do either…but *you* are." She ran a shaking hand through Ichi's hair, holding the covers up against her chest with the other. She gave Ichi the saddest smile he had ever seen. "I can't stay here anymore. I can't. So please, come back here at midnight and do what you have to do. Just…end it for me, one way or the other."

Ichi didn't know what to say, so he kissed her furiously instead. He pushed Claire back against the bed and she let him do so. He bit into her neck and shoulders, of half a mind to rip the diamond necklace away, then ran kisses down her chest and back up again to her mouth. But when he looked into Claire's beautiful blue eyes, he could see that something had changed. She was looking at him differently, as if he had unknowingly done something to alter her opinion of him.

"Claire, what's going on in your head?" he asked, his voice rough and unsteady against her lips.

Claire let out half a sob before she managed to reign it back in. "If you get me out of here, I'll tell you."

But before Ichi could press the issue any further, he heard a cough behind him and turned to see Vic standing awkwardly by the door with the doctor. Ichi hadn't even heard them come in. He looked back at Claire, and he saw that her expression had changed again; now she looked determined and resolute. She kissed Ichi gently again. "Come back later, okay?" she said, so Ichi turned away from her and bowled past Vic and the doctor for the corridor behind him. As he made his way up to the twelfth floor, Ichi wondered how he could possibly make the decision Claire was asking him to make, and what could possibly have happened to her to make her ask Ichi to make it in the first place.

Vic

Claire was awake. Finally, after three days, she was awake. And Vic hadn't been the first person to talk to her, which as he entered the lab Vic was certain was going to be his downfall. But when Ichi locked eyes with him, it became apparent that Claire hadn't told the other man anything about Vic, and how he had been John for a time. *I might be able to save you yet, princess,* Vic thought, not daring to hope.

412

He allowed the doctor to fuss over Claire's heart rate and blood pressure for a minute or two, waiting for the woman to vacate the room so that Vic could have some privacy with Claire. He mentally noted that he would have to bring some clothes down for Claire now that she was awake; Claire was currently clinging onto the white sheets that were the only thing protecting her decency as if her life depended on it.

When the doctor finally left the two of them alone, Vic smiled at Claire as he sat down on her bed, knowing that he'd have to get as close as possible to talk to her as *quietly* as possible; after all, this was a conversation that Michael absolutely could not hear. "Hey, princess," he said after a few moments of silence, and the tension in the air that Vic hadn't even realised was there was broken. Claire let out a shaky laugh as she reached out a hand to take a hold of Vic's. Her hand was shaking just as badly as her laugh had been, so Vic closed his fingers around Claire's as tightly as possible to help ground her.

"Hey, stranger," she replied, and Vic thought for a moment that she was going to cry.

"Claire…" Vic began, but his voice trailed off when he saw the look on Claire's face.

"*Don't*," she warned. "Don't you dare apologise."

"But –"

"No, Vic!" Claire interrupted, loud enough that Vic had half a mind to cover her mouth to keep her quiet. Claire sighed, rubbing her temple with her left hand as she did so. "I don't mean to be angry…sorry," she added on, much quieter this time. She looked up at Vic. "You have a lot of explaining to do, but it can wait."

Vic frowned at her. "It can?"

"Yes," Claire replied, her voice calm and certain. Then she ripped a piece of paper that she had written all over in half, folding the two pieces over themselves before giving them both to Vic. "The larger one is for you, Vic; read it as soon as you leave the lab, okay?"

Vic nodded his assent. "And the other one?" Claire laughed at that, ringing alarm bells in Vic's head because it made her sound a little insane.

"That's for the big, bad boss. Can you give it to him just after midnight?"

"Why?" Vic asked, knowing that the extreme confusion he was feeling was written plain as day across his face.

"Because I'm asking you to," Claire replied simply. "But don't read it; you owe me that much, Vic."

"Why is it that when you finally have a request for me it's to *not* do something you know I'll badly want to do?"

Claire smiled at him and squeezed his hand. "Good thing I have a much bigger request for you to deal with, then."

Vic leant in closer to Claire. "And that would be?"

Claire took a second to breathe in deeply. "You need to help me get Ichi out of here."

Vic looked at her, shell-shocked. *That was not what I was expecting her to say at all.* But Claire was deathly serious; Vic could tell by the look in her eyes. "Why does he need help getting out of here?" Vic eventually asked. Claire glanced at the paper in his hands, and understanding dawned on Vic as she did so. *Okay, so these are instructions. How very prepared of you, princess.*

Claire brought a hand up to Vic's face; she ran it up through his hair before collapsing against his chest, crying. "Claire? Hey, Claire! What's wrong?" Vic asked, all thoughts of Ichi lost to the wind.

Claire glanced up at him through thick, wet eyelashes. "I always wanted to do that," Claire whispered.

"Do what, princess?" Vic replied softly.

"Run my hand through your hair," she said. "You did it all the time, before. I always wondered what it would feel like to do it myself." Vic kissed her forehead before holding onto her tightly, knowing more than ever that he would save Ichi for Claire, because he loved her and he would do anything for her...even if that *anything* involved helping out his psychotic love rival.

"You can play with my hair as much as you want, Claire. You know I'd do anything for you."

"Then you'll do it? Help me save Ichi?" Claire murmured into his chest. She lifted her head up to look at Vic, and she looked genuinely hopeful. Vic tried to ignore the fact that that hope was all for Ichi, and not for him.

"Of course I will," he replied, and Claire breathed a sigh of relief. Then she gave him a look of eternal gratitude and mouthed the words *thank you*.

Vic didn't think that he had ever hated Ichi more than in that moment.

Claire

Once Vic had left, Claire collapsed against her pillows, sighing. She was barely keeping it together, and she knew it. *But I have to organise everything, otherwise it won't work,* Claire thought. *And if it doesn't work then I will never get out of here, alive or dead.* She closed her eyes, wishing that she had more than thirteen hours to work with but knowing that that was impossible.

When Claire opened her eyes again, she was distinctly aware of the fact that she must have fallen asleep; it felt like she had lost some of the precious time that she had left to her. Claire clutched the covers to her chest, wondering how long Vic would be with some of her clothes. She scanned the room around her, just in case he had brought them down but hadn't wanted to disturb her sleep, but couldn't see anything that resembled a pile of fabric. On the opposite wall, Claire saw the dress that she had worn to the awards ball hanging up, looking beautiful and innocuous on its hanger. Then Claire put a hand on the necklace still lying heavily against her breastbone.

I want this damn thing off, she thought, bringing her hands around to the back of her neck to attempt to undo to catch. But Ichi had been right; it was caught up in several strands of her hair – too many for her to simply pull the necklace away to break them. Claire dragged a hand over her face, exasperated by this one, tiny thing that she couldn't think her way out of. Then she heard the door to the lab click open, followed by the sound of footsteps.

"I'm sure you have much bigger things to worry about than getting that off, Miss Danvers," Michael said casually as he closed the gap between himself and Claire. Then he stood by her bedside, regarding her critically in silence, as if waiting for Claire to say something.

Claire realised that she didn't have the energy to be polite to Michael at that particular moment in time. "Go away," she told him, not looking at him as she said so. Michael chuckled, then Claire heard the scrape of chair legs on the tiled floor that meant Michael most definitely intended *not* to go away. It was only after he had sat down by her side that Claire glanced over at him. "You finally decided I could wake up, then," she said flatly.

Michael's eyes seemed to glitter with amusement as he replied simply, "Yes." Claire said nothing in response, because she didn't trust herself not to give anything away about her returned memories. Eventually, Michael asked, "What do you remember before you fell unconscious?"

"Everything," Claire replied, laughing internally at the fact that she had indeed just told Michael that her memories had returned, if he chose to look at her answer that way.

Michael frowned slightly. "What happened at the awards ceremony, from your perspective? I've had reports from Ichi and Vic, but they are decidedly…biased." Claire wondered for a moment what had happened between the two men after she ran away from Ichi and then, later, collapsed.

Claire decided to give as succinct an answer as possible. "I got drunk," she said, "and got into an argument with Ichi. Then I ran off towards the closest selection of hard spirits that I could find and drank some more, and then I passed out."

"Something tells me that that is an incredibly edited version of what happened to you."

"Forgive me for not jumping at the opportunity to provide you with information that, for once, you don't actually have." Claire was satisfied to see that she seemed to have struck a nerve with Michael. *The way I'm feeling now, I'm tempted to flat-out tell him to fuck off, like I should have done back when I was eighteen.*

But Michael seemed to have picked up on her thoughts, for he raised an eyebrow and said, "You don't seem to be in the most cooperative of moods, Miss Danvers."

Claire rolled her eyes. "You had me put in a coma."

"I sent two men out to kill you ten months ago; surely that's far worse?"

Claire let out a bark of laughter and made to run a hand through her hair; it was only in lifting her arm that she remembered that doing so would allow the sheets covering her to fall, so she quickly put it back down. "You sent two men out to *kidnap* me – there's a difference," she corrected. Claire figured that informing Michael that she knew her assassination had been a sham was probably not the best idea she had ever had, but at this point she found that she didn't care. Michael leant forward in interest.

"Vic told you that just after you arrived here, if I recall."

Claire rolled her eyes again. "Look at me naively forgetting that you watch over everything that happens here." She paused, thinking back on the memory. "He wanted me to know that Ichi was being played and never had any control over what happened to me from the very beginning."

"How noble of him to tell you." *I wonder if Vic ever got into trouble for telling me,* Claire thought, deciding that if her plan didn't go awry then she would ask Vic about it herself. *Not that it matters anymore, I suppose.* Claire glanced up at Michael through strands of hair that she was itching to brush away from her face – he was leaning slightly to one side against the chair's left arm rest, chin propped up on his hand. Claire thought that it appeared as if Michael happened slept; there were dark shadows under his eyes. He frowned at her. "Why are you staring at me as if you hope I won't notice?" Claire felt her cheeks grow warm, and was suddenly very glad of all of the hair in front of her face.

"Did my being asleep really cause you to lose so much of your own? I'd be flattered, if you weren't the homicidal psychopath who had me kidnapped." But before anything else could be said – and it looked to Claire as if Michael had *a lot* to say in response – Roger came in through the door, carrying a tray of food. The man gave Claire a smile.

"You need to eat, Sleeping Beauty," he said, placing the tray down in her lap. It was only soup and bread, but Claire realised that that was probably about all she could stomach right now in the first place.

"I agree; she's in a terrible mood," Michael commented. Claire ignored him.

She looked up at Roger. "Thank you," she said, pulling the sheets covering her up a little higher before picking up the bowl to drink directly from it. She saw out of the corner of her eye that Michael had noticed her doing so.

Roger gave her another smile before turning to Michael. "Alexis caught me on my way down here – she needs to speak to you." Claire couldn't help but flinch slightly at the mention of her sister's name; she sincerely hoped that Michael hadn't noticed.

Michael waved a hand dismissively at nobody in particular. "Tell her she can wait, Roger. I think I'll keep Miss Danvers company whilst she eats."

"Fantastic," Claire replied scathingly.

Roger raised two bushy eyebrows at her before laughing loudly. "I really had missed your sarcasm in the rec hall, dear!"

"I rather missed being conscious," Claire replied quietly, and Roger's grin disappeared.

"I can see that this is a serious conversation I'm interrupting," he said. He walked towards the door before turning to look at Claire one more time. "No scrimping on your food, Miss Danvers – you need it all, okay? And be careful with *him* –" Roger pointed to Michael, who smiled wanly, "– since he's liable to devour you whole if you keep speaking to him like that."

Michael laughed humourlessly at Roger's comment, but Claire could tell that he agreed with every word of it. "Consider myself warned," Claire said, and then: "Thanks again, Roger," as the man exited the lab.

And then there was silence for a while as Claire delicately drank her soup, being particularly careful to ensure that her covers did not fall. Eventually, because she couldn't take Michael simply staring at her any more, she asked, "What was it about my mother that you liked so much?" Claire was gratified to see that the question had taken Michael by surprise.

"What makes you think that I liked her in the first place?"

"Just an assumption," Claire replied. She looked down into her almost-empty bowl. "She was pretty much a full-on bitch to me after I turned sixteen, so I forget sometimes that she's generally a lovely person to everybody else."

Michael laughed; Claire grew uneasy when she noticed that he had pulled his chair in a little closer to her side. "And why did that happen?" Michael asked. Claire threw him a look, wondering whether it was dangerous to continue the current topic of conversation. *But so long as I can keep Michael talking about anything* other *than what happened on the night I collapsed, then I don't care what we talk about,* Claire thought, resolute. *I might even get some answers as to what my parents did to Michael in the first place.* But Claire wasn't particularly expecting much on that front, considering everything she had learned of Michael's twisted personality so far.

She sighed. "My dad said it was because I was reminding her too much of herself, back when she was my age."

"He would be correct; I do recall telling you on several occasions that you're a lot like her."

"You never specified that you meant I was like my mother when she was *younger*," Claire argued. Michael shrugged his shoulders slightly as if the clarification didn't matter to him. Claire turned away from him, thinking hard about the comparison between herself and her mother.

"Don't disappear off into your head, Miss Danvers," she vaguely heard Michael warn her.

She glanced back at him through her hair. "But I'm not that much like her; not really."

"How could you possibly know that? Obviously you never knew her when she was your age."

Claire laughed bitterly. "I didn't have to; she was always so driven by a genuine desire to help other people – it's all anybody ever said about her as I grew up. But I never had that desire…all I wanted to do was please her and my dad, so I tried to follow in their footsteps. All I managed to do was make her hate me." Claire paused, because she realised that tears were stinging her eyes. *I am not going to cry in front of him,* Claire repeated to herself over and over again, until the stinging subsided.

Michael watched her with growing interest. "That sounds slightly melodramatic," he said. "Although, knowing Joanna, it may have actually been true." Claire gave him a look, because she knew that Michael wasn't going to elaborate on just how well he had known her mother. "You can't have only bad memories of her," he added on quietly as an afterthought.

"Of course I don't," Claire replied, staring at the almost-empty bowl in front of her. She carefully moved it and the tray it was on over to the small table on her left hand side. She closed her eyes for a moment. "There was this one time when I was five, and it's such a stupid thing that I don't even know why I remember it," Claire eventually said. "I was in the park with my mother eating ice cream, even though it was so cold outside, but that's when we always ate it, even when I got older."

Claire paused, almost smiling at the idea, but then she remembered who she was talking to and the vaguely-realised smile disappeared. *Why am I even telling him this in the first place?* Claire wondered, but she knew that Michael wouldn't let her stop her story halfway through now that she had started it. So she continued, keeping her head down as she spoke. "It was my favourite thing about winter; eating ice cream in the snow with my mother. But this one time, I dropped mine on the ice because I kept watching everyone else in the park. 'For God's sake Claire!' she told me, 'look at what you're doing rather than looking at strangers!' But then she shared her ice cream with me anyway. And – and then…" Claire let the sentence trail off as she realised the terrible mistake that she had just made, for now, with her perfect recall of everything that had ever happened to her, Claire knew that she hadn't been watching every stranger in the park; only one in particular. *And of course it's Michael, because that's just how my life fucking works now, isn't it?* Claire thought despairingly. In her head, late-teenage Michael looked so young compared to his current self, and he had watched Claire and her mother with a sullen face before finally coming over to talk to them.

"And then…?" Michael asked, forcing Claire out of her head again. Claire didn't think she could face looking at him.

"And then nothing," Claire said. "She was wonderful to me until I got really into genetics. I have all of these happy memories of her, but I guess it's just the bad ones that are stuck in my head right now. Can't say I blame myself for that, considering what my parents have landed me in." There was silence then, and Claire willed Michael to be satisfied with her half-lie with all of her might.

"You met me before," Michael finally said, and Claire felt her heart plummet into her stomach. "When you were eighteen," Michael continued. "Do you —"

"I remember," Claire interrupted, grabbing onto something that was much more logical for her to remember now, at twenty-three. She glanced up to see Michael looking at her suspiciously.

"You've never mentioned anything about it prior to now."

"I didn't want to. I wish I *had* forgotten it," Claire replied, because she sincerely wanted it to have never happened in the first place.

"You rather convinced me that you had never seen me before when you were first brought here."

Claire tried to keep her face as blank as possible as she forced herself to match Michael's stare. "I was terrified; forgive me for not immediately recalling I had met you several years prior when I was drunk."

Michael chuckled. "You weren't drunk when I initially arrived." Claire didn't respond, because Michael was correct. She fished around in her brain for something else to say instead.

"I had thought it was strange, for my mum to introduce you as an old friend, when you were so much younger than her," Claire finally managed, attempting to steer the conversation away from further suspicion over her memories returning.

Michael looked at her as if he knew exactly what Claire was doing. "Twelve and a half years younger, to be precise," he replied. He flashed an amused grin at Claire. "Around the same age difference between the two of us, interestingly enough." Claire felt her stomach squirm uncomfortably at the comment, but it disappeared as she came to a sudden realisation.

"You met my mother when you were a child," she said, knowing it to be true as she said it.

Michael raised an eyebrow at her. "You're very sharp."

"No, I just put some very obvious pieces of information together," Claire replied. "That's not being sharp; it's called using your common sense."

"Something many people lack these days."

Claire clung onto the topic with everything she had, hoping to turn the conversation away from herself once and for all. "Did you hate my dad?" she asked.

"Ha!" Michael let out, genuine laughter playing across his lips. "What a question."

But he didn't make an effort to answer it, so Claire asked another. "Did you love my mother?"

Michael glanced up at the ceiling, looking as close to pensive as Claire thought was possible for the man. "Possibly," he replied.

Claire frowned at him. "That's not a full answer."

"And who are you to tell me how to answer that question?"

"Are you going to kill her?" Claire blurted out before she could stop herself, and she brought a hand up to cover her mouth after the words came out, horrified.

Michael smiled dangerously at her. "Probably. I'll kill your father first though. Did you really want to hear the answer to that question?"

"Possibly."

"I thought you deemed that an inappropriate response?"

Claire looked away from him. "I changed my mind," she muttered, and she realised that she couldn't deal with the fake-casual conversation that she was having anymore. Claire brought her hands up to drag her hair away from her face, thinking that the sheets covering her couldn't possibly fall in the second it would take her to complete the action. But her hair snagged painfully on the necklace that was already caught up in it, and Claire winced before bringing her arms down as quickly as possible.

Michael was out of his chair and leaning over her before Claire had an opportunity to blink, lacing a hand through her hair when he got there. "What are you –" Claire began to say, startled, then panicked herself into silence when Michael brought out a knife. Claire tried to push him away, but Michael kept his grip on her hair nonetheless. He grinned at her, then brought the knife behind Claire's neck and cut through the hairs caught in the necklace in one fluid motion. Then he undid the catch, and the heavy piece of jewellery slipped down over Claire's breastbone to rest somewhere on her navel, beneath the sheets.

Michael pushed Claire back against the bed, removing his knife from behind her neck as he did so. He fixed her with a hard stare until Claire forced herself to match it. Her mind had gone completely blank; she had no idea what she was supposed to do.

"You're lying to me, Miss Danvers," Michael informed her in an undertone. Claire could feel him remove the hand that was entwined in her hair in order to trace the line of her collarbone. "You'd be wise to tell me everything that you remember before things…escalate."

"How could things possibly escalate further than they have done already?!" Claire bit out. She was terrified by the look in Michael's grey eyes; she had seen the same look in them when she was eighteen. Michael smirked at her as he allowed his hand to snake down Claire's front to retrieve the necklace; his fingertips moved slowly and softly across her skin. Claire felt her breath catch in her throat. *No, no, no! What's happening here? What am I supposed to do?!*

But then Michael curled his fingers around the necklace and brought it back up, very deliberately brushing against Claire's breasts as he did so. "Oh, I think if you piece some *very obvious pieces of information* together, you can work it out." Michael's face was far too close to Claire's by this point; she could feel strands of his ordinarily impeccably swept-back hair brushing her forehead. He watched her carefully, waiting to see if she would do or say anything. It reminded her horribly of a time when Ichi had done the exact same thing to her, back in the abominable classroom, and she felt herself panic even more than she already was at the very thought of the memory. *Please,* Claire begged silently. *Don't let him do anything to me. Please oh please oh please…what did I ever do to deserve this?*

It was all Claire could do not to breathe a very obvious sigh of relief when Michael finally stepped away from her. He wandered over to the door without a word, bent down to retrieve something, then came back to her bedside.

"I almost forgot," Michael began, as if the last five minutes had never happened. "Vic brought down some clothes for you; I told him I'd bring them in." He placed a bag on Claire's lap, and Claire clutched it to her chest as soon as he let it go.

Claire took as deep a breath as she dared to, to try and steady her nerves. "…you could have led with that," she mumbled, not trusting her voice.

Michael laughed. "And what kind of hot-blooded male, when faced with a beautiful naked female, leads with the statement 'I have some clothes for you'? You're more naïve than I thought, Miss Danvers." Claire didn't want to look up at him, but she instinctively knew that Michael wouldn't go away until she did. She brought her eyes up to his very slowly; Michael's expression was serious again. "By all means," he continued, "Delay giving me the answers I want from you for as long as you wish; it will only prolong the length of time that I have to allow things to *escalate*." He paused, cocking his head to one side slightly as he watched Claire.

"Are you done?" Claire finally said, remembering as she uttered them that they also belonged to that horrific memory of Ichi in the classroom.

"How cold of you, Miss Danvers, to use those words on me," Michael remarked, causing a shiver to run down Claire's spine at the idea that Michael knew where the statement came from. "At least come up with something different to say…I feel like I should have earned some originality from you by now." Then he walked back over to the door, turning to face Claire just as Roger had done earlier when he reached it. "Take some time to seriously consider how long you think it's wise to lie to me. I'm sure you know that we'll be picking up this conversation far sooner than you would probably like."

And then he was gone, leaving Claire struggling to process the last half hour of her life. *I'm running out of time, I'm running out of time,* she kept thinking, finally beginning to fully realise what a terrible mistake it had been to pin all of her hopes of escape onto the man who, without his memories, was just as deplorable as Michael himself.

CHAPTER 38
Torn

Ichi

Ichi still didn't know how to deal with the request Claire had made, and it was fast approaching ten in the evening. *I have two hours left and I'm no closer to figuring out what I'm going to do,* Ichi thought, frustrated. He had weighed up the pros and cons of both options Claire had given him whilst mindlessly exercising in the gym, then mindlessly eating in the rec hall and, finally, mindlessly throwing knives into equally mindless, empty targets. He had packed and unpacked a bag holding everything he'd need to run away with Claire ten times over, only to turn to his knives and sharpen them methodically instead. He had also arranged getaway cars to use across the mainland should they ever reach it; after all, if he was going to escape with Claire then he had to do it properly, otherwise Ichi would merely be signing his own death warrant and dooming Claire to a captivity she could no longer stand.

Ichi's pro and con list for killing Claire ran as follows:

Pros

I finally get to kill her.

If she's dead I don't have to obsess over her any more.

It would piss everybody off.

I get to slice into her body and watch her slowly bleed to death for all of the crap she's made me go through.

She can't choose Vic over me if she's dead.

I finally get to kill her.

Cons

I can't have sex with her if she's dead.

She's probably the only person I enjoy conversing with, and I can't do that if she's dead.

There's no guarantee I won't still obsess over her once she's dead.

There's no turning back if I kill her.

Vic or Michael will probably kill me.

She's actually okay with me doing it.

His pro and con list for running away with Claire was much simpler:

Pros

She doesn't have to die.

I get to be with her.

Cons

She wouldn't necessarily stay with me.

Vic or Michael will probably kill me.

Ichi sighed. He knew that, when it came right down to it, his decision rested entirely on whether he truly wanted Claire to remain alive. Everything else was purely hypothetical, since Ichi couldn't possibly know exactly what would happen after he chose to either kill her or help her escape. He threw his currently-packed bag against the wall, infuriated.

"This shouldn't be so fucking hard," Ichi muttered under his breath, though he knew that it was probably the most important, and therefore most difficult, decision he had ever had to make in his life. He knew that the *correct* answer was to help Claire escape. However, there was that ever-incessant voice in the back of his head telling him that he had wanted to destroy Claire from the very beginning. Even now, that cold, primal desire of his to see the life drain from her eyes was causing Ichi to reach out for his favourite knife once more, desperate to see its blade stained crimson.

But then Ichi glanced over at his bed, thinking of the many nights he had spent in it with Claire over the past couple of months, and his resolve to kill her vanished. *How can I even be contemplating doing something like that?* Ichi criticised. *Am I really so fucked up in the head that I can't see past the initial high I'd get from taking Claire's life? In the long run, I gain far more from keeping Claire alive.*

Ichi knew that every thought he was having on the matter was purely selfish, though he also knew why that was. Because if he thought about what Claire would want, Ichi found that he kept drawing a blank. He stood up to pace his room, restless with his indecision. *If running away was truly preferable to dying as I would reasonably assume,* Ichi thought, *Then Claire would have simply asked me to help her escape. By giving me the choice to either break her out of here or kill her, she made it clear that both options were equally as appealing. Which means...*

"Which means that there's something about staying alive that Claire would rather die to avoid," Ichi finished aloud. He crashed onto his bed, running a hand over his face in exasperation. *How am I supposed to make this decision in one night?* And then Ichi looked up at the ceiling, staring at nothing for a long time. He didn't want to think about what was bothering him most, but it kept creeping back up on him.

How could you ask me to make this decision in the first place, Claire? Ichi was supposed to be the awful human being – the one who was expected to say cruel things and act despicably. Not *Claire.* Never Claire. Ichi was struggling to come to terms with the fact that she had given him no reasonable explanation as to why *he* had to be the one to make the decision. *Why not Vic, after all?* Ichi pondered. *He would help you escape in a heartbeat, no doubt about it, and you wouldn't have to risk dying at my hands for it.* Ichi didn't want Claire to do that, of course, since that would mean that she had chosen Vic over himself, and Ichi reckoned that such a decision might make him go insane. *I'd end up pursuing them and killing them both, and maybe Claire knows that.*

In that respect, Ichi was glad that Claire had at least gone to him rather than to Vic for help, but knowing that didn't make his decision any easier. He sighed. *What is it that you've remembered that's worth dying for,*

Claire? And would I agree with you if I knew? He glanced at the time on his phone. *11.03pm. Wonderful.*

Ichi closed his eyes for a moment, bracing himself for whichever decision it was that he would make in less than an hour's time. *Fifty-seven minutes to go and counting. Let's see just how deplorable a human being I truly am.*

Vic

After having read Claire's instructions, Vic was left speechless. He sat on his bed, head overloaded with so many drastically differing emotions that Vic wasn't entirely sure how to process them all.

He was relieved; Claire's memories had returned to her, seemingly completely, and even though she must still have had a hundred questions to ask Vic, she chose to trust him entirely. For that Vic was grateful – he didn't know what he could have done to regain Claire's trust if he had managed to fully lose it, which he had been worried was a very real possibility.

Vic was furious. Claire's plan was unnecessarily insane, and all so she could get Ichi out of Michael's complex as well as herself. *It's up to him if he wants to stay and work for Michael,* Vic thought. *So why does she want to risk everything just to get him out of here?* Vic stood up and kicked the wall closest to him in his frustration. *Why can't she just be selfish this one time and focus on getting herself out? What am I missing from the bigger picture that means I can't understand her thought process here?*

Vic was happy, because Claire regaining her memories didn't cause her to have a full-on breakdown, as Vic had become increasingly concerned that she had been heading towards one over the past few weeks. If anything, she seemed far more in control than she had been in a long time. He had always had a lot of respect for Claire, but seeing her manage to work out an escape from nothing had caused that respect to increase drastically. Claire was *strong,* and Vic loved her for it.

But that only made Vic's heartbreak worse, because until he heard directly from Claire why she needed to help Ichi escape from Michael's complex, the only logical conclusion that he could reach was that Claire was doing so because she loved the other man. Vic fell back onto his bed again, sighing heavily. *Even if she* does *love him, I can't blame her. I can't. I wasn't there for her like I should have been.* Vic knew that to be bitterly true; he had been so scared of Claire remembering who Vic had been before she was kidnapped that he hadn't dared to get as close to Claire as he had wanted to over the past ten months. *I dodged her questions and kept her at bay, all because I didn't know what she would do if she remembered. I should have had more faith in her.*

And now it might be too late. But... Vic glanced at Claire's note again. *Whether she's in love with Ichi or not, she knows that he's too dangerous to have around once she's out of here.* He thought back to how he had told Ichi that he was his only ally in the fight to figure out what Michael's full intentions towards Claire were and began to feel just the slightest bit guilty. He shook his head. *I never said he was my ally in keeping Claire safe,* Vic countered, *only in finding out what was going on. And I don't need to do that if I can keep Claire away from here.*

Vic stood up once more, deciding to check in on Claire for one final time before everything went down. He looked at his phone; it was quarter past eleven. *There's really not long left until we see if we truly can outsmart Michael.*

Vic was surprised when he ran almost directly into Ichi when he exited onto the stairwell. "What the –" he exclaimed, just as Ichi called out something similar. The two men took a step back from each other; Vic saw that Ichi looked very slightly out of breath. He raised a suspicious eyebrow. "What are you doing, Ich?"

"Running," Ichi replied simply.

"Can't you do that in the gym?"

Ichi laughed humourlessly. "Not unless I want Ryan to keep talking to me. Which I don't."

Vic gave him a half-smile. "I don't blame you." He paused, regarding Ichi carefully. "Is Claire on your mind?"

Ichi laughed again. "She's always on my mind." Vic blinked twice, surprised by Ichi's honesty. Ichi frowned at him. "What?" he fired at Vic defensively.

Vic shook his head. "Nothing, it's nothing. Just…" He sighed, eyes on the floor. "I just don't understand you, I suppose."

"Join the club," Ichi grumbled, causing Vic to whip his head back up to look at him.

"Excuse me?"

Ichi scratched his head, his frown deepening. "I don't really understand myself right now, either. I don't really *feel* like myself. Or, rather," Ichi stopped to consider his answer, "Whoever I am now is not who I was ten months ago, and I don't know if I'm prepared for that."

"It's called character development, you idiot," Vic reprimanded. "Growing up. Evolution. Whatever. Just grow some balls and let it happen. If you keep regressing out of fear – nah, you definitely don't do anything out of fear – or some selfish, baseless desire to keep things uncomplicated, then you're going to lose her." Vic didn't know when he had found the time to analyse Ichi's behaviour, yet as he said the words he realised that he must have, and it made Vic feel even worse about the idea of abandoning him once the other man had helped Claire escape.

Ichi glared at him. "You think I don't know that?!" he barked, running a hand through his hair as he did so. "I know what she wants me to be, or what she hopes I can truly become, but I can't…people don't just change overnight, Vic." Vic almost laughed at the irony of it all, but he kept it to himself.

He gave Ichi a look. "Well, all you can do is work it out. And if you come to the conclusion that you're not what you should be for Claire, then do her a favour and get out of her life." Ichi rolled his eyes at Vic's request.

"As if I'd do that," he remarked, beginning to head up the stairs as he did so. "You seriously think I'd ever become a decent enough person to leave her alone? Hah…" And with that Ichi was gone, leaving Vic unsure about whether or not he should feel any guilt towards Ichi. *He's done so many despicable things to Claire,* he thought. *I shouldn't have to feel guilty.* But Vic couldn't help but acknowledge that most of the terrible behaviour that Ichi displayed towards Claire had only really occurred in the first few months of her having been a captive in Michael's building. By comparison, he had been a saint ever since Claire had put him in his place in February.

430

Though the good behaviour might only have been because Claire was sleeping with him...

Vic was brought out of his reverie when he almost ran into yet another person, this time Marie. She smiled at him, and Vic almost felt like telling her everything simply because of that smile. But then Marie frowned at him and said, "Don't even think about it, Vic."

Vic raised his hands in feigned ignorance. "Think about what, Marie?"

"Just don't tell me, whatever it is."

Vic fixed her with a serious gaze. "I wish you would let me."

Marie shook her head. "You don't. Because if you tell me, I'll have to tell *him*," she said quietly. "I don't want to tell him, so just don't tell me." Vic reached over and hugged her tightly, and Marie happily reciprocated.

"You're too good for here, you know. I always told you that."

"*You're* the one who's too good for here, Vic, not me," Marie replied. She giggled. "You asking me to run away with you? Don't tempt me."

"Then I won't," Vic mumbled into her hair. "I just...I just wish..." Marie broke away from Vic's arms to look up at him, and her eyes were sad.

"I have a feeling I might not be seeing you again for a long time, Vic."

"I have that feeling too." Then Marie gently squeezed Vic's hand, giving him one last smile before departing up the stairs. When Vic walked down the final two flights to the sub-basement floor, he was surprised to find Alexis lingering in the corridor near the lab; he made his footsteps louder so that she would notice his approach. Alexis glanced over at him, a scowl on her face.

"Do you guys ever leave Claire alone? Imran was just in there talking to her for over *two hours*. Two hours!"

"So why are you still loitering in the corridor, if he's finally left?"

Alexis scowled at him again. "You know I won't go in there."

"And why not?"

"It's...complicated."

Vic crossed his arms, disapproval written all over his face. "It's only complicated because you made it that way. What's so hard about going in there and making sure she's okay?" Alexis' scowl disappeared at the same time as she turned to face away from Vic.

"Because it's too late. Probably." Vic was glad that Alexis had her back turned, because he flinched at the statement. *Has Alexis worked something out about Claire's escape plans? How could she possibly have done that? Or...* Vic felt his face grow cold. *Or is it Michael who's worked something out?*

Vic glanced at his phone; it was after half past eleven. "Well, if you're not going to go in and speak to her, stop hanging around the corridor," Vic said, walking past Alexis towards the lab door. "It's Ichi-level creepy."

"Oh, that burns, Vic," Alexis replied, feigning hurt. She gave him what Vic could almost consider a smile. "Keep looking after her, okay?"

"Always," he said, before turning from her to enter the code for the lab.

CHAPTER 39
Madness

Claire

I've gone insane. I have officially gone mad, Claire thought as she considered the note she had given to Vic to pass on to Michael. *I should never have written that, I should have...* Claire sighed. She had written it before Michael had come in to speak to her, and how could she have known how that conversation was going to go? *Everything I wrote was in a moment of rebelliousness, but that's definitely not how I'm feeling any more,* she lamented, pulling at a stray strand of wool in her favourite, oversized blue jumper as she did so.

The fact that Vic had chosen that jumper, as well as the one t-shirt of his that Claire had inadvertently claimed for herself months ago, as the clothes for her to wear whilst she was down in the lab made Claire smile, despite her situation. *Such classic Vic behaviour, trying to make sure I feel as comfortable as possible.* But now was not a time to be comfortable; now was the time for Claire to worry and cross-examine every decision that she had made that day, and she was beginning to question and regret more and more of them.

Which means I must have lost my mind when I made them, Claire concluded, since it seemed like the only logical answer as to why she would make all of the decisions she had made in the first place. She wondered what the time was, knowing that there couldn't be any longer than an hour left until Ichi had to make the decision to kill Claire or help her escape. Claire shivered at the thought. But she stood resolute about having asked Ichi to make the decision in the first place; he was Claire's best chance for evading Michael without Michael suspecting that it was going to happen. *But knowing Michael, he'll suspect anybody close to me as capable of helping me escape anyway. I just hope he keeps his eyes more on* Vic *than he does on Ichi.*

Though Claire was nervous about what was going to happen when Ichi showed up, it wasn't because she could potentially lose her life – on that front, she was oddly calm. *If I'm dead I don't have to think about any of this anymore. Michael won't get the research in my head and I won't have to betray Ichi.* For that was what she feared the most about him helping her escape – knowing that she was planning to then abandon him in favour of running off with Vic once she was a safe distance from the complex. *I'm a terrible person,* Claire thought, *but I can't deal with having Ichi around until I can fix him. I just need to keep him away from Michael until I've worked out how to do that.* Claire laughed bitterly; everything she had to do once she escaped was horrendously difficult, and she had to do most of it on her own.

But then she saw Vic through the glass door and the knot in her stomach subsided a little. *He'll do everything he possibly can to help me...maybe I* won't *have to do most of it on my own.* Claire felt abruptly stupid for thinking that it might be better to have Ichi simply kill her now. *If he kills me then I can't fix him, and I can't make sure that Olivia is kept safe, and I can't try to talk some sense into Alexis.* She glanced up at Vic as he entered the door and smiled. *And I can't get to know Vic for precisely who he is, either.* All of these were wishes she very much wanted to come true, and suddenly Claire was filled with an overwhelming desire to stay alive.

"I didn't know you knew the code for the door," she told Vic as he came over and sat beside her.

"There are perks to having worked for Michael for so long," he replied. Vic wasn't smiling; the look on his face worried Claire to no end. *Has something gone wrong?* Claire couldn't help but wonder. *Has Michael figured something out?!* But before Claire could vocalise any of her worries, Vic took her hands in both of his and rested his forehead down on top of them.

"Vic...?" Claire ventured, but she stopped talking when Vic made a soft shushing sound; it tickled the skin on her hands as it left his lips, and Claire abruptly felt her face heat up.

"Are you sure about everything, princess?" Vic mumbled against her hands, a barely audible question that Michael's security cameras would struggle to pick up.

Claire smiled down at Vic even though he couldn't see it. "As sure as I'll ever be, Vic," she replied, gently extricating her hands from underneath his as she spoke. The movement caused Vic to sit back up, and Claire was shocked to see that his pale blue eyes were overly bright.

"And what about after everything? What about your future? Are you sure about that?" Claire struggled not to flinch. Vic didn't know exactly what she had asked Ichi to do, and she didn't plan on telling him. And yet even so, there was something in Vic's tone of voice, in the shine of his eyes, which suggested that he knew Claire most definitely wasn't sure whether she would still be alive when the day ended.

So Claire brought her hands up to run them through Vic's hair, and he leant willingly into the motion. Then she kissed him gently, and Vic's eyes opened in shock. "Of course," Claire said, hiding the lie behind a radiant smile that her mother would have been proud of. "I want that first date with John, after all. Hope he doesn't mind that I stood him up for nearly a year." Vic laughed softly; a genuine sound that reminded Claire of how much he had laughed with her when she had first been kidnapped. Claire realised just how rarely the man had laughed over the past few months, and she was filled with pre-emptive regret that she may never be able to hear Vic's laugh again. So Claire kissed him again, this time on his forehead, and then on the tip of his nose, and eventually she showered him with light, fluttering kisses all over his face that had Vic spluttering with laughter.

"I'm sure he won't mind that you stood him up, princess," Vic eventually managed to get out between chuckles. "I'm fairly certain that he'd wait years and years for you." His words made the atmosphere in the room return to something much heavier, and Vic sighed. Claire watched him glance at his phone. "I better go," he told her, keeping his head down as he spoke.

Claire felt her stomach tie up in knots. "What time is it, Vic?"

"Quarter to midnight," Vic replied, not looking at her.

It was Claire's turn to sigh. "I better try to get some sleep, then," she lied, and Vic stood up and began to walk away. It was only as he took his final few steps towards the door that Claire remembered her note to Michael once more. "Ah, Vic, wait!" Claire called out after him, so Vic paused in his tracks and turned to face her.

"What is it, princess?"

But Claire couldn't get the words out to ask him to destroy the message she had given him; they simply wouldn't leave her lips. "I –" she began, and then: "Um, ah…" *Damn it, why can't I ask him?* Claire thought, frustrated.

Vic raised a curious eyebrow. "What is it?"

Claire sighed, defeated. But then she thought of something else to say. "The Lambert glacier," she murmured, smiling slightly, "That's the largest glacier in the world, right?"

Vic looked confused for a moment, but then a grin spread across his face as understanding came to him. "I asked you if you knew the answer to that months ago."

Claire nodded. "You were testing me, right?"

Vic laughed softly. "Guess you passed…eventually." He gave Claire one final smile. And then, though he was clearly not entirely convinced that Claire's question had been the one she originally wanted to vocalise, Vic left.

Claire collapsed against her pillows, hating herself. *If I get out of here alive, baiting Michael is something I will one hundred percent regret.* And yet it was too late to change her mind now; clearly some part of her had decided that the risk was worth it, even though most of her knew that it was absolutely not. Then Claire felt her skin grow cold.

If I get out of here alive. If I get out of here alive. It was a big *if*, and Claire was now more determined than ever to survive. *I'll happily spend the rest of my life repaying Ichi for getting me out of here alive.* But she had to betray him first, and Claire was dreading that more than anything else in what was left of her potentially frightfully short life span.

Ichi

It was time, and Ichi still hadn't made a decision. It was time, yet he was no closer to working out if what he *should* do and what he *wanted* to do could line up. But what he did know was that, no matter how much time was given to him, Ichi would never be one hundred percent certain that his decision would be the right one.

He looked at his phone. *Five to midnight. Let's do this...whatever 'this' is.* Ichi roughly slung his bag onto his back then carefully placed his knives into the inner pockets of his leather jacket. He added a gun for good measure. Ichi's favourite knife, the one he had intended to kill Claire with in the first place, he slid into a sheath on his hip. Then he grabbed a chair from beside his dining table and left his room for the elevator. As he passed Claire's room, however, he paused. *Regardless of what happens, that won't be 'Claire's room' anymore; it'll go back to being room 1202.* Ichi laughed ruefully. *And mine will go back to being room 1201...it's not like I'll be coming back here again, regardless of my decision.*

It took the elevator what felt like an age to arrive at the twelfth floor, and Ichi clucked his tongue in impatience, despite the impending decision that was waiting for him on the sub-basement floor. When the elevator finally arrived, Ichi rushed into it, dragging the chair behind him. He stabbed the sub-basement floor button, hoping against hope that nobody else would enter the lift whilst he was in it as the doors slid shut.

Do I kill her or do I let her live? Do I escape with her or run off on my own, leaving her in a pool of her own blood? Ichi felt like he was indulging in some macabre version of pulling the petals from daisies, except 'I love her, I love her not' was replaced with something far more final.

And then, before Ichi knew it, the elevator doors pinged open onto the sub-basement floor, and Ichi knew he had run out of time. Hands shaking slightly with pre-emptive adrenaline, Ichi lodged the chair he had brought down with him between the elevator doors, preventing them from closing, and stalked purposefully down the corridor towards the lab, even though he did not yet know what his purpose was.

He didn't look at Claire through the glass door as he entered the code she had given him; Ichi had memorised it earlier. But because his hands were shaking, he made a mistake when entering the sixteenth number and the light by the lock remained red. Muttering a curse under his breath, Ichi forced himself to close his eyes for a moment to regain his composure, then he entered the code for a second time. He was relieved to see the light change to green, and he hauled the door open using slightly too much strength, causing it to bang against the wall. *Stop messing this up!* Ichi admonished, but he kept his self-frustration from showing on his face.

When he finally locked eyes with Claire he was shocked to see that she didn't look nervous at all. If anything, her expression was stiff and resolute, as if she had spent the entire day preparing herself for Ichi's decision. He supposed that she had. Ichi's hand shifted to the knife by his hip as he walked towards her, considering allowing his ever-present bloodlust to make his impossible decision for him. But Claire caught on to the movement and she gulped slightly in response. It was only then that Ichi noticed how red her eyes were.

"...okay," was all Claire said, in an agonised tone that belied her calm facial expression. And then Ichi saw how small Claire looked underneath her massive blue jumper; how her shoulders were shaking just as much as Ichi's hands were. She looked *vulnerable,* once Ichi got passed the façade she had put on. *And that was just for me, so I could make this decision on my own. If you don't want to die, just tell me, God damn it!* He glanced down at the knife by his hip, temporary fury at Claire's lack of vocal opinion towards her own life causing him to unsheathe it. But then he put it back just as quickly as he had taken it out and brought out his gun instead. He shot both security cameras in quick succession, then ran over to Claire's bedside, grabbed her and flung her over his shoulder, not giving Claire a chance to react.

He bolted out of the lab and down the corridor, knowing that he had probably wasted too much time messing about with the code for the door and making his decision. But Ichi could think about his mistakes later; for now, all he had to do was get Claire up onto the roof of the complex. He threw her into the lift before vaulting over the chair himself, dragging it back into the lift as he pressed the button for the roof.

It felt as if the door took an eternity to close, and Ichi found himself holding his breath until it did. But as it began its slow ascent upwards, he took several, shaky breaths to regain his composure. "Run for the green helicopter," he said quietly, not looking at Claire. Ichi heard her get up off

438

the floor of the elevator to stand by his side. Claire made to touch his arm with an unsteady hand, but Ichi turned towards her and wrapped his arms tightly around her instead.

"Ichi, I –" Claire began, but Ichi interrupted her.

"The green one," he said again. "I need to ruin the other one, but you have to get to the green one. If I get taken out, then leave by yourself."

"But I –"

"Just do it!" Ichi yelled at her, knowing he was being unfair. He pulled away from Claire slightly to lift her head up with a curled finger under her chin. "Even if you don't know how to…just do it. Work it out. But I'll get there, so it'll be okay." Claire's eyes were full of tears, but she closed her eyes and took a deep breath, and when she opened her eyes again they were gone. She kissed Ichi gently, and it felt unlike any other time that Ichi had been kissed by her. He wondered why.

Claire broke away from the kiss to smile at him slightly. "The green one. Got it," she said, glancing at the elevator display at the same time Ichi did; they had just passed the tenth floor. Ichi grabbed Claire's hand and brought it up to his mouth, kissing each of her fingertips in turn – it satisfied him to see her face grow ever so slightly redder each time.

He never let his eyes leave hers as he said, "We can do this. *You* can do this." For the first time in his life, Ichi knew exactly what to say to make Claire feel better, even if he wasn't sure where any of the words had come from.

Claire bit her lip slightly. "So let's do this," she replied, just as the elevator reached the rooftop.

Michael

There were many things Michael had learned about Claire Danvers in the time he had known her, but perhaps the most important aspect of her personality for Michael to understand right now was her ability to be simultaneously an excellent and a terrible liar. He was poring over CCTV footage on two computer monitors; on the left monitor was the live feed from the lab, showing Claire lying restlessly on the bed there. The footage on the right monitor was also from the lab, and also of Claire, but it was a month old.

There was a lot of footage of Claire working away in the lab in the dead of night, rummaging through cupboards and freezers for the drugs and solutions that she needed to experiment on herself. And she had experimented on herself *a lot* – personally, Michael didn't understand how she hadn't noticed the track marks littering the crook of her left arm yet.

Michael had picked up on the fact that Claire had no idea that she was working down in the lab every night very quickly – a few nights of observing her fall unconscious underneath the fourth floor stairs or on the carpet of her room, only to wake up in a wordless panic hours later, was all it took to confirm his suspicions. And once he had worked out that Claire had no idea what she was doing...

Michael grinned at the CCTV footage. He had started joining her in the lab, watching what Claire was doing in person. She didn't seem to care, so long as he never interrupted her. On the occasions that he had out of curiosity, Claire would swat his hand away and tell him to find something less dangerous to do. It reminded Michael so much of the way Joanna Danvers had scolded him in the past that he found himself laughing at Claire every time she said as much, but Claire just gazed sightlessly through him and continued with her work.

Claire never told him what she was doing, or whether she had any memory of her parents' research, whilst she was in one of her late-night trances. Michael had engaged her in conversation several times, but if he tried to bring up anything to do with lab work Claire stayed resolutely silent. But Michael wasn't stupid; he knew that there were only so many plausible explanations for Claire experimenting on herself. The most obvious was that she was trying to remove the memory block that her parents had put on her, and this remained Michael's favourite theory. It was also possible that Claire remembered everything whilst she was in a trance, and was attempting to reproduce her parents' research on herself, but Michael deemed this less likely because Claire had always seemed averse to the idea of being an experimental lab rat for her parents. It made him question how Claire ended up going into the late-night trances in the first place – whether that was also something her parents had done to her, or whether it was a side-effect from them not blocking her memory efficiently enough.

What is it that you've remembered now, Miss Danvers? Michael wondered, turning his gaze to the live CCTV footage from the lab. Vic had entered through the door to sit by Claire's side; he dropped his head onto Claire's hands and was muttering about something that Michael couldn't hear. Michael frowned; Vic had been overly emotional ever since Claire had collapsed at the awards ball, and Michael didn't like that at all – it made the man dangerous and unreliable. Vic had always been a generally good and moral person on the outside, which was why he was a great undercover agent, but he had also been emotionally detached on the inside, which made him even better for working for Michael. Which was why, when Claire Danvers came into the picture, Michael had been so shocked at how strongly the man seemed to fall for her. Michael smiled grimly. *It's hardly as if I don't understand why, but... it's annoying, to say the least.*

He had no idea what Vic was up to, other than it obviously involving keeping Claire safe. But Vic had no reason to believe that Claire was unsafe, even if her memories had returned. After all, Michael had promised to let her go if she gave him access to her parents' research, and Vic had never seen Michael break a deal. *So what's making him so uneasy, then?* Michael was growing increasingly frustrated that he couldn't work it out; it was as if he were missing a single piece of a very complicated puzzle.

Or maybe several pieces. He looked closely at Claire as she spoke to Vic; she had a smile on her face that was hiding everything she was feeling – and Michael would know, since it was what he did himself. He had learned that Claire was very good at keeping things to herself, and that the only way to get some semblance of an honest answer from her was to shock her with something, enough that she would forget to lie and act emotionally. Bringing up her parents had been a sure-fire way to get Claire to talk honestly, whether she wanted to or not. Then Michael thought of the other times he had managed to get through Claire's otherwise unbreakable exterior and grinned.

She reacts to me. *Even before she remembered who I was, she reacted to me.* For Michael was quite certain that Claire had lied about remembering who he was prior to her collapse at the awards ball – it had been one of her, albeit few, terrible lies, but Michael supposed he couldn't blame her. He had deliberately put her on the spot, after all. Her reaction to Roger bringing up Alexis had also affirmed that Claire remembered who her sister was, thus also confirming that she hadn't known who she was beforehand. *Alexis will be pleased to hear that, I'm sure,* Michael thought, knowing that the other woman had ignored Claire largely in part because she wasn't sure if Claire was merely pretending not to know who she was or not.

Taking the risk of sending Claire to the awards ball on the hunch that she would regain her memories had definitely been worth it. The only problem was that Michael couldn't be certain if Claire had remembered everything that had been blocked before or only parts of it. *And she's certainly not telling me that she remembers.* That was the problem with Claire being both an awful and a perfect liar – Michael knew that something was wrong, but Claire had a hundred plausible excuses for why that was, none of which related to her recovering her memories. And so long as Claire refused to admit to having regained her memories, Michael couldn't force her to uphold her end of their deal.

He glanced at the left monitor to see Claire kiss Vic, and frowned. *I think it's about time I separate her from everyone…particularly Vic and Ichi.* Ichi was a wildcard, Michael knew, but he understood Ichi's way of thinking far more than he understood Vic's. Ichi wouldn't want to think about what would happen after Claire's memories returned, because it would mean that Michael would let her go. Which meant Ichi's most likely course of action was to make sure Claire stayed in the building, where he could get to her. In that respect, Ichi was far less of a threat to Michael's plans than Vic was, who he figured was more likely than not going to help her escape if Claire had remembered something that she didn't want Michael to get a hold of.

And on that front I am absolutely certain. Michael leaned back against his chair, closing his eyes for a moment. He had waited for so long to get to this point, and he wasn't about to let Claire Danvers slip through his fingers now. *Especially not when she's beginning to grasp the full extent of what I want from her.* When he opened his eyes, he saw Vic exit the lab, leaving Claire alone again. *Ah, Vic, if only you knew that that was the last time you'll ever see her,* Michael thought maliciously, deciding in that moment that he would move Claire to the basement floor in the next few hours. And that was *Michael's* floor, not anybody else's. He wondered how Ichi would react, or Alexis, now that her sister knew who she was, but in reality Michael didn't care. They were merely his employees, after all; his pawns. And they had moved as he had needed them to move, at least up until this point.

He was interrupted from his thoughts by a knock on the door. "Come in, Vic," Michael called over to the door, taking an educated guess at who it was likely to be. When Vic entered, Michael smiled wanly at him. "I don't recall having asked you to come in and see me," he said as Vic sat down.

Vic frowned at him, looked down at his hands, then back up at Michael. "I have something to give you." Michael raised an eyebrow at him, leaning forward as he did so. But Vic made no move to give whatever it was over to him, so Michael crossed his arms against his chest as he leant back against his chair again.

"I'm not going to sit around all night waiting for you to hand it over, Vic," he said. He looked at Vic critically. "Why so reluctant?" Vic made a face, then brought out a folded piece of paper from the inside of his jacket.

"Because it's from Claire," Vic muttered, keeping a hold of the note as if the last thing he wanted to do was to hand it over.

"Give it to me," Michael ordered, the tone of his voice leaving no room for argument. It helped to have an authoritative air at times; Michael used it to hide how he was feeling rather a lot. And right now, he was definitely both excited and deathly curious – two things he did not want Vic seeing on his face and hearing in his tone, since they were directed at Claire. So Vic very reluctantly handed the note over to Michael, who picked it out of his hand immediately.

He glanced over at Vic expectantly. "You don't need to be here for me to read this."

Vic seemed to swallow slightly. "May I speak freely, Michael?"

Michael looked down at the paper in his hands, then back up at the other man. "If you keep it short."

Vic tilted his head up to gaze at the ceiling, pinching the bridge of his nose between his fingertips for a second. Then he brought his head back down to stare at Michael, his expression serious. "What are you planning to do to Claire once – if – she remembers how to access her parents' research?"

Michael matched Vic's hard stare. "I don't see why that's any of your concern." He could see the vein in Vic's temple twitch slightly at his answer, and had to hold back a smirk.

"You said that you would let her go free, to live safely with Olivia."

"I never said precisely that," Michael corrected. Vic furrowed his brow but said nothing. Michael laughed slightly at the other man. "Ah, Vic, you weren't there, else you would have ensured that Miss Danvers agreed to somewhat less ambiguous terms."

"Meaning…?"

"Meaning I told her that, when she gave me all of her parents' research, I would give both Miss Danvers and her sister their lives to do with as they please. That's not the same as me telling her she could go free to live safely with her sister."

Vic stood up abruptly, fury written all over his face. "What the hell are you —"

"Oh, rest assured Vic, I mean neither Miss Danvers nor her sister any harm," Michael interrupted, smiling easily. "I simply vocalised my terms in such a way that, if I perhaps needed something else from her, I wouldn't be breaking my own word."

"That doesn't sound like it fits into letting her 'live as she pleases' at all!" Vic protested.

"If Miss Danvers gives me everything I need from her in the first place, then she has nothing to fear and can do what she wants." Michael paused, allowing the smile to disappear from his face before continuing. "Which is why having her admit to regaining her memories is *in her best interests,* Vic. But is it so unlike me to have a loophole in a deal to ensure I get everything I need out of it?"

Vic clucked his tongue. "No, it's exactly like you."

Michael sighed. "I appreciate your concern for Miss Danvers, but it's misplaced nonetheless. All things considered, she has been treated very well here, in my building. You know fine well that there are numerous ways her captivity here could have been handled, and it was *me* who decided that the way would be tolerable for her."

It was Vic's turn to sigh. "I know, I know." He looked at Michael. "You know I'm going to resign the second Claire is let out of here, right?"

Michael grinned at him. "I may have had a notion. I'll miss having you work for me, though; you really are a truly spectacular undercover agent."

Vic smiled slightly at that. "I know." And then he was gone, leaving Michael to dwell over just how many half-truths he had told Vic. *Well, not so much half-truths as* quarter-truths, *but when have I ever given anybody even that much?*

Then Michael remembered the note in his hand. Feeling vaguely impressed that Vic's conversation had been interesting enough to cause him to forget about it in the first place, Michael leant back against his chair for a third time as he unfolded the piece of paper to read it.

> *You said you were quite certain you would see me again five years ago – well done on forcing that to be true. But you've had a year to see me and all you've done is compare me to my mother...not a great way to appeal to my better nature, for future information. You can keep that in mind for next time...if you can find me.*

> *Claire (not Miss Danvers)*

Michael read and reread Claire's handwriting several times before her words sank in, by which point a movement out of the corner of his eye caused him to glance up at his computer monitors. Something had caused the live footage in the lab to cut out, so he rewound the feed. And there was Ichi, pulling out a gun and firing at the cameras. Michael was out of his office and running down the stairs in a second, anger and dread building up in equal quantities.

When he reached the lab, both Alexis and Vic were already there, staring at the empty bed. "I heard gunshots," Alexis said, explaining her presence. Michael supposed Vic didn't need an excuse to come back down and see Claire. Michael wordlessly turned from the two of them to run to the elevator, which was on the third floor. Michael stabbed the button to call the lift, but then realised that Ichi was likely to block it when it reached the roof.

"The stairs," he muttered, before slamming the door to the stairwell open to run up it. He heard two sets of footsteps follow behind him. Michael didn't allow himself to think as he passed floor after floor during his ascent upwards, using his now abominable rage to fuel his legs into taking each flight of stairs faster than the one before.

When he reached the rooftop, Alexis and Vic close behind, Michael watched as Ichi leapt deftly from one of his helicopters to run to the other, which Claire was in. She had managed to get the engine going, and the propellers were beginning to stutter into life. Michael ran towards her, pulling a gun out of his suit jacket as he did so. He fired a bullet at Ichi but the other man dodged it as if he had been expecting it, sparing Michael a glance before jumping into the helicopter just as it began to leave the ground. Michael shot his gun at him again, but it only just managed to graze the side of Ichi's arm.

"Get back here, Miss Danvers!" Michael demanded furiously over the deafening sound of the spinning propellers. Claire looked down at him from the cockpit as the helicopter gained more height, a terrified but determined expression on her face.

"Never!" she shouted back at him, defiant, and then both she and Ichi were out of reach. Michael broke away from Claire's gaze to look at the other helicopter, which Vic was in, but the other man shook his head at Michael.

"Ichi shot out the control panel!" Vic yelled over to him. Michael ran his hands through his swept-back hair, not quite believing what he had just witnessed. *Ichi wasn't supposed to do this. Ichi was supposed to keep her here. Claire wasn't supposed to* want *to leave with Ichi.* Alexis walked over to join him, just as Vic did the same.

"Get. Her. Back." Michael snarled through gritted teeth, eyes on the rapidly disappearing helicopter in the sky. Vic nodded his assent, then left for the stairs. Alexis stayed by Michael's side.

"And Ichi?" she asked.

Michael didn't look at her. "Kill him."

"I don't think that would be wise, if you want Claire to do as you say."

"Don't presume to know what I need to do!" he shouted into Alexis' face, turning on her in a second.

Alexis didn't so much as flinch at the outburst. "I think there's some information you may need now, that wasn't relevant before." Michael stared at her, barely able to stop himself from screaming at her again. Alexis gave him a level stare. "We should head back down to your office…I don't much like the idea of you throwing me off the top of the complex for what I have to say."

CHAPTER 40
Driving with the Brakes On

Claire

Hours had passed since Ichi had helped her so narrowly escape from Michael's complex, and Claire still hadn't quite managed to process it. They had abandoned Michael's helicopter as soon as they had reached the mainland, and now they were in their third consecutive car. Claire had had no idea where they were until they passed the border into Scotland, and now Claire was beginning to feel terribly homesick looking at the increasingly familiar landscape surrounding her.

Ichi drove quickly – well over the speed limit – but as it was about four in the morning nobody had stopped the car to tell them to slow down. And he didn't look as if he *ever* intended to slow down – if anything, Claire thought that Ichi was driving even faster than he had been an hour ago. He didn't seem bothered by the fact that Michael had shot him in the arm, but Claire supposed that it looked as if nothing at all was bothering Ichi right now; he kept an expressionless face looking out at the road in front of them, not once turning to Claire to speak to her or even acknowledge her presence.

Does he regret having helped me escape? Claire worried. Where Ichi was calm and still, Claire was fidgety and on edge. Her eyes took in everything around her, telling her that the motorways were too bright and the country roads too dark, and she worried that her time in Michael's complex had caused her to become oversensitive to such drastic light changes. And her ears seemed to pick up every little sound, even over the hum of the car engine. Claire shivered. *Michael could be right behind us, he could be tracking us right now, he could...* but Claire's train of thought was interrupted by Ichi, finally, speaking to her.

"Do you have somewhere in mind that you want to go?" he asked quietly. Claire gaped at him for a few seconds, surprised to hear his voice, but then she forced her thoughts away from Michael to the task at hand.

"Yes," she replied, nodding her head slightly. "There's a cabin in the Trossachs that I used to go to in the summer with a friend's family. It should be empty right now."

"*Should?*" Ichi echoed, frowning, but he still didn't look at her. In the distance, Claire could see the horizon beginning to lighten. It made her feel odd.

Claire glanced at Ichi before turning her gaze to the floor. "Well, I...I don't really know what the date is, so..."

"It's June fourteenth," Ichi replied in a clipped tone. Claire found herself worrying once more about what was running through Ichi's head, but then she saw the sun beginning to rise above the horizon, and she realised why she had felt so odd seeing it.

"Stop the car, Ichi," Claire murmured, transfixed by the red and gold hues bleeding through the murky blue sky.

"Why?"

"Just stop the car!" The words had come out much sharper than Claire had intended, but it caused Ichi to turn off of the country road they were currently driving along onto a nondescript patch of grass nonetheless.

There was silence once more as Claire sat, still as a statue, watching the sun slowly rise higher and higher above the earth, until the light hit the windshield of the car. Claire raised a hand up to protect her eyes from it, and realised that she was crying. A quick glance to her right confirmed that Ichi was watching her.

"Why are you crying?" he asked, confused. Claire tried to swallow a sob but found that she couldn't.

"I haven't seen the sun in – oh my God, I don't even know –"

"Three hundred and fourteen days," Ichi interjected, so quickly that Claire suspected that the number had been in his head all night. Claire turned to stare at him.

"Why do you even know that?"

Ichi laughed ruefully. "Why wouldn't I keep track of the number of days that you've been around to torment me?" Claire let out another sob at that, and turned away from Ichi to brush tears away from her eyes.

"That's not fair," she cried, thinking about how she had actually known Ichi for months longer than that, and until she worked out how to fix him he could never know. But thinking that made Claire feel even worse, and she felt more tears escape from her eyes to run down her cheeks. Then she felt Ichi's hand run through her hair, turning her head to face him again.

"I know," was all he said, and Claire thought that there might have been just a hint of sympathy in his expression, but when she blinked it was gone. Ichi seemed to hesitate for a second before continuing. "Claire, do you…do you regret escaping with me?"

Claire felt her mouth open at the question. "Why would you ask that?"

Ichi frowned at her. "Because ever since we got away, it's looked like you do. And I don't know what I'm supposed to do if you regret this."

Claire let out a laugh that almost sounded like she was crying again. She brought her hand up to cover Ichi's, still entwined in her hair. "There may be a lot of things I regret from the past year, and there will be a million things I'll regret in the future, I'm sure, but running away with you is definitely not one of them."

Ichi breathed a sigh of relief that Claire hadn't realised he had been holding onto, and he smiled slightly. Then it widened into a full-on grin. "Being on the run should be…interesting."

"What makes you think that?" Claire asked, puzzled. Ichi undid his seatbelt and then Claire's, reaching over her to pull a lever by her side, dropping her seat back abruptly. It didn't take Claire long to realise what Ichi was getting at. She laughed again, and it sounded far more genuine this time. "Can you seriously not wait until we get to an actual bed?" she reprimanded as Ichi clambered on top of her.

"Beds are boring," Ichi replied off-handily. "And no, I can't wait. You were unconscious for three days, after all."

Claire shook her head slightly at the comment. "Three whole days? How ever did you cope?"

"Badly." Claire looked into Ichi's eyes properly then, and she saw how serious he was about the sentiment. A wave of guilt at the fact that she would abandon the man in front of her washed over Claire once again, and Ichi must have seen something flit across her face, for he frowned. "What is it? You've had that look about you every time I noticed you staring at me all night." In the back of her mind, Claire couldn't help but feel surprised at how perceptive Ichi was being about her feelings, considering who he was.

She responded by leaning forwards slightly to kiss the end of his nose. The gentle action seemed to confuse Ichi more than anything. "I just have a lot to think about," Claire replied quietly, choosing to skirt around the truth instead of having to lie. She pulled Ichi down closer to her with a hand on the back of his neck, running it up the back of his head to feel his hair between her fingertips. "But I only want to think about you right now." Ichi grazed his teeth against Claire's bottom lip before biting into it slightly. Claire could feel his heartbeat against her chest; it was hammering away as quickly as her own.

"About bloody time," he growled into her mouth before kissing her, and Claire desperately reciprocated. *I can give in, just one more time. Just one more time.* Claire had never wanted time to stand still more than she did in that moment, when all she could think about was Ichi and all he could think about was her, knowing that the sun rising higher and higher in the sky was counting down the hours she had left to be with him.

But by the time Ichi had ripped her clothes off, Claire wasn't thinking about anything at all.

Ichi

He knew that there was more going on in Claire's head than she was letting on, and that failing to discuss it immediately was likely a decision that Ichi would later regret, but for the moment Ichi couldn't care less. He didn't think anything could beat the feeling of Claire's skin against his own, or her shuddering breath against his neck as he bit into hers, or even the fact that he was seeing Claire in the golden, morning sunlight for the first time

451

in his life. She was beautiful, and she was his, and Ichi knew that he would do anything to keep it that way.

Anything, I'll do anything, he promised, knowing that he had never had a truer thought before in his entire life. But then he felt Claire's fingers crawl across his back, pulling him closer to her, and he threw the thought away in his desperation to get lost in the woman beneath him.

Alexis

"Claire *knew* Ichi before her memory loss?!" Michael exclaimed from behind his desk. He had calmed down somewhat in the time it took to get down to the basement floor, though Alexis was aware that anything she said might cause him to explode once more. She warily took a seat opposite Michael's desk, steeling herself for the barrage of questions that she should have pre-emptively addressed months ago, but hadn't wanted to.

She sighed. "Yes."

Michael narrowed his eyes at her. "And Ichi didn't know because…?"

Alexis laughed bitterly. "That should be obvious." Michael looked at her sharply then – a warning against being sarcastic. Alexis matched his stare unflinchingly. "His memories have been blocked," she said, "Probably by my parents, like Claire's were. Or, you know, he could have majorly banged his head, but I find that unlikely." Alexis chuckled at that final thought; even before her parents had experimented on Ichi, he had never been the type to fall over. He had always moved so gracefully, never looking at his feet or stumbling. It was so unlike Claire that Alexis laughed again, then stopped suddenly when she remembered who she was talking to.

Michael raised an eyebrow at her, leaning back into his chair slightly. "What's so funny? I don't see anything amusing about this situation."

Alexis shook her head. "It's nothing." And then she was silent, waiting to hear what Michael's next question would be.

"I'm assuming your parents had a reason for blocking his memories," Michael said eventually, and Alexis nodded in answer.

"He was their test subject. Before Claire, anyway. Their human guinea pig." Alexis felt herself getting angry at the thought, as she always did; it helped to hide the fact that Michael didn't know that she herself had been a test subject, or knew what her parents' secret research had been about in the first place. And for her own safety, as well as Claire and Olivia's, it had to remain that way.

Michael frowned at her. "And you considered this piece of information *irrelevant* before now?"

Alexis shrugged slightly. "When we found Ichi last year, it was obvious that he had no recollection of what had happened to him, else he'd have remembered me." It still broke her heart, even now, when she thought about what Ichi had become after her parents had blocked his memories. Claire had promised her that she would fix him, after all. Clearly she had failed. Alexis tried her best not to blame her sister for the monster her parents had created – she knew it had been a lofty task to fix Ichi – but the fact remained that if Claire had managed to stick to her promise, then Ichi wouldn't have become a psychopathic killer.

"You get lost inside your own head as frequently as your sister does, you know," Michael commented, clearly impatient with Alexis at having paused halfway through her explanation.

Alexis ignored the jibe. "If Claire had recognised Ichi when he was sent to kidnap her with Vic, I'd have told you about them knowing each other." She paused, thinking about how incredibly lucky she and Ichi and Claire had been that her sister had had no recollection of what had happened to any of them. Alexis had only gone to Michael in order to get the help required to seek revenge against her parents, after all, and kidnapping Claire had seemed like the best way to force their parents out of hiding. *Well, dad at the very least,* Alexis thought bitterly. When Alexis had broached the idea to Michael, she had been surprised at how easily he had agreed to it. She had been relieved at that; Alexis had been convinced it would have taken a lot more time and effort on her part in order to prevent Michael from outright killing one of her sisters to force her parents out.

He probably realised that that wasn't the best way to get a hold of their research, Alexis supposed, sparing her boss a glance. He was watching her carefully, waiting to see what she would say next. Alexis didn't care for the research, personally, to the point that her own apathy surprised her at times. *Before my parents experimented on me, I'd have cared about this man getting his hands on something so dangerous. But now...* Alexis knew that she was a different person than who she was before – not as drastically different as Ichi, but different nonetheless. She was sharper, more calculative, and more ruthless. She still felt sporadic bouts of rage now and again, but she knew how to handle them. It was only when she had seen Claire violently attack Vic several weeks prior that Alexis had realised that her sister had also been experimented on in the same way that she had been. *And Claire had no idea why she felt that way. She must have been so terrified.* Alexis felt herself put her head into her hands, dismayed at the thought. *Why on earth did you let them do that to you, you idiot? Idiot, idiot, idiot. You hated what they had done to me and Ichi!*

"Alexis." Michael's voice brought Alexis out of her head again, but she was surprised by the fact that he didn't sound angry. She looked at him, waiting for him to continue. He kept his expression mild as he said, "I've never questioned your desire to see your parents dead, and I won't do so now. You always knew that I needed their research before that happened, and you have been extremely helpful so far in putting the pieces together that I've needed in order to do so." Alexis felt a twinge of guilt at that; being the reason that her sister had been kidnapped and kept in captivity for a year was not exactly something Alexis was proud of. Michael's gaze sharpened, and he leant forward slightly. "However, the situation has changed, and I can see by the look on your face that you know that too."

Alexis shifted uncomfortably in her seat; it disturbed her how much Michael managed to glean from watching a person's behaviour, and she knew that he had picked up far too much from Claire when he had spoken to her in the lab before her escape. "When did you figure out that she literally had all of the research in her head, rather than simply knowing where it was?" Alexis found herself asking.

Michael smiled slightly. "I've had a...notion...for months now."

Alexis let out a bark of humourless laughter. "But of course you had."

"Were your sister and Ichi in love with each other before their memories were blocked?" Alexis flinched at the sudden question, and she muddled through how best to answer it in her head before replying.

454

"Possibly," she said eventually. "I mean, I wasn't there, in the lab, so I wouldn't know. I only knew who Ichi was in the first place near the end – the fact that my parents were illegally experimenting on people was one of the main reasons I left, after all." *Lies, all lies,* Alexis thought. She knew that Claire and Ichi had fallen for each other; it had only served to fuel Alexis' jealousy towards her sister at the time, and she could remember all too clearly how frequently she had caught Ichi following her sister's every move with his eyes, even before he had decided to start talking to her. *He never looked at* me *like that.* Alexis was surprised to realise that she still felt bitter about that, even now.

"The look on your face implies that 'possibly' means 'absolutely'."

Alexis schooled her expression somewhat. "Do you honestly think I'd sleep with someone I knew my sister to be in love with?"

"Yes," Michael replied, so quickly that Alexis was slightly affronted. But instead of falling for the bait and asking why her boss thought as much, Alexis decided to bring the conversation back round to the matter at hand.

"So what's your plan now?"

Michael regarded her for a few seconds. "You must have some ideas about where your sister might go."

"Of course I do," she replied, "But I can't say the same about Ichi."

"Ichi isn't pulling the strings here; wherever they're heading, it'll be your sister's choice."

Alexis narrowed her eyes. "How can you be so sure?"

Michael laughed lightly. "You don't know your sister half as well as you should, Alexis. Or Ichi, for that matter." Alexis wondered for a moment how it was possible for Michael to know more about her sister's habits and personality than she did, but then she remembered that Michael had spent much of the past year watching her sister's every move on camera.

"In that case, I know of a few places to check out. I need a helicopter though."

"One will be arriving within the hour." Michael's expression had grown very serious. "Don't disappoint me, Alexis. Get her back. And Ichi, too, if you can. Seems like he's the best leverage I could have on hand against her." He glanced up at the ceiling of his office thoughtfully. "And Vic, too, for that matter."

Alexis was filled with a sudden fear. "You won't hurt her, will you?" she asked, not even attempting to hide the concern from her voice.

Michael smiled. "If you're asking me that, then you really don't know me very well at all, Alexis."

"I make a point not to. What do you mean?"

Michael stared at her briefly, and for a moment Alexis saw something in his eyes that she hadn't noticed before. "I'd never physically hurt your sister...well, not unless she wanted me to." He chuckled, and Alexis frowned.

"That's not a particularly reassuring answer."

"I never said I'd give you one."

Alexis swallowed slightly, then asked a question she had been thinking about since the evening of the awards ball. "What exactly do you want from my sister, Michael?"

"Nothing life-threatening," he answered, grinning.

Alexis ran a hand over her face. "Why do I work for you?" she mumbled, mostly to herself.

"Because you needed someone to give you all of the money and resources required to track down and kill your parents without taking either of your sisters' lives in the process."

Alexis rolled her eyes. "That was a rhetorical question." The dread she had felt before had not entirely abated, but Alexis resigned herself to the fact that Michael was unlikely to ever give her a completely honest answer. *I'll just have to work it out for myself, I suppose.* She glanced at Michael; he still looked as if he hadn't slept since the awards ball, and his dark blonde hair was in disarray. It was such a stark contrast to how he normally appeared that Alexis wondered for a second which appearance aligned itself more with who Michael actually was.

"You're as bad as your sister for staring, Alexis," Michael said quietly. He leant forwards and placed his elbows on his desk, linking his fingers together as he did so to rest his chin upon them. "Does my being tired look *that* out of place?"

"Yes," Alexis replied. "Especially when the reason you look as such is because of my sister." Then Alexis thought of something that had been bothering her for months. "Why do you never call her 'Claire' to her face?" she asked. "It's always 'Miss Danvers'."

Michael smirked at the question. "Am I not allowed to be polite to my own hostage?" He chuckled at Alexis' resultant stony face before amending his answer. "Because the false politeness irks her, though she'd never admit to it out loud. I've been waiting to see how long it takes for her to call me up on it; turns out it took precisely the entire time that she was here to do so."

Alexis frowned. "False politeness? Huh. Why do I not believe that?" It was only in voicing her confusion that she realised she was likely better off not getting an answer from Michael about it. But Michael didn't say anything anyway, giving her nothing but a level stare in response.

"Can you find Vic for me before you leave?" he asked as Alexis got up for the door. She nodded in assent, then began dutifully looking for the man in question, trying not to think about her concerns over Michael's intentions towards Claire too much. *Just how ignorant am I allowed to be before it puts her or Olivia in danger?* Alexis wondered as she traversed floor after floor looking for Vic. *If I can find Claire and bring her back, I'll convince her to give Michael the research he wants, for her own wellbeing. Even if she doesn't want to, I'll make her do it. And then...* Alexis paused from her search to stare at nothing for a moment, then shook her head and focussed on locating Vic.

But after two rounds of the complex, Alexis had no choice but to conclude that Vic was nowhere to be found, so she went back to Michael's office. "Michael," she said when she got there, "Vic isn't here."

Her boss looked up at her sharply. "You're certain?" Alexis nodded her head. Michael's face darkened, and she found herself edging backwards half a step in response to the look he gave her.

"Find your sister," Michael murmured, stony-faced. "Find her before Vic does." And for the first time in over a year, Alexis felt a seed of doubt

457

begin to grow in the back of her mind, telling her that choosing to work for Michael had been a terrible, horrible mistake.

CHAPTER 41
Rolling in the Deep

Ichi

Ichi liked the lodge that Claire had directed him to. It was a lot larger than he had been expecting, with a very expensive-looking outdoor hot tub that Ichi imagined barely saw any use, considering where the lodge was geographically located. All he knew was that if he didn't use it with Claire whilst he was there, then Ichi would likely regret it for the rest of his life. There was also a fireplace located in the living room of the lodge, as well as a well-equipped kitchen, four bedrooms and two bathrooms.

Ichi let out a low whistle when he wandered into the main bedroom. "Who did you say owns this place again?" he called out over his shoulder.

"I didn't." Claire brushed past him and crouched down low by the bed, apparently looking for something underneath it. She pulled out a large, dark purple bag after a few seconds, letting out a sigh of relief as she opened it up and inspected its contents. "It belongs to a family we were close with. We would stay here for most of July back when I was in high school."

"Who's 'we'?" Ichi walked over to kneel down beside Claire as she zipped the bag back up. "And what's in there?"

"Me, Olivia and –" Claire stopped abruptly, and her eyes went glassy for a moment. Then she shook her head slightly. "Just the two of us, and the family. They had daughters close in age to us."

Ichi frowned at her, suspicious. "And the bag?" Claire unzipped the bag again so that Ichi could see the contents. It was loaded full of clothes; Ichi thought he also spied a torch and a wallet.

"Emergency supplies, in case we ran out of clothes or whatever whilst we were out here," Claire explained. She laughed softly. "Though most of the clothes likely won't fit anymore, since they were bought when I was about fourteen." Ichi turned from her to rummage through his own bag, picking out a mobile phone and charger from it before throwing them into Claire's purple one. Claire raised an eyebrow at him.

"I have a few of them for jobs," he explained. Ichi stood up to fall backwards onto the bed. It was incredibly comfortable, and it was only in sinking into the soft fabric of the duvet that Ichi realised that he was exhausted. "I can just buy you new clothes," he added on, after a few seconds of silence. "I *am* a hired killer with several off-shore bank accounts full of money, after all." Knowing that his blasé attitude towards his occupation would irk Claire, he glanced over to see her reaction, hoping to see an annoyed pout upon her lips that he could kiss away. Instead Claire looked incredibly sad.

Ichi sat up and leant down to pull Claire up onto the bed by her arms. She let him do so without complaint, but the look on her face didn't change. So Ichi pushed her down against the bed, kissing her again and again because he didn't know what else to do. Eventually, Claire pushed him away slightly to look up at him, her dark blue eyes glittering.

Ichi traced the edge of her upper lip with a finger; it was trembling slightly. "What are you thinking about?" he murmured, wondering if Claire would deflect the question as she had done his questions in the car. "You told me you'd explain everything once we got away from Michael's complex."

Claire's eyes widened slightly at the mention of Michael's name. "I'm – I'm scared, Ichi. I'm *terrified*. I keep wondering whether I should have just made you kill me, then this would all be over." Ichi nearly slapped her, then; his hand was millimetres from her face before he managed to stop it. Claire flinched slightly at the motion.

"Don't you *dare* say that!" he said angrily, balling his hand up into her hair instead of hitting her. "Don't you dare say that I made the wrong decision! If you want to end your life then you can bloody well do it yourself!" Then Ichi made a noise of surprise when Claire flung her arms around his neck, pulling him towards her so that she could bury her face against his shoulder. He felt her lashes brush against his skin, fluttering and wet.

"Thank you," she sobbed, "Thank you, thank you, thank you."

Ichi didn't think he had ever been so confused. "Claire, you're not making any sense. Are you happy I saved your life or aren't you?"

"Can't I be both?" she murmured into his neck.

Ichi kissed the top of her head. "Not if you want me to understand." Claire pulled away from him, taking her arms back to brush away her tears with her right hand.

"I'm just a coward," she replied. "If you had killed me then it would have all been over. I wouldn't have to worry about keeping my parents' damnable research hidden, or making sure Olivia – and even my parents – remain safe..." She looked up at Ichi, and he saw a fear in her eyes one hundred times stronger than any fear he had ever caused in her. "I don't want to ever go back to that place. I don't want him to *ever* get a hold of me." Ichi didn't have to ask who 'him' was referring to; he wondered if Claire was making a conscious decision to avoid Michael's name. Claire closed her eyes, taking several deep breaths before continuing, and she seemed altogether more like herself when she opened them again. "But I'm glad you saved me, Ichi. Truly, I am. I don't want to die. I want to *live*. It's just that I don't know how long it's going to take before I get to live the life I want, or if I'll ever get to live that life at all."

"You're talking as if you have to do all of this without me, you idiot," Ichi chided, knocking Claire's forehead with his knuckles as he spoke. She gave him a small smile, then reached up and kissed him. Somewhat satisfied that at least some of Claire's problems had been dealt with for now, Ichi ran his fingers through her hair as he kissed her back, sliding his other hand underneath her jumper to feel the smooth skin of her stomach. Claire squirmed pleasantly at his touch.

"I'd kill for a shower," she said, and Ichi chuckled at her choice of words.

"How about settling for a go in that hot tub outside instead?" he grinned. Claire rolled her eyes at the idea, but she returned the smile nonetheless, and Ichi knew that she was completely fine with it.

But then there was the sound of footsteps outside, and both Ichi and Claire froze. He stood up silently, reaching for the gun inside his leather jacket as he did so. When he heard someone fiddling with the front door, he undid the safety catch. He vaguely heard Claire get up to follow him through to the living room, and he gestured for her to stay behind him. But when the door opened, Claire grabbed for his left arm, gesturing the gun away from the person entering the cabin.

"Claire, what are you –" he began, but Claire interrupted him.

"Put it away, Ichi, it's just –"

"Vic." Ichi said, finishing the sentence for her. He watched the other man carefully as Vic closed the door behind him before turning to face both Ichi and Claire. "Claire, what's going on?" Ichi asked, suspicious and confused.

"Ichi, put the gun away," Claire begged again, tugging more insistently on his arm.

"Why are you here, Vic?"

The other man looked pointedly at Claire. "For her, obviously."

Ichi glanced down at Claire; her eyes pleading with him to understand something that he simply didn't. "But you don't need Vic's help if I'm here," Ichi said, frowning at her. She didn't look at him.

"I know that," she replied as she tried to pull the gun away from Ichi's hand. He tightened his grip on it instead.

"If you know that," he said through gritted teeth, "Then why is Vic here?" Then he saw the look Claire gave Vic, and Vic gave her, and he understood. "Ahh. I understand now."

"Ichi –"

"Just shut up, Claire." He pulled away from her arm so that he could walk away, running his free hand through his hair as he struggled to accept that he had been duped. "I was just a decoy, wasn't I? Michael's eyes were on Vic. It's so fucking obvious now." He threw a glance at Claire. "You should feel proud of yourself – you managed to outsmart Michael. And *me.*"

"Ichi –"

"*Shut up! Just shut up!*" Ichi marched back over to Claire, but Vic got to her first and pulled her out of the way. "Get the fuck out of my way, Vic!" Ichi screamed at the other man, but Vic merely pulled Claire in closer against his chest.

"This is exactly why you can't be around her, Ich," Vic said quietly. Ichi stared at him, bug-eyed. He swept his gaze down to Claire, who looked as if she might burst into tears again.

"What does he mean, Claire?" Ichi asked her, forcing his voice down to a lower volume. He saw her glance at the gun still held in his left hand.

"Ichi, I...I can't trust you like this. You know I can't," Claire stammered, still not looking at him.

"What do you mean *'like this'?!*" Ichi yelled, raising his voice again. "Claire, fucking look at me! Look at me and tell me what you mean!" He felt the gun trembling in his hand, and for half a second he considered pointing it at her. And Vic could clearly tell what was going through his head, for he pushed Claire behind him.

"Ichi, put the damn gun down, or I swear to God I'll –"

"As if I care what you'll do!" Ichi interrupted, taking a step towards them. But when Vic made to stop him, Claire put a hand out and Vic paused. She took a few steps forwards herself, away from Vic and towards Ichi, and looked up at him with furtive eyes that meant Ichi already knew he wasn't going to get the truth that he desired.

"I can't tell you right now," she said quietly.

Ichi grabbed her. "The hell you can't! Just open your mouth and let the fucking words come out, it's that simple!"

"No it's not!" Claire screamed, finding her voice at last. She pushed Ichi away. "You are not in a position to tell me what I can and cannot do right now. *Nobody can!*" Out of the corner of his eye Ichi saw Vic flinch, and he realised that perhaps he wasn't the only one with many desperate questions for the woman in front of him. Claire glared at him, eyes blazing. "I'm the only one who gets to decide that, and right now I'm telling *you* that I can't give you any of the answers you need. Can you not be patient for once in your life?"

"I've already used up a lifetime of patience on you, Claire!"

"This has gone on for too long," Vic interjected, taking a step towards Claire. "Princess, we need to go." Ichi swung his gaze wildly from Vic and back to Claire, again and again.

"Claire, I just…don't understand. What have I got to do so that you'll let me understand?" And Ichi's words caused Claire's anger to dissipate, and she returned to looking small and fragile.

"Don't go back to the complex. Please, don't go back to *him*," she begged.

Ichi shook his head in frustration. "What has that got to do with anything?"

Claire's eyes went wide. "It's got to do with *everything*." She paused, glancing down at the shaking gun in Ichi's hand once more. "Please, just…hide. Don't let him find you. And when I can tell you everything, *I'll* find you. Can you do that?"

"Like hell I can!" Ichi screamed, bringing his left arm up as he spoke. "Now tell me what the fuck is –"

The last thing Ichi saw before Vic knocked him out was Claire mouthing *I'm sorry* to him, but by then the words meant nothing.

Alexis

She found Ichi lying face-down on the floor of the cabin. It had been the first place Alexis had headed to in her search for Claire, knowing her sister well enough that she could eliminate all obvious places such as her flat, their parents' house or her university from her list pre-emptively. So Alexis ran on the hunch that Claire would aim for as obscure a place as possible whilst still remaining practical. And what was more practical that a currently-abandoned cabin full of clothes and emergency supplies that Claire could make use of without endangering the lives of anyone she knew? It was so *Claire* that it annoyed Alexis that it had been this easy for her to locate her.

What she hadn't expected was only finding Ichi. After searching the cabin to confirm that Claire wasn't there, Alexis returned to his side to shake him awake. "Ichi?" she ventured. "Ichi, what happened?"

"Vic…" Ichi muttered as he came to. "Completely…duped. Fucking bitch." Alexis watched as he sat up and rubbed his head, wincing as he felt the bump no doubt growing on the back of it.

"Tell me *exactly* what happened," Alexis ordered, once it was obvious that Ichi had regained enough of his senses. He frowned at the authoritarian tone of her voice, but then proceeded to explain what had happened nonetheless. When he was finished, Alexis groaned. "Michael's not going to like this, not at all."

Hearing Michael's name caused Ichi to look up at her in surprise. "Shouldn't you be trying to kill me or something?" he asked, voice devoid of all emotion.

Alexis let out a hollow laugh. "You're way too valuable for that, you know. So how about it; wanna come back with me and help Michael and me track Claire and Vic down?" Ichi looked at her oddly then, but Alexis resisted the urge to ask why.

"Why am I valuable?"

Alexis shifted uncomfortably on the spot. "You'll know. Eventually."

"What the hell is it that I don't get to know?!" Ichi suddenly raged at her, standing up to throw a lamp down to the floor. Alexis flinched as the ceramic and glass shattered everywhere. Slowly, she got up to her feet.

"I'm not going to apologise for withholding information from you, Ichi," she told him, keeping her voice level. He didn't look at her. "Michael has been withholding information from the very beginning, after all."

"Like how Claire's assassination was a fucking sham?" Ichi bit out.

Alexis looked at him, surprised. "Who told you that?"

"Claire."

Alexis sighed. "Of course she did. Vic told her?"

"Who else?"

Alexis took a few steps towards him. "Look, Ichi," she began, "Come back with me. Come back with me, and Michael will be able to fill in a few of the gaps in your knowledge. Not all, but a few. You *do* want to get Claire back, don't you?" Ichi looked at her then, and his eyes were cold and dead.

It reminded Alexis horribly of when she had first found him with his memories blocked, covered in blood and surrounded by corpses.

"As if you had to ask that."

"Then come with me."

But as the two of them made their way back to Michael's island, Alexis was struck by a disturbing thought. *If I surround myself with monsters, how long will it be until I'm one of those monsters myself?*

CHAPTER 42
When I'm Alone

Ichi

Ichi had intended never to set foot inside Michael's complex again. And yet here he was, sitting in Michael's office as if the past twelve hours hadn't happened. He shifted uncomfortably in his seat as Michael stared at him with haggard, dispassionate eyes; Ichi decided that he'd rather like to never find out what the other man was thinking about at that moment.

Alexis was sitting beside him, waiting patiently for Michael to break the silence that pervaded the air. She seemed to be bothered by something, but whatever it was it was evident that she had no desire to talk about it.

Eventually, Ichi couldn't take the silence any longer. "Alexis said you could 'fill in some of the gaps' in my knowledge," he said blankly.

Michael let out a chuckle that didn't reach his eyes. "What, no 'I'm sorry for running off with your captive, Michael'? I'm wounded, Ichi," Michael remarked casually, even as his eyes remained hard and unforgiving.

Ichi looked away. "As if I'd apologise for something like that," he replied, "And I'd do it again if she asked me to. I never cared much whether I worked for you in the first place anyway." Ichi realised that he sounded almost petulant, but he didn't care.

Michael laughed again, and this time his eyes seemed to light up a little in amusement. "Yes, well, Miss Danvers seems to have some kind of hold over every person she comes into contact with." He paused; Ichi was suddenly reminded that, whilst Claire had been unconscious, both he and Vic had begun to wonder about what Michael's true intentions had been towards Claire. And now that he was thinking about it again, it was all he wanted to know. Michael continued: "And for the moment, you're more use to me alive than dead, so I suppose it's your lucky day."

It was Ichi's turn to let out a short, derisive laugh. "I don't feel so lucky."

"She outsmarted all of us, Ich," came Alexis' voice to his left. "I wouldn't be so hard on yourself." Ichi had a lot he wanted to say in response, but he forced himself to stay silent. He still hadn't quite processed what Claire had done to him, and it was something he reckoned he would have to go over in his head a thousand times or more before he could even begin to hope to understand it.

"Yes, I never thought for a moment that she was manipulative enough to use both yourself and Vic like she did, Ichi, and yet here we are," Michael said, leaning back against his chair in order to stare up at the ceiling. Ichi thought that the other man looked somewhat impressed.

"So how do you plan on getting her back?" Ichi asked, cutting straight to the point.

"Oh, first things first," Michael replied. He smiled a bland smile again. "There are some things you wish to know. So ask away, and I'll see if I'm inclined to answer your questions."

Ichi felt a niggling anger in the back of his head at how blasé Michael was acting towards his lack of knowledge, but he forced it back. He closed his eyes for a second. *What's the thing I want to know the most?* he wondered, but of course he knew that already.

"Ichi?" Alexis ventured, when he still hadn't answered. Ichi spared her a glance before fixing Michael with a hard stare of his own.

"What did Claire remember that has her so fucking terrified of you?" He felt Alexis staring at him, aghast, but he didn't care.

Michael smiled slightly. "Interesting first question. I think I'll pass." Ichi clucked his tongue in protest, but Michael continued speaking before he could say anything on the matter. "There are several things that she could have remembered that would illicit that kind of reaction from her, so I'm not exactly at liberty to say what in particular has her so spooked." But the look on Michael's face told Ichi otherwise; the man clearly had a strong notion as to why Claire was so scared of him now – scared enough to ask Ichi to take her life so that she could avoid the man in question. Michael

468

raised an eyebrow at him. "Next question," he said, in a tone that brooked no argument.

Ichi thought about it for a moment, then said, "Vic told me that you were hoping that hearing her buzzword would trigger her memories at the awards ball. But it wasn't her father who said the words, so how did you know that it would work?"

Michael's smile grew wider, and he turned his computer monitor screen around to show both Ichi and Alexis some CCTV footage. Ichi watched in shock as he saw Claire working in the lab night after night after night. Alexis let out a low whistle. "So she experimented on herself. Huh. How ironic."

Ichi frowned at her. "Ironic how, exactly?"

Michael waved a hand dismissively at him. "We'll get to that later." He paused the CCTV footage before continuing. "You knew she was blacking out, Ichi, and I know that you were preventing her from going anywhere during those times in the last two weeks of her being here. That...annoyed me. You could have messed everything up."

Ichi felt his temper flare on Claire's behalf, even though he was currently livid with her. "It was practically killing her, being like that every night." He paused, then added on as an afterthought: "And she kept going on about things I didn't understand when she was in her trances, and I couldn't take it."

Michael looked surprised. "I didn't know that."

"Well, even you can't possibly know everything," Ichi replied, irritated.

Michael laughed. "And you know even less. At the end of the day my plan worked, and Miss Danvers regained her memories. And didn't die in the process, which is obviously rather important."

"And now she's gone, so what use is anything?" Ichi fired back. "She has the password to her parents' research in her head, and there's no way she'll give it to –"

"It's not a password, Ichi," Michael interrupted.

Ichi frowned. "Then what...?"

Michael grinned dangerously; it was enough to make Ichi flinch. "Miss Danvers has every last piece of that research stored in her head. She, quite literally, *is* the research." Ichi stared at him, shell-shocked. *What the hell happened to you, Claire?* he thought numbly. *Why couldn't you just tell me about this yourself?*

"Why didn't she tell you about it herself, Ich?" Alexis asked him, voicing the very question he was going over himself.

He stared at her blankly. "She said she couldn't trust me whilst I was *like this.* Hell if I know what that means. She told me I'd have to wait for her to find me again before she told me anything." It looked to Ichi as if Alexis flinched at his explanation, but by this point he was getting too tired to care. He didn't add on how Claire hadn't wanted him to return to working for Michael; that alone he kept private.

"Well, that was certainly a wise decision on her behalf," Michael said quietly, almost to himself. "I wonder when I'll stop underestimating her..."

"That's why I told you from the beginning not to!" Alexis snapped. "She's much smarter than you, though you won't care to admit it."

To Ichi's surprise, Michael took the criticism. "Then I'll just have to start using much more under-handed techniques to out-smart her." He fixed his gaze on Ichi. "That's where you come in. And Alexis too now, I suppose." Ichi looked over at the woman on his left.

"The hell would Claire care about you using Alexis against her?" he asked, infuriated at his continued lack of understanding of the situation he was in. Alexis gave him a bashful look, then turned to gaze at the floor.

Michael grinned again. "Ah, Ichi, you really don't know a thing. Meet Alexis Joanna Danvers, Claire Danvers' older sister. It appears that you have a rather specific taste in women."

"What...?" Ichi mouthed, ignoring the jibe. He couldn't believe what he was hearing. "Alexis, if you're her...then why –"

"I'll talk to you about it later, Ich," Alexis mumbled, then she looked up at Michael and asked, "Now that he knows, can we get on to the game plan?"

Michael gave her a blank smile. "I guess we can." He sat up a little straighter in his chair. "Now, although the obvious goal is to bring back Miss Danvers –"

"It's really weird for you to call her that in front of the two of us, now Ichi knows that I'm also a Miss Danvers, Michael," Alexis interrupted, and Michael chuckled.

"I suppose you're correct. So whilst the obvious goal is to bring back Claire –" Ichi found that hearing Claire's name on Michael's tongue made him feel uncomfortable, though he couldn't pinpoint why, "– what I have learned about her over the past year, and particularly with her escape, is that *she won't tell me anything.* So what we need, first and foremost, is leverage."

Ichi blinked at him, not quite understanding what Michael was saying. "Leverage?" he echoed.

"Yes," Michael continued, "Leverage. The right leverage will have Miss Da...Claire...rushing back, without anybody having to pursue her."

It dawned on Ichi what he meant then. "You mean to do something to Olivia?" Michael shook his head, and Ichi saw him look at Alexis.

"Not harming Olivia is one of the very few things I cannot do. Or, rather, will not do. Claire would never forgive that."

"What do you care what Claire will or will not forgive?" Ichi bit out testily.

Michael smirked at him. "Oh, rather a lot, if I'm to get everything I want from her." And there was that uncomfortable feeling in the pit of Ichi's stomach again. He glanced at Alexis to see if she was feeling the same way as he was, but she remained impassive. Ichi wondered if he was simply imagining things in his exhaustion, but he was fairly certain that that wasn't the case.

"So, what leverage then?" Ichi asked.

Michael's smirk turned into a grin. "Why, her parents, of course. And unlike Olivia, I have no qualms about putting them through hell until their daughter shows up. I'm sure you feel the same way, Ichi."

471

Ichi felt the familiar stirrings of excitement at the prospect in his body, but then narrowed his eyes at the other man. "I thought Claire hated her parents."

"No, she still loves them, no matter what she says," Alexis muttered to his left. "She's too soft."

Ichi clucked his tongue. "After what she just did today, I wouldn't say that about her at all."

"Alexis is correct," Michael said, bringing the conversation back to its main topic. "What I have learned from my conversations with Claire is that she's still attached to her parents, even if, on the surface, she hates them."

"But that might have changed now that she has her memories back," Ichi argued. "If they experimented on her, I mean. I'd say that that's pretty reasonable cause to hate one's parents." Out of the corner of his eye, he saw Alexis glance at him.

"I spoke to her after she regained consciousness, if you do recall," Michael pointed out. "I can tell you with reasonable certainty that she still cares for them both, regardless of what they did to her."

Ichi was silent for a few moments. Then he said, "So, find Claire's parents and bring them back. Find a way to tell Claire we have them, then torture them until she gives up the research. That's essentially it, yes?" Michael nodded his assent. Then Ichi remembered something, and he grinned.

"I don't suppose I can tell her about this plan before-the-fact?" Both Michael and Alexis looked at him, surprised. He shrugged his shoulders. "I put a phone in her bag," he explained, "And she might still have it on her."

Michael returned his grin. "I don't see why not. Please send her my regards."

As Ichi opened the phone to dial the only number he had saved to it, he caught Alexis looking at him almost sadly. But he was too excited and angry and exhausted to care, so he ignored what it could have meant entirely.

I'll make you come back to me, Claire, Ichi promised as he put the phone up to his ear. *And when you do, I'll make you suffer for having ever left.*

Vic

Claire had her eyes closed to the sun, letting it wash over her as Vic watched. They were on the deck of a cruise ship, having boarded an hour ago. It had always been his intention to escape somewhere warm and sunny with Claire, who hadn't been outside in so long. Now Vic knew for certain that it had been the right choice – even with so much going on for her to think about, Claire's face looked serene as she took in the sun. Neither of them were dressed for warm weather in the slightest, but Vic knew that they could rectify that by going to the shops on-board the ship. *And besides, it won't get properly hot until we're well away from Scotland anyway,* he mused. Vic planned to give Claire the full two weeks of the cruise for pure recovery purposes, and then…

I don't know what happens then, Vic forced himself to admit. *I don't know what she wants – she won't speak to me.* That much was true; Claire hadn't spoken more than five words strung together since they had left Ichi in that cabin. All she had done was cry, which was terrible, or fitfully sleep whilst crying, which was even worse. Vic hadn't wanted to press her on anything, however, so he let her be. *But now I think I need to get some answers. And I need to give* her *some too.*

"Claire…" he began, and Claire half-opened one eye to glance at him.

"You can explain why you were John later," she said, closing her eyes again. "I swear that I'll let you. I want to know after all. Just…not right now."

Vic sighed. "And what about what happened to you? What exactly did you remember?"

Claire flinched, but she tried to hide it. "I can't tell you right now," she mumbled. Vic frowned, for that was exactly what she had told Ichi.

"Claire, you know that you can tell me any –"

"I know."

"Then why –"

She opened her eyes fully to fix Vic with a hard stare. "I've trusted you all this time Vic, often blindly," she said. "Can't you do the same for me this once?"

Vic gave her a small smile, then ruffled her hair even as he remembered that Marie had warned him against doing it. The thought of Marie made his heart twist painfully, but he put it to the side for now. "You know I'll do anything for you, princess," he said, forcing his deathly curiosity at bay. "Just know that you can tell me whenever you want, regardless of how bad you think things are, okay?"

Claire returned his smile with one of her own, but it didn't quite reach her eyes. "Yeah, okay."

Then they lay back on their deck chairs in silence, listening to the excited prattle of other cruise ship guests go about their business around them. But a few minutes later, the silence was interrupted by the sound of buzzing, and Vic frowned.

"That's coming from your bag, Claire," he murmured, immediately concerned. Claire made a grab for her bag, unzipping it and pulling out a phone as her face grew paler and paler. She stared at it for a second, then before Vic could tell her not to, she flipped it open and held it to her ear.

Vic didn't have to hear his voice to know that it was Ichi on the other side of the receiver.

Claire

"I almost expected you not to pick up," came Ichi's voice over the phone. And for a moment, Claire wondered why in the world she had answered in the first place. She glanced over at the ship's railing on her left. *I should just throw it overboard. I should just…but I owe him this much, at least.*

"Ichi," she finally said. "I'm sor –"

"Cut the apologies," Ichi interrupted. Claire waited for him to say something else, but he didn't.

"I can't let you catch me," she finally said. She heard Ichi chuckle down the phone; it caused a shiver to run down her spine.

"As if you had to tell me that. It doesn't matter, anyway. I'll make you come to *me*, so where you are right now doesn't matter."

Claire frowned. "Ichi, I won't –"

"Michael's going to find your parents," Ichi interrupted again, and Claire went cold. "And when he does, I'm going to cut them up nice and slowly until you come back."

"You're…you've gone back to…"

"What choice did you leave me with, Claire? Oh, nice of you to tell me that I'd been fucking your sister before you, by the way." Claire thought that she might faint; she vaguely felt Vic put a hand on her shoulder to steady her, but she didn't look at him.

"Ichi, what – what have they told you?" *He can't know, oh my God he can't know.*

Ichi chuckled again, and it was the worst sound Claire had ever heard. "I think it's my turn to leave you in the dark, Claire." She could practically see Ichi smirking down the phone as he no doubt heard her breathing accelerate in panic. "For your parents' best interests, you should probably just come back now, to limit the amount of pain I put them through before I slice their throats open," he continued.

"Ichi…please," Claire begged, but she couldn't find any other words to say.

"That won't work on me anymore, you bitch," he spat out. And then: "If you want to know precisely when we find your parents, I suggest not losing this phone." There was a pause, then Ichi added on as an afterthought, "Michael says hi." And then the line went dead, and Ichi's voice was gone. Claire let the phone drop into her lap, hand gone numb from shock. *No, this isn't happening,* she thought. *Alexis can't have told him. Alexis can't have told* Michael! *But then…what do I really know about Alexis? What do I –*

Claire was brought out of her head abruptly by Vic pulling her into his arms, and she realised she was crying. "It's okay, Claire, you're going to be okay," Vic told her, voice calm and soothing. "Just throw the phone away; don't listen to anything he said. Just throw it away." But Claire shook her head against his chest, struggling to hold back a sob.

"I can't, not when they –"

"Not when they what, Claire? What did Ichi tell you?" But then Claire froze. There was somebody much worse than her parents that Ichi could get a hold of, and now that she had broken her deal with Michael by running away, that person wasn't safe anymore.

"Vic, do you know where Olivia is?" she asked suddenly, pulling away from Vic's chest to stare at him. "Please tell me that you do!" Vic stroked her hair reassuringly.

"Of course I do, princess. It's where we're headed, after all."

Claire let out a cry of relief. "When will we reach her?"

"In two weeks; why?"

Claire felt her eyes go wide. "No! We need to get to her *now!*" Vic put a finger to her lips to quieten her, but Claire didn't care.

"You think I'd leave her unprotected?" Vic scolded. "I'd have never left her unguarded, princess, not after I promised your parents to keep their daughters safe." It was then that Claire realised that Vic didn't know who Alexis was, and she wondered whether she should tell him. *It can wait. She's not my sister right now, anyway,* Claire thought bitterly.

She sighed. "Okay, I'll wait two weeks," she finally said.

Vic frowned at her. "What did Ichi say to you, Claire?" he asked again.

Claire felt herself shiver involuntarily at the very thought of Ichi's voice down the phone. "He's working for *him* again," she replied blankly. "Ichi and Alexis are working with him to find my parents, to…to hurt them until I go back." She hated the look Vic gave her then, as if he expected it to work, and that he would have to formulate a plan to prevent her from going back. So Claire fixed him with a straight stare, forcing the tears out of her voice. "Vic, they may as well be dead to me. No, I'm serious," she added on when she saw the disbelief on Vic's face. "They left me to die in that damn complex, so I'll treat them with the same indifference. The only person I'd break for is Olivia, so that's who we're going to protect."

"And then?" Claire thought about how heavily-laden that question was. *And then I try to fix everything.* But instead of saying that, she smiled, and reached a hand out to run it through Vic's hair, which was shining gloriously in the sunlight.

476

"And then we can work it out from there." Vic put a hand over hers, and despite everything that had happened, and how much the world was crumbling around her, Claire felt her heart flutter. She felt her smile grow a little wider. "But until then, I think John and I have some catching up to do."

Vic returned the smile with a laugh so genuine that Claire could have cried. She saw how his pale blue eyes creased up with it, how the sides of his mouth curved upwards with the sound, and she knew that she had made the right choice in asking Vic to help her.

"I think they do, too," Vic agreed, and Claire felt just the slightest stirring of hope that, with his help, she might be able to fix everything – and everyone – that she had helped her parents to destroy.